THE WORLD'S CLASSICS
BASil

WILKIE COLLINS was born in London in 1824, the son of a popular landscape painter. In 1846 he entered Lincoln's Inn as a law student; in 1851 he was called to the bar, and in the same year met Dickens for the first time. Adopting literature as a profession and collaborating with Dickens, he contributed to *Household Words* and *All the Year Round*. *Basil*, his second novel, was published in 1852. Among his best-known works are *The Woman in White* (1860) and *The Moonstone* (1868). The 'original' of the woman in white was Mrs Caroline Graves with whom Wilkie Collins lived for most of his life from 1859 until his death, though he had three children by Martha Rudd. He died in 1889.

DOROTHY GOLDMAN is Deputy Director and Senior Lecturer in Literature in the School of Continuing Education of the University of Kent at Canterbury. She has written on Dorothy Canfield and Kate Chopin and her interest in Wilkie Collins stems from a lifelong devotion to detective fiction. She is currently preparing a collection of essays on women's response to World War I.

THE WORLD'S CLASSICS

══

WILKIE COLLINS

Basil

══

Edited with an Introduction by

DOROTHY GOLDMAN

Oxford   New York

OXFORD UNIVERSITY PRESS

Oxford University Press, Walton Street, Oxford OX2 6DP

Oxford New York
Athens Auckland Bangkok Bombay
Calcutta Cape Town Dar es Salaam Delhi
Florence Hong Kong Istanbul Karachi
Kuala Lumpur Madras Madrid Melbourne
Mexico City Nairobi Paris Singapore
Taipei Tokyo Toronto

and associated companies in
Berlin Ibadan

Oxford is a trade mark of Oxford University Press

Introduction, Note on the Text, Select Bibliography,
Explanatory Notes © Dorothy Goldman 1990
Chronology © Catherine Peters and Dorothy Goldman 1990

First issued as a World's Classics paperback 1990

British Library Cataloguing in Publication Data

Data available

Library of Congress Cataloging in Publication Data
Collins, Wilkie, 1824–1889.
Basil/William Wilkie Collins; edited with an introduction by
Dorothy Goldman.
p. cm.—(The World's classics)
The text is that of the 1852 rev. ed.
Bibliography: p.
1. Goldman, Dorothy. II. Title. III. Series.
PR4494.B3 1989 823'.8—dc20 89-31674
ISBN 0-19-282195-4

7 9 10 8 6

Printed in Great Britain by
BPC Paperbacks Ltd
Aylesbury, Bucks

CONTENTS

INTRODUCTION

What distinguishes the true sensation genre, as it appears in its prime during the 1860s, is the violent yoking of romance and realism, traditionally the two contradictory modes of literary perception.... The chosen territory of the sensation novelists lies somewhere between the possible and the improbable, ideally at their point of intersection. (Winifred Hughes, *The Maniac in the Cellar*[1])

BASIL (1852) anticipates this characterization of the sensation novel by a decade. In its Letter of Dedication Collins announces his commitment to realism, the possible, and the bourgeois, all of which he subsumes in the Actual: 'the more of the Actual I could garner up as a text to speak from, the more certain I might feel of the genuineness and value of the Ideal which was sure to spring out of it' (xxxv–xxxvi). The Actual will, however, not be mundane: 'I have not thought it either politic or necessary, while adhering to realities, to adhere to every-day realities only.' The ability to fuse realism and romance grew out of Collins's earlier work—journalism, biography, historical romance, travel writing. To the reader of his best-known books, *The Moonstone*, or *The Woman in White*, these early works appear inexplicable, but paradoxically it is from them that *Basil*, his first characteristic novel, springs.

Of the articles and short stories which Collins reportedly wrote and published while still in his teens and articled to a London tea-merchant, only one is extant. Published in 1843 when he was only nineteen, 'The Last Stage Coachman' is a sub-Dickensian conceit crudely yoking the probable and the impossible in an as yet unsophisticated manner. The piece's emaciated and miserable hero explains to the narrator the social effects of the coming of the railway—his own decline,

---

[1] Winifred Hughes, *The Maniac in the Cellar: Sensation Novels of the 1860s* (Princeton, New Jersey, 1980), p. 16.

the bankruptcy of the landlord of the coaching-inn, and the death of an ostler rescuing horses from the railway line. Their conversation is fantastically interrupted, however, when

a fully equipped Stage Coach appeared in the clouds, with a railway director strapped fast to each wheel, and a stoker between the teeth of each of the four horses. In place of luggage, fragments of broken steam carriages, and red carpet bags filled with other mementoes of railway accidents, occupied the roof.[2]

The last stage coachman joyously takes his place and disappears from view. Five years later Collins formally recognized the imaginative potential of combining antithetical *genres* when he described his grandfather's *Memoirs of a Picture* as 'a curious combination of the serious purpose of biography with the gay license of fiction'.[3] This potential was first fully realized in *Basil* where it was used to suggest the instability of conventional life which lies at the heart of Collins's fiction.

Little is known about Collins's first novel, written in 1845 or 1846 without his family's knowledge and probably destroyed. His own description makes one regret its loss:

The scene of the story is the island of Tahiti, before the period of its discovery by European navigators! My youthful imagination ran riot among the noble savages, in scenes which caused the respectable British publisher to declare that it was impossible to put his name on the title-page of such an novel. For the moment I was a little discouraged. But I got over it, and began another novel.[4]

Nuel Pharr Davis suggests that this 'wildly impractical, rather mad novel'[5] may paradoxically be the outcome of mundane research: Ellis's *Polynesian Researches* and Hall's *Fragments of Voyages and Travels* were both in the Collins family library. If so, it initiated a pattern of establishing the

[2] Wilkie Collins, 'The Last Stage Coachman', *Illuminated Magazine* (Aug. 1843), 211.

[3] Wilkie Collins, *The Memoirs of the Life of William Collins, Esq. RA* (London, 1848), i. 9.

[4] Quoted in George W. Towle, 'Wilkie Collins', *Appleton's Journal of Popular Literature, Science and Art* (3 Sept. 1870), 279.

[5] Nuel Pharr Davis, *The Life of Wilkie Collins* (Urbana, 1950), p. 42.

exotic on a factually researched basis which would continue throughout Collins's writing career, and nowhere more than in his first published novel, *Antonina; or, the Fall of Rome*, begun in April 1846. Collins showed the first chapters to his father who was impressed enough to allow him to give up his apprenticeship and enrol as a law student at Lincoln's Inn, a profession traditionally allowing more time for writing. He continued work on the novel during that winter but in February 1847 his father died and he put it aside to write a filial biography: the 'gay license of fiction' was literally abandoned for 'the serious purpose of biography'.

The Memoirs of the Life of William Collins, Esq. R.A. is not a psychological portrait—it contains surprisingly little about his father's personal life—but a factual account of the career of a professional painter. The aspect of his father's technique which Collins especially admired was his insistence on accuracy; the artist's search for authenticity is suggestive of the novelist's research for his fiction. Of one picture,

the most amusing criticism . . . proceeded from Mr. Collins's gardener; who, as a great skittle-player, was called in to test the correctness of the picture, as to its main subject. 'Well!' cried the horticultural functionary, with genuine delight—'this is as down-right a tough game, as ever I *see*.' Such a 'dictum,' coming from such a quarter, was to the painter [a] decisive . . . testimony to the truth of his picture. (ii. 9)

His father's preference for working from originals provides more than an artistic analogy to the son's preference for grounding imaginative works on a documentary base; it had a specific influence on his work. He too used originals in the *Memoirs*, including numerous and lengthy quotations from his father's journal and friends' letters. The future novelist was already developing a technique which would eventuate in personal narratives. William Collins had been a popular and successful painter, and with some skilful lobbying by its author, the biography was widely and politely reviewed. Its reception encouraged Collins to continue work on his historical romance dealing with the fall of Rome and the victories of Alaric the Goth. He wrote much of the remainder in the spring and summer of 1848 in Paris, calling upon his memories of a childhood visit to Italy: in September 1836, when Wilkie was twelve, the family had gone abroad for almost two years, a trip which included several months in Rome.

Collins seems to have been less at home with the classics than many of his contemporaries, and he relied upon Gibbon's *The History of the Decline and Fall of the Roman Empire* as a major source for *Antonina*. In the Preface he is at pains to stress the historical accuracy of the novel, which will include 'various historical illustrations of the period which the Author's researches among conflicting but equally important authorities . . . enabled him to garner up'. He describes the 'one main object of his anxiety, viz., to make his plot invariably arise and proceed out of, the great historical events of the era, exactly in the order in which they occurred'. However, 'the bare outline of historic fact' will be filled 'with the colouring of romantic fancy'; over and above historical facts, there is historical fiction. Goisvintha forces from her brother Hermanric a promise to avenge her children, slaughtered by the Romans. Antonina, innocent daughter of a Christian fanatic, becomes the object of both Goisvintha's desire for revenge and Hermanric's love during the siege of Rome. She is only saved when Goisvintha is murdered by a pagan fanatic, who amazingly turns out to be the long lost brother of Antonina's father. Throughout this clumsy novel family relationships are exposed in contrasting portraits of children and parents, brother and sister, brother and brother; and the power of religion is suggested by a comparison of Christian and pagan fanaticism. The twists of the sub-Bulwer-Lytton plot are, however, always bizarre and unconvincing. The implausibility of *Antonina* is only matched by its unwieldy, rhetorical, and over-blown prose.

Collins's next book could hardly present a greater contrast. *Rambles Beyond Railways: Notes in Cornwall Taken A-Foot* (1851) is another example of Collins's penchant for mixed perception—an accurate, even documentary description of an outlandish journey over 'the most untrodden ground that we could select'[6] with Collins's tone, both informal and funny, that of a traveller in exotic and wonderful parts. In all the works preceding *Basil* Collins insists with varying degrees of success on the relationship between factual research and fantasy, authenticity and bizarrerie; he utilizes both the outlandish and documentary personal narratives. In *Basil* a new element cements the connection. In domestic crime Collins found factual evidence for the penetration of polite society by the outlandish and the violent, and in doing so introduced a disconcerting moral ambiguity into his fiction. His novels, from *Basil* onwards, use domestic crime as the intersecting point of his double vision of Victorian society.

How does Collins realize the relationship between realism and romance, how does he connect the factual and the interpretative? R. P. Laidlaw identifies Collins's consistent use of doubles as the 'basic structuring motif in studying the relationship between a totally secular and objective order and the subjective'.[7] *Basil* is a long way from the almost random comparisons of *Antonina*; the structuring doubles now reveal a consistent relationship between surface and hidden realities. Barickman, MacDonald, and Stark describe this as '[s]ymbolic pairing and polarities in characterization, plot, dramatic scene, and description. Together these techniques of indirect presentation form a major ironic structure, a counterplot to the novel's direct method.'[8] *Basil* is the first example in Collins's writing of the revelation of the subjective constituting a psychological counterplot which functions as a subversive revelation of the hidden sexual tensions within Victorian culture.

In *Basil* the eponymous narrator and protagonist is emotionally torn between two women, Margaret Sherwin

[6] Wilkie Collins, *Rambles Beyond Railways: Notes in Cornwall Taken A-Foot* (London, 1851), i. 7.

[7] R. P. Laidlaw, ' "Awful Images and Associations": A Study of Wilkie Collins's *The Moonstone*', *Southern Review: An Australian Journal of Literary Studies*, 9 (Nov. 1976), 211.

[8] Richard Barickman, Susan MacDonald, and Myra Stark, *Corrupt Relations: Dickens, Thackeray, Trollope, Collins and the Victorian Sexual System* (New York, 1982), p. 33.

and his own sister Clara, who subtextually form dual aspects of one woman. Basil contrasts his relationship and duties to the two in a manner which establishes them as rivals for his love. He calls his marriage to Margaret, which is to remain both secret and unconsummated for a year, 'the parting day for Clara, and the marriage day for me' (92). He feels guilty at the growth of his feelings for Margaret: 'My first look at my sister made me feel as if I had been detected in a crime. . . . Was she searching my heart, and discovering the new love rising, an usurper already, in the place where the love of her had reigned before?' (38, 40)

The contrast exists on both the physical and the spiritual levels. Clara has blue eyes and an 'absence of any colour in her complexion' (18) whereas Margaret:

was dark. Her hair, eyes, and complexion were darker than usual in English women. . . . The fire in her large dark eyes . . . was latent. Their languor, when she was silent—that voluptuous languor of black eyes—was still fugitive and unsteady. The smile about her full lips (to other eyes they might have looked *too* full) struggled to be eloquent, yet dared not. (30)

Basil dreams of two women, one dark, one fair. The latter was

descending from . . . bright summits; and her robe was white, and pure, and glistening. Her face was illumined with a light . . . and her footsteps . . . left a long track of brightness, that sparkled far behind her, like the track of the stars when the winter night is clear and cold. . . . Meanwhile, the woman from the dark wood still approached . . . her eyes were lustrous and fascinating, as the eyes of a serpent. . . . Her lips were parted with a languid smile; and she drew back the long hair, which lay over her cheeks, her neck, her bosom, as I was gazing on her. (45)

The fair woman beckons to him, but the dark woman approaches and

I touched her hand, and in an instant the touch ran through me like fire. . . . I was drawn along in the arms of the dark woman, with my blood burning and my breath failing me, until we entered the secret recesses that lay amid the unfathomable depths of trees. There she encircled me in the folds of her dusky robe, and laid her cheek close to mine, and murmured a mysterious music in my ear, amid the midnight silence and darkness of all around us. . . . I had forgotten the woman of the fair hills, and had given myself up, heart, and soul, and body, to the woman from the dark woods. (46–7)

It is unnecessary to spell out the sexuality suggested by the dark dream woman, or the chastity and purity surrounding the fair woman in this simple stereotypical contrast.

The contrast and implicit connection between the the two women continues in the manner in which Basil learns of their respective worth. The central scene of the novel, a scene of shocking sexual intensity, is presented aurally. A year after his unconsummated wedding, on the eve of the very day when he is to claim Margaret as his wife, Basil follows her and her father's confidential clerk Mannion, to a hotel; from the room next to theirs 'I listened; and through the thin partition, I heard voices—*her* voice, and *his* voice. *I heard and I knew*—knew my degredation in all its infamy, knew my wrongs in all their nameless horror' (160). This scene is the first example of Collins's use of confrontational tableaux to establish the interaction of text and sub-text. *The Moonstone* and *The Woman in White* both contain pivotal moments of equal intensity and significance.

When Mannion leaves the hotel Basil attacks him, beating his face into a recently macadamized road and mutilating him horribly. The shock is too much for Basil, however, and he collapses. During his recovery he learns, again through hearing activity outside his room, of Clara's loyal love for him:

The first sense of which I regained the use, was the sense of hearing; and the first sound that I recognised, was of a light footstep which mysteriously approached, paused, and then retired again gently outside my door. The hearing of this sound was my first pleasure . . . I could now hear [Clara pronounce] my name—once, twice, three times—very softly and imploringly, as if to beg the answer which I was still too weak to give. But I knew the voice: I knew it was Clara's. . . . The next sound. . . . was . . . the soft rustling of a woman's dress. And yet, I heard in it innumerable harmonies. . . . I knew that the rustling dress was Clara's. (175–6)

This doubling of sexual and chaste women requires a pair of male doubles to explore possible responses and it is in this light that we should understand the relationship of Basil and Mannion. Mannion, the more knowing, is conscious of the connection between them: ' "there is something . . . which urges me . . . to link myself to you for life . . . a fatality . . . perpetuating itself in you and me" ' (252). The most telling parallels between the two men occur in their relationships with Margaret. Each corresponds secretly with her by letter via the same maid. Each is betrayed by her in his absence. Mannion says that he went to France, ' "confident that my short absence would not weaken the result of years of steady influence over Margaret" ' (241), but on his return she is married; similarly, Basil goes to visit his family for a week and when he comes back Mannion has reasserted his domination over her. Mannion's description of Basil as ' "the man who, in my absence, had stepped between me and my prize . . . had snatched from me the long-delayed reward" ' (242) could equally have been spoken by Basil of Mannion. They are both present at Margaret's deathbed, though Mannion is hidden: ' "I shared her last moments with you, to the very end" ' (303). Charles Rycroft stresses the similarity between this scene and that of Basil's betrayal when he points out significantly that 'this time it is Mannion who listens from an adjoining room'.[9] At her grave, Mannion 'stopped at the foot of it--stopped opposite me, as I stood at the head' (302).

It is as if there is only one courtship/seduction of Margaret, as if Mannion and Basil are the same person, forming a single protagonist, incapable of dealing with what then become the conflicting demands of romantic and sexual love. Mannion is the sexually aware and sexually active element, Basil the sentimental and passive element who responds to sexuality

---

[9] Charles Rycroft, 'A Detective Story: Psychoanalytic Observations', *Psychoanalytic Quarterly*, 26 (1957), 242.

with repugnance and guilt. Rycroft suggests that in 'the ideal detective story the detective or hero would discover that he himself is the criminal for whom he has been seeking' and that Mannion represents the hero's 'unadmitted impulses'.[10] This recognition that Mannion's guilt is Basil's guilt explains the latter's exaggerated sense of shame: 'I have traced the history of my errors and misfortunes, *of the wrong I have done* and the punishment I have suffered for it' (311; my emphasis). In simple narrative terms Basil has been the victim, not the sinner; it is he who has been wronged.

The analysis of the pervasive and powerful nature of human sexuality extends beyond the two central pairs of doubles to include a man who has come to terms with sexuality and love and a woman who is destroyed by it. Basil's brother, Ralph, is his opposite. The contrast between them is made clear when Basil defends himself to his father: ' "My brother's faults towards you, and towards his family, are not such faults as mine, Sir. . . . I have *not* imitated his vices; I have acted as he would *not* have acted" ' (196–7). Yet, at the end of the book the virtuous Basil is the broken man, living in retirement with his sister: 'I have suffered too much; I have been wounded too sadly, to range myself with the heroes of Ambition, and fight my way upwards from the ranks. The glory and the glitter which I once longed to look on as my own, would dazzle and destroy me, now' (342). The formerly dissolute Ralph is 'now the head of our family; now aroused by his new duties to a sense of his new position—Ralph, already emancipated from many of his habits which once enthralled and degraded him' (342). He has been reclaimed from his licentious ways by his devotion to a woman of whom society disapproves. 'He . . . contracted, what would be termed in the continental code of morals, a reformatory attachment to a woman older than himself, who was living separated from her husband, when he met with her' (17). Ralph is quite explicit about her reforming qualities:

[10] Rycroft, pp. 230, 243.

'The fact is, the morganatic Mrs. Ralph . . . wanted to see England, and I was tired of being abroad. So . . . we're going to live quietly, somewhere in the Brompton neighbourhood. That woman has been my salvation. . . . She has broke me of gaming altogether; I was going to the devil as fast as I could, when she stopped me.' (257)

The narrator's confused sexuality is not endorsed by the author.

Before we meet Margaret's mother, Mrs Sherwin is presented as a woman of simple but clear ideas, who knows her place and the virtues associated with it. Commenting on Margaret's regular trips to market, the maid says: ' "Master don't like it; but Missus begged and prayed she might; for Missus says she won't be fit to be married, if she knows nothing about housekeeping, and prices, and what's good meat, and what isn't, and all that, you know" ' (52). But Mrs Sherwin is also a sad and frightened woman, bullied by her husband and disregarded by her daughter:

the restless timidity of her expression; the mixture of useless hesitation and involuntary rapidity in every one of her actions all furnished the same significant betrayal of a life of incessant fear and restraint . . . in that mild, wan face of hers in those painful startings and hurryings when she moved; in that tremulous, faint utterance when she spoke   *there*, I could see one of those ghastly heart-tragedies laid open before me, which are acted and re-acted, scene by scene, and year by year, in the secret theatre of the home. (75–6)

William H. Marshall is surely right when he says that Mrs Sherwin 'appears insane because her orderly orientation recurringly collapses when it faces the chaos in which she must live',[11] but it is important to recognize that it is the specifically sexual chaos implicit in a secret, unconsummated marriage and a seduction which causes her rapid deterioration. When the affair becomes known, her husband writes to Basil that 'my wife, whose wretched health has been a trouble and annoyance to us for years past, has now, I grieve

[11] William H. Marshall, *Wilkie Collins* (New York, 1970), p. 118.

to say, under pressure of this sad misfortune, quite lost her reason' (184).

The passions which underlie polite behaviour are further suggested by the literal revelation of two spectre-faces which have been hidden beneath conventional façades. Margaret's only becomes apparent on her death-bed but is suggested in Mannion's description of her seduction—' "We had some interviews . . . at which I spoke such words to her as would have left their mark on the face of a Jezebel, or a Messalina" ' (248). The revelation of Mannion's true face is more complex. Initially his facial unresponsiveness is emphasized, and only alters when he begins to ensnare Basil. After their first private interview, a flash of lightning 'gave such a hideously livid hue, such a spectral look of ghastliness and distortion to his features, that he absolutely seemed to be glaring and grinning . . . like a fiend, in the one instant of its duration' (130). The inhuman aspect of his features is finally made visible to everyone by Basil: 'I had already stooped towards him, as he lay insensible beneath me, to lift him again, and beat out of him, on the granite, not life only, but the semblance of humanity as well' (164). His success is evident at Margaret's funeral, when Mannion appears with 'that appalling face . . . its hideous deformity of feature, its fierce and changeless malignity of expression glaring . . . with the same unearthly look of fury and triumph which . . . had [first appeared] through the flashing lightning . . . the fiend-face' (302–4). Basil has exposed the inner man. In Basil's delirium, after the attack, there is a symbolic variant on these facial revelations: Mannion and Margaret 'each laid a talon on my shoulder—each raised a veil which was one hideous net-work of twining worms. I saw through the ghastly corruption of their faces the look that told me who they were—the monstrous iniquities incarnate in monstrous forms; the fiend-souls made visible in fiend-shapes' (174). The revelation of the true characters of Margaret and Mannion in their faces is an early but clear example of Collins's need to bring to the surface hidden pressures, repressed motives, and secret beliefs, which has often been crudely marginalized as the need to explain 'who-dun-it'.

Confirmation of both the themes Collins was trying to resolve in *Basil* and their technical realization comes from three short stories written about the same time. In 'The Twin Sisters: A True Story' (1851), Streatfield falls in love with an unknown girl on a balcony. From a shopkeeper and a family servant he learns her name and within six weeks they are engaged. Only at the banquet on their wedding eve does he meet her twin sister Clara, when he blurts out, ' "*That* is the face I saw in the balcony!—*that* woman is the only woman I can ever marry!" '[12] He explains that he had not known that his fiancée was a twin, and that when he first met her, ' "I felt an unaccountable impression that she was the same as, and yet different from, the lady whom I had seen in the balcony" ' (283). The marriage is cancelled, the wedding guests disperse, Streatfield marries Clara. Three elements deserve our special attention here: Streatfield's falling in love at first sight with a complete stranger—just as Basil does; his use of a shopkeeper and a servant to assist his pursuit of her—as Basil discovers Margaret's father to be a shopkeeper and uses a servant to make initial contact with her; and most important of all, the fact that she is a twin, literally a double. In *Basil*, Margaret and the significantly named Clara are not twins, but they are variants on one person. Similarly, 'Nine O'Clock!' (1852) confirms Collins's interest in male doubles: 'If I was certain of anything in the world, I was certain that I had seen my brother in the study . . . and equally certain that I had seen his double . . . in the garden.'[13]

A third story of this period, 'Mad Monkton', confirms the connection Collins suggests between sexuality and insanity.[14]

[12] Wilkie Collins, 'The Twin Sisters: A True Story', *Bentley's Miscellany* (1851), xxix. 280.

[13] Wilkie Collins, 'Nine O'Clock!', ibid. (Aug. 1852), xxxii. 226.

[14] This story, although written in February 1852, was not published until 1855, in the November and December issues of *Fraser's Magazine*. Submitted originally to *Household Words* it was rejected by Dickens because it dealt with hereditary insanity.

The narrator's father has forbidden his ward, Ada Elmslie, to marry Alfred Monkton, the last survivor of a family thought to be tainted by hereditary insanity, but on his death they become engaged. It 'seemed, however, as if there was some fatality at work to prevent' their wedding.[15] Monkton leaves England for Italy, obsessed with the need to find the unburied body of his uncle Stephen and return it to the Monkton family vault. During his fruitless search the narrator renews his acquaintance. The common opinion that Monkton's mental health is failing seems to be supported by his belief in a family curse: the Monkton line will die out if the body of any member of the family is left unburied. He has determined not to marry until he has found his uncle's body and brought it back to England. He confesses to the narrator that ' "*Stephen Monkton himself stands there at this moment*" ' (132), and that the apparition has accompanied him ever since his death:

'Think . . . think of what I must have suffered at looking always on that hideous vision, whenever I looked on my betrothed wife! Think of my taking her hand, and seeming to take it through the figure of the apparition! Think of the calm angel-face and the tortured spectre-face being always together, whenever my eyes met hers! (138)

Out of pity the narrator agrees to help him and his common sense brings the search to a successful conclusion. A storm on their journey home forces them to abandon ship, leaving the coffin to sink to the bottom of the sea. Monkton, dragged unwilling from the wreck, subsequently suffers from brain fever, and is soon himself buried in the family vault. Set against *Basil* interesting comparisons come to light: an unfulfilled engagement, the suggestion of sexual voyeurism, hidden faces, and more, especially the psychosexual metaphor of the plot.

The melodrama of 'Mad Monkton', however, is modified in *Basil* where increasingly psychological explanations of

---

[15] Wilkie Collins, 'Mad Monkton', from *The Biter Bit & Other Stories* (Gloucester, 1983), p. 114.

what had happened are made concrete in realistic, even commonplace, imagery. The first time Basil sees Margaret at home she is teasing a canary with a piece of sugar: 'The bird hopped and fluttered up and down in his prison after the sugar, chirping as if he enjoyed playing *his* part of the game with his mistress' (37). Clearly Basil is suggested by the figure of the caged bird—forbidden to consummate his marriage, teased by the offer of pleasure. It is this bird which is destroyed by Mrs Sherwin's cat—by which we may understand that Mrs Sherwin could remove Basil, Margaret's plaything, were she to tell him what she knows. The servant who rescues the cat appeals to Margaret's compassion for her ailing mother but Margaret's only reply is, ' "I don't care! The cat has killed my bird, and the cat shall be killed for doing it!—it shall!!—it shall!!—it shall!!!" ' (134)—and indeed with Mrs Sherwin's death, symbolically, it is. By illustrating the hidden springs of human behaviour (Margaret's passionate nature, Basil's sexual passivity, Mrs Sherwin's spiritual weakness) by such a homely image Collins reinforces their existence in the same world which his readers inhabit.

The narrative method of *Basil* reveals Collins's increasingly sophisticated use of realism in other ways. Marshall points out that Collins uses 'the accumulation and then the synthesis into meaningful narrative of the private records (letters, journals, expiational accounts, and the like) of various characters' (31) in a technique similar to the one he used in the *Memoirs*. Such accounts are incorporated into a first person narrative which thus combines constant appeals to documentary evidence with first-hand experience. Almost immediately after the excesses of Basil's Poe-like delirium the book moves into a semi-documentary mode with newspaper extracts describing Mannion's injuries. It is often suggested that Collins used first-person narratives to bring the flavour of the court-room into his detective fiction, yet its salient features are present in a biography and a novel which cannot be categorized as detective fiction. More likely Collins recognized that a realistic structure could be used to show that the enormities he described and analysed were not the figments of his fevered brain,[16] but part of the comfortable middle-class existence of his characters—and by extension his readers. However, as the reviews were to show, in *Basil* he did not achieve his object.

Collins was not unused to helping his work to get favourable reviews. The *Leader*, the *Atlas*, the *Morning Post*, and *Bentley's Miscellany* obliged in November and December 1852. The last, by including *Basil* in a double review with Thackeray's *The History of Henry Esmond*, even implied that the books were of equal worth. But more representative were the reviews in the *Westminster Review* and in the *Athenaeum*, where D. O. Maddyn wrote that *Basil* 'is a tale of criminality, almost revolting from its domestic horrors. The vicious atmosphere in which the drama of the tale is enveloped, weighs on us like a nightmare. . . . its subject is faulty and unwholesome.'[17] The *Westminster Review*'s criticism was harsher in that it went closer to the heart of what Collins was attempting to do and denied its artistic validity. Authors of this type of fiction,

though professedly taking their incidents from real life, seem to revel in scenes of fury and passion, such as, happily, real life seldom affords. . . . Mr. Collins . . . has taken his tale from what we are willing to hope is, if real, a perfectly exceptional case. The incident which forms the foundation of the whole, is absolutely disgusting; and it is kept so perseveringly before the eyes of the reader in all its

[16] Even the usually sympathetic Edmund Yates mentions 'that weird imagination'. See 'Mr. Wilkie Collins in Gloucester Place', *Celebrities at Home* (London, 1879), p. 148.

[17] D. O. Maddyn, unsigned review, *Athenaeum* (4 Dec. 1852), 1323. Such opinions were to dog *Basil* even after Collins's death. An unsigned obituary notice in the *Athenaeum* (28 Sept. 1889, 418) calls *Basil* 'crude in some parts and coarse in others'. In the same year Swinburne called it 'violent and unlovely', full of 'violence and cruelty' ('Wilkie Collins', *Fortnightly Review* [1 Nov. 1889], NS cclxxv. 590, 591) and even Yates, who had earlier tried to defend it ('The main incident of the story may appear objectionable to many, on grounds particularly English, and not particularly defensible' ['W. Wilkie Collins', *Train*, June 1857, iii. 356]), after his death bowed to accepted critical opinion by calling the novel 'a remarkably unpleasant story' ('The Novels of Wilkie Collins', *Temple Bar* [Aug. 1890], lxxxix. 530).

hateful details, that all interest is destroyed in the loathing which it occasions. . . . There are some subjects on which it is not possible to dwell without offence . . . and Mr. Collins . . . [spares] us no revolting details. . . . [He] makes a woman given up to evil the heroine of his piece, and dwells on the details of animal appetite with a persistency which can serve no moral purpose, and may minister to evil passions even while professing condemnation of them.[18]

Collins had expected some such attack and wrote in the novel's original Letter of Dedication:

Nobody who admits that the business of fiction is to exhibit human life, can deny that scenes of misery and crime must of necessity . . . form part of that exhibition. . . . [I do not address myself to those] who shrink from . . . subjects which they think of in private . . . whose innocence is in the word, and not in the thought. (vi–vii)

It is clear, however, from the additions which he made to the Dedication when the book was republished in 1862, that some of the criticism had hurt—'On its appearance, [*Basil*] was condemned off-hand . . . as an outrage on . . . 'proprietary' (xxxix). His explanation that 'a certain class of readers' had misinterpreted 'certain perfectly innocent passages' is, however, quite unconvincing. The book is a shocking analysis of psychosexual behaviour and he knew it.

[18] Unsigned review, *Westminster Review* (Oct. 1853), lx. 372–3.

edition. Occasionally, he substitutes a more correct or
precise word for a vaguer one. He thus reined in both
narrative and descriptive styles, at times overcharged and
emotion-bullying rhetoric. (The adjective 'smoky', for

NOTE ON THE TEXT

An early draft manuscript of the novel is extant (British
Library Add. MS. 41060, folios 1–86). It is not printer's copy
and therefore one or more lost manuscripts stand between it
and the first edition. On the verso of two manuscript pages
Collins jotted four alternative titles: *Basil; or Pages from the
Story of a Young Man's Life*, *Basil; a Young Man's Confession*,
Basil; or Leaves from the History of a Young Man's Life, and
Basil; or The Love Secret.

Basil; A Story of Modern Life was published in three volumes
in 1852 by Richard Bentley, London. Volume One contains
a Letter of Dedication and Part I, Chs. I–XIII; Volume Two
contains Part II, Chs I–VII and Part III, Chs. I–IV; Volume
Three contains Part III, Chs. I–IV [*sic*], Journal and Letters
I–III. *Basil* was reprinted in 1856, reset, in one volume, by
James Blackwood, London, without any alterations.

Collins carefully revised *Basil*—eliminating the subtitle—
for publication in 1862, in one volume, by Sampson Low,
Son & Co., London. Part I, Ch. VII conflates the first
edition's Part I, Chs. VII and VIII; Part I, Chs. IX–XIII are
renumbered VIII–XII. The first edition's Volume Three, Part
III, Chs. I–IV are renumbered Part III, Chs. V–VIII. The text
of this World's Classics edition is that of the 1862 revised
edition, reprinted from the same plates as 'a new edition'
in 1873 by Smith, Elder.

Collins's 1862 revisions involved over a thousand
deletions— of single words, phrases, and paragraphs, and of
page-length and longer passages, including two lengthy
scenes (on the omnibus just before Basil sees Margaret for the
first time, and when Basil walks through London awaiting
Margaret and Mannion's departure from her aunt's party).
Only very occasionally is anything substituted for these
deletions, and there are no expansions of text. Characterist-
ically, Collins removed items from a doubled or trebled
phrase or clause, a common rhetorical formula in the first

edition. Occasionally, he substituted a more correct or precise word for a vaguer one. He thus reined in both narrative and dialogue and toned down highly charged and emotion-building rhetoric. (The adjective 'sinister', for example, was a repeated casualty.) While tightening the pace of the novel, Collins's revisions entailed some loss in sustaining certain of its more psychologically probing, transcendental, or *outré* themes: the Notes on pp. 345–56 draw attention to some of these.

SELECT BIBLIOGRAPHY

BIBLIOGRAPHY

Kirk H. Beetz, *Wilkie Collins: An Annotated Bibliography, 1889–1976* (New York: The Scarecrow Author Bibliographies 50, 1976).

—— 'Wilkie Collins and *The Leader*', *Victorian Periodicals Review*, vol. xv, no. 1 (Spring 1982), 20–9.

Andrew Gasson, 'Wilkie Collins: A collector's and bibliographer's challenge', *The Private Library*, 3rd ser., 3 (Summer 1980), 51–77.

BIOGRAPHY

William M. Clarke, *The Secret Life of Wilkie Collins* (London, 1988).

Wilkie Collins, 'Books Necessary for a Liberal Education', *Pall Mall Gazette*, 43 (11 Feb. 1886), 2.

Wilkie Collins, 'How I Write My Books: Related in a Letter to a Friend', *The Globe*, 26 Nov. 1887.

Wilkie Collins, 'Reminiscences of a Story-teller', *Universal Review*, 1 (May–Aug. 1888), 182–92.

Nuel Pharr Davis, *The Life of Wilkie Collins* (Urbana, 1956).

Kenneth Robinson, *Wilkie Collins: A Biography* (London, 1951, repr. 1974).

Dorothy L. Sayers, *Wilkie Collins: A Biographical and Critical Study*, ed. E. R. Gregory (Toledo: Friends of the University of Toledo Libraries, 1977).

CRITICAL STUDIES

Robert Ashley, *Wilkie Collins* (London, 1952).

Emile D. Forgues, 'Etudes sur le roman Anglais. Les romans de Wilkie Collins', *Revue des Deux Mondes*, 2ème, 12 (15 Nov. 1855), 815–48.

Winifred Hughes, *The Maniac in the Cellar: Sensation Novels of the 1860s* (Princeton, New Jersey: Princeton University Press, 1980).

Sue Lonoff, *Wilkie Collins and His Victorian Readers* (New York, 1982).

William Marshall, *Wilkie Collins* (New York: Twayne's English Authors Series 94, 1970).

Norman Page, ed., *Wilkie Collins: The Critical Heritage* (London, 1974).

Charles Rycroft, 'The Analysis of a Detective Story', *Imagination and Reality: Psycho-Analytical Essays 1951–1961* (London: Hogarth Press, 1968).

A CHRONOLOGY OF
WILKIE COLLINS

begins collaboration with Dickens in *The Wreck of the Golden Mary* (December).   32

1857 (January–June) *The Dead Secret* serialized in *Household Words*, published in volume form (June).

(6 January) *The Frozen Deep* performed by Dickens's theatrical company at Tavistock House.

(August) *The Lighthouse* performed at the Olympia Theatre.

(September) Tours Cumberland, Lancashire, and Yorkshire with Dickens, their account appearing as *The Lazy Tour of Two Idle Apprentices* in *Household Words* (October).

Collaborates with Dickens on *The Perils of Certain English Prisoners*.   33

1858 (October) *The Red Vial* produced at the Olympic Theatre; a failure.   34

1859 From this year no longer living with his mother; lives for the rest of his life (with one interlude) with Mrs Caroline Graves. (January–February) Living at 124 Albany Street; (May–December) Living at 2a Cavendish Street.

(October) *The Queen of Hearts*, a collection of short stories, published.

(26 November–25 August 1860) *The Woman in White* serialized in *All the Year Round*.

(December) Moves to 12 Harley Street.   35

1860 (August) *The Woman in White* published in volume form: a best-seller in Britain and the United States, and rapidly translated into most European languages.   36

1861 (January) Resigns from *All the Year Round*.   37

1862 (15 March–17 January 1863) *No Name* serial-

1871 (14 May) Second daughter, Harriet Constance
     Dawson, born at 33 Bolsover Street.
     (May) Caroline Graves again living with
     Collins.
     (October) *The Woman in White* produced at the
     Olympic Theatre.
     (October–March 1872) *Poor Miss Finch* serial-
     ized in *Cassell's Magazine*.   47

1872 (February) *Poor Miss Finch* published in volume
     form.   48

1873 (February) Dramatic version of *Man and Wife*
     performed at the Prince of Wales theatre.
     (9 April) Brother, Charles Allston Collins, dies.
     (May) *The New Magdalen* published in volume
     form; dramatic version performed at the
     Olympic Theatre.
     Miss or Mrs? And Other Stories in Outline
     published.
     (September–March 1874) Tours United States
     and Canada, giving readings from his work.   49

1874 (November) *The Frozen Deep and Other Stories*.
     (25 December) Son, William Charles Dawson,
     born, 10 Taunton Place, Regent's Park.   50

1875 Copyrights in Collins's work transferred to
     Chatto & Windus, who become his main
     publisher.
     The Law and the Lady serialized in *The London
     Graphic*; published in volume form.   51

1876 (April) *Miss Gwilt* (dramatic version of *Armadale*)
     performed at the Globe Theatre.
     The Two Destinies, published in volume form.   52

1877 (September) Dramatic version of *The Moonstone*
     performed at the Olympic Theatre.
     My Lady's Money and Percy and the Prophet,
     short stories, published.   53

1878 *The Haunted Hotel* published in volume form.   54

BASIL

LETTER OF DEDICATION.

TO CHARLES JAMES WARD, Esq.*

It has long been one of my pleasantest anticipations to look forward to the time when I might offer to you, my old and dear friend, some such acknowledgment of the value I place on your affection for me, and of my grateful sense of the many acts of kindness by which that affection has been proved, as I now gladly offer in this place. In dedicating the present work to you, I fulfil therefore a purpose which, for some time past, I have sincerely desired to achieve; and, more than that, I gain for myself the satisfaction of knowing that there is one page, at least, of my book, on which I shall always look with unalloyed pleasure—the page that bears your name.

I have founded the main event out of which this story springs, on a fact within my own knowledge.* In afterwards shaping the course of the narrative thus suggested, I have guided it, as often as I could, where I knew by my own experience, or by experience related to me by others, that it would touch on something real and true in its progress. My idea was that the more of the Actual I could garner up as a text to speak from, the more certain I might feel

of the genuineness and value of the Ideal which was sure
to spring out of it. Fancy and Imagination, Grace and
Beauty, all those qualities which are to the work of Art
what scent and colour are to the flower, can only grow
towards heaven by taking root in earth. Is not the noblest
poetry of prose fiction the poetry of every-day truth?

Directing my characters and my story, then, towards the
light of Reality wherever I could find it, I have not hesitated
to violate some of the conventionalities of sentimental fiction. For instance, the first love-meeting of two of the
personages in this book, occurs (where the real love-meeting
from which it is drawn, occurred) in the very last place
and under the very last circumstances which the artifices of
sentimental writing would sanction. Will my lovers excite
ridicule instead of interest, because I have truly represented
them as seeing each other where hundreds of other lovers
have first seen each other, as hundreds of people will readily
admit when they read the passage to which I refer? I am
sanguine enough to think not.

So again, in certain parts of this book where I have
attempted to excite the suspense or pity of the reader, I
have admitted as perfectly fit accessories to the scene the
most ordinary street-sounds that could be heard, and the
most ordinary street-events that could occur, at the time
and in the place represented—believing that by adding to
truth, they were adding to tragedy—adding by all the force
of fair contrast—adding as no artifices of mere writing
possibly could add, let them be ever so cunningly introduced
by ever so crafty a hand.

Allow me to dwell a moment longer on the story which
these pages contain.

Believing that the Novel and the Play are twin-sisters in the family of Fiction; that the one is a drama narrated, as the other is a drama acted; and that all the strong and deep emotions which the Play-writer is privileged to excite, the Novel-writer is privileged to excite also, I have not thought it either politic or necessary, while adhering to realities, to adhere to every-day realities only. In other words, I have not stooped so low as to assure myself of the reader's belief in the probability of my story, by never once calling on him for the exercise of his faith. Those extraordinary accidents and events which happen to few men, seemed to me to be as legitimate materials for fiction to work with—when there was a good object in using them—as the ordinary accidents and events which may, and do, happen to us all. By appealing to genuine sources of interest *within* the reader's own experience, I could certainly gain his attention to begin with; but it would be only by appealing to other sources (as genuine in their way) *beyond* his own experience, that I could hope to fix his interest and excite his suspense, to occupy his deeper feelings, or to stir his nobler thoughts.

In writing thus—briefly and very generally—(for I must not delay you too long from the story), I can but repeat, though I hope almost unnecessarily, that I am now only speaking of what I have *tried* to do. Between the purpose hinted at here, and the execution of that purpose contained in the succeeding pages, lies the broad line of separation which distinguishes between the will and the deed. How far I may fall short of another man's standard, remains to be discovered. How far I have fallen short of my own, I know painfully well.

One word more on the manner in which the purpose of the following pages is worked out—and I have done.

Nobody who admits that the business of fiction is to exhibit human life, can deny that scenes of misery and crime must of necessity, while human nature remains what it is, form part of that exhibition. Nobody can assert that such scenes are unproductive of useful results,* when they are turned to a plainly and purely moral purpose. If I am asked why I have written certain scenes in this book, my answer is to be found in the universally-accepted truth which the preceding words express. I have a right to appeal to that truth; for I guided myself by it throughout. In deriving the lesson* which the following pages contain, from those examples of error and crime which would most strikingly and naturally teach it, I determined to do justice to the honesty of my object by speaking out. In drawing the two characters, whose actions bring about the darker scenes of my story, I did not forget that it was my duty, while striving to pourtray them naturally, to put them to a good moral use; and at some sacrifice, in certain places, of dramatic effect (though I trust with no sacrifice of truth to Nature), I have shown the conduct of the vile, as always, in a greater or less degree, associated with something that is selfish, contemptible, or cruel in motive. Whether any of my better characters may succeed in endearing themselves to the reader, I know not: but this I do certainly know:—that I shall in no instance cheat him out of his sympathies in favour of the bad.

To those persons who dissent from the broad principles here adverted to; who deny that it is the novelist's vocation to do more than merely amuse them; who shrink from all honest and serious reference, in books, to subjects which they think of in private and talk of in public everywhere; who see covert implications where nothing is implied, and improper allusions where nothing improper is alluded to; whose innocence is in the word, and not in the thought; whose morality stops at the tongue, and never gets on to the heart—to those persons, I should consider it loss of time, and worse, to offer any further explanation of my motives, than the sufficient explanation which I have given already. I do not address myself to them in this book, and shall never think of addressing myself to them in any other.

Those words formed part of the original introduction to this novel. I wrote them nearly ten years since; and what I said then, I say now.

"Basil" was the second work of fiction which I produced. On its appearance, it was condemned off-hand, by a certain class of readers, as an outrage on their sense of propriety. Conscious of having designed and written my story with the strictest regard to true delicacy, as distinguished from false—I allowed the prurient misinterpretation of certain perfectly innocent passages in this book to assert itself as offensively as it pleased, without troubling myself to protest against an expression of opinion which aroused in me no other feeling than a feeling of contempt. I knew that "Basil" had nothing to fear from pure-minded readers; and I left these pages to stand or fall on such merits as they possessed. Slowly and surely, my story forced its way through all adverse criticism, to a place in the public favour which it has never lost since. Some of the most valued friends I now possess, were made for me

by " Basil." Some of the most gratifying recognitions of
my labours which I have received, from readers personally
strangers to me, have been recognitions of the purity
of this story, from the first page to the last. All the indulgence I need now ask for " Basil," is indulgence for
literary defects, which are the result of inexperience
which no correction can wholly remove; and which no one
sees more plainly, after a lapse of ten years, than the writer
himself.

I have only to add, that the present edition of this book
is the first which has had the benefit of my careful revision.
While the incidents of the story remain exactly what they
were, the language in which they are told has been, I hope,
in many cases greatly altered for the better.

                                        WILKIE COLLINS.

Harley Street, London,
    July, 1862.

BASIL.

PART I.

I.

WHAT am I now about to write?

The history of little more than the events of one year, out of the twenty-four years of my life.

Why do I undertake such an employment as this?

Perhaps, because I think that my narrative may do good; because I hope that, one day, it may be put to some warning use.* I am now about to relate the story of an error, innocent in its beginning, guilty in its progress, fatal in its results; and I would fain hope that my plain and true record will show that this error was not committed altogether without excuse. When these pages are found after my death, they will perhaps be calmly read and gently judged, as relics solemnized by the atoning shadows of the grave. Then, the hard sentence against me may be repented of; the children of the next generation of our house may be taught to speak charitably of my memory, and may often, of their own accord, think of me kindly in the thoughtful watches of the night.

Prompted by these motives, and by others which I feel, but cannot analyse, I now begin my self-imposed occupation. Hidden amid the far hills of the far West of England, surrounded only by the few simple inhabitants of a fishing hamlet on the Cornish coast, there is little fear that my attention will be distracted from my task ; and as little chance that any indolence on my part will delay its speedy accomplishment. I live under a threat of impending hostility, which may descend and overwhelm me, I know not how soon, or in what manner. An enemy, determined and deadly, patient alike to wait days or years for his opportunity, is ever lurking after me in the dark. In entering on my new employment, I cannot say of my time, that it may be mine for another hour ; of my life, that it may last till evening.

Thus, it is as no leisure work that I begin my narrative— and begin it, too, on my birthday ! On this day I complete my twenty-fourth year ; the first new year of my life which has not been greeted by a single kind word, or a single loving wish. But one look of welcome can still find me in my solitude—the lovely morning look of nature, as I now see it from the casement of my room. Brighter and brighter shines out the lusty sun from banks of purple, rainy cloud ; fishermen are spreading their nets to dry on the lower declivities of the rocks ; children are playing round the boats drawn up on the beach ; the sea-breeze blows fresh and pure towards the shore—all objects are brilliant to look on, all sounds are pleasant to hear, as my pen traces the first lines which open the story of my life.

II.

I am the second son of an English gentleman of large fortune. Our family is, I believe, one of the most ancient in this country. On my father's side, it dates back beyond the Conquest ; on my mother's, it is not so old, but the pedigree is nobler. Besides my elder brother, I have one sister, younger than myself. My mother died shortly after giving birth to her last child.

Circumstances which will appear hereafter, have forced me

to abandon my father's name. I have been obliged in honour to resign it; and in honour I abstain from mentioning it here. Accordingly, at the head of these pages, I have only placed my Christian name—not considering it of any importance to add the surname which I have assumed; and which I may, perhaps, be obliged to change for some other, at no very distant period. It will now, I hope, be understood from the outset, why I never mention my brother and sister but by their Christian names; why a blank occurs wherever my father's name should appear; why my own is kept concealed in this narrative, as it is kept concealed in the world.

The story of my boyhood and youth*has little to interest—nothing that is new. My education was the education of hundreds of others in my rank of life. I was first taught at a public school, and then went to college to complete what is termed "a liberal education."

My life at college has not left me a single pleasant recollection.* I found sycophancy established there, as a principle of action; flaunting on the lord's gold tassel in the street; enthroned on the lord's dais in the dining-room. The most learned student in my college—the man whose life was most exemplary, whose acquirements were most admirable—was shown me sitting, as a commoner, in the lowest place. The heir to an Earldom, who had failed at the last examination, was pointed out a few minutes afterwards, dining in solitary grandeur at a raised table, above the reverend scholars who had turned him back as a dunce. I had just arrived at the University, and had just been congratulated on entering "a venerable seminary of learning and religion."

Trite and common-place though it be, I mention this circumstance attending my introduction to college, because it formed the first cause which tended to diminish my faith in the institution to which I was attached. I soon grew to regard my university training as a sort of necessary evil, to be patiently submitted to. I read for no honours, and joined no particular set of men. I studied the literature of France, Italy, and Germany; just kept up my classical knowledge sufficiently to take my degree; and left college with no other reputation than a reputation for indolence and reserve.

When I returned home, it was thought necessary, as I was a younger son, and could inherit none of the landed property of the family, except in the case of my brother's dying without children, that I should belong to a profession. My father had the patronage of some valuable "livings;"* and good interest with more than one member of the government. The church, the army, the navy, and, in the last instance, the bar, were offered me to choose from. I selected the last.

My father appeared to be a little astonished at my choice; but he made no remark on it, except simply telling me not to forget that the bar was a good stepping-stone to parliament. My real ambition, however, was, not to make a name in parliament, but a name in literature. I had already engaged myself in the hard, but glorious service of the pen; and I was determined to persevere. The profession which offered me the greatest facilities for pursuing my project, was the profession which I was ready to prefer. So I chose the bar.

Thus, I entered life under the fairest auspices. Though a younger son, I knew that my father's wealth, exclusive of his landed property, secured me an independent income far beyond my wants. I had no extravagant habits; no tastes that I could not gratify as soon as formed; no cares or responsibilities of any kind. I might practise my profession or not, just as I chose. I could devote myself wholly and unreservedly to literature, knowing that, in my case, the struggle for fame could never be identical—terribly, though gloriously identical—with the struggle for bread. For

me, the morning sunshine of life was sunshine without a
cloud

I might attempt, in this place, to sketch my own character
as it was at that time. But what man can say—I will
sound the depth of my own vices, and measure the height of
my own virtues; and be as good as his word? We can
neither know nor judge ourselves; others may judge, but
cannot know us: God alone judges and knows too. Let
my character appear—as far as any human character can
appear in its integrity, in this world—in my actions, when I
describe the one eventful passage in my life which forms the
basis of this narrative. In the mean time, it is first necessary that I should say more about the members of my
family. Two of them, at least, will be found important to
the progress of events in these pages. I make no attempt
to judge their characters: I only describe them—whether
rightly or wrongly, I know not—as they appeared to *me*.

III.

I always considered my father—I speak of him in the
past tense, because we are now separated for ever; because
he is henceforth as dead to me as if the grave had closed
over him—I always considered my father to be the proudest
man I ever knew; the proudest man I ever heard of. His
was not that conventional pride, which the popular notions
are fond of characterising by a stiff, stately carriage; by a
rigid expression of features; by a hard, severe intonation
of voice; by set speeches of contempt for poverty and rags,
and rhapsodical braggadocio about rank and breeding. My
father's pride had nothing of this about it. It was that
quiet, negative, courteous, inbred pride, which only the
closest observation could detect; which no ordinary ob-
servers ever detected at all.

Who that observed him in communication with any of

the farmers on any of his estates—who that saw the manner in which he lifted his hat, when he accidentally met any of those farmers' wives—who that noticed his hearty welcome to the man of the people, when that man happened to be a man of genius—would have thought him proud? On such occasions as these, if he had any pride, it was impossible to detect it. But seeing him when, for instance, an author and a new-made peer of no ancestry entered his house together—observing merely the entirely different manner in which he shook hands with each—remarking that the polite cordiality was all for the man of letters, who did not contest his family rank with him, and the polite formality all for the man of title, who did—you discovered where and how he was proud in an instant. Here lay his fretful point. The aristocracy of rank, as separate from the aristocracy of ancestry, was no aristocracy for *him*. He was jealous of it; he hated it. Commoner though he was, he considered himself the social superior of any man, from a baronet up to a duke, whose family was less ancient than his own.

Among a host of instances of this peculiar pride of his which I could cite, I remember one, characteristic enough to be taken as a sample of all the rest. It happened when I was quite a child, and was told me by one of my uncles—now dead—who witnessed the circumstance himself, and always made a good story of it to the end of his life.

A merchant of enormous wealth, who had recently been raised to the peerage, was staying at one of our country houses. His daughter, my uncle, and an Italian Abbé were the only guests besides. The merchant was a portly, purple-faced man, who bore his new honours with a curious mixture of assumed pomposity and natural good-humour. The Abbé was dwarfish and deformed, lean, sallow, sharp-featured, with bright bird-like eyes, and a low, liquid voice. He was a political refugee, dependent for the bread he ate, on the money he received for teaching languages. He might have been a beggar from the streets; and still my father would have treated him as the principal guest in the house, for this all-sufficient reason—he was a direct descendant of one of the oldest of those famous Roman families whose names are part of the history of the Civil Wars in Italy.

On the first day, the party assembled for dinner comprised the merchant's daughter, my mother, an old lady who had once been her governess, and had always lived with her since her marriage, the new Lord, the Abbé, my father, and my uncle. When dinner was announced, the peer advanced in new-blown dignity, to offer his arm as a matter of course to my mother. My father's pale face flushed crimson in a moment. He touched the magnificent merchant-lord on the arm, and pointed significantly, with a low bow, towards the decrepid old lady who had once been my mother's governess. Then walking to the other end of the room, where the penniless Abbé was looking over a book in a corner, he gravely and courteously led the little, deformed, limping language-master, clad in a long, threadbare, black coat, up to my mother (whose shoulder the Abbé's head hardly reached), held the door open for them to pass out first, with his own hand; politely invited the new nobleman, who stood half-paralysed between confusion and astonishment, to follow with the tottering old lady on his arm; and then returned to lead the peer's daughter down to dinner himself. He only resumed his wonted expression and manner, when he had seen the little Abbé—the squalid, half-starved representative of mighty barons of the olden time—seated at the highest place of the table by my mother's side.

It was by such accidental circumstances as these that you discovered how far he was proud. He never boasted of his ancestors; he never even spoke of them, except when he was questioned on the subject; but he never

forgot them. They were the very breath of his life; the
deities of his social worship: the family treasures to be
held precious beyond all lands and all wealth, all ambitions
and all glories, by his children and his children's children
to the end of their race.

In home-life he performed his duties towards his family
honourably, delicately, and kindly. I believe in his own
way he loved us all; but we, his descendants, had to share
his heart with his ancestors—we were his household property as well as his children. Every fair liberty was
given to us; every fair indulgence was granted to us. He
never displayed any suspicion, or any undue severity. We
were taught by his direction, that to disgrace our family,
either by word or action, was the one fatal crime which
could never be forgotten and never be pardoned. We were
formed, under his superintendence, in principles of religion,
honour, and industry; and the rest was left to our own
moral sense, to our own comprehension of the duties and
privileges of our station. There was no one point in his
conduct towards any of us that we could complain of; and
yet there was something always incomplete in our domestic
relations.

It may seem incomprehensible, even ridiculous, to some
persons, but it is nevertheless true, that we were none of us
ever on intimate terms with him. I mean by this, that he
was a father to us, but never a companion. There was
something in his manner, his quiet and unchanging manner
which kept us almost unconsciously restrained. I never in
my life felt less at my ease—I knew not why at the time—
than when I occasionally dined alone with him. I never
confided to him my schemes for amusement as a boy; or
mentioned more than generally my ambitious hopes, as a
young man. It was not that he would have received such
-confidences with ridicule or severity, he was incapable of
it; but that he seemed above them, unfitted to enter into

them, too far removed by his own thoughts from such thoughts as ours. Thus, all holiday councils were held with old servants; thus, my first pages of manuscript, when I first tried authorship, were read by my sister, and never penetrated into my father's study.

Again, his mode of testifying displeasure towards my brother or myself, had something terrible in its calmness, something that we never forgot, and always dreaded as the worst calamity that could befall us.

Whenever, as boys, we committed some boyish fault, he never displayed outwardly any irritation—he simply altered his manner towards us altogether. We were not soundly lectured, or vehemently threatened, or positively punished in any way; but, when we came in contact with him, we were treated with a cold, contemptuous politeness (especially if our fault showed a tendency to anything mean or ungentlemanlike) which cut us to the heart. On these occasions, we were not addressed by our Christian names; if we accidentally met him out of doors, he was sure to turn aside and avoid us; if we asked a question, it was answered in the briefest possible manner, as if we had been strangers. His whole course of conduct said, as though in so many words—You have rendered yourselves unfit to associate with your father; and he is now making you feel that unfitness as deeply as he does. We were left in this domestic purgatory for days, sometimes for weeks together. To our boyish feelings (to mine especially) there was no ignominy like it, while it lasted.

I know not on what terms my father lived with my mother. Towards my sister, his demeanour always exhibited something of the old-fashioned, affectionate gallantry of a former age. He paid her the same attention that he would have paid to the highest lady in the land. He led her into the dining-room, when we were alone, exactly as he would have led a duchess into a banqueting-hall. He would allow us, as boys, to quit the breakfast-table before he had risen himself; but never before she had left it. If a servant failed in duty towards *him*, the servant was often forgiven; if towards *her*, the servant was sent away on the spot. His daughter was in his eyes the representative of her mother: the mistress of his house, as well as his child. It was curious to see the mixture of high-bred courtesy and fatherly love in his manner, as he just gently touched her forehead with his lips, when he first saw her in the morning.

In person, my father was of not more than middle height. He was very slenderly and delicately made; his head small, and well set on his shoulders—his forehead more broad than lofty—his complexion singularly pale, except in moments of agitation, when I have already noticed its tendency to flush all over in an instant. His eyes, large and gray, had something commanding in their look; they gave a certain unchanging firmness and dignity to his expression, not often met with. They betrayed his birth and breeding, his old ancestral prejudices, his chivalrous sense of honour, in every glance. It required, indeed, all the masculine energy of look about the upper part of his face, to redeem the lower part from an appearance of effeminacy, so delicately was it moulded in its fine Norman outline. His smile was remarkable for its sweetness—it was almost like a woman's smile. In speaking, too, his lips often trembled as women's do. If he ever laughed, as a young man, his laugh must have been very clear and musical; but since I can recollect him, I never heard it. In his happiest moments, in the gayest society, I have only seen him smile.

There were other characteristics of my father's disposition and manner, which I might mention; but they will appear to greater advantage, perhaps, hereafter, connected with circumstances which especially called them forth.

everybody. Though I was his favourite both, both at school and college, I never quarrelled with him in my life. I always let him ridicule my dress, manners, and habits in his

IV.

When a family is possessed of large landed property, the individual of that family who shows least interest in its welfare; who is least fond of home, least connected by his own sympathies with his relatives, least ready to learn his duties or admit his responsibilities, is often that very individual who is to succeed to the family inheritance—the eldest son.

My brother Ralph was no exception to this remark. We were educated together. After our education was completed, I never saw him, except for short periods. He was almost always on the continent, for some years after he left college. And when he returned definitely to England, he did not return to live under our roof. Both in town and country he was our visitor, not our inmate.

I recollect him at school—stronger, taller, handsomer than I was; far beyond me in popularity among the little community we lived with; the first to lead a daring exploit, the last to abandon it; now at the bottom of the class, now at the top—just that sort of gay, boisterous, fine-looking, dare-devil boy, whom old people would instinctively turn round and smile after, as they passed him by in a morning walk.

Then, at college, he became illustrious among rowers and cricketers, renowned as a pistol shot, dreaded as a single-stick player: No wine parties in the university were such wine parties as his; tradesmen gave him the first choice of everything that was new; young ladies in the town fell in love with him by dozens; young tutors with a tendency to dandyism, copied the cut of his coat and the tie of his cravat; even the awful heads of houses looked leniently on his delinquencies. The gay, hearty, handsome young English gentleman carried a charm about him that subdued

everybody. Though I was his favourite butt, both at schoo.
and college, I never quarrelled with him in my life. I always let him ridicule my dress, manners, and habits in his
own reckless, boisterous way, as if it had been a part of
his birthright privilege to laugh at me as much as he
chose.

Thus far, my father had no worse anxieties about him
than those occasioned by his high spirits and his heavy debts.
But when he returned home—when the debts had been
paid, and it was next thought necessary to drill the free,
careless energies into something like useful discipline—then
my father's trials and difficulties began in earnest.

It was impossible to make Ralph comprehend and appreciate his position, as he was desired to comprehend and appreciate it. The steward gave up in despair all attempts
to enlighten him about the extent, value, and management
of the estates he was to inherit. A vigorous effort was
made to inspire him with ambition; to get him to go into
parliament. He laughed at the idea. A commission in
the Guards was next offered to him. He refused it, because
he would never be buttoned up in a red coat; because he
would submit to no restraints, fashionable or military; because, in short, he was determined to be his own master.
My father talked to him by the hour together, about his
duties and his prospects, the cultivation of his mind, and
the example of his ancestors; and talked in vain. He
yawned and fidgetted over the emblazoned pages of his
own family pedigree, whenever they were opened before
him.

In the country, he cared for nothing but hunting and
shooting—it was as difficult to make him go to a grand
county dinner-party, as to make him go to church. In
town, he haunted the theatres, behind the scenes as well as
before; entertained actors and actresses at Richmond;
ascended in balloons at Vauxhall;* went about with detec-

tive policemen, seeing life among pickpockets and house-breakers ; belonged to a whist club, a supper club, a catch club, a boxing club, a pic-nic club,* an amateur theatrical club ; and, in short, lived such a careless, convivial life, that my father, outraged in every one of his family preju-dices and family refinements, almost ceased to speak to him, and saw him as rarely as possible. Occasionally, my sister's interference reconciled them again for a short time ; her influence, gentle as it was, was always powerfully felt for good, but she could not change my brother's nature. Per-suade and entreat as anxiously as she might, he was always sure to forfeit the paternal favour again, a few days after he had been restored to it.

At last, matters were brought to their climax by an awk-ward love adventure of Ralph's with one of our tenants' daughters. My father acted with his usual decision on the occasion. He determined to apply a desperate remedy : to let the refractory eldest son run through his career in free-dom, abroad, until he had well wearied himself, and could return home a sobered man. Accordingly, he procured for my brother an *attaché's* place in a foreign embassy, and insisted on his leaving England forthwith. For once in a way, Ralph was docile. He knew and cared nothing about diplomacy ; but he liked the idea of living on the con-tinent,* so he took his leave of home with his best grace. My father saw him depart, with ill-concealed agitation and apprehension ; although he affected to feel satisfied that, flighty and idle as Ralph was, he was incapable of volun-tarily dishonouring his family, even in his most reckless moods.

After this, we heard little from my brother. His letters were few and short, and generally ended with petitions for money. The only important news of him that reached us, reached us through public channels.

He was making quite a continental reputation—a repu-

tation, the bare mention of which made my father wince.
He had fought a duel; he had imported a new dance from
Hungary; he had contrived to get the smallest groom
that ever was seen behind a cabriolet; he had carried off
the reigning beauty among the opera-dancers* of the day
from all competitors; a great French cook had composed
a great French dish, and christened it by his name; he was
understood to be the "unknown friend," to whom a literary
Polish countess had dedicated her "Letters against the
restraint of the Marriage Tie;" a female German metaphy-
sician, sixty years old, had fallen (Platonically) in love with
him, and had taken to writing erotic romances in her old
age. Such were some of the rumours that reached my
father's ears on the subject of his son and heir!

After a long absence, he came home on a visit. How
well I remember the astonishment he produced in the
whole household! He had become a foreigner in manners
and appearance. His mustachios were magnificent; miniature toys in gold and jewellery hung in clusters from his
watch-chain; his shirt-front was a perfect filigree of lace and
cambric. He brought with him his own boxes of choice
liqueurs and perfumes; his own smart, impudent, French
valet; his own travelling bookcase of French novels,* which
he opened with his own golden key. He drank nothing
but chocolate in the morning; he had long interviews with
the cook, and revolutionized our dinner table. All the
French newspapers were sent to him by a London agent.
He altered the arrangements of his bed-room; no servant
but his own valet was permitted to enter it. Family
portraits that hung there, were turned to the walls, and
portraits of French actresses and Italian singers were stuck
to the back of the canvasses. Then he displaced a beautiful
little ebony cabinet which had been in the family three
hundred years; and set up in its stead a Cyprian temple* of
his own, in miniature, with crystal doors, behind which

hung locks of hair, rings, notes written on blush-coloured paper, and other love-tokens kept as sentimental relics. His influence became all-pervading among us. He seemed to communicate to the house the change that had taken place in himself, from the reckless, racketty young Englishman to the super-exquisite foreign dandy. It was as if the fiery, effervescent atmosphere of the Boulevards of Paris had insolently penetrated into the old English mansion, and ruffled and infected its quiet native air, to the remotest corners of the place.

My father was even more dismayed than displeased by the alteration in my brother's habits and manners—the eldest son was now farther from his ideal of what an eldest son should be, than ever. As for friends and neighbours, Ralph was heartily feared and disliked by them, before he had been in the house a week. He had an ironically patient way of listening to their conversation; an ironically respectful manner of demolishing their old-fashioned opinions, and correcting their slightest mistakes, which secretly aggravated them beyond endurance. It was worse still, when my father, in despair, tried to tempt him into marriage, as the one final chance of working his reform; and invited half the marriageable young ladies of our acquaintance to the house, for his especial benefit.

Ralph had never shown much fondness at home, for the refinements of good female society. Abroad, he had lived as exclusively as he possibly could, among women whose characters ranged downwards by infinitesimal degrees, from the mysteriously doubtful to the notoriously bad. The highly-bred, highly-refined, highly-accomplished young English beauties had no charm for him. He detected at once the domestic conspiracy of which he was destined to become the victim. He often came up-stairs, at night, into my bed-room; and while he was amusing himself by derisively kicking about my simple clothes and simple toilette apparatus; while he was laughing in his old careless way at my quiet habits and monotonous life, used to slip in, parenthetically, all sorts of sarcasms about our young lady guests. To him, their manners were horribly inanimate; their innocence, hypocrisy of education. Pure complexions and regular features were very well, he said, as far as they went; but when a girl could not walk properly, when she shook hands with you with cold fingers, when having good eyes she could not make a stimulating use of them, then it was time to sentence the regular features and pure complexions to be taken back forthwith to the nursery from which they came. For *his* part, he missed the conversation of his witty Polish Countess, and longed for another pan-cake-supper with his favourite *grisettes.**

The failure of my father's last experiment with Ralph soon became apparent. Watchful and experienced mothers began to suspect that my brother's method of flirtation was dangerous, and his style of waltzing improper. One or two ultra-cautious parents, alarmed by the laxity of his manners and opinions, removed their daughters out of harm's way, by shortening their visits. The rest were spared any such necessity. My father suddenly discovered that Ralph was devoting himself rather too significantly to a young married woman who was staying in the house. The same day he had a long private interview with my brother. What passed between them, I know not; but it must have been something serious. Ralph came out of my father's private study, very pale and very silent; ordered his luggage to be packed directly; and the next morning departed, with his French valet, and his multifarious French goods and chattels, for the continent.

Another interval passed; and then we had another short visit from him. He was still unaltered. My father's temper suffered under this second disappointment. He became more fretful and silent; more apt to take offence than had been his wont. I particularly mention the change thus produced in his disposition, because that change was destined, at no very distant period, to act fatally upon me.

On this last occasion, also, there was another serious disagreement between father and son; and Ralph left England again in much the same way that he had left it before.

Shortly after that second departure, we heard that he had altered his manner of life. He had contracted, what would be termed in the continental code of morals, a reformatory attachment to a woman older than himself, who was living separated from her husband, when he met with her. It was this lady's lofty ambition to be Mentor and mistress, both together! And she soon proved herself to be well qualified for her courageous undertaking. To the astonishment of everyone who knew him, Ralph suddenly turned economical; and, soon afterwards, actually resigned his post at the embassy, to be out of the way of temptation! Since that, he has returned to England; has devoted himself to collecting snuff-boxes and learning the violin; and is now living quietly in the suburbs of London, still under the inspection of the resolute female missionary who first worked his reform.

Whether he will ever become the high-minded, high-principled country gentleman, that my father has always desired to see him, it is useless for me to guess. On the domains which he is to inherit, I shall never perhaps set foot again: in the halls where he will one day preside as master, I shall never more be sheltered. Let me now quit the subject of my elder brother, and turn to a theme which is nearer to my heart; dear to me as the last remembrance left that I can love; precious beyond all treasures in my solitude and my exile from home.

My sister!—well may I linger over your beloved name in such a record as this. A little farther on, and the darkness of crime and grief will encompass me; here, my recollec-

tions of you kindle like a pure light before my eyes—
doubly pure by contrast with what lies beyond.   May *your*
kind eyes, love, be the first that fall on these pages, when
the writer has parted from them for ever!   May *your* tender hand be the first that touches these leaves, when mine
is cold!   Backward in my narrative, Clara, wherever I have
but casually mentioned my sister, the pen has trembled and
stood still.   At this place, where all my remembrances of
you throng upon me unrestrained, the tears gather fast and
thick beyond control; and for the first time since I began
my task, my courage and my calmness fail me.

It is useless to persevere longer.   My hand trembles;
my eyes grow dimmer and dimmer.   I must close my
labours for the day, and go forth to gather strength and
resolution for to-morrow on the hill-tops that overlook the
sea.

V.

My sister Clara is four years younger than I am.   In
form of face, in complexion, and—except the eyes—in features, she bears a striking resemblance to my father.   Her
expression, however, must be very like what my mother's
was.   Whenever I have looked at her in her silent and
thoughtful moments, she has always appeared to freshen,
and even to increase, my vague, childish recollections of our
lost mother.   Her eyes have that slight tinge of melancholy
in their tenderness, and that peculiar softness in their repose, which is only seen in blue eyes.   Her complexion,
pale as my father's when she is neither speaking nor moving,
has in a far greater degree than his the tendency to flush,
not merely in moments of agitation, but even when she is
walking, or talking on any subject that interests her.
Without this peculiarity, her paleness would be a defect.
With it, the absence of any colour in her complexion but

the fugitive uncertain colour which I have described, would to some eyes debar her from any claims to beauty. And a beauty perhaps she is not—at least, in the ordinary acceptation of the term.

The lower part of her face is rather too small for the upper, her figure is too slight, the sensitiveness of her nervous organization is too constantly visible in her actions and her looks. She would not fix attention and admiration in a box at the opera; very few men passing her in the street, would turn round to look after her; very few women would regard her with that slightingly attentive stare, that steady depreciating scrutiny, which a dashing decided beauty so often receives (and so often triumphs in receiving) from her personal inferiors among her own sex. The greatest charms that my sister has on the surface, come from beneath it.

When you really knew her, when she spoke to you freely, as to a friend—then, the attraction of her voice, her smile, her manner, impressed you indescribably. Her slightest words and her commonest actions interested and delighted you, you knew not why. There was a beauty about her unassuming simplicity, her natural—exquisitely natural—kindness of heart, and word, and manner, which preserved its own unobtrusive influence over you, in spite of all other rival influences, be they what they might. You missed and thought of her, when you were fresh from the society of the most beautiful and the most brilliant women. You remembered a few kind, pleasant words of hers when you forgot the wit of the wittiest ladies, the learning of the most learned. The influence thus possessed, and unconsciously possessed, by my sister over every one with whom she came in contact—over men especially—may, I think, be very simply accounted for, in very few sentences.

We live in an age when too many women appear to be ambitious of morally unsexing themselves before society, by

aping the language and the manners of men—especially in
reference to that miserable modern dandyism of demeanour,
which aims at repressing all betrayal of warmth of feeling;
which abstains from displaying any enthusiasm on any subject whatever; which, in short, labours to make the fashionable imperturbability of the face the faithful reflection of
the fashionable imperturbability of the mind. Women of
this exclusively modern order, like to use slang expressions
in their conversation; assume a bastard-masculine abruptness in their manners, a bastard-masculine licence in their
opinions; affect to ridicule those outward developments of
feeling which pass under the general appellation of " sentiment." Nothing impresses, agitates, amuses, or delights
them in a hearty, natural, womanly way. Sympathy looks
ironical, if they ever show it: love seems to be an affair of
calculation, or mockery, or contemptuous sufferance, if they
ever feel it.

To women such as these, my sister Clara presented as
complete a contrast as could well be conceived. In this
contrast lay the secret of her influence, of the voluntary
tribute of love and admiration which followed her wherever
she went.

Few men have not their secret moments of deep feeling
—moments when, amid the wretched trivialities and hypocrisies of modern society, the image will present itself to
their minds of some woman, fresh, innocent, gentle, sincere;
some woman whose emotions are still warm and impressible,
whose affections and sympathies can still appear in her actions, and give the colour to her thoughts; some woman in
whom we could put as perfect faith and trust, as if we were
children; whom we despair of finding near the hardening
influences of the world; whom we could scarcely venture
to look for, except in solitary places far away in the country;
in little rural shrines, shut up from society, among woods
and fields, and lonesome boundary-hills. When any women

happen to realise, or nearly to realise, such an image as this, they possess that universal influence which no rivalry can ever approach. On them really depends, and by them is really preserved, that claim upon the sincere respect and admiration of men, on which the power of the whole sex is based—the power so often assumed by the many, so rarely possessed but by the few.

It was thus with my sister. Thus, wherever she went, though without either the inclination, or the ambition to shine, she eclipsed women who were her superiors in beauty, in accomplishments, in brilliancy of manners and conversation—conquering by no other weapon than the purely feminine charm of everything she said, and every-thing she did.

But it was not amid the gaiety and grandeur of a London season that her character was displayed to the greatest advantage. It was when she was living where she loved to live, in the old country-house, among the old friends and old servants who would every one of them have died a hundred deaths for her sake, that you could study and love her best. Then, the charm there was in the mere presence of the kind, gentle, happy young English girl, who could enter into everybody's interests, and be grateful for everybody's love, possessed its best and brightest influence. At picnics, lawn-parties, little country gatherings of all sorts, she was, in her own quiet, natural manner, always the presiding spirit of general comfort and general friendship. Even the rigid laws of country punctilio relaxed before her unaffected cheerfulness and irresistible good-nature. She always contrived—nobody ever knew how—to lure the most formal people into forgetting their formality, and becoming natural for the rest of the day. Even a heavy-headed, lumbering, silent country squire, was not too much for her. She managed to make him feel at his ease, when no one else would undertake the task : she could listen patiently to his confused speeches about dogs, horses, and the state of the crops, when other conversations were proceeding in which she was really interested; she could receive any little grateful attention that he wished to pay her—no matter how awkward or ill-timed—as she received attentions from any one else, with a manner which showed she considered it as a favour granted to her sex, not as a right accorded to it.

So, again, she always succeeded in diminishing the long list of those pitiful affronts and offences, which play such important parts in the social drama of country society. She was a perfect Apostle-errant of the order of Reconciliation; and wherever she went, cast out the devil Sulkiness from all his strongholds—the lofty and the lowly alike. Our good rector used to call her his Volunteer Curate; and declare that she preached by a timely word, or a persuasive look, the best practical sermons on the blessings of peace-making that were ever composed.

With all this untiring good-nature, with all this resolute industry in the task of making every one happy whom she approached, there was mingled some indescribable influence, which invariably preserved her from the presumption, even of the most presuming people. I never knew anybody venturesome enough—either by word or look—to take a liberty with her. There was something about her which inspired respect as well as love. My father, following the bent of his peculiar and favourite ideas, always thought it was the look of her race in her eyes, the ascendancy of her race in her manners. I believe it to have proceeded from a simpler and a better cause. There is a goodness of heart, which carries the shield of its purity over the open hand of its kindness: and that goodness was hers.

To my father, she was more, I believe, than he himself over imagined—or will ever know, unless he should lose her. He was often, in his intercourse with the world, wounded severely enough in his peculiar prejudices and peculiar refinements—he was always sure to find the first respected, and the last partaken by *her*. He could trust in her implicitly, he could feel assured that she was not only willing, but able, to share and relieve his domestic troubles and anxieties. If he had been less fretfully anxious about his eldest son; if he had wisely distrusted from the first his own powers of persuading and reforming, and had allowed Clara to exercise her influence over Ralph more constantly and more completely than he really did, I am persuaded that the long-expected epoch of my brother's transformation would have really arrived by this time, or even before it.

The strong and deep feelings of my sister's nature lay far below the surface—for a woman, too far below it. Suffering was, for her, silent, secret, long enduring; often almost entirely void of outward vent or development. I never remember seeing her in tears, except on rare and very serious occasions. Unless you looked at her narrowly, you would judge her to be little sensitive to ordinary griefs and troubles. At such times, her eyes only grew dimmer and less animated than usual; the paleness of her complexion became rather more marked; her lips closed and trembled involuntarily—but this was all: there was no sighing, no weeping, no speaking even. And yet she suffered acutely. The very strength of her emotions was in their silence and their secresy. I, of all others—I, guilty of infecting with my anguish the pure heart that loved me—ought to know this best!

How long I might linger over all that she has done for *me*! As I now approach nearer and nearer to the pages which are to reveal my fatal story, so I am more and more tempted to delay over those better and purer remembrances of my sister which now occupy my mind. The first little presents—innocent girlish presents—which she secretly sent to me at school; the first sweet days of our uninterrupted intercourse, when the close of my college life restored me to home; her first inestimable sympathies with my first fugitive vanities of embryo authorship, are thronging back fast and fondly on my thoughts, while I now write.

But these memories must be calmed and disciplined. I must be collected and impartial over my narrative—if it be only to make that narrative show fairly and truly, without suppression or exaggeration, all that I have owed to her.

Not merely all that I *have* owed to her; but all that I owe to her now. Though I may never see her again, but in my thoughts; still she influences, comforts, cheers me on to hope, as if she were already the guardian spirit of the cottage where I live. Even in my worst moments of despair,* I can still remember that Clara is thinking of me and sorrowing for me: I can still feel that remembrance, as an invisible hand of mercy which supports me, sinking; which raises me, fallen; which may yet lead me safely and tenderly to my hard journey's end.

VI.

I have now completed all the preliminary notices of my near relatives, which it is necessary to present in these pages; and may proceed at once to the more immediate subject of my narrative.

Imagine to yourself that my father and my sister have been living for some months at our London residence; and that I have recently joined them, after having enjoyed a short tour on the continent.

My father is engaged in his parliamentary duties. We see very little of him. Committees absorb his mornings—debates his evenings. When he has a day of leisure occasionally, he passes it in his study, devoted to his own affairs.

He goes very little into society—a political dinner, or a scientific meeting are the only social relaxations that tempt him.

My sister leads a life which is not much in accordance with her simple tastes. She is wearied of balls, operas, flower-shows, and all other London gaieties besides; and heartily longs to be driving about the green lanes again in her own little poney-chaise, and distributing plum-cake prizes to the good children at the Rector's Infant School. But the female friend who happens to be staying with her, is fond of excitement; my father expects her to accept the invitations which he is obliged to decline; so she gives up her own tastes and inclinations as usual, and goes into hot rooms among crowds of fine people, hearing the same glib compliments, and the same polite inquiries, night after night, until, patient as she is, she heartily wishes that her fashionable friends all lived in some opposite quarter of the globe, the farther away the better.

My arrival from the continent is the most welcome of events to her. It gives a new object and a new impulse to her London life.

I am engaged in writing a historical romance—indeed, it is principally to examine the localities in the country where my story is laid, that I have been abroad.* Clara has read the first half-dozen finished chapters, in manuscript, and augurs wonderful success for my fiction when it is published. She is determined to arrange my study with her own hands; to dust my books, and sort my papers herself. She knows that I am already as fretful and precise about my literary goods and chattels, as indignant at any interference of house-maids and dusters with my library treasures, as if I were a veteran author of twenty years' standing; and she is resolved to spare me every apprehension on this score, by taking all the arrangements of my study on herself, and keeping the key of the door when I am not in need of it.*

We have our London amusements, too, as well as our London employments. But the pleasantest of our relaxations are, after all, procured for us by our horses. We ride every day—sometimes with friends, sometimes alone together. On these latter occasions, we generally turn our horses' heads away from the parks, and seek what country sights we can get in the neighbourhood of London. The northern roads are generally our favourite ride.

Sometimes we penetrate so far that we can bait our horses at a little inn which reminds me of the inns near our country home. I see the same sanded parlour, decorated with the same old sporting prints, furnished with the same battered, deep-coloured mahogany table, and polished elm tree chairs, that I remember in our own village inn. Clara, also, finds bits of common, out of doors, that look like *our* common; and trees that might have been transplanted expressly for her, from *our* park.

These excursions we keep a secret, we like to enjoy them entirely by ourselves. Besides, if my father knew that his daughter was drinking the landlady's fresh milk, and his son the landlord's old ale, in the parlour of a suburban roadside inn, he would, I believe, be apt to suspect that both his children had fairly taken leave of their senses.

Evening parties I frequent almost as rarely as my father. Clara's good nature is called into requisition to do duty for me, as well as for him. She has little respite in the task. Old lady relatives and friends, always ready to take care of her, leave her no excuse for staying at home. Sometimes I am shamed into accompanying her a little more frequently than usual; but my old indolence in these matters soon possesses me again. I have contracted a bad habit of writing at night—I read almost incessantly in the day time. It is only because I am fond of riding, that I am ever willing to interrupt my studies, and ever ready to go out at all.

Such were my domestic habits, such my regular occupations and amusements, when a mere accident changed every purpose of my life, and altered me irretrievably from what I was then, to what I am now.

It happened thus:

VII.

I had just received my quarter's allowance of pocket-money, and had gone into the city to cash the cheque at my father's bankers.

The money paid, I debated for a moment how I should return homewards. First I thought of walking: then of taking a cab. While I was considering this frivolous point, an omnibus passed me, going westward. In the idle impulse of the moment, I hailed it, and got in.

It was something more than an idle impulse though. If I had at that time no other qualification for the literary career on which I was entering, I certainly had this one—an aptitude for discovering points of character in others: and its natural result, an unfailing delight in studying characters of all kinds, wherever I could meet with them.

I had often before ridden in omnibuses to amuse myself by observing the passengers.* An omnibus has always appeared to me, to be a perambulatory exhibition-room of the eccentricities of human nature. I know not any other sphere in which persons of all classes and all temperaments are so oddly collected together, and so immediately contrasted and confronted with each other. To watch merely the different methods of getting into the vehicle, and taking their seats, adopted by different people, is to study no incomplete commentary on the infinitesimal varieties of human character—as various even as the varieties of the human face.*

Thus, in addition to the idle impulse, there was the idea of amusement in my thoughts, as I stopped the public vehicle, and added one to the number of the conductor's passengers.

There were five persons in the omnibus when I entered it. Two middle-aged ladies, dressed with amazing splendour in silks and satins, wearing straw-coloured kid gloves, and carrying highly-scented pocket handkerchiefs, sat apart at the end of the vehicle; trying to look as if they occupied it under protest, and preserving the most stately gravity and silence. They evidently felt that their magnificent outward adornments were exhibited in a very unworthy locality, and among a very uncongenial company.

One side, close to the door, was occupied by a lean, withered old man, very shabbily dressed in black, who sat eternally mumbling something between his toothless jaws. Occasionally, to the evident disgust of the genteel ladies, he wiped his bald head and wrinkled forehead with a ragged blue cotton handkerchief, which he kept in the crown of his hat.

Opposite to this ancient sat a dignified gentleman and a sickly vacant-looking little girl. Every event of that day is so indelibly marked on my memory, that I remember, not only this man's pompous look and manner, but even the words he addressed to the poor squalid little creature by his side. When I entered the omnibus, he was telling her in a loud voice how she ought to dispose of her frock and her feet when people got into the vehicle, and when they got out. He then impressed on her the necessity in future life, when she grew up, of always having the price of her fare ready before it was wanted, to prevent unnecessary delay. Having delivered himself of this good advice, he began to hum, keeping time by drumming with his thick Malacca cane. He was still proceeding with this amusement—producing some of the most acutely unmusical sounds I ever heard—when the omnibus stopped to give admission to two ladies.* The first who got in was an elderly person—pale and depressed—evidently in delicate health. The second was a young girl.

Among the workings of the hidden life within us which we may experience but cannot explain, are there any more remarkable than those mysterious moral influences constantly exercised, either for attraction or repulsion, by one human being over another? In the simplest, as in the most important affairs of life, how startling, how irresistible is their power! How often we feel and know, either pleasurably or painfully, that another is looking on us, before we have ascertained the fact with our own eyes! How often we prophesy truly to ourselves the approach of a friend or enemy, just before either have really appeared! How strangely and abruptly we become convinced, at a first introduction, that we shall secretly love this person and loathe that, before experience has guided us with a single fact in relation to their characters !*

I have said that the two additional passengers who entered the vehicle in which I was riding, were, one of them, an elderly lady; the other, a young girl. As soon as the latter had seated herself nearly opposite to me, by her companion's side, I felt her influence on me directly—an influence that I cannot describe—an influence which I had never experienced in my life before, which I shall never experience again.

I had helped to hand her in, as she passed me ; merely touching her arm for a moment. But how the sense of that touch was prolonged! I felt it thrilling through me—thrilling in every nerve, in every pulsation of my fast-throbbing heart.

Had I the same influence over her? Or was it I that received, and she that conferred, only ? I was yet destined to discover; but not then—not for a long, long time.

Her veil was down when I first saw her. Her features

and her expression were but indistinctly visible to me. I could just vaguely perceive that she was young and beautiful; but, beyond this, though I might imagine much, I could see little.

From the time when she entered the omnibus, I have no recollection of anything more that occurred in it. I neither remember what passengers got out, or what passengers got in. My powers of observation, hitherto active enough, had now wholly deserted me. Strange! that the capricious rule of chance should sway the action of our faculties!— that a trifle should set in motion the whole complicated machinery of their exercise, and a trifle suspend it.

We had been moving onward for some little time, when the girl's companion addressed an observation to her. She heard it imperfectly, and lifted her veil while it was being repeated. How painfully my heart beat! I could almost hear it—as her face was, for the first time, freely and fairly disclosed!

She was dark. Her hair, eyes, and complexion were darker than usual in English women. The form, the look altogether, of her face, coupled with what I could see of her figure, made me guess her age to be about twenty. There was the appearance of maturity already in the shape of her features; but their expression still remained girlish, unformed, unsettled. The fire in her large dark eyes, when she spoke, was latent. Their languor, when she was silent —that voluptuous languor of black eyes—was still fugitive and unsteady. The smile about her full lips (to other eyes, they might have looked *too* full) struggled to be eloquent, yet dared not. Among women, there always seems something left incomplete—a moral creation to be superinduced on the physical—which love alone can develop, and which maternity perfects still further, when developed. I thought, as I looked on her, how the passing colour would fix itself brilliantly on her round, olive cheek; how the expression that still hesitated to declare itself, would speak out at last, would shine forth in the full luxury of its beauty, when she heard the first words, received the first kiss, from the man she loved!

While I still looked at her, as she sat opposite speaking to her companion, our eyes met. It was only for a moment—but the sensation of a moment often makes the thought of a life; and that one little instant made the new life of my heart. She put down her veil again immediately.; her lips moved involuntarily as she lowered it: I thought I could discern, through the lace, that the slight movement ripened to a smile.

Still there was enough left to see—enough to charm. There was the little rim of delicate white lace, encircling the lovely, dusky throat; there was the figure visible, where the shawl had fallen open, slender, but already well developed in its slenderness, and exquisitely supple; there was the waist, naturally low, and left to its natural place and natural size; there were the little millinery and jewellery ornaments that she wore—simple and common-place enough in themselves—yet each a beauty, each a treasure, on *her*. There was all this to behold, all this to dwell on, in spite of the veil. The veil! how little of the woman does it hide, when the man really loves her!

We had nearly arrived at the last point to which the omnibus would take us, when she and her companion got out. I followed them, cautiously and at some distance.

She was tall—tall at least for a woman. There were not many people in the road along which we were proceeding; but even if there had been, far behind as I was walking, I should never have lost her—never have mistaken any one else for her. Already, strangers though we were, I felt that I should know her, almost at any distance, only by her walk.

They went on until we reached a suburb of new houses,

intermingled with wretched patches of waste land, half built over. Unfinished streets, unfinished crescents, unfinished squares, unfinished shops, unfinished gardens, surrounded us. At last they stopped at a new square, and rang the bell at one of the newest of the new houses. The door was opened, and she and her companion disappeared. The house was partly detached. It bore no number; but was distinguished as North Villa. The square—unfinished like everything else in the neighbourhood—was called Hollyoake Square.

I noticed nothing else about the place at that time. Its newness and desolateness of appearance revolted me, just then. I had satisfied myself about the locality of the house, and I knew that it was her home; for I had approached sufficiently near, when the door was opened, to hear her inquire if anybody had called in her absence. For the present, this was enough. My sensations wanted repose; my thoughts wanted collecting. I left Hollyoake Square at once, and walked into the Regent's Park, the northern portion of which was close at hand.

Was I in love?—in love with a girl whom I had accidentally met in an omnibus? Or, was I merely indulging a momentary caprice—merely feeling a young man's hot, hasty admiration for a beautiful face? These were questions which I could not then decide. My ideas were in utter confusion, all my thoughts ran astray. I walked on, dreaming in full day—I had no distinct impressions, except of the stranger beauty whom I had just seen. The more I tried to collect myself, to resume the easy, equable feelings with which I had set forth in the morning, the less self-possessed I became. There are two emergencies in which the wisest man may try to reason himself back from impulse to principle; and try in vain:—the one when a woman has attracted him for the first time; the other, when, for the first time, also, she has happened to offend him.

I know not how long I had been walking in the park, thus absorbed yet not thinking, when the clock of a neighbouring church struck three, and roused me to the remembrance that I had engaged to ride out with my sister at two o'clock. It would be nearly half-an-hour more before I could reach home. Never had any former appointment of mine with Clara been thus forgotten! Love had not yet turned me selfish, as it turns all men, and even all women, more or less. I felt both sorrow and shame at the neglect of which I had been guilty; and hastened homeward.

The groom, looking unutterably weary and discontented, was still leading my horse up and down before the house. My sister's horse had been sent back to the stables. I went in; and heard that, after waiting for me an hour, Clara had gone out with some friends, and would not be back before dinner.

No one was in the house but the servants. The place looked dull, empty, inexpressibly miserable to me; the distant roll of carriages along the surrounding streets had a heavy boding sound; the opening and shutting of doors in the domestic offices below, startled and irritated me; the London air seemed denser to breathe than it had ever seemed before. I walked up and down one of the rooms, fretful and irresolute. Once I directed my steps towards my study; but retraced them before I had entered it. Reading or writing was out of the question at that moment.

I felt the secret inclination strengthening within me to return to Hollyoake Square; to try to see the girl again, or at least to ascertain who she was. I strove—yes, I can honestly say, strove to repress the desire. I tried to laugh it off, as idle and ridiculous; to think of my sister, of the book I was writing, of anything but the one subject that pressed stronger and stronger on me, the harder I struggled against it. The spell of the syren was over me. I went out, hypocritically persuading myself, that I was only animated by a capricious curiosity to know the girl's name, which once satisfied, would leave me at rest on the matter, and free to laugh at my own idleness and folly as soon as I got home again.

I arrived at the house. The blinds were all drawn down over the front windows, to keep out the sun. The little slip of garden was left solitary—baking and cracking in the heat. The square was silent; desolately silent, as only a suburban square can be. I walked up and down the glaring pavement, resolved to find out her name before I quitted the place. While still undecided how to act, a shrill whistling —sounding doubly shrill in the silence around—made me look up.

A tradesman's boy—one of those town Pucks of the highway; one of those incarnations of precocious cunning, inveterate mischief, and impudent humour, which great cities only can produce—was approaching me with his empty tray under his arm. I called to him to come and speak to me. He evidently belonged to the neighbourhood, and might be made of some use.

His first answer to my inquiries, showed that his master served the household at North Villa. A present of a shilling secured his attention at once to the few questions of any importance which I desired to put to him. I learned from his replies, that the name of the master of the house was "Sherwin:" and that the family only consisted of Mr. and Mrs. Sherwin, and the young lady, their daughter.

My last inquiry addressed to the boy was the most important of all. Did he know what Mr. Sherwin's profession or employment was?

His answer startled me into perfect silence. Mr. Sherwin kept a large linen-draper's shop in one of the great London thoroughfares! The boy mentioned the number, and the side of the way on which the house stood—then asked me if I wanted to know anything more. I could only tell him by a sign that he might leave me, and that I had heard enough.

Enough? If he had spoken the truth, I had heard too much.

A linen-draper's shop—a linen-draper's daughter! Was I still in love?—I thought of my father; I thought of the name I bore; and this time, though I might have answered the question, I dared not.

But the boy might be wrong. Perhaps, in mere mischief, he had been deceiving me throughout. I determined to seek the address he had mentioned, and ascertain the truth for myself.

I reached the place : there was the shop, and there the name "Sherwin" over the door. One chance still remained. This Sherwin and the Sherwin of Hollyoake Square might not be the same.

I went in and purchased something. While the man was tying up the parcel, I asked him whether his master lived in Hollyoake Square. Looking a little astonished at the question, he answered in the affirmative.

"There was a Mr. Sherwin I once knew," I said, forging in those words the first link in the long chain of deceit which was afterwards to fetter and degrade me—"a Mr. Sherwin who is now, as I have heard, living somewhere in the Hollyoake Square neighbourhood. He was a bachelor— I don't know whether my friend and your master are the same ?"

"Oh dear no, Sir! My master is a married man, and has one daughter—Miss Margaret—who is reckoned a very fine young lady, Sir!" And the man grinned as he spoke—a grin that sickened and shocked me.

I was answered at last : I had discovered all. Margaret! —I had heard her name, too. Margaret!—it had never hitherto been a favourite name with me. Now I felt a sort of terror as I detected myself repeating it, and finding a new, unimagined poetry in the sound.

Could this be love?—pure, first love for a shopkeeper's daughter, whom I had seen for a quarter of an hour in an omnibus, and followed home for another quarter of an hour? The thing was impossible. And yet, I felt a strange unwillingness to go back to our house, and see my father and sister, just at that moment.

I was still walking onward slowly, but not in the direction of home, when I met an old college friend of my brother's, and an acquaintance of mine—a reckless, good-humoured, convivial fellow. He greeted me at once, with uproarious cordiality; and insisted on my accompanying him to dine at his club.

If the thoughts that still hung heavy on my mind were only the morbid, fanciful thoughts of the hour, here was a man whose society would dissipate them. I resolved to try the experiment, and accepted his invitation.

At dinner, I tried hard to rival him in jest and joviality; I drank much more than my usual quantity of wine—but it was useless. The gay words came fainting from my heart, and fell dead on my lips. The wine fevered, but did not exhilarate me. Still, the image of the dark beauty of the morning was the one reigning image of my thoughts—still, the influence of the morning, at once sinister and seductive, kept its hold on my heart.

I gave up the struggle. I longed to be alone again. My friend soon found that my forced spirits were flagging; he tried to rouse me, tried to talk for two, ordered more wine; but everything failed. Yawning at last, in undisguised despair, he suggested a visit to the theatre.

I excused myself—professed illness—hinted that the wine had been too much for me. He laughed, with something of contempt as well as good-nature in the laugh; and went away to the play by himself, evidently feeling that I was still as bad a companion as he had found me at college, years ago.

As soon as we parted I felt a sense of relief. I hesitated, walked backwards and forwards a few paces in the street; and then, silencing all doubts, leaving my inclinations to guide me as they would—I turned my steps for the third time in that one day to Hollyoake Square.

The fair summer evening was tending towards twilight; the sun stood fiery and low in a cloudless horizon; the last loveliness of the last quietest daylight hour was fading on the violet sky, as I entered the square.

I approached the house. She was at the window—it was thrown wide open. A bird-cage hung rather high up, against the shutter-pannel. She was standing opposite to it, making a plaything for the poor captive canary of a piece of sugar, which she rapidly offered and drew back again, now at one bar of the cage, and now at another. The bird hopped and fluttered up and down in his prison after the sugar, chirping as if he enjoyed playing *his* part of the game with his mistress. How lovely she looked! Her dark hair, drawn back over each cheek so as just to leave the lower part of the ear visible, was gathered up into a thick simple knot behind, without ornament of any sort. She wore a plain white dress fastening round the neck, and descending over the bosom in numberless little wavy plaits. The cage hung just high enough to oblige her to look up to it. She was laughing with all the glee of a child; darting the piece of sugar about incessantly from place to place. Every moment, her head and neck assumed some new and lovely turn—every moment her figure naturally fell into the position which showed its pliant symmetry best. The last-left glow of the evening atmosphere was shining on her—the farewell pause of daylight over the kindred daylight of beauty and youth.

I kept myself concealed behind a pillar of the garden-gate; I looked, hardly daring either to move or breathe; for I feared that if she saw or heard me, she would leave the window. After a lapse of some minutes, the canary touched the sugar with his beak.

"There, Minnie!" she cried laughingly, "you have caught the runaway sugar, and now you shall keep it!"

For a moment more, she stood quietly looking at the cage; then raising herself on tip-toe, pouted her lips caressingly to the bird, and disappeared in the interior of the room.

The sun went down; the twilight shadows fell over the dreary square; the gas lamps were lighted far and near; people who had been out for a breath of fresh air in the fields, came straggling past me by ones and twos, on their way home—and still I lingered near the house, hoping she might come to the window again; but she did not re-appear· At last, a servant brought candles into the room, and drew down the Venetian blinds. Knowing it would be useless to stay longer, I left the square.

I walked homeward joyfully. That second sight of her completed what the first meeting had begun. The impressions left by it made me insensible for the time to all boding reflections, careless of exercising the smallest self-restraint. I gave myself up to the charm that was at work on me. Prudence, duty, memories and prejudices of home, were all absorbed and forgotten in love—love that I encouraged, that I dwelt over in the first reckless luxury of a new sensation.

I entered our house, thinking of nothing but how to see her, how to speak to her, on the morrow; murmuring her name to myself, even while my hand was on the lock of my study door. The instant I was in the room, I involuntarily shuddered and stopped speechless. Clara was there! I was not merely startled; a cold, faint sensation came over me. My first look at my sister made me feel as if I had been detected in a crime.

She was standing at my writing-table, and had just finished stringing together the loose pages of my manuscript, which had hitherto laid disconnectedly in a drawer. There was a grand ball somewhere, to which she was going that night. The dress she wore was of pale blue crape (my father's favourite colour, on *her*). One white flower was placed in her light brown hair. She stood within the soft steady light of my lamp, looking up towards the door from the leaves she had just tied together. Her slight figure appeared slighter than usual, in the delicate material that now clothed it. Her complexion was at its palest: her face looked almost statue-like in its purity and repose. What a contrast to the other living picture which I had seen at sunset!

The remembrance of the engagement that I had broken came back on me avengingly, as she smiled, and held my manuscript up before me to look at. With that remembrance there returned, too—darker than ever—the ominous doubts which had depressed me but a few hours since. I tried to steady my voice, and felt how I failed in the effort, as I spoke to her:

"Will you forgive me, Clara, for having deprived you of your ride to-day? I am afraid I have but a bad excuse—"

"Then don't make it, Basil; or wait till papa can arrange it for you, in a proper parliamentary way, when he comes back from the House of Commons to-night. See how I have been meddling with your papers; but they were in such confusion I was really afraid some of these leaves might have been lost."

"Neither the leaves nor the writer deserve half the pains you have taken with them; but I am really sorry for breaking our engagement. I met an old college friend—there was business too, in the morning—we dined together—he would take no denial."

"Basil, how pale you look! Are you ill?"

"No; the heat has been a little too much for me—nothing more."

"Has anything happened? I only ask, because if I can be of any use—if you want me to stay at home—"

"Certainly not, love. I wish you all success and pleasure at the ball."

For a moment she did not speak; but fixed her clear, kind eyes on me more gravely and anxiously than usual. Was she searching my heart, and discovering the new love rising, an usurper already, in the place where the love of her had reigned before?

Love! love for a shopkeeper's daughter! That thought came again, as she looked at me! and, strangely mingled with it, a maxim I had often heard my father repeat to Ralph—"Never forget that your station is not yours, to do as you like with. It belongs to us, and belongs to your children. You must keep it for them, as I have kept it for you."

"I thought," resumed Clara, in rather lower tones than before, "that I would just look into your room before I went to the ball, and see that everything was properly arranged for you, in case you had any idea of writing to-night; I had just time to do this while my aunt, who is going with me, was upstairs altering her toilette. But perhaps you don't feel inclined to write?"

"I will try at least."

"Can I do anything more? Would you like my nosegay left in the room?—the flowers smell so fresh! I can easily get another. Look at the roses, my favourite white roses, that always remind me of my own garden at the dear old Park!"

"Thank you, Clara; but I think the nosegay is fitter for your hand than my table."

"Good night, Basil."

"Good night."

She walked to the door, then turned round, and smiled as

if she were about to speak again; but checked herself, and merely looked at me for an instant. In that instant, however, the smile left her face, and the grave, anxious expression came again. She went out softly. A few minutes afterwards the roll of the carriage which took her and her companion to the ball, died away heavily on my ear. I was left alone in the house—alone for the night.

VIII.

My manuscript lay before me, set in order by Clara's careful hand. I slowly turned over the leaves one by one; but my eye only fell mechanically on the writing. Yet one day since, and how much ambition, how much hope, how many of my heart's dearest sensations and my mind's highest thoughts dwelt in those poor paper leaves, in those little crabbed marks of pen and ink! Now I could look on them indifferently—almost as a stranger would have looked. The days of calm study, of steady toil of thought, seemed departed for ever. Stirring ideas; store of knowledge patiently heaped up; visions of better sights than this world can show, falling freshly and sunnily over the pages of my first book; all these were past and gone—withered up by the hot breath of the senses—doomed by a paltry fate, whose germ was the accident of an idle day!

I hastily put the manuscript aside. My unexpected interview with Clara had calmed the turbulent sensations of the evening: but the fatal influence of the dark beauty remained with me still. How could I write?

I sat down at the open window. It was at the back of the house, and looked out on a strip of garden—London garden—a close-shut dungeon for nature, where stunted trees and drooping flowers seemed visibly pining for the free air and sunlight of the country, in their sooty atmosphere, amid their prison of high brick walls. But the place gave room for the air to blow in it, and distanced the tumult of the busy streets. The moon was up, shrined round tenderly by a little border-work of pale yellow light. Elsewhere, the awful void of night was starless; the dark lustre of space shone without a cloud.

A presentiment arose within me, that in this still and solitary hour would occur my decisive, my final struggle with myself. I felt that my heart's life or death was set on the hazard of the night.

This new love that was in me; this giant sensation of a day's growth, was first love. Hitherto, I had been heartwhole. I had known nothing of the passion, which is the absorbing passion of humanity. No woman had ever before stood between me and my ambitions, my occupations, my amusements. No woman had ever before inspired me with the sensations which I now felt.

In trying to realise my position, there was this one question to consider; was I still strong enough to resist the temptation which accident had thrown in my way? I had this one incentive to resistance: the conviction that, if I succumbed, as far as my family prospects were concerned, I should be a ruined man.

I knew my father's character well: I knew how far his affections and his sympathies might prevail over his prejudices—even over his principles—in some peculiar cases; and this very knowledge convinced me that the consequences of a degrading marriage contracted by his son (degrading in regard to rank), would be terrible: fatal to one, perhaps to both. Every other irregularity—every other offence even—he might sooner or later forgive. *This* irregularity, *this* offence, never—never, though his heart broke in the struggle. I was as sure of it, as I was of my own existence at that moment.

I loved her! All that I felt, all that I knew, was summed up in those few words! Deteriorating as my passion was in its effect on the exercise of my mental powers, and on my candour and sense of duty in my intercourse with home, it was a pure feeling towards *her*. This is truth. If I lay on my death-bed, at the present moment, and knew that, at the Judgment Day, I should be tried by the truth or false-hood of the lines just written, I could say with my last breath: So be it; let them remain.

But what mattered my love for her? However worthy of it she might be, I had misplaced it, because chance—the same chance which might have given her station and family —had placed her in a rank of life far—too far—below mine. As the daughter of a " gentleman," my father's welcome, my father's affection, would have been bestowed on her, when I took her home as my wife. As the daughter of a tradesman, my father's anger, my father's misery, my own ruin perhaps besides, would be the fatal dower that a marriage would confer on her. What made all this dif-ference? A social prejudice. Yes: but a prejudice which had been a principle—nay, more, a religion—in our house, since my birth; and for centuries before it.

(How strange that foresight of love which precipitates the future into the present! Here was I thinking of her as my wife, before, perhaps, she had a suspicion of the passion with which she had inspired me—vexing my heart, weary-ing my thoughts, before I had even spoken to her, as if the perilous discovery of our marriage were already at hand! I have thought since how unnatural I should have considered this, if I had read it in a book.)

How could I best crush the desire to see her, to speak to her, on the morrow? Should I leave London, leave Eng-land, fly from the temptation, no matter where, or at what sacrifice? Or should I take refuge in my books—the calm, changeless old friends of my earliest fireside hours? Had I resolution enough to wear my heart out by hard, serious, slaving study? If I left London on the morrow, could I feel secure, in my own conscience, that I should not return the day after!

While, throughout the hours of the night, I was thus vainly striving to hold calm counsel with myself, the base thought never occurred to me, which might have occurred to some other men, in my position : Why marry the girl, because I love her ? Why, with my money, my station, my opportunities, obstinately connect love and marriage as one idea ; and make a dilemma and a danger where neither need exist ? Had such a thought as this, in the faintest, the most shadowy form, crossed my mind, I should have shrunk from it, have shrunk from myself, with horror. Whatever fresh degradations may be yet in store for me, this one consoling and sanctifying remembrance must still be mine. My love for Margaret Sherwin was worthy to be offered to the purest and perfectest woman that ever God created.

The night advanced—the noises faintly reaching me from the streets, sank and ceased—my lamp flickered and went out—I heard the carriage return with Clara from the ball —the first cold clouds of day rose and hid the waning orb of the moon—the air was cooled with its morning freshness : the earth was purified with its morning dew—and still I sat by my open window, striving with my burning love-thoughts of Margaret; striving to think collectedly and usefully—abandoned to a struggle ever renewing, yet never changing ; and always hour after hour, a struggle in vain.

At last I began to think less and less distinctly—a few moments more, and I sank into a restless, feverish slumber. Then began another, and a more perilous ordeal for me —the ordeal of dreams. Thoughts and sensations which had been more and more weakly restrained with each succeeding hour of wakefulness, now rioted within me in perfect liberation from all control.

This is what I dreamed :

I stood on a wide plain. On one side, it was bounded by thick woods, whose dark secret depths looked unfathomable to the eye: on the other, by hills, ever rising higher and higher yet, until they were lost in bright, beautifully white clouds, gleaming in refulgent sunlight. On the side above the woods, the sky was dark and vaporous. It seemed as if some thick exhalation had arisen from beneath the trees, and overspread the clear firmament throughout this portion of the scene.

As I still stood on the plain and looked around, I saw a woman coming towards me from the wood. Her stature was tall; her black hair flowed about her unconfined; her robe was of the dun hue of the vapour and mist which hung above the trees, and fell to her feet in dark thick folds. She came on towards me swiftly and softly, passing over the ground like cloud-shadows over the ripe corn-field or the calm water.

I looked to the other side, towards the hills; and there was another woman descending from their bright summits; and her robe was white, and pure, and glistening. Her face was illumined with a light, like the light of the harvest-moon; and her footsteps, as she descended the hills, left a long track of brightness, that sparkled far behind her, like the track of the stars when the winter night is clear and cold. She came to the place where the hills and the plain were joined together. Then she stopped, and I knew that she was watching me from afar off.

Meanwhile, the woman from the dark wood still approached; never pausing on her path, like the woman from the fair hills. And now I could see her face plainly. Her eyes were lustrous and fascinating, as the eyes of a serpent —large, dark and soft, as the eyes of the wild doe. Her lips were parted with a languid smile; and she drew back the long hair, which lay over her cheeks, her neck, her bosom, while I was gazing on her.

Then, I felt as if a light were shining on me from the other side. I turned to look, and there was the woman from the hills beckoning me away to ascend with her towards the bright clouds above. Her arm, as she held it forth, shone fair, even against the fair hills; and from her outstretched hand came long thin rays of trembling light, which penetrated to where I stood, cooling and calming wherever they touched me.

But the woman from the woods still came nearer and nearer, until I could feel her hot breath on my face. Her eyes looked into mine, and fascinated them, as she held out her arms to embrace me. I touched her hand, and in an instant the touch ran through me like fire, from head to foot. Then, still looking intently on me with her wild bright eyes, she clasped her supple arms round my neck, and drew me a few paces away with her towards the wood.

I felt the rays of light that had touched me from the beckoning hand, depart; and yet once more I looked towards the woman from the hills. She was ascending again towards the bright clouds, and ever and anon she stopped and turned round, wringing her hands and letting her head droop, as if in bitter grief. The last time I saw her look towards me, she was near the clouds. She covered her face with her robe, and knelt down where she stood. After this I discerned no more of her. For now the woman from the woods clasped me more closely than before, pressing her warm lips on mine; and it was as if her long hair fell round us both, spreading over my eyes like a veil, to hide from them the fair hill-tops, and the woman who was walking onward to the bright clouds above.

I was drawn along in the arms of the dark woman, with my blood burning and my breath failing me, until we entered the secret recesses that lay amid the unfathomble depths of trees. There, she encircled me in the folds of her dusky robe, and laid her cheek close to mine, and murmured a mysterious music in my ear, amid the midnight silence and darkness of all around us. And I had no thought of returning to the plain again; for I had forgotten the woman from the fair hills, and had given myself up, heart, and soul, and body, to the woman from the dark woods.

Here the dream ended, and I awoke.

It was broad daylight. The sun shone brilliantly, the sky was cloudless. I looked at my watch; it had stopped Shortly afterwards I heard the hall clock strike six.

My dream was vividly impressed on my memory, especially the latter part of it. Was it a warning of coming events, foreshadowed in the wild visions of sleep? But to what purpose could this dream, or indeed any dream, tend? Why had it remained incomplete, failing to show me the visionary consequences of my visionary actions? What superstition to ask! What a waste of attention to bestow it on such a trifle as a dream!

Still, this trifle had produced one abiding result. I knew it not then; but I know it now. As I looked out on the reviving, re-assuring sunlight, it was easy enough for me to dismiss as ridiculous from my mind, or rather from my conscience, the tendency to see in the two shadowy forms of my dream, the types of two real living beings, whose names almost trembled into utterance on my lips; but I could not also dismiss from my heart the love-images which that dream had set up there for the worship of the senses. Those results of the night still remained within me, growing and strengthening with every minute.

If I had been told beforehand how the mere sight of the morning would reanimate and embolden me, I should have scouted the prediction as too outrageous for consideration; yet so it was. The moody and boding reflections, the fear and struggle of the hours of darkness were gone with the daylight. The love-thoughts of Margaret alone remained, and now remained unquestioned and unopposed. Were my

convictions of a few hours since, like the night-mists that
fade before returning sunshine? I knew not. But I was
young; and each new morning is as much the new life of
youth, as the new life of Nature.

So I left my study and went out. Consequences might
come how they would, and when they would; I thought of
them no more. It seemed as if I had cast off every melancholy thought, in leaving my room; as if my heart had
sprung up more elastic than ever, after the burden that had
been laid on it during the night. Enjoyment for the present, hope for the future, and chance and fortune to trust
in to the very last! This was my creed, as I walked into
the street, determined to see Margaret again, and to tell
her of my love before the day was out. In the exhilaration
of the fresh air and the gay sunshine, I turned my steps
towards Hollyoake Square, almost as light-hearted as a boy
let loose from school, joyously repeating Shakespeare's lines
as I went:

> " Hope is a lover's staff; walk hence with that,
> And manage it against despairing thoughts." *

IX.

London was rousing everywhere into morning activity, as
I passed through the streets. The shutters were being removed from the windows of public-houses: the drink-vam-
pyres that suck the life of London, were opening their eyes
betimes to look abroad for the new day's prey! Small
tobacco and provision-shops in poor neighbourhoods; dirty
little eating-houses, exhaling greasy-smelling steam, and
displaying a leaf of yesterday's paper, stained and fly-blown,
hanging in the windows—were already plying, or making
ready to ply, their daily trade. Here, a labouring man,
late for his work, hurried by; there, a hale old gentleman
started for his early walk before breakfast. Now a market-

cart, already unloaded, passed me on its way back to the country ; now, a cab, laden with luggage and carrying pale, sleepy-looking people, rattled by, bound for the morning train or the morning steamboat. I saw the mighty vitality of the great city renewing itself in every direction; and I felt an unwonted interest in the sight.* It was as if all things, on all sides, were reflecting before me the aspect of my own heart.

But the quiet and torpor of the night still hung over Hollyoake Square. That dreary neighbourhood seemed to vindicate its dreariness by being the last to awaken even to a semblance of activity and life. Nothing was stirring as yet at North Villa. I walked on, beyond the last houses, into the sooty London fields ; and tried to think of the course I ought to pursue in order to see Margaret, and speak to her, before I turned homeward again. After the lapse of more than half an hour, I returned to the square, without plan or project ; but resolved, nevertheless, to carry my point.

The garden-gate of North Villa was now open. One of the female servants of the house was standing at it, to breathe the fresh air, and look about her, before the duties of the day began. I advanced ; determined, if money and persuasion could do it, to secure her services.

She was young (that was one chance in my favour!)— plump, florid, and evidently not by any means careless about her personal appearance (that gave me another!) As she saw me approaching her, she smiled ; and passed her apron hurriedly over her face—carefully polishing it for my inspection, much as a broker polishes a piece of furniture when you stop to look at it.

"Are you in Mr. Sherwin's service ?"—I asked, as I got to the garden gate.

"As plain cook, Sir," answered the girl, administering to her face a final and furious rub of the apron.

"Should you be very much surprised if I asked you to do me a great favour?"

"Well—really, Sir—you're quite a stranger to me—I'm *sure* I don't know!" She stopped, and transferred the apron-rubbing to her arms.

"I hope we shall not be strangers long. Suppose I begin our acquaintance, by telling you that you would look prettier in brighter cap-ribbons, and asking you to buy some, just to see whether I am not right?"

"It's very kind of you to say so, Sir; and thank you. But cap and ribbons are the last things I can buy while I'm in *this* place. Master's master and missus too, here; and drives us half wild with the fuss he makes about our caps and ribbons. He's such an austerious man, that he will have our caps as he likes 'em. It's bad enough when a missus meddles with a poor servant's ribbons; but to have master come down into the kitchen, and—Well, it's no use telling *you* of it, Sir—and—and thank you, Sir, for what you've given me, all the same!"

"I hope this is not the last time I shall make you a present. And now I must come to the favour I want to ask of you: can you keep a secret?"

"That I can, Sir! I've kep' a many secrets since I've been out at service."

"Well: I want you to find me an opportunity of speaking to your young lady—"

"To Miss Margaret, Sir?"

"Yes. I want an opportunity of seeing Miss Margaret, and speaking to her in private—and not a word must be said to her about it, beforehand."

"Oh Lord, Sir! I couldn't dare to do it!"

"Come! come! Can't you guess why I want to see your young lady, and what I want to say to her?"

The girl smiled, and shook her head archly. "Perhaps you're in love with Miss Margaret, Sir!—But I couldn't do it! I couldn't dare to do it!"

"Very well; but you can tell me at least, whether Miss Margaret ever goes out to take a walk?"

"Oh, yes, Sir; mostly every day."

"Do you ever go out with her?—just to take care of her when no one else can be spared?"

"Don't ask me—please, Sir, don't!" She crumpled her apron between her fingers, with a very piteous and perplexed air. "I don't know you; and Miss Margaret don't know you, I'm sure—I couldn't, Sir, I really couldn't!"

"Take a good look at me! Do you think I am likely to do you or your young lady any harm? Am I too dangerous a man to be trusted? Would you believe me on my promise?"

"Yes, Sir, I'm sure I would!—being so kind and so civil to me, too!" (a fresh arrangement of the cap followed this speech.)

"Then suppose I promised, in the first place, not to tell Miss Margaret that I had spoken to you about her at all. And suppose I promised, in the second place, that, if you told me when you and Miss Margaret go out together, I would only speak to her while she was in your sight, and would leave her the moment you wished me to go away. Don't you think you could venture to help me, if I promised all that?"

"Well, Sir, that would make a difference, to be sure. But then, it's master I'm so afraid of—couldn't you speak to master first, Sir?"

"Suppose you were in Miss Margaret's place, would *you* like to be made love to, by your father's authority, without your own wishes being consulted first? would you like an offer of marriage, delivered like a message, by means of your father? Come, tell me honestly, would you?"

She laughed, and shook her head very expressively. I knew the strength of my last argument, and repeated it: "Suppose you were in Miss Margaret's place?"

"Hush! don't speak so loud," resumed the girl in a confidential whisper. "I'm sure you're a gentleman. I should like to help you—if I could only dare to do it, I should indeed!"

"That's a good girl," I said. "Now tell me, when does Miss Margaret go out to-day; and who goes with her?"

"Dear! dear!—it's very wrong to say it; but I must. She'll go out with me to market, this morning, at eleven o'clock. She's done it for the last week. Master don't like it; but Missus begged and prayed she might; for Missus says she won't be fit to be married, if she knows nothing about housekeeping, and prices, and what's good meat, and what isn't, and all that, you know."

"Thank you a thousand times! you have given me all the help I want. I'll be here before eleven, waiting for you to come out."

"Oh, please don't, Sir—I wish I hadn't told you—I oughtn't, indeed I oughtn't!"

"No fear—you shall not lose by what you have told me—I promise all I said I would promise—good bye. And mind, not a word to Miss Margaret till I see her!"

As I hurried away, I heard the girl run a few paces after me—then stop—then return, and close the garden gate, softly. She had evidently put herself once more in Miss Margaret's place; and had given up all idea of further resistance as she did so.

How should I occupy the hours until eleven o'clock? Deceit whispered :—Go home; avoid even the chance of exciting suspicion, by breakfasting with your family as usual. And as deceit counselled, so I acted.

I never remember Clara more kind, more ready with all those trifling little cares and attentions which have so exquisite a grace, when offered by a woman to a man, and especially by a sister to a brother, as when she and I and my father assembled together at the breakfast-table. I now recollect with shame how little I thought about her, or spoke to her on that morning; with how little hesitation or self-reproach I excused myself from accepting an engagement which she wished to make with me for that day. My father was absorbed in some matter of business; to *him* she could not speak. It was to *me* that she addressed all her wonted questions and remarks of the morning. I hardly listened to them; I answered them carelessly and briefly. The moment breakfast was over, without a word of explanation I hastily left the house again.

As I descended the steps, I glanced by accident at the dining-room window. Clara was looking after me from it. There was the same anxious expression on her face which it had worn when she left me the evening before. She smiled as our eyes met—a sad, faint smile that made her look unlike herself. But it produced no impression on me then: I had no attention for anything but my approaching interview with Margaret. My life throbbed and burned within me, in that direction: it was all coldness, torpor, insensibility, in every other.

I reached Hollyoake Square nearly an hour before the appointed time. In the suspense and impatience of that long interval, it was impossible to be a moment in repose. I walked incessantly up and down the square, and round and round the neighbourhood, hearing each quarter chimed from a church clock near, and mechanically quickening my pace the nearer the time came for the hour to strike. At last, I heard the first peal of the eventful eleven. Before the clock was silent, I had taken up my position within view of the gate of North Villa.

Five minutes passed—ten—and no one appeared. In my impatience, I could almost have rung the bell and entered the house, no matter who might be there, or what might be the result. The first quarter struck; and at that very moment I heard the door open, and saw Margaret, and

the servant with whom I had spoken, descending the
steps.

They passed out slowly through the garden gate, and
walked down the square, away from where I was standing.
The servant noticed me by one significant look, as they went
on. Her young mistress did not appear to see me. At
first, my agitation was so violent that I was perfectly incapable of following them a single step. In a few moments I
recovered myself; and hastened to overtake them, before
they arrived at a more frequented part of the neighbourhood.

As I approached her side, Margaret turned suddenly and
looked at me, with an expression of anger and astonishment
in her eyes. The next instant, her lovely face became tinged
all over with a deep, burning blush; her head drooped a
little; she hesitated for a moment; and then abruptly
quickened her pace. Did she remember me? The mere
chance that she did, gave me confidence : I—

—No! I cannot write down the words that I said to her.
Recollecting the end to which our fatal interview led, I re-
coil at the very thought of exposing to others, or of preserving in any permanent form, the words in which I first confessed my love. It may be pride—miserable, useless pride
—which animates me with this feeling: but I cannot overcome it. Remembering what I do, I am ashamed to write,
ashamed to recal, what I said at my first interview with
Margaret Sherwin. I can give no good reason for the sensations which now influence me; I cannot analyse them;
and I would not if I could.

Let it be enough to say that I risked everything, and
spoke to her. My words, confused as they were, came
hotly, eagerly, and eloquently from my heart. In the space
of a few minutes, I confessed to her all, and more than all,
that I have here painfully related in many pages. I made
use of my name and my rank in life—even now, my cheeks

burn while I think of it—to dazzle her girl's pride, to make her listen to me for the sake of my station, if she would not for the sake of my suit, however honourably urged. Never before had I committed the meanness of trusting to my social advantages, what I feared to trust to myself. It is true that love soars higher than the other passions; but it can stoop lower as well.

Her answers to all that I urged were confused, commonplace, and chilling enough. I had surprised her—frightened her—it was impossible she could listen to such addresses from a total stranger—it was very wrong of me to speak, and of her to stop and hear me—I should remember what became me as a gentleman, and should not make such advances to her again—I knew nothing of her—it was impossible I could really care about her in so short a time—she must beg that I would allow her to proceed unhindered.

Thus she spoke; sometimes standing still, sometimes moving hurriedly a few steps forward. She might have expressed herself severely, even angrily; but nothing she could have said would have counteracted the fascination that her presence exercised over me. I saw her face, lovelier than ever in its confusion, in its rapid changes of expression; I saw her eloquent eyes once or twice raised to mine, then instantly withdrawn again—and so long as I could look at her, I cared not what I listened to. She was only speaking what she had been educated to speak; it was not in her words that I sought the clue to her thoughts and sensations; but in the tone of her voice, in the language of her eyes, in the whole expression of her face. All these contained indications which reassured me. I tried everything that respect, that the persuasion of love could urge, to win her consent to our meeting again; but she only answered with repetitions of what she had said before, walking onward rapidly while she spoke. The servant, who had hitherto lingered a few paces behind, now advanced to her young mistress's side, with a significant look, as if to remind me of my promise. Saying a few parting words, I let them proceed: at this first interview, to have delayed them longer would have been risking too much.

As they walked away, the servant turned round, nodding her head and smiling, as if to assure me that I had lost nothing by the forbearance which I had exercised. Margaret neither lingered nor looked back. This last proof of modesty and reserve, so far from discouraging, attracted me to her more powerfully than ever. After a first interview, it was the most becoming virtue she could have shown. All my love for her before, seemed as nothing compared with my love for her now that she had left me, and left me without a parting look.

What course should I next pursue? Could I expect that Margaret, after what she had said, would go out again at the same hour on the morrow? No: she would not so soon abandon the modesty and restraint that she had shown at our first interview. How communicate with her? how manage most skilfully to make good the first favourable impression which vanity whispered I had already produced? I determined to write to her.

How different was the writing of that letter, to the writing of those once-treasured pages of my romance, which I had now abandoned for ever! How slowly I worked; how cautiously and diffidently I built up sentence after sentence, and doubtingly set a stop here, and laboriously rounded off a paragraph there, when I toiled in the service of ambition! Now, when I had given myself up to the service of love, how rapidly the pen ran over the paper; how much more freely and smoothly the desires of the heart flowed into words, than the thoughts of the mind! Composition was an instinct now, an art no longer. I could write eloquently, and yet write without pausing for an expression or blotting a word—It was the slow progress up the hill, in the service of ambition; it was the swift (too swift) career down it, in the service of love!

There is no need to describe the contents of my letter to Margaret; they comprised a mere recapitulation of what I had already said to her. I insisted often and strongly on the honourable purpose of my suit; and ended by entreating her to write an answer, and consent to allow me another interview.

The letter was delivered by the servant. Another present, a little more timely persuasion, and above all, the regard I had shown to my promise, won the girl with all her heart to my interests. She was ready to help me in every way, as long as her interference could be kept a secret from her master.

I waited a day for the reply to my letter; but none came. The servant could give me no explanation of this silence. Her young mistress had not said one word to her about me, since the morning when we had met. Still not discouraged, I wrote again. The letter contained some lover's threats this time, as well as lover's entreaties; and it produced its effect —an answer came.

It was very short—rather hurriedly and tremblingly written—and simply said that the difference between my rank and hers made it her duty to request of me, that neither by word nor by letter should I ever address her again.

"Difference in rank,"—that was the only objection then! "Her duty"—it was not from inclination that she refused me! So young a creature; and yet so noble in self-sacrifice, so firm in her integrity! I resolved to disobey her injunction, and see her again. My rank! What was my rank? Something to cast at Margaret's feet, for Margaret to trample on!

Once more I sought the aid of my faithful ally, the servant. After delays which half maddened me with impatience, insignificant though they were, she contrived to fulfil my wishes. One afternoon, while Mr. Sherwin was away at business, and while his wife had gone out, I succeeded in gaining admission to the garden at the back of the house where Margaret was then occupied in watering some flowers.

She started as she saw me, and attempted to return to the house. I took her hand to detain her. She withdrew it, but neither abruptly nor angrily. I seized the opportunity, while she hesitated whether to persist or not in retiring; and repeated what I had already said to her at our first interview (what is the language of love but a language of repetitions?). She answered, as she had answered me in her letter: the difference in our rank made it her duty to discourage me.

" But if this difference did not exist," I said : " if we were both living in the same rank, Margaret—"

She looked up quickly ; then moved away a step or two, as I addressed her by her Christian name.

" Are you offended with me for calling you Margaret so soon ? I do not *think* of you as Miss Sherwin, but as Margaret—are you offended with me for speaking as I think ?"

No : she ought not to be offended with me, or with anybody, for doing that.

" Suppose this difference in rank, which you so cruelly insist on, did not exist, would you tell me not to hope, not to speak then, as coldly as you tell me now ?"

I must not ask her that—it was no use—the difference in rank *did* exist.

" Perhaps I have met you too late ?—perhaps you are already—"

" No ! oh, no !"—she stopped abruptly, as the words passed her lips. The same lovely blush which I had before seen spreading over her face, rose on it now. She evidently felt that she had unguardedly said too much: that she had given me an answer in a case where, according to every established love-law of the female code, I had no right to expect one.* Her next words accused me—but in very low and broken tones—of having committed an intrusion which she should hardly have expected from a gentleman in my position.

"I will regain your better opinion," I said, eagerly catching at the most favourable interpretation of her last words, "by seeing you for the next time, and for all times after, with your father's full permission. I will write to-day, and ask for a private interview with him. I will tell him all I have told you: I will tell him that you take a rank in beauty and goodness, which is the highest rank in the land—a rar higher rank than mine—the only rank I desire." (A smile, which she vainly strove to repress, stole charmingly to her lips.) "Yes, I will do this; I will never leave him till his answer is favourable—and then what would be yours? One word, Margaret; one word before I go—"

I attempted to take her hand a second time; but she broke from me, and hurried into the house.

What more could I desire? What more could the modesty and timidity of a young girl concede to me?

The moment I reached home, I wrote to Mr. Sherwin. The letter was superscribed "Private;" and simply requested an interview with him on a subject of importance, at any hour he might mention. Unwilling to trust what I had written to the post, I sent my note by a messenger—not one of our own servants, caution forbade that—and instructed the man to wait for an answer: if Mr. Sherwin was out, to wait till he came home.

After a long delay—long to *me;* for my impatience would fain have turned hours into minutes—I received a reply. It was written on gilt-edged letter-paper, in a handwriting vulgarised by innumerable flourishes. Mr. Sherwin presented his respectful compliments, and would be happy to have the honour of seeing me at North Villa, if quite convenient, at five o'clock to-morrow afternoon.

I folded up the letter carefully : it was almost as precious as a letter from Margaret herself. That night I passed sleeplessly, revolving in my mind every possible course that I could take at the interview of the morrow. It would be a difficult and a delicate business. I knew nothing of Mr. Sherwin's character; yet I must trust him with a secret which I dared not trust to my own father. Any proposals for paying addresses to his daughter, coming from one in my position, might appear open to suspicion. What could I say about marriage ? A public, acknowledged marriage was impossible : a private marriage might be a bold, if not fatal proposal. I could come to no other conclusion, reflect as anxiously as I might, than that it was best for me to speak candidly at all hazards. I could be candid enough when it suited my purpose !

It was not till the next day, when the time approached for my interview with Mr. Sherwin, that I thoroughly roused myself to face the plain necessities of my position. Determined to try what impression appearances could make on him, I took unusual pains with my dress; and more, I applied to a friend whom I could rely on as likely to ask no questions—I write this in shame and sorrow : I tell truth here, where it is hard penance to tell it—I applied, I say, to a friend for the loan of one of his carriages to take me to North Villa; fearing the risk of borrowing my father's carriage, or my sister's—knowing the common weakness of rank-worship and wealth-worship in men of Mr. Sherwin's order, and meanly determining to profit by it to the utmost. My friend's carriage was willingly lent me. By my directions, it took me up at the appointed hour, at a shop where I was a regular customer

X.

On my arrival at North Villa, I was shown into what I presumed was the drawing-room.

Everything was oppressively new. The brilliantly-varnished door cracked with a report like a pistol when it was opened; the paper on the walls, with its gaudy pattern of birds, trellis-work, and flowers, in gold, red, and green on a white ground, looked hardly dry yet; the showy window-curtains of white and sky-blue, and the still showier carpet of red and yellow, seemed as if they had come out of the shop yesterday; the round rosewood table was in a painfully high state of polish; the morocco-bound picture books that lay on it, looked as if they had never been moved or opened since they had been bought; not one leaf even of the music on the piano was dogs-eared or worn. Never was a richly furnished room more thoroughly comfortless than this — the eye ached at looking round it. There was no repose anywhere. The print of the Queen, hanging lonely on the wall, in its heavy gilt frame, with a large crown at the top, glared on you: the paper, the curtains, the carpet glared on you: the books, the wax-flowers in glass cases, the chairs in flaring chintz-covers, the china plates on the door, the blue and pink glass vases and cups ranged on the chimney-piece, the over-ornamented chiffoniers with Tonbridge toys* and long-necked smelling bottles on their upper shelves—all glared on you. There was no look of shadow, shelter, secrecy, or retirement in any one nook or corner of those four gaudy walls. All surrounding objects seemed startlingly near to the eye; much nearer than they really were. The room would have given a nervous man the headache, before he had been in it a quarter of an hour.

I was not kept waiting long. Another violent crack from the new door, announced the entrance of Mr. Sherwin himself.

He was a tall, thin man : rather round-shouldered ; weak at the knees, and trying to conceal the weakness in the breadth of his trowsers. He wore a white cravat, and an absurdly high shirt collar. His complexion was sallow ; his eyes were small, black, bright, and incessantly in motion—indeed, all his features were singularly mobile : they were affected by nervous contractions and spasms which were constantly drawing up and down in all directions the brow, the mouth, and the muscles of the cheek. His hair had been black, but was now turning to a sort of iron-grey ; it was very dry, wiry, and plentiful, and part of it projected almost horizontally over his forehead. He had a habit of stretching it in this direction, by irritably combing it out, from time to time, with his fingers. His lips were thin and colourless, the lines about them being numerous and strongly marked. Had I seen him under ordinary circumstances, I should have set him down as a little-minded man ; a small tyrant in his own way over those dependent on him ; a pompous parasite to those above him—a great stickler for the conventional respectabilities of life, and a great believer in his own infallibility. But he was Margaret's father ; and I was determined to be pleased with him.

He made me a low and rather a cringing bow—then looked to the window, and seeing the carriage waiting for me at his door, made another bow, and insisted on relieving me of my hat with his own hand. This done, he coughed, and begged to know what he could do for me.

I felt some difficulty in opening my business to him. It was necessary to speak, however, at once—I began with an apology.

"I am afraid, Mr. Sherwin, that this intrusion on the part of a perfect stranger—"

"Not entirely a stranger, Sir, if I may be allowed to say so."

"Indeed !"

"I had tne great pleasure, Sir, and profit, and—and, indeed, advantage—of being shown over your town residence last year, when the family were absent from London. A very beautiful house—I happen to be acquainted with the steward of your respected father : he was kind enough to allow me to walk through the rooms. A treat ; quite an intellectual treat—the furniture and hangings, and so on, arranged in such a chaste style—and the pictures, some of the finest pieces I ever saw—I was delighted—quite delighted, indeed."

He spoke in under-tones, laying great stress upon particular words that were evidently favourites with him—such as, "indeed." Not only his eyes, but his whole face, seemed to be nervously blinking and winking all the time he was addressing me, In the embarrassment and anxiety which I then felt, this peculiarity fidgetted and bewildered me more than I can describe. I would have given the world to have had his back turned, before I spoke to him again.

"I am delighted to hear that my family and my name are not unknown to you, Mr. Sherwin," I resumed. "Under those circumstances, I shall feel less hesitation and difficulty in making you acquainted with the object of my visit."

"Just so. May I offer you anything ?—a glass of sherry, a—"

"Nothing, thank you. In the first place, Mr. Sherwin, I have reasons for wishing that this interview, whatever results it may lead to, may be considered strictly confidential. I am sure I can depend on your favouring me thus far ?"

"Certainly—most certainly—the strictest secrecy of course—pray go on."

He drew his chair a little nearer to me. Through all his blinking and winking, I could see a latent expression of cunning and curiosity in his eyes. My card was in his hand : he was nervously rolling and unrolling it, without a moment's cessation, in his anxiety to hear what I had to say.

"I must also beg you to suspend your judgment until you have heard me to the end. You may be disposed to view—to view, I say, unfavourably at first—in short, Mr. Sherwin, without further preface, the object of my visit is connected with your daughter, with Miss Margaret Sherwin—"

"My daughter! Bless my soul—God bless my soul, I really can't imagine—"

He stopped, half-breathless, bending forward towards me, and crumpling my card between his fingers into the smallest possible dimensions.

"Rather more than a week ago," I continued, "I accidentally met Miss Sherwin in an omnibus, accompanied by a lady older than herself—"

"My wife; Mrs. Sherwin," he said, impatiently motioning with his hand, as if "Mrs. Sherwin" were some insignificant obstacle to the conversation, which he wished to clear out of the way as fast as possible.

"You will not probably be surprised to hear that I was struck by Miss Sherwin's extreme beauty. The impression she made on me was something more, however, than a mere momentary feeling of admiration. To speak candidly, I felt—You have heard of such a thing as love at first sight. Mr. Sherwin?"

"In books, Sir." He tapped one of the morocco-bound volumes on the table, and smiled—a curious smile, partly deferential and partly sarcastic.

"You would be inclined to laugh, I dare say, if I asked you to believe that there is such a thing as love at first sight, *out* of books. But, without dwelling further on that, it is my duty to confess to you, in all candour and honesty, that the impression Miss Sherwin produced on me was such as to make me desire the privilege of becoming acquainted with her. In plain words, I discovered her place of residence by following her to this house."

"Upon my soul this is the most extraordinary proceeding——!"

"Pray hear me out, Mr. Sherwin: you will not condemn my conduct, I think, if you hear all I have to say."

He muttered something unintelligible; his complexion turned yellower; he dropped my card, which he had by this time crushed into fragments; and ran his hand rapidly through his hair until he had stretched it out like a penthouse over his forehead—blinking all the time, and regarding me with a lowering, sinister expression of countenance. I saw that it was useless to treat him as I should have treated a gentleman. He had evidently put the meanest and the foulest construction upon my delicacy and hesitation in speaking to him: so I altered my plan, and came to the point abruptly—"came to business," as he would have called it.

"I ought to have been plainer, Mr. Sherwin; I ought perhaps to have told you at the outset, in so many words, that I came to—" (I was about to say, "to ask your daughter's hand in marriage;" but a thought of my father moved darkly over my mind at that moment, and the words would not pass my lips).

"Well, Sir! to what?"

The tone in which he said this was harsh enough to rouse me. It gave me back my self-possession immediately.

"To ask your permission to pay my addresses to Miss Sherwin—or, to be plainer still, if you like, to ask of you her hand in marriage."

The words were spoken. Even if I could have done so I would not have recalled what I had just said; but still, I trembled in spite of myself, as I expressed in plain, blunt words what I had only rapturously thought over, or delicately hinted at to Margaret, up to this time.

"God bless me!" cried Mr. Sherwin, suddenly sitting back bolt upright in his chair, and staring at me in such surprise, that his restless features were actually struck with immobility for the moment—"God bless me, this is quite another story. Most gratifying, most astonishing—highly flattered I am sure; highly indeed, my dear Sir! Don't suppose, for one moment, I ever doubted your honourable feeling. Young gentlemen in your station of life do sometimes fail in respect towards the wives and daughters of their—in short, of those who are not in their rank exactly. But that's not the question—quite a misunderstanding—extremely stupid of me, to be sure. *Pray* let me offer you a glass of wine!"

"No wine, thank you, Mr. Sherwin. I must beg your attention a little longer, while I state to you, in confidence, how I am situated with regard to the proposals I have made. There are certain circumstances—"

"Yes—yes?"

He bent forward again eagerly towards me, as he spoke; looking more inquisitive and more cunning than ever.

"I have acknowledged to you, Mr. Sherwin, that I have found means to speak to your daughter—to speak to her twice. I made my advances honourably. She received them with a modesty and a reluctance worthy of herself, worthy of any lady, the highest lady in the land." (Mr. Sherwin looked round reverentially to his print of the Queen; then looked back at me, and bowed solemnly.) "Now, although in so many words she directly discouraged me—it is her due that I should say this—still, I think I may without vanity venture to hope that she did so as a matter of duty, more than as a matter of inclination."

"Ah—yes, yes! I understand. She would do nothing without my authority, of course?"

"No doubt that was one reason why she received me as she did; but she had another, which she communicated to me in the plainest terms — the difference in our rank of life."

"Ah! she said that, did she? Exactly so—she saw a difficulty there? Yes — yes! high principles, Sir — high principles, thank God!"

"I need hardly tell you, Mr. Sherwin, how deeply I feel the delicate sense of honour which this objection shows on your daughter's part. You will easily imagine that it is no objection to *me*, personally. The happiness of my whole life depends on Miss Sherwin; I desire no higher honour, as I can conceive no greater happiness, than to be your daughter's husband. I told her this: I also told her that I would explain myself on the subject to you. She made no objection; and I am, therefore, I think, justified in considering that if you authorised the removal of scruples which do her honour at present, she would not feel the delicacy she does now at sanctioning my addresses."

"Very proper—a very proper way of putting it. Practical, if I may be allowed to say so. And now, my dear Sir, the next point is: how about your own honoured family— eh?"

"It is exactly there that the difficulty lies. My father, on whom I am dependent as the younger son, has very strong prejudices—convictions I ought perhaps to call them —on the subject of social inequalities."

"Quite so—most natural; most becoming, indeed, on the part of your respected father. I honour his convictions, Sir. Such estates, such houses, such a family as his—connected, I believe, with the nobility, especially on your late lamented mother's side. My dear Sir, I emphatically repeat it, your father's convictions do him honour; I respect them as much as I respect him; I do, indeed."

"I am glad you can view my father's ideas on social subjects in so favourable a light, Mr. Sherwin. You will be less surprised to hear how they are likely to affect me in the step I am now taking."

"He disapproves of it, of course — strongly, perhaps. Well, though my dear girl is worthy of any station; and a man like me, devoted to mercantile interests, may hold his head up anywhere as one of the props of this commercial country,"(he ran his fingers rapidly through his hair, and tried to look independent), "still I am prepared to admit, under all the circumstances—I say under all the circumstances—that his disapproval is very natural, and was very much to be expected—very much indeed."

"He has expressed no disapproval, Mr. Sherwin."

"You don't say so!"

"I have not given him an opportunity. My meeting with your daughter has been kept a profound secret from him, and from every member of my family; and a secret it must remain. I speak from my intimate knowledge of my father, when I say that I hardly know of any means that he would not be capable of employing to frustrate the purpose of this visit, if I had mentioned it to him. He has been the kindest and best of fathers to me; but I firmly believe, that if I waited for his consent, no entreaties of mine, or of any one belonging to me, would induce him to give his sanction to the marriage I have come to you to propose."

"Bless my soul! this is carrying things rather far, though —dependent as you are on him, and all that. Why, what on earth can we do—eh?"

"We must keep both the courtship and the marriage secret."

"Secret! Good gracious, I don't at all see my way—"

"Yes, secret—a profound secret among ourselves, until I can divulge my marriage to my father, with the best chance of—"

"But I tell you, Sir, I can't see my way through it at all. Chance! what chance would there be, after what you have told me?"

"There might be many chances. For instance, when the marriage was solemnised, I might introduce your daughter to my father's notice—without disclosing who she was—and leave her, gradually and unsuspectedly, to win his affection and respect (as with her beauty, elegance, and amiability, she could not fail to do), while I waited until the occasion was ripe for confessing everything. Then if I said to him, 'This young lady, who has so interested and delighted you, is my wife;' do you think, with that powerful argument in my favour, he could fail to give us his pardon? If, on the other hand, I could only say, ' This young lady is about to become my wife,' his prejudices would assuredly induce him to recall his most favourable impressions, and refuse his consent. In short, Mr. Sherwin, before marriage, it would be impossible to move him—after marriage, when opposition could no longer be of any avail, it would be quite a different thing : we might be sure of producing, sooner or later, the most favourable results. This is why it would be absolutely necessary to keep our union secret at first."

I wondered then—I have since wondered more—how it was that I contrived to speak thus, so smoothly and so unhesitatingly, when my conscience was giving the lie all the while to every word I uttered.

"Yes, yes ; I see—oh, yes, I see !" said Mr. Sherwin, rattling a bunch of keys in his pocket, with an expression of considerable perplexity ; "but this is a ticklish business, you know—a very queer and ticklish business indeed. To have a gentleman of your birth and breeding for a son-in-law, is of course—but then there is the money question. Suppose you failed with your father after all—*my* money is out in my speculations—*I* can do nothing. Upon my word, you have placed me in a position that I never was placed in before."

"I have influential friends, Mr. Sherwin, in many directions—there are appointments, good appointments, which would be open to me, if I pushed my interests. I might provide in this way against the chance of failure."

" Ah!—well—yes. There's something in that, certainly."

" I can only assure you that my attachment to Miss Sherwin is not of a nature to be overcome by any pecuniary considerations. I speak in all our interests, when I say that a private marriage gives us a chance for the future, as opportunities arise of gradually disclosing it. My offer to you may be made under some disadvantages and difficulties, perhaps; for, with the exception of a very small independence, left me by my mother, I have no certain prospects.* But I really think my proposals have some compensating advantages to recommend them——"

" Certainly! most decidedly so! I am not insensible, my dear Sir, to the great advantage, and honour, and so forth. But there is something so unusual about the whole affair. What would be my feelings, if your father should not come round, and my dear girl was disowned by the family? Well, well! that could hardly happen, I think, with her accomplishments and education, and manners too, so distinguished—though perhaps I ought not to say so. Her schooling alone was a hundred a-year, Sir, without including extras——"

" I am sure, Mr. Sherwin——"

" ——A school, Sir, where it was a rule to take in nothing lower than the daughter of a professional man—they only waived the rule in my case—the most genteel school, perhaps, in all London! A drawing-room-deportment day once every week—the girls taught how to enter a room and leave a room with dignity and ease—a model of a carriage door and steps, in the back drawing-room, to practise the girls (with the footman of the establishment in attendance) in getting into a carriage and getting out again, in a lady-like manner! No duchess has had a better education than *my* Margaret!——"

"Permit me to assure you, Mr. Sherwin——"

"And then, her knowledge of languages—her French, and Italian, and German, not discontinued in holidays, or after she left school (she has only just left it); but all kept up and improved every evening, by the kind attention of Mr. Mannion——"

"May I ask who Mr. Mannion is?" The tone in which I put this question, cooled his enthusiasm about his daughter's education immediately. He answered in his former tones, and with one of his former bows:

"Mr. Mannion is my confidential clerk, Sir—a most superior person, most highly talented, and well read, and all that."

"Is he a young man?"

"Young! Oh, dear no! Mr. Mannion is forty, or a year or two more, if he's a day—an admirable man of business, as well as a great scholar. He's at Lyons now, buying silks for me. When he comes back I shall be delighted to introduce——"

"I beg your pardon, but I think we are wandering away from the point, a little."

"I beg *yours*—so we are. Well, my dear Sir, I must be allowed a day or two—say two days—to ascertain what my daughter's feelings are, and to consider your proposals, which have taken me very much by surprise, as you may in fact see. But I assure you I am most flattered, most honoured, most anxious——"

"I hope you will consider *my* anxieties, Mr. Sherwin, and let me know the result of your deliberations as soon as possible."

"Without fail, depend upon it. Let me see: shall we say the second day from this, at the same time, if you can favour me with a visit?"

"Certainly."

"And between that time and this, you will engage not to hold any communication with my daughter?"

"I promise not, Mr. Sherwin—because I believe that your answer will be favourable."

"Ah, well—well! lovers, they say, should never despair. A little consideration, and a little talk with my dear girl—really now, won't you change your mind and have a glass of sherry? (No again?) Very well, then, the day after to-morrow, at five o'clock."

With a louder crack than ever, the bran-new* drawing-room door was opened to let me out. The noise was instantly succeeded by the rustling of a silk dress, and the banging of another door, at the opposite end of the passage. Had anybody been listening? Where was Margaret?

Mr. Sherwin stood at the garden-gate to watch my departure, and to make his farewell bow. Thick as was the atmosphere of illusion in which I now lived, I shuddered involuntarily as I returned his parting salute, and thought of him as my father-in-law!

XI.

The nearer I approached to our own door, the more reluctance I felt to pass the short interval between my first and second interview with Mr. Sherwin, at home. When I entered the house, this reluctance increased to something almost like dread. I felt unwilling and unfit to meet the eyes of my nearest and dearest relatives. It was a relief to me to hear that my father was not at home. My sister was in the house: the servant said she had just gone into the library, and inquired whether he should tell her that I had come in. I desired him not to disturb her, as it was my intention to go out again immediately.

I went into my study, and wrote a short note there to Clara; merely telling her that I should be absent in the country for two days. I had sealed and laid it on the table for the servant to deliver, and was about to leave the room, when I heard the library door open. I instantly drew back, and half-closed my own door again. Clara had got the book she wanted, and was taking it up to her own sitting-room. I waited till she was out of sight, and then left the house. It was the first time I had ever avoided my sister —my sister, who had never in her life asked a question, or uttered a word that could annoy me; my sister, who had confided all her own little secrets to my keeping, ever since we had been children. As I thought on what I had done, I felt a sense of humiliation which was almost punishment enough for the meanness of which I had been guilty.

I went round to the stables, and had my horse saddled immediately. No idea of proceeding in any particular direction occurred to me. I simply felt resolved to pass my two days' ordeal of suspense away from home—far enough away to keep me faithful to my promise not to see Margaret. Soon after I started, I left my horse to his own guidance, and gave myself up to my thoughts and recollections, as one by one they rose within me. The animal took the direction which he had been oftenest used to take during my residence in London—the northern road.

It was not until I had ridden half a mile beyond the suburbs that I looked round me, and discovered towards what part of the country I was proceeding. I drew the rein directly, and turned my horse's head back again, towards the south. To follow the favourite road which I had so often followed with Clara; to stop perhaps at some place where I had often stopped with her, was more than I had the courage or the insensibility to do at that moment.

I rode as far as Ewell,* and stopped there: the darkness had overtaken me, and it was useless to tire my horse by going on any greater distance. The next morning, I was up almost with sunrise; and passed the greater part of the day in walking about among villages, lanes, and fields, just as chance led me. During the night, many thoughts that I had banished for the last week had returned—those thoughts of evil omen under which the mind seems to ache, just as the body aches under a dull, heavy pain, to which we can assign no particular place or cause. Absent from Margaret, I had no resource against the oppression that now overcame me. I could only endeavour to alleviate it by keeping incessantly in action; by walking or riding, hour after hour, in the vain attempt to quiet the mind by wearying out the body. Apprehension of the failure of my application to Mr. Sherwin had nothing to do with the vague gloom which now darkened my thoughts; they kept too near home for that. Besides, what I had observed of Margaret's father, especially during the latter part of my interview with him, showed me plainly enough that he was trying to conceal, under exaggerated surprise and assumed hesitation, his secret desire to profit at once by my offer; which, whatever conditions might clog it, was infinitely more advantageous in a social point of view, than any he could have hoped for. It was not his delay in accepting my proposals, but the burden of deceit, the fetters of concealment forced on me by the proposals themselves, which now hung heavy on my heart.

That evening I left Ewell, and rode towards home again, as far as Richmond, where I remained for the night and the forepart of the next day. I reached London in the afternoon; and got to North Villa—without going home first— about five o'clock.

The oppression was still on my spirits. Even the sight of the house where Margaret lived failed to invigorate or arouse me.

On this occasion, when I was shown into the drawing-room, both Mr. and Mrs. Sherwin were awaiting me there.

On the table was the sherry which had been so perseveringly pressed on me at the last interview, and by it a new pound cake. Mrs. Sherwin was cutting the cake as I came in, while her husband watched the process with critical eyes. The poor woman's weak white fingers trembled as they moved the knife under conjugal inspection.

"Most happy to see you again—most happy indeed, my dear Sir," said Mr. Sherwin, advancing with hospitable smile and outstretched hand. "Allow me to introduce my better half, Mrs. S."

His wife rose in a hurry, and curtseyed, leaving the knife sticking in the cake; upon which Mr. Sherwin, with a stern look at her, ostentatiously pulled it out, and set it down rather violently on the dish.

Poor Mrs. Sherwin!* I had hardly noticed her on the day when she got into the omnibus with her daughter—it was as if I now saw her for the first time. There is a natural communicativeness about women's emotions. A happy woman imperceptibly diffuses her happiness around her; she has an influence that is something akin to the influence of a sunshiny day. So, again, the melancholy of a melancholy woman is invariably, though silently, infectious; and Mrs. Sherwin was one of this latter order. Her pale, sickly, moist-looking skin; her large, mild, watery, light-blue eyes; the restless timidity* of her expression; the mixture of useless hesitation and involuntary rapidity in every one of her actions—all furnished the same significant betrayal of a life of incessant fear and restraint; of a disposition full of modest generosities and meek sympathies, which had been crushed down past rousing to self-assertion, past ever seeing the light. There, in that mild, wan face of hers—in those painful startings and hurryings when she moved; in that tremulous, faint utterance when she spoke—*there*, I could see one of those ghastly heart-tragedies laid open before me, which are acted and re-acted, scene by scene, and year by

year, in the secret theatre of home; tragedies which are
ever shadowed by the slow falling of the black curtain that
drops lower and lower every day—that drops, to hide all at
last, from the hand of death.

"We have had very beautiful weather lately, Sir," said
Mrs. Sherwin, almost inaudibly; looking as she spoke, with
anxious eyes towards her husband, to see if she was justified in uttering even those piteously common-place words.
"Very beautiful weather to be sure," continued the poor
woman, as timidly as if she had become a little child again,
and had been ordered to say her first lesson in a stranger's
presence.

"Delightful weather, Mrs. Sherwin. I have been enjoy-
ing it for the last two days in the country—in a part of
Surrey (the neighbourhood of Ewell) that I had not seen
before."

There was a pause. Mr. Sherwin coughed; it was evidently a warning matrimonial peal that he had often rung
before—for Mrs. Sherwin started, and looked up at him
directly.

"As the lady of the house, Mrs. S., it strikes me that you
might offer a visitor, like this gentleman, some cake and
wine, without making any particular hole in your manners!"

"Oh dear me! I beg your pardon! I'm very sorry, I'm
sure"—and she poured out a glass of wine, with such a
trembling hand that the decanter tinkled all the while against
the glass. Though I wanted nothing, I ate and drank something immediately, in common consideration for Mrs. Sherwin's embarrassment.

Mr. Sherwin filled himself a glass—held it up admiringly
to the light—said, "Your good health, Sir, your very good
health;" and drank the wine with the air of a connoisseur,
and a most expressive smacking of the lips. His wife (to
whom he offered nothing) looked at him all the time with
the most reverential attention.

"You are taking nothing yourself, Mrs. Sherwin," I said.

"Mrs. Sherwin, Sir," interposed her husband, "never drinks wine, and can't digest cake. A bad stomach—a very bad stomach. Have another glass yourself. Won't you, indeed? This sherry stands me in six shillings a bottle—ought to be first-rate wine at that price: and so it is. Well, if you won't have any more, we will proceed to business. Ha! ha! business as *I* call it; pleasure I hope it will be to *you*."

Mrs. Sherwin coughed—a very weak, small cough, half-stifled in its birth.

"There you are again!" he said, turning fiercely towards her—"Coughing again! Six months of the doctor—a six months' bill to come out of my pocket—and no good done —no good, Mrs. S."

"Oh, I am much better, thank you—it was only a little—"

"Well, Sir, the evening after you left me, I had what you may call an explanation with my dear girl. She was naturally a little confused and—and embarrassed, indeed. A very serious thing of course, to decide at her age, and at so short a notice, on a point involving the happiness of her whole life to come."

Here Mrs. Sherwin put her handkerchief to her eyes—quite noiselessly; for she had doubtless acquired by long practice the habit of weeping in silence. Her husband's quick glance turned on her, however, immediately, with anything but an expression of sympathy.

"Good God, Mrs. S.! what's the use of going on in that way?" he said, indignantly. "What is there to cry about? Margaret isn't ill, and isn't unhappy—what on earth's the matter now? Upon my soul this is a most annoying circumstance: and before a visitor too! You had better leave me to discuss the matter alone—you always *were* in the way of business, and it's my opinion you always will be."

Mrs. Sherwin prepared, without a word of remonstrance, to leave the room. I sincerely felt for her; but could say nothing. In the impulse of the moment, I rose to open the door for her; and immediately repented having done so. The action added so much to her embarrassment that she kicked her foot against a chair, and uttered a suppressed exclamation of pain as she went out.

Mr. Sherwin helped himself to a second glass of wine, without taking the smallest notice of this.

"I hope Mrs. Sherwin has not hurt herself?" I said.

"Oh dear no! not worth a moment's thought—awkwardness and nervousness, nothing else—she always was nervous —the doctors (all humbugs) can do nothing with her—it's very sad, very sad indeed; but there's no help for it."

By this time (in spite of all my efforts to preserve some respect for him, as Margaret's father) he had sunk to his proper place in my estimation.

"Well, my dear Sir," he resumed, "to go back to where I was interrupted by Mrs. S. Let me see: I was saying that my dear girl was a little confused, and so forth. As a matter of course, I put before her all the advantages which such a connection as yours promised—and at the same time, mentioned some of the little embarrassing circumstances—the private marriage, you know, and all that—besides telling her of certain restrictions in reference to the marriage, if it came off, which I should feel it my duty as a father to impose; and which I shall proceed, in short, to explain to you. As a man of the world, my dear Sir, you know as well as I do, that young ladies don't give very straightforward answers on the subject of their prepossessions in favour of young gentlemen. But I got enough out of her to show me that you had made pretty good use of your time—no occasion to despond, you know—I leave *you* to make her speak plain; it's more in your line than mine, more a good deal. And now let us come to the business part of the transaction. All I have to say is this :—if you agree to my proposals, then I agree to yours. I think that's fair enough—Eh?"

"Quite fair, Mr. Sherwin."

"Just so. Now, in the first place, my daughter is too young to be married yet. She was only seventeen last birthday."

"You astonish me! I should have imagined her three years older at least."

"Everybody thinks her older than she is—everybody, my dear Sir—and she certainly looks it. She's more formed, more developed I may say, than most girls at her age. However, that's not the point. The plain fact is, she's too young to be married now—too young in a moral point of view ; too young in an educational point of view ;* too young altogether. Well : the upshot of this is, that I could not give my consent to Margaret's marrying, until another year is out—say a year from this time. One year's courtship for the finishing off of her education, and the formation of her constitution—you understand me, for the formation of her constitution."

A year to wait! At first, this seemed a long trial to endure, a trial that ought not to be imposed on me. But the next moment, the delay appeared in a different light. Would it not be the dearest of privileges to be able to see Margaret, perhaps every day, perhaps for hours at a time? Would it not be happiness enough to observe each development of her character, to watch her first maiden love for me, advancing nearer and nearer towards confidence and maturity the oftener we met? As I thought on this, I answered Mr. Sherwin without further hesitation.

"It will be some trial," I said, "to my patience, though none to my constancy, none to the strength of my affection —I will wait the year."

"Exactly so," rejoined Mr. Sherwin ; "such candour and such reasonableness were to be expected from one who is quite the gentleman. And now comes my grand difficulty in this business—in fact, the little stipulation I have to make."

He stopped, and ran his fingers through his hair, in all directions; his features fidgetting and distorting themselves ominously, while he looked at me.

" Pray explain yourself, Mr. Sherwin. Your silence gives me some uneasiness at this particular moment, I assure you."

" Quite so—I understand. Now, you must promise me not to be huffed—offended, I should say—at what I am going to propose."

" Certainly not."

" Well, then, it may seem odd; but under all the circumstances—that is to say, as far as the case concerns you personally—I want you and my dear girl to be married at once, and yet not to be married exactly, for another year. I don't know whether you understand me ?"

" I must confess I do not."

He coughed rather uneasily; turned to the table, and poured out another glass of sherry—his hand trembling a little as he did so. He drank off the wine at a draught; cleared his throat three or four times after it; and then spoke again.

" Well, to be still plainer, this is how the matter stands: If you were a party in our rank of life, coming to court Margaret with your father's full approval and permission— when once you had consented to the year's engagement, everything would be done and settled; the bargain would have been struck on both sides; and there would be an end of it. But, situated as you are, I can't stop here safely— I mean, I can't end the agreement exactly in this way."

He evidently felt that he got fluent on wine; and helped himself, at this juncture, to another glass.

" You will see what I am driving at, my dear Sir, directly," he continued. "Suppose now, you came courting my daughter for a year, as we settled; and suppose your father found it out—we should keep it a profound secret of course: but still, secrets are sometimes found out, nobody knows how. Suppose, I say, your father got scent of the thing, and the match was broken off; where do you think Margaret's reputation would be? If it happened with somebody in her own station, we might explain it all, and be believed: but happening with somebody in yours, what would the world say? Would the world believe you had ever intended to marry her? That's the point—that's the point precisely."

"But the case could not happen—I am astonished you can imagine it possible. I have told you already, I am of age."

"Properly urged—very properly, indeed. But you also told me, if you remember, when I first had the pleasure of seeing you, that your father, if he knew of this match, would stick at nothing to oppose it—*at nothing*—I recollect you said so. Now, knowing this, my dear Sir—though I have the most perfect confidence in *your* honour, and *your* resolution to fulfil your engagement — I can't have confidence in your being prepared beforehand to oppose all your father might do if he found us out; because you can't tell yourself what he might be up to, or what influence he might set to work over you. This sort of mess is not very probable, you will say; but if it's at all possible — and there's a year for it to be possible in—by George, Sir, I must guard against accidents, for my daughter's sake—I must indeed!"

"In Heaven's name, Mr. Sherwin, pass over all these impossible difficulties of yours! and let me hear what you have finally to propose."

"Gently, my dear Sir! gently, gently, gently! I propose this, to begin with: that you should marry my daughter—

privately marry her—in a week's time.   Now, pray compose
yourself!"   (I was looking at him in speechless astonishment.)   "Take it easy; pray take it easy!   Supposing,
then, you marry her in this way, I make one stipulation.   I
require you to give me your word of honour to leave her
at the church door; and for the space of one year never to
attempt to see her, except in the presence of a third party.
At the end of that time, I will engage to give her to you,
as your wife in fact, as well as in name.   There! what do
you say to that—eh?"

I was too astounded, too overwhelmed, to say anything at
that moment; Mr. Sherwin went on:

"This plan of mine, you see, reconciles everything.   If
any accident *does* happen, and we are discovered, why your
father can do nothing to stop the match, because the match
will have been already made.   And, at the same time, I secure
a year's delay, for the formation of her constitution, and the
finishing of her accomplishments, and so forth.   Besides,
what an opportunity this gives of sailing as near the wind
as you choose, in breaking the thing, bit by bit, to your
father, without fear of consequences, in case he should run
rough after all.   Upon my honour, my dear Sir, I think I
deserve some credit for hitting on this plan—it makes everything so right and straight, and suits of course the wishes
of all parties!   I need hardly say that you shall have every
facility for seeing Margaret, under the restrictions—under
the restrictions, you understand.   People may talk about
your visits; but having got the certificate, and knowing it's
all safe and settled, I shan't care for that.   Well, what do
you say? take time to think, if you wish it—only remember that I have the most perfect confidence in your honour,
and that I act from a fatherly feeling for the interests of
my dear girl!"   He stopped, out of breath from the extraordinary volubility of his long harangue.

Some men more experienced in the world, less mastered

by love than I was, would, in my position, have recognised in this proposal an unfair trial of self-restraint—perhaps, something like an unfair humilation as well. Others would have detected the selfish motives which suggested it : the mean distrust of my honour, integrity, and firmness of purpose which it implied; and the equally mean anxiety on Mr. Sherwin's part to clench his profitable bargain at once, for fear it might be repented of. I discerned nothing of this. As soon as I had recovered from the natural astonishment of the first few moments, I only saw in the strange plan proposed to me,* a certainty of assuring—no matter with what sacrifice, what hazard, or what delay—the ultimate triumph of my love. When Mr. Sherwin had ceased speaking, I replied at once :

"I accept your conditions—I accept them with all my heart."

He was hardly prepared for so complete and so sudden an acquiescence in his proposal, and looked absolutely startled by it, at first. But soon resuming his self-possession—his wily, "business-like" self-possession—he started up, and shook me vehemently by the hand.

"Delighted—most delighted, my dear Sir, to find how soon we understand each other, and that we pull together so well. We must have another glass; hang it, we really must! a toast, you know; a toast you can't help drinking— your wife! Ha! ha!—I had you there!—my dear, dear Margaret, God bless her!"

"We may consider all difficulties finally settled then," I said, anxious to close my interview with Mr. Sherwin as speedily as possible.

"Decidedly so. Done, and double done, I may say. There will be a little insurance on your life, that I shall ask you to effect for dear Margaret's sake; and perhaps, a memorandum of agreement, engaging to settle a certain proportion of any property you may become possessed of, on her and her children. You see I am looking forward to my grandfather days already! But this can wait for a future occasion—say in a day or two."

"Then I presume there will be no objection to my seeing Miss Sherwin now?"

"None whatever—at once, if you like. This way, my dear Sir; this way," and he led me across the passage, into the dining-room.

This apartment was furnished with less luxury, but with more bad taste (if possible) than the room we had just left. Near the window sat Margaret—it was the same window at which I had seen her, on the evening when I wandered into the square, after our meeting in the omnibus. The cage with the canary-bird hung in the same place. I just noticed —with a momentary surprise—that Mrs. Sherwin was sitting far away from her daughter, at the other end of the room; and then placed myself by Margaret's side. She was dressed in pale yellow—a colour which gave new splendour to her dark complexion and magnificently dark hair. Once more, all my doubts, all my self-upbraidings vanished, and gave place to the exquisite sense of happiness, the glow of joy and hope and love which seemed to rush over my heart, the moment I looked at her.

After staying in the room about five minutes, Mr. Sherwin whispered to his wife, and left us. Mrs. Sherwin still kept her place; but she said nothing, and hardly turned to look round at us more than once or twice. Perhaps she was occupied by her own thoughts; perhaps, from a motive of delicacy, she abstained even from an appearance of watching her daughter or watching me. Whatever feelings influenced her, I cared not to speculate on them. It was enough that I had the privilege of speaking to Margaret uninterruptedly; of declaring my love at last, without hesitation and without reserve.

How much I had to say to her, and how short a time

seemed to be left me that evening to say it in! How short a time to tell her all the thoughts of the past which she had created in me; all the self-sacrifice to which I had cheerfully consented for her sake; all the anticipations of future happiness which were concentrated in her, which drew their very breath of life, only from the prospect of her rewarding love! She spoke but little; yet even that little it was a new delight to hear. She smiled now; she let me take her hand, and made no attempt to withdraw it. The evening had closed in; the darkness was stealing fast upon us; the still, dead-still figure of Mrs. Sherwin, always in the same place and the same attitude, grew fainter and fainter to the eye, across the distance of the room—but no thought of time, no thought of home ever once crossed my mind. I could have sat at the window with Margaret the long night through; without an idea of numbering the hours as they passed.

Ere long, however, Mr. Sherwin entered the room again, and effectually roused me by approaching and speaking to us. I saw that I had stayed long enough, and that we were not to be left together again, that night. So I rose and took my leave, having first fixed a time for seeing Margaret on the morrow. Mr. Sherwin accompanied me with great ceremony to the outer door. Just as I was leaving him, he touched me on the arm, and said in his most confidential tones:

"Come an hour earlier, to-morrow; and we'll go and get the licence together. No objection to that—eh? And the marriage, shall we say this day week? Just as *you* like, you know—don't let me seem to dictate. Ah! no objection to that, either, I see, and no objection on Margaret's side, I'll warrant! With respect to consents, in the marrying part of the business, there's complete mutuality—isn't there? Good night: God bless you!"

XII.

That night I went home with none of the reluctance or
the apprehension which I had felt on the last occasion, when
I approached our own door. The assurance of success contained in the events of the afternoon, gave me a trust in
my own self-possession—a confidence in my own capacity
to parry all dangerous questions—which I had not experienced before. I cared not how soon, or for how long a
time, I might find myself in company with Clara or my
father. It was well for the preservation of my secret that
I was in this frame of mind; for, on opening my study door,
I was astonished to see both of them in my room.

Clara was measuring one of my over-crowded book-shelves,
with a piece of string; and was apparently just about to
compare the length of it with a vacant space on the wall
close by, when I came in. Seeing me, she stopped; and
looked round significantly at my father, who was standing
near her, with a file of papers in his hand.

"You may well feel surprised, Basil, at this invasion of
your territory," he said, with peculiar kindness of manner
—"you must, however, apply there, to the prime minister
of the household," pointing to Clara, "for an explanation.
I am only the instrument of a domestic conspiracy on your
sister's part."

Clara seemed doubtful whether she should speak. It
was the first time I had ever seen such an expression in her
face, when she looked into mine.

"We are discovered, papa," she said, after a momentary
silence, "and we must explain; but you know I always
leave as many explanations as I can to you."

"Very well," said my father smiling; "my task in this
instance will be an easy one. I was intercepted, Basil, on
my way to my own room by your sister, and taken in here

to advise about a new set of bookcases for you, when I ought to have been attending to my own money matters. Clara's idea was to have had these new bookcases made in secret, and put up as a surprise, some day when you were not at home. However, as you have caught her in the act of measuring spaces, with all the skill of an experienced carpenter, and all the impetuosity of an arbitrary young lady who rules supreme over everybody, further concealment is out of the question. We must make a virtue of necessity, and confess everything."

Poor Clara! This was her only return for ten days' utter neglect—and she had been half afraid to tell me of it herself. I approached and thanked her; not very gratefully, I am afraid, for I felt too confused to speak freely. It seemed like a fatality. The more evil I was doing in secret, evil to family ties and family principles, the more good was unconsciously returned to me by my family, through my sister's hands.

"I made no objection, of course, to the bookcase plan," continued my father. "More room is really wanted for the volumes on volumes that you have collected about you; but I certainly suggested a little delay in the execution of the project. The bookcases will, at all events, not be required here for five months to come. This day week we return to the country."

I could not repress a start of astonishment and dismay Here was a difficulty which I ought to have provided for; but which I had most unaccountably never once thought of, although it was now the period of the year at which on all former occasions we had been accustomed to leave London. This day week too! The very day fixed by Mr. Sherwin for my marriage!

"I am afraid, Sir, I shall not be able to go with you and Clara so soon as you propose. It was my wish to remain in London some time longer." I said this in a low voice,

without venturing to look at my sister. But I could not
help hearing her exclamation as I spoke, and the tone in
which she uttered it.

My father moved nearer to me a step or two, and looked
in my face intently, with the firm, penetrating expression
which peculiarly characterized him.

"This seems an extraordinary resolution," he said, his
tones and manner altering ominously while he spoke. "I
thought your sudden absence for the last two days rather
odd; but this plan of remaining in London by yourself is
really incomprehensible. What can you have to do?"

An excuse—no! not an excuse; let me call things by
their right names in these pages—a *lie* was rising to my
lips; but my father checked the utterance of it. He detected my embarrassment immediately, anxiously as I strove
to conceal it.

"Stop," he said coldly, while the red flush which meant
so much when it rose on *his* cheek, began to appear there
for the first time. "Stop! If you must make excuses, Basil,
I must ask no questions. You have a secret which you
wish to keep from me; and I beg you *will* keep it. I have
never been accustomed to treat my sons as I would not
treat any other gentlemen with whom I may happen to be
associated. If they have private affairs, I cannot interfere
with those affairs. My trust in their honour is my only
guarantee against their deceiving me; but in the intercourse
of gentlemen that is guarantee enough. Remain here as
long as you like: we shall be happy to see you in the
country, when you are able to leave town."

He turned to Clara. "I suppose, my love, you want me
no longer. While I settle my own matters of business,
you can arrange about the book-cases with your brother.
Whatever you wish, I shall be glad to do." And he left
the room without speaking to me, or looking at me again.
I sank into a chair, feeling disgraced in my own estimation

by the last words he had spoken to me. His trust in my honour was his only guarantee against my deceiving him. As I thought over that declaration, every syllable of it seemed to sear my conscience; to brand Hypocrite on my heart.

I turned towards my sister. She was standing at a little distance from me, silent and pale, mechanically twisting the measuring-string, which she still held between her trembling fingers; and fixing her eyes upon me so lovingly, so mournfully, that my fortitude gave way when I looked at her. At that instant, I seemed to forget everything that had passed since the day when I first met Margaret, and to be restored once more to my old way of life and my old home-sympathies. My head drooped on my breast, and I felt the hot tears forcing themselves into my eyes.

Clara stepped quietly to my side; and sitting down by me in silence, put her arm round my neck.

When I was calmer, she said gently:

"I have been very anxious about you, Basil; and perhaps I have allowed that anxiety to appear more than I ought. Perhaps I have been accustomed to exact too much from you—you have been too ready to please me. But I have been used to it so long; and I have nobody else that I can speak to as I can to you. Papa is very kind; but he can't be what you are to me exactly; and Ralph does not live with us now, and cared little about me, I am afraid, when he did. I have friends, but friends are not—"

She stopped again; her voice was failing her. For a moment, she struggled to keep her self-possession—struggled as only women can—and succeeded in the effort. She pressed her arm closer round my neck; but her tones were steadier and clearer when she resumed:

"It will not be very easy for me to give up our country rides and walks together, and the evening talk that we always had at dusk in the old library at the park. But I think I can resign all this, and go away alone with papa, for the first time, without making you melancholy by anything I say or do at parting, if you will only promise that when you are in any difficulty you will let me be of some use. I think I could always be of use, because I should always feel an interest in anything that concerned you. I don't want to intrude on your secret; but if that secret should ever bring you trouble or distress (which I hope and pray it may not), I want you to have confidence in my being able to help you, in some way, through any mischances. Let me go into the country, Basil, knowing that you can still put trust in *me*, even though a time should come when you can put trust in no one else—let me know this: *do* let me!"

I gave her the assurance she desired—gave it with my whole heart. She seemed to have recovered all her old influence over me by the few simple words she had spoken. The thought crossed my mind, whether I ought not in common gratitude to confide my secret to her at once, knowing as I did, that it would be safe in her keeping, however the disclosure might startle or pain her. I believe I should have told her all, in another minute, but for a mere accident—the trifling interruption caused by a knock at the door.

It came from one of the servants. My father desired to see Clara on some matter connected with their impending departure for the country. She was unfit enough to obey such a summons at such a time; but with her usual courage in disciplining her own feelings into subserviency to the wishes of any one whom she loved, she determined to obey immediately the message which had been delivered to her. A few moments of silence; a slight trembling soon repressed; a parting kiss for me; these few farewell words of encouragement at the door; "Don't grieve about what papa has said; you have made *me* feel happy about you, Basil; I will make *him* feel happy too," and Clara was gone.

With those few minutes of interruption, the time for the

disclosure of my secret had passed by. As soon as my sister was out of the room, my former reluctance to trust it to home-keeping returned, and remained unchanged throughout the whole of the long year's probation which I had engaged to pass. But this mattered little. As events turned out, if I had told Clara all, the end would have come in the same way, the fatality would have been accomplished by the same means.

I went out shortly after my sister had left me. I could give myself to no occupation at home, for the rest of that night; and I knew that it would be useless to attempt to sleep just then. As I walked through the streets, bitter thoughts against my father rose in my mind—bitter thoughts against his inexorable family pride, which imposed on me the concealment and secrecy, under the oppression of which I had already suffered so much—bitter thoughts against those social tyrannies, which take no account of human sympathy and human love, and which my father now impersonated, as it were, to my ideas. Gradually these reflections merged in others that were better. I thought of Clara again; consoling myself with the belief, that, however my father might receive the news of my marriage, I might count upon my sister as certain to love my wife and be kind to her, for my sake. This thought led my heart back to Margaret—led it gently and happily. I went home, calmed and reassured again—at least for the rest of the night.

The events of that week, so fraught with importance for the future of my life, passed with ominous rapidity.

The marriage license was procured; all remaining preliminaries with Mr. Sherwin were adjusted; I saw Margaret every day, and gave myself up more and more unreservedly to the charm that she exercised over me, at each succeeding interview. At home, the bustle of approaching departure; the farewell visitings; the multitudinous minor arrangements preceding a journey to the country, seemed to hurry the hours on faster and faster, as the parting day for Clara, and the marriage day for me, drew near. Incessant interruptions prevented any more lengthened or private conversations with my sister; and my father was hardly ever accessible for more than five minutes together, even to those who specially wished to speak with him. Nothing arose to embarrass or alarm me now, out of my intercourse with home.

The day came. I had not slept during the night that preceded it; so I rose early to look out on the morning.

It is strange how frequently that instinctive belief in omens and predestinations, which we flippantly term Superstition, asserts its natural prerogative even over minds trained to repel it, at the moment of some great event in our lives. I believe this has happened to many more men than ever confessed it; and it happened to me. At any former period of my life, I should have laughed at the bare imputation of a " superstitious" feeling ever having risen in my mind. But now, as I looked on the sky, and saw the black clouds that overspread the whole firmament, and the heavy rain that poured down from them, an irrepressible sinking of the heart came over me. For the last ten days the sun had shone almost uninterruptedly—with my marriage-day came the cloud, the mist and the rain. I tried to laugh myself out of the forebodings which this suggested, and tried in vain.

The departure for the country was to take place at an early hour. We all breakfasted together; the meal was hurried over comfortlessly and silently. My father was either writing notes, or examining the steward's accounts, almost the whole time; and Clara was evidently incapable of uttering a single word, without risking the loss of her self-possession. The silence was so complete, while we sat together at the table, that the fall of the rain outside (which had grown softer and thicker as the morning advanced), and the quick, quiet tread of the servants, as they moved about the room, were audible with a painful distinctness. The oppression of our last family breakfast in London, for that year, had an influence of wretchedness which I cannot describe—which I can never forget.

At last the hour of starting came. Clara seemed afraid to trust herself even to look at me now. She hurriedly drew down her veil the moment the carriage was announced. My father shook hands with me rather coldly. I had hoped he would have said something at parting; but he only bade me farewell in the simplest and shortest manner. I had rather he would have spoken to me in anger than restrained himself as he did, to what the commonest forms of courtesy required. There was but one more slight, after this, that he could cast on me; and he did not spare it. While my sister was taking leave of me, he waited at the door of the room to lead her down stairs, as if he knew by intuition that this was the last little parting attention which I had hoped to show her myself.

Clara whispered (in such low, trembling tones that I could hardly hear her):

"Think of what you promised in your study, Basil, whenever you think of *me*: I will write often."

As she raised her veil for a moment, and kissed me, I felt on my own cheek the tears that were falling fast over hers. I followed her and my father down stairs. When they reached the street, she gave me her hand—it was cold and powerless. I knew that the fortitude she had promised to show, was giving way, in spite of all her efforts to preserve it; so I let her hurry into the carriage without detaining her by any last words. The next instant she and my father were driven rapidly from the door.

When I re-entered the house, my watch showed me that I had still an hour to wait, before it was time to go to North Villa.

Between the different emotions produced by my impressions of the scene I had just passed through, and my anticipations of the scene that was yet to come, I suffered in that one hour as much mental conflict as most men suffer in a life. It seemed as if I were living out all my feelings in this short interval of delay, and must die at heart when it was over. My restlessness was a torture to me; and yet I could not overcome it. I wandered through the house from room to room, stopping nowhere. I took down book after book from the library, opened them to read, and put them back on the shelves the next instant. Over and over again I walked to the window to occupy myself with what was passing in the street; and each time I could not stay there for one minute together. I went into the picture-gallery, looked along the walls, and yet knew not what I was looking at. At last I wandered into my father's study—the only room I had not yet visited.

A portrait of my mother hung over the fireplace: my eyes turned towards it, and for the first time I came to a long pause. The picture had an influence that quieted me; but what influence I hardly knew. Perhaps it led my spirit up to the spirit that had gone from us—perhaps those secret voices from the unknown world, which only the soul can listen to, were loosed at that moment, and spoke within me. While I sat looking up at the portrait, I grew strangely and suddenly calm before it. My memory flew back to a long illness that I had suffered from, as a child, when my little cradle-couch was placed by my mother's bedside, and she used to sit by me in the dull evenings and hush me to sleep. The remembrance of this brought with it a dread imagining that she might now be hushing my spirit, from her place among the angels of God. A stillness and awe crept over me; and I hid my face in my hands.

The striking of the hour from a clock in the room, startled

me back to the outer world. I left the house and went at once to North Villa.

Margaret and her father and mother were in the drawing-room when I entered it. I saw immediately that neither of the two latter had passed the morning calmly. The impending event of the day had exercised its agitating influence over them, as well as over me. Mrs. Sherwin's face was pale to her very lips: not a word escaped her. Mr. Sherwin endeavoured to assume the self-possession which he was evidently far from feeling, by walking briskly up and down the room, and talking incessantly—asking the most common-place questions, and making the most common-place jokes. Margaret, to my surprise, showed fewer symptoms of agitation than either of her parents. Except when the colour came and went occasionally on her cheek, I could detect no outward evidences of emotion in her at all.

The church was near at hand. As we proceeded to it, the rain fell heavily, and the mist of the morning was thickening to a fog. We had to wait in the vestry for the officiating clergyman. All the gloom and dampness of the day seemed to be collected in this room—a dark, cold, melancholy place, with one window which opened on a burial-ground steaming in the wet. The rain pattered monotonously on the pavement outside. While Mr. Sherwin exchanged remarks on the weather with the clerk, (a tall, lean man, arrayed in a black gown), I sat silent, near Mrs. Sherwin and Margaret, looking with mechanical attention at the white surplices which hung before me in a half-opened cupboard —at the bottle of water and tumbler, and the long-shaped books, bound in brown leather, which were on the table. I was incapable of speaking—incapable even of thinking— during that interval of expectation.

At length the clergyman arrived, and we went into the church—the church, with its desolate array of empty pews, and its chill, heavy, week-day atmosphere. As we ranged ourselves round the altar, a confusion overspread all my faculties. My sense of the place I was in, and even of the ceremony in which I took part, grew more and more vague and doubtful every minute. My attention wandered throughout the whole service. I stammered and made mistakes in uttering the responses. Once or twice I detected myself in feeling impatient at the slow progress of the ceremony—it seemed to be doubly, trebly longer than its usual length. Mixed up with this impression was another, wild and monstrous as if it had been produced by a dream—an impression that my father had discovered my secret, and was watching me from some hidden place in the church; watching through the service, to denounce and abandon me publicly at the end. This morbid fancy grew and grew on me until the termination of the ceremony, until we had left the church and returned to the vestry once more.

The fees were paid; we wrote our names in the books and on the certificate; the clergyman quietly wished me happiness; the clerk solemnly imitated him; the pew-opener smiled and curtseyed; Mr. Sherwin made congratulatory speeches, kissed his daughter, shook hands with me, frowned a private rebuke at his wife for shedding tears, and, finally, led the way with Margaret out of the vestry. The rain was still falling, as they got into the carriage. The fog was still thickening, as I stood alone under the portico of the church, and tried to realise to myself that I was married.

Married! The son of the proudest man in England, the inheritor of a name written on the roll of Battle Abbey, wedded to a linen-draper's daughter! And what a marriage! What a condition weighed on it! What a probation was now to follow it! Why had I consented so easily to Mr. Sherwin's proposals? Would he not have given way. if I had only been resolute enough to insist on my own conditions?

How useless to inquire! I had made the engagement

and must abide by it—abide by it cheerfully until the year was over, and she* was mine for ever. This must be my all-sufficing thought for the future. No more reflections on consequences, no more forebodings about the effect of the disclosure of my secret on my family --the leap into a new life had been taken, and, lead where it might, it was a leap that could never be retraced!

Mr. Sherwin had insisted, with the immovable obstinacy which characterises all feeble-minded people in the management of their important affairs, that the first clause in our agreement (the leaving my wife at the church-door) should be performed to the letter. As a due compensation for this, I was to dine at North Villa that day. How should I employ the interval that was to elapse before the dinner-hour?

I went home, and had my horse saddled. I was in no mood for remaining in an empty house, in no mood for calling on any of my friends—I was fit for nothing but a gallop through the rain. All my wearing and depressing emotions of the morning, had now merged into a wild excitement of body and mind. When the horse was brought round, I saw with delight that the groom could hardly hold him. "Keep him well in hand, Sir," said the man, " he's not been out for three days." I was just in the humour for such a ride as the caution promised me.

And what a ride it was, when I fairly got out of London ; and the afternoon brightening of the foggy atmosphere, showed the smooth, empty high road before me! The dashing through the rain that still fell ; the feel of the long, powerful, regular stride of the horse under me ; the thrill of that physical sympathy which establishes itself between the man and the steed; the whirling past carts and wag-gons, saluted by the frantic barking of dogs inside them; the flying by roadside alehouses, with the cheering of boys and half-drunken men sounding for an instant behind me, then lost in the distance—this was indeed to occupy, to hurry on, to annihilate the tardy hours of solitude on my wedding day, exactly as my heart desired!

I got home wet through; but with my body in a glow from the exercise, with my spirits boiling up at fever heat. When I arrived at North Villa, the change in my manner astonished every one. At dinner, I required no pressing now to partake of the sherry which Mr. Sherwin was so fond of extolling, nor of the port which he brought out afterwards, with a preliminary account of the vintage-date of the wine, and the price of each bottle. My spirits, factitious as they were, never flagged. Every time I looked at Margaret, the sight of her stimulated them afresh. She seemed pre-occupied, and was unusually silent during dinner; but her beauty was just that voluptuous beauty which is loveliest in repose. I had never felt its influence so powerful over me as I felt it then.

In the drawing-room, Margaret's manner grew more familiar, more confident towards me than it had ever been before. She spoke to me in warmer tones, looked at me with warmer looks. A hundred little incidents marked our wedding-evening—trifles that love treasures up—which still remain in my memory. One among them, at least, will never depart from it: I first kissed her on that evening.

Mr. Sherwin had gone out of the room; Mrs. Sherwin was at the other end of it, watering some plants at the window; Margaret, by her father's desire, was showing me some rare prints. She handed me a magnifying glass, through which I was to look at a particular part of one of the engravings, that was considered a master-piece of delicate workmanship. Instead of applying the magnifying test to the print, for which I cared nothing, I laughingly applied it to Margaret's face. Her lovely lustrous black eye seemed to flash into mine through the glass; her warm, quick breathing played on my cheek—it was but for an instant,

and in that instant I kissed her for the first time. What
sensations the kiss gave me then!—what remembrances it
has left me now!

It was one more proof how tenderly, how purely I loved
her, that, before this time, I had feared to take the first
love-privilege which I had longed to assert, and might well
have asserted, before. Men may not understand this; women, I believe, will.

The hour of departure arrived; the inexorable hour
which was to separate me from my wife on my wedding
evening. Shall I confess what I felt, on the first perform-
ance of my ill-considered promise to Mr. Sherwin? No:
I kept this a secret from Margaret; I will keep it a secret
here.

I took leave of her as hurriedly and abruptly as possible
—I could not trust myself to quit her in any other way.
She had contrived to slip aside into the darkest part of the
room, so that I only saw her face dimly at parting.

I went home at once. When I lay down to sleep—then
the ordeal which I had been unconsciously preparing for
myself throughout the day, began to try me. Every
nerve in my body, strung up to the extremest point of
tension since the morning, now at last gave way. I felt
my limbs quivering, till the bed shook under me. I was
possessed by a gloom and horror, caused by no thought, and
producing no thought: the thinking faculty seemed paralysed within me, altogether. The physical and mental re-
action, after the fever and agitation of the day, was so sudden
and severe, that the faintest noise from the street now
terrified—yes, literally terrified me. The whistling of the
wind—which had risen since sunset—made me start up in
bed, with my heart throbbing, and my blood all chill. When
no sounds were audible, then I listened for them to come
—listened breathlessly, without daring to move. At last,
the agony of nervous prostration grew more than I could

bear—grew worse even than the child's horror of walking in the darkness, and sleeping alone on the bed-room floor, which had overcome me, almost from the first moment when I laid down. I groped my way to the table and lit the candle again; then wrapped my dressing-gown round me, and sat shuddering near the light, to watch the weary hours out till morning.

And this was my wedding-night! This was how the day ended which had begun by my marriage with Margaret Sherwin!

PART II.

I.

AN epoch in my narrative has now arrived. Up to the time of my marriage, I have appeared as an active agent in the different events I have described. After that period, and—with one or two exceptional cases—throughout the whole year of my probation, my position changed with the change in my life, and became a passive one.

During this interval year, certain events happened, some of which, at the time, excited my curiosity, but none my apprehension—some affected me with a temporary disappointment, but none with even a momentary suspicion. I can now look back on them, as so many timely warnings which I treated with fatal neglect. It is in these events that the history of the long year through which I waited to claim my wife as my own, is really comprised. They marked the lapse of time broadly and significantly; and to them I must now confine myself, as exclusively as may be, in the present portion of my narrative.

It will be first necessary, however, that I should describe what was the nature of my intercourse with Margaret, during the probationary period which followed our marriage.

Mr. Sherwin's anxiety was to make my visits to North Villa as few as possible : he evidently feared the consequences of my seeing his daughter too often. But on this point, I was resolute enough in asserting my own interests, to overpower any resistance on his part. I required him to concede to me the right of seeing Margaret every day—leaving all arrangements of time to depend on his own convenience. After the due number of objections, he reluctantly acquiesced in my demand. I was bound by no engagement whatever, limiting the number of my visits to Margaret; and I let him see at the outset, that I was now ready in my turn, to impose conditions on him, as he had already imposed them on me.

Accordingly, it was settled that Margaret and I were to meet every day. I usually saw her in the evening. When any alteration in the hour of my visit took place, that alteration was produced by the necessity (which we all recognised alike) of avoiding a meeting with any of Mr. Sherwin's friends.

Those portions of the day or the evening which I spent with Margaret, were seldom passed altogether in the Elysian idleness of love. Not content with only enumerating his daughter's school-accomplishments to me at our first interview, Mr. Sherwin boastfully referred to them again and again, on many subsequent occasions; and even obliged Margaret to display before me, some of her knowledge of languages—which he never forgot to remind us had been lavishly paid for out of his own pocket. It was at one of these exhibitions that the idea occurred to me of making a new pleasure for myself out of Margaret's society, by teaching her really to appreciate and enjoy the literature which she had evidently hitherto only studied as a task. My fancy revelled by anticipation in all the delights of such an employment as this. It would be like acting the story of Abelard and Heloise over again—reviving all the poetry and romance in which those immortal love-studies of old had begun, with none of the guilt and none of the misery that had darkened their end.

I had a definite purpose, besides, in wishing to assume

the direction of Margaret's studies. Whenever the secret of my marriage was revealed, my pride was concerned in being able to show my wife to every one, as the all-sufficient excuse for any imprudence I might have committed for her sake. I was determined that my father, especially, should have no other argument against her than the one ungracious argument of her birth—that he should see her, fitted by the beauty of her mind, as well as by all her other beauties, for the highest station that society could offer. The thought of this gave me fresh ardour in my project; I assumed my new duties without delay, and continued them with a happiness which never once suffered even a momentary decrease.

Of all the pleasures which a man finds in the society of a woman whom he loves, are there any superior, are there many equal, to the pleasure of reading out of the same book with her? On what other occasion do the sweet familiarities of the sweetest of all companionships last so long without cloying, and pass and re-pass so naturally, so delicately, so inexhaustibly between you and her? When is your face so constantly close to hers as it is then?—when can your hair mingle with hers, your cheek touch hers, your eyes meet hers, so often as they can then? That is, of all times, the only time when you can breathe with her breath for hours together; feel every little warming of the colour on her cheek marking its own changes on the temperature of yours; follow every slight fluttering of her bosom, every faint gradation of her sighs, as if *her* heart was beating, *her* life glowing, within yours. Surely it is then—if ever —that we realize, almost revive, in ourselves, the love of the first two of our race, when angels walked with them on the same garden paths, and their hearts were pure from the pollution of the fatal tree!

Evening after evening passed away—one more happily than another—in what Margaret and I called our lessons.

Never were lessons of literature so like lessons of love! We read oftenest the lighter Italian poets—we studied the poetry of love, written in the language of love. But, as for the steady, utilitarian purpose I had proposed to myself of practically improving Margaret's intellect, that was a purpose which insensibly and deceitfully abandoned me as completely as if it had never existed. The little serious teaching I tried with her at first, led to very poor results. Perhaps, the lover interfered too much with the tutor; perhaps, I had over-estimated the fertility of the faculties I designed to cultivate—but I cared not, and thought not to inquire where the fault lay, then. I gave myself up unreservedly to the exquisite sensations which the mere act of looking on the same page with Margaret procured for me; and neither detected, nor wished to detect, that it was I who read the difficult passages, and left only a few even of the very easiest to be attempted by her.

Happily for my patience under the trial imposed on me by the terms on which Mr. Sherwin's restrictions, and my promise to obey them, obliged me to live with Margaret, it was Mrs. Sherwin who was generally selected to remain in the room with us. By no one could such ungrateful duties of supervision as those imposed on her, have been more delicately and more considerately performed.

She always kept far enough away to be out of hearing when we whispered to each other. We rarely detected her even in looking at us. She had a way of sitting for hours together in the same part of the room, without ever changing her position, without occupation of any kind, without uttering a word, or breathing a sigh. I soon discovered that she was not lost in thought, at these periods (as I had at first supposed) : but lost in a strange lethargy of body and mind; a comfortless, waking trance, into which she fell from sheer physical weakness—it was like the vacancy and feebleness of a first convalescence, after a long illness. She never changed: never looked better, never worse. I often spoke to her: I tried hard to show my sympathy, and win her confidence and friendship. The poor lady was always thankful, always spoke to me gratefully and kindly, but very briefly. She never told me what were her sufferings or her sorrows. The story of that lonely, lingering life was an impenetrable mystery for her own family—for her husband and her daughter, as well as for me. It was a secret between her and God.

With Mrs. Sherwin as the guardian to watch over Margaret, it may easily be imagined that I felt none of the heavier oppressions of restraint. Her presence, as the third person appointed to remain with us, was not enough to repress the little endearments to which each evening's lesson gave rise; but was just sufficiently perceptible to invest them with the character of stolen endearments, and to make them all the more precious on that very account. Mrs. Sherwin never knew, I never thoroughly knew myself till later, how much of the secret of my patience under my year's probation lay in her conduct, while she was sitting in the room with Margaret and me.

In this solitude where I now write—in the change of life and of all life's hopes and enjoyments which has come over me—when I look back to those evenings at North Villa, I shudder as I look. At this moment, I see the room again —as in a dream—with the little round table, the reading lamp, and the open books. Margaret and I are sitting together: her hand is in mine; my heart is with hers. Love, and Youth, and Beauty—the mortal Trinity of this world's worship—are there, in that quiet softly-lit room; but not alone. Away in the dim light behind, is a solitary figure, ever mournful and ever still. It is a woman's form; but how wasted and how weak!—a woman's face; but how ghastly and changeless, with those eyes that are vacant, those lips that are motionless, those cheeks that the blood

never tinges, that the freshness of health and happiness
shall never visit again! Woful, warning figure of dumb
sorrow and patient pain, to fill the background of a picture
of Love, and Beauty, and Youth!

I am straying from my task. Let me return to my narrative : its course begins to darken before me apace, while I
now write.

The partial restraint and embarrassment, caused at first
by the strange terms on which my wife and I were living
together, gradually vanished before the frequency of my
visits to North Villa. We soon began to speak with all
the ease, all the unpremeditated frankness of a long intimacy. Margaret's powers of conversation were generally
only employed to lead me to exert mine. She was never
tired of inducing me to speak of my family. She listened
with every appearance of interest, while I talked of my
father, my sister, or my elder brother ; but whenever she
questioned me directly about any of them, her inquiries invariably led away from their characters and dispositions, to
their personal appearance, their every-day habits, their dress,
their intercourse with the gay world, the things they spent
their money on, and other topics of a similar nature.

For instance; she always listened, and listened attentively, to what I told her of my father's character, and
of the principles which regulated his life. She showed
every disposition to profit by the instructions I gave her beforehand, about how she should treat his peculiarities when
she was introduced to him. But, on all these occasions,
what really interested her most, was to hear how many servants waited on him; how often he went to Court; how
many lords and ladies he knew ; what he said or did to his
servants, when they committed mistakes ; whether he was
ever angry with his children for asking him for money ; and
whether he limited my sister to any given number of dresses
in the course of the year ?

Again; whenever our conversation turned on Clara, if I began by describing her kindness, her gentleness and goodness, her simple winning manners—I was sure to be led insensibly into a digression about her height, figure, complexion, and style of dress. The latter subject especially interested Margaret; she could question me on it, over and over again. What was Clara's usual morning dress? How did she wear her hair? What was her evening dress? Did she make a difference between a dinner party and a ball? What colours did she prefer? What dressmaker did she employ? Did she wear much jewellery? Which did she like best in her hair, and which were most fashionable, flowers or pearls? How many new dresses did she have in a year; and was there more than one maid especially to attend on her?

Then, again: Had she a carriage of her own? What ladies took care of her when she went out? Did she like dancing? What were the fashionable dances at noblemen's houses? Did young ladies in the great world practise the pianoforte much? How many offers had my sister had? Did she go to Court, as well as my father? What did she talk about to gentlemen, and what did gentlemen talk about to her? If she were speaking to a duke, how often would she say "your Grace" to him? and would a duke get her a chair, or an ice, and wait on her just as gentlemen without titles waited on ladies, when they met them in society?

My replies to these and hundreds of other questions like them, were received by Margaret with the most eager attention. On the favourite subject of Clara's dresses, my answers were an unending source of amusement and pleasure to her. She especially enjoyed overcoming the difficulties of interpreting aright my clumsy, circumlocutory phrases in attempting to describe shawls, gowns, and bonnets; and taught me the exact millinery language which I ought to have made use of, with an arch expression of triumph and a burlesque earnestness of manner, that always enchanted me. At that time, every word she uttered, no matter how frivolous, was the sweetest of all music to my ears. It was only by the stern test of after-events that I learnt to analyse her conversation. Sometimes, when I was away from her, I might think of leading her girlish curiosity to higher things; but when we met again, the thought vanished; and it became delight enough for me simply to hear her speak, without once caring or considering what she spoke of.

Those were the days when I lived happy and unreflecting in the broad sunshine of joy which love showered round me —my eyes were dazzled; my mind lay asleep under it. Once or twice, a cloud came threatening, with chill and shadowy influence; but it passed away, and then the sunshine returned—to *me*, the same sunshine that it was before.

II.

The first change that passed over the calm uniformity of the life at North Villa, came in this manner:

One evening, on entering the drawing-room, I missed Mrs. Sherwin; and found to my great disappointment that her husband was apparently settled there for the evening. He looked a little flurried, and was more restless than usual. His first words, as we met, informed me of an event in which he appeared to take the deepest interest.

"News, my dear sir!" he said. "Mr. Mannion has come back—at least two days before I expected him!"

At first, I felt inclined to ask who Mr. Mannion was, and what consequence it could possibly be to me that he had come back. But immediately afterwards, I remembered that this Mr. Mannion's name had been mentioned during my first conversation with Mr. Sherwin; and then I recalled to mind the description I had heard of him, as "confidential clerk;" as forty years of age; and as an educated man, who had made his information of some use to Margaret in keeping up the knowledge she had acquired at school. I knew no more than this about him, and I felt no curiosity to discover more from Mr. Sherwin.

Margaret and I sat down as usual with our books about us.

There had been something a little hurried and abrupt in her manner of receiving me, when I came in. When we began to read, her attention wandered incessantly; she looked round several times towards the door. Mr. Sherwin walked about the room without intermission, except when he once paused on his restless course, to tell me that Mr. Mannion was coming that evening; and that he hoped I should have no objection to be introduced to a person who was "quite like one of the family, and well enough read to be sure to please a great reader like me." I asked myself rather impatiently, who was this Mr. Mannion, that his arrival at his employer's house should make a sensation? When I whispered something of this to Margaret, she smiled rather uneasily, and said nothing.

At last the bell was rung. Margaret started a little at the sound. Mr. Sherwin sat down; composing himself into rather an elaborate attitude—the door opened, and Mr. Mannion came in.

Mr. Sherwin received his clerk with the assumed superiority of the master in his words; but his tones and manner flatly contradicted them. Margaret rose hastily, and then as hastily sat down again, while the visitor very respectfully took her hand, and made the usual inquiries. After this, he was introduced to me; and then Margaret was sent away to summon her mother down stairs. While she was out of the room, there was nothing to distract my attention from Mr. Mannion. I looked at him with a curiosity and interest, which I could hardly account for at first.

If extraordinary regularity of feature were alone sufficient
to make a handsome man, then this confidential clerk of
Mr. Sherwin's was assuredly one of the handsomest men I
ever beheld. Viewed separately from the head (which was
rather large, both in front and behind) his face exhibited,
throughout, an almost perfect symmetry of proportion.
His bald forehead was smooth and massive as marble; his
high brow and thin eyelids had the firmness and immobility
of marble, and seemed as cold; his delicately-formed lips,
when he was not speaking, closed habitually, as changelessly
still as if no breath of life ever passed them. There was
not a wrinkle or line anywhere on his face. But for the
baldness in front, and the greyness of the hair at the back
and sides of his head, it would have been impossible from
his appearance to have guessed his age, even within ten
years of what it really was.

Such was his countenance in point of form; but in that
which is the outward assertion of our immortality—in expression—it was, as I now beheld it, an utter void. Never
had I before seen any human face which baffled all inquiry
like his. No mask could have been made expressionless
enough to resemble it; and yet it looked like a mask.
It told you nothing of his thoughts, when he spoke:
nothing of his disposition, when he was silent. His cold
grey eyes gave you no help in trying to study him. They
never varied from the steady, straightforward look, which
was exactly the same for Margaret as it was for me; for
Mrs. Sherwin as for Mr. Sherwin—exactly the same whether
he spoke or whether he listened; whether he talked of
indifferent, or of important matters. Who was he? What
was he? His name and calling were poor replies to those
questions. Was he naturally cold and unimpressible at
heart? or had some fierce passion, some terrible sorrow,
ravaged the life within him, and left it dead for ever after?
Impossible to conjecture! There was the impenetrable

face before you, wholly inexpressive—so inexpressive that it did not even look vacant—a mystery for your eyes and your mind to dwell on—hiding something; but whether vice or virtue you could not tell.

He was dressed as unobtrusively as possible, entirely in black; and was rather above the middle height. His manner was the only part of him that betrayed anything to the observation of others. Viewed in connection with his station, his demeanour (unobtrusive though it was) proclaimed itself as above his position in the world. He had all the quietness and self-possession of a gentleman. He maintained his respectful bearing, without the slightest appearance of cringing; and displayed a decision, both in word and action, that could never be mistaken for obstinacy or over-confidence. Before I had been in his company five minutes, his manner assured me that he must have descended to the position he now occupied.

On his introduction to me, he bowed without saying anything. When he spoke to Mr. Sherwin, his voice was as void of expression as his face: it was rather low in tone, but singularly distinct in utterance. He spoke deliberately, but with no emphasis on particular words, and without hesitation in choosing his terms.

When Mrs. Sherwin came down, I watched her conduct towards him. She could not repress a slight nervous shrinking, when he approached and placed a chair for her. In answering his inquiries after her health, she never once looked at him; but fixed her eyes all the time on Margaret and me, with a sad, anxious expression, wholly indescribable, which often recurred to my memory after that day. She always looked more or less frightened, poor thing, in her husband's presence; but she seemed positively awe-struck before Mr. Mannion.

In truth, my first observation of this so-called clerk, at North Villa, was enough to convince me that he was

master there—master in his own quiet, unobtrusive way.
That man's character, of whatever elements it might be
composed, was a character that ruled.   I could not see this
in his face, or detect it in his words; but I could discover
it in the looks and manners of his employer and his employer's family, as he now sat at the same table with them.
Margaret's eyes avoided his countenance much less frequently than the eyes of her parents; but then he rarely
looked at her in return—rarely looked at her at all, except
when common courtesy obliged him to do so.

If any one had told me beforehand, that I should suspend
my ordinary evening's occupation with my young wife, for
the sake of observing the very man who had interrupted it,
and that man only Mr. Sherwin's clerk, I should have
laughed at the idea. Yet so it was. Our books lay neglected
on the table—neglected by me, perhaps by Margaret too,
for Mr. Mannion.

His conversation, on this occasion at least, baffled all curiosity as completely as his face.   I tried to lead him to
talk. He just answered me, and that was all; speaking with
great respect of manner and phrase, very intelligibly, but
very briefly.   Mr. Sherwin—after referring to the business
expedition on which he had been absent, for the purchase of
silks at Lyons—asked him some questions about France and
the French, which evidently proceeded from the most ludi-
crous ignorance both of the country and the people.   Mr.
Mannion just set him right; and did no more.   There was
not the smallest inflection of sarcasm in his voice, not the
slightest look of sarcasm in his eye, while he spoke. When
we talked among ourselves, he did not join in the conversation; but sat quietly waiting until he might be pointedly
and personally addressed again.   At these times a suspicion
crossed my mind that he might really be studying my character, as I was vainly trying to study his; and I often
turned suddenly round on him, to see whether he was look-

ing at me. This was never the case. His hard, chill grey eyes were not on me, and not on Margaret: they rested most frequently on Mrs. Sherwin, who always shrank before them.

After staying little more than half an hour, he rose to go away. While Mr. Sherwin was vainly pressing him to remain longer, I walked to the round table at the other end of the room, on which the book was placed that Margaret and I had intended to read during the evening. I was standing by the table when he came to take leave of me. He just glanced at the volume under my hand, and said in tones too low to be heard at the other end of the room:

"I hope my arrival has not interrupted any occupation to-night, Sir. Mr. Sherwin, aware of the interest I must feel in whatever concerns the family of an employer whom I have served for years, has informed me in confidence—a confidence which I know how to respect and preserve—of your marriage with his daughter, and of the peculiar circumstances under which the marriage has been contracted. I may at least venture to congratulate the young lady on a change of life which must procure her happiness, having begun already by procuring the increase of her mental resources and pleasures." He bowed, and pointed to the book on the table.

"I believe, Mr. Mannion," I said, "that you have been of great assistance in laying a foundation for the studies to which I presume you refer."

"I endeavoured to make myself useful in that way, Sir, as in all others, when my employer desired it." He bowed again, as he said this; and then went out, followed by Mr. Sherwin, who held a short colloquy with him in the hall.

What had he said to me? Only a few civil words, spoken in a very respectful manner. There had been nothing in his tones, nothing in his looks, to give any peculiar significance to what he uttered. Still, the moment his back was turned,

I found myself speculating whether his words contained any hidden meaning; trying to recall something in his voice or manner which might guide me in discovering the real sense he attached to what he said. It seemed as if the most powerful whet to my curiosity, were supplied by my own experience of the impossibility of penetrating beneath the unassailable surface which this man presented to me.

I questioned Margaret about him. She could not tell me more than I knew already. He had always been very kind and useful; he was a clever man, and could talk a great deal sometimes, when he chose; and he had taught her more of foreign languages and foreign literature in a month, than she had learned at school in a year. While she was telling me this, I hardly noticed that she spoke in a very hurried manner, and busied herself in arranging the books and work that lay on the table. My attention was more closely directed to Mrs. Sherwin. To my surprise, I saw her eagerly lean forward while Margaret was speaking, and fix her eyes on her daughter with a look of penetrating scrutiny, of which I could never have supposed a person usually so feeble and unenergetic to be capable. I thought of transferring to her my questionings on the subject of Mr. Mannion; but at that moment her husband entered the room, and I addressed myself for further enlightenment to him.

"Aha!"—cried Mr. Sherwin, rubbing his hands triumphantly—"I knew Mannion would please you. I told you so, my dear Sir, if you remember, before he came. Curious looking person—isn't he?"

"So curious, that I may safely say I never saw a face in the slightest degree resembling his in my life. Your clerk, Mr. Sherwin, is a complete walking mystery that I want to solve. Margaret cannot give me much help, I am afraid. When you came in, I was about to apply to Mrs. Sherwin for a little assistance."

"Don't do any such thing! You'll be quite in the wrong box there. Mrs. S. is as sulky as a bear, whenever Mannion and she are in company together. Considering her behaviour to him, I wonder he can be so civil to her as he is."

"What can you tell me about him yourself, Mr. Sherwin?"

"I can tell you there's not a house of business in London has such a managing man as he is: he's my factotum—my right hand, in short; and my left too, for the matter of that. He understands my ways of doing business; and, in fact, carries things out in first-rate style. Why, he'd be worth his weight in gold, only for the knack he has of keeping the young men in the shop in order. Poor devils! they don't know how he does it; but there's a particular look of Mr. Mannion's that's as bad as transportation and hanging to them, whenever they see it. I'll pledge you my word of honour he's never had a day's illness, or made a single mistake, since he's been with me. He's a quiet, steady-going, regular dragon at his work—he is! And then, so obliging in other things. I've only got to say to him: 'Here's Margaret at home for the holidays;' or, 'Here's Margaret a little out of sorts, and going to be nursed at home for the half-year—what's to be done about keeping up her lessons? I can't pay for a governess (bad lot, governesses!) and school too.'—I've only got to say that; and up gets Mannion from his books and his fireside at home, in the evening—which begins to be something, you know, to a man of his time of life—and turns tutor for me, gratis; and a first-rate tutor, too! That's what I call having a treasure! And yet, though he's been with us for years, Mrs. S. there won't take to him!—I defy her or anybody else to say why, or wherefore!"

"Do you know how he was employed before he came to you?"

"Ah! now you've hit it—that's where you're right in

saying he's a mystery.   What he did before I knew him, **is** more than I can tell—a good deal more.   He came to me with a capital recommendation and security, from a gentleman whom I knew to be of the highest respectability.   I had a vacancy in the back office, and tried him, and found out what he was worth, in no time—I flatter myself I've a knack at that with everybody.   Well: before I got used to his curious-looking face, and his quiet ways, I wanted badly enough to know something about him, and who his connections were.   First, I asked his friend who had recommended him—the friend wasn't at liberty to answer for anything but his perfect trustworthiness.   Then I asked Mannion himself point-blank about it, one day.   He just told me that he had reasons for keeping his family affairs to himself—nothing more—but you know the way he has with him ; and, damn it, he put the stopper on me, from that time to this. I wasn't going to risk losing the best clerk that ever man had, by worrying him about his secrets.   They didn't interfere with business, and didn't interfere with me ; so I put my curiosity in my pocket.   I know nothing about him, but that he's my right-hand man, and the honestest fellow that ever stood in shoes.   He may be the Great Mogul himself, in disguise, for anything I care !   In short, *you* may be able to find out all about him, my dear Sir ; but *I* can't."

"There does not seem much chance for me, Mr. Sherwin, after what you have said."

"Well : I'm not so sure of that—plenty of chances here, you know.   You'll see him often enough : he lives near, and drops in constantly of evenings.   We settle business matters that won't come into business hours, in my private snuggery up stairs.   In fact, he's one of the family ; treat him as such, and get anything out of him you can—the more the better, as far as regards that.   Ah! Mrs. S., you may stare, Ma'am ; but I say again, he's one of the family ;

may be, he'll be my partner some of these days—you'll have to get used to him then, whether you like it or not."

"One more question: is he married or single?"

"Single, to be sure—a regular old bachelor, if ever there was one yet."

During the whole time we had been speaking, Mrs. Sherwin had looked at us with far more earnestness and attention than I had ever seen her display before. Even her languid faculties seemed susceptible of active curiosity on the subject of Mr. Mannion—the more so, perhaps, from her very dislike of him. Margaret had moved her chair into the background, while her father was talking; and was apparently little interested in the topic under discussion. In the first interval of silence, she complained of headache, and asked leave to retire to her room.

After she left us, I took my departure: for Mr. Sherwin evidently had nothing more to tell me about his clerk that was worth hearing. On my way home, Mr. Mannion occupied no small share of my thoughts. The idea of trying to penetrate the mystery connected with him was an idea that pleased me; there was a promise of future excitement in it of no ordinary kind. I determined to have a little private conversation with Margaret about him; and to make her an ally in my new project. If there really had been some romance connected with Mr. Mannion's early life—if that strange and striking face of his was indeed a sealed book which contained a secret story, what a triumph and a pleasure, if Margaret and I should succeed in discovering it together!

When I woke the next morning, I could hardly believe that this tradesman's clerk had so interested my curiosity that he had actually shared my thoughts with my young wife, during the evening before. And yet, when I next saw him, he produced exactly the same impression on me again.

III.

Some weeks passed away; Margaret and I resumed our usual employments and amusements; the life at North Villa ran on as smoothly and obscurely as usual—and still I remained ignorant of Mr. Mannion's history and Mr. Mannion's character. He came frequently to the house, in the evening; but was generally closeted with Mr. Sherwin, and seldom accepted his employer's constant invitation to him to join the party in the drawing-room. At those rare intervals when we did see him, his appearance and behaviour were exactly the same as on the night when I had met him for the first time; he spoke just as seldom, and resisted just as resolutely and respectfully the many attempts made on my part to lead him into conversation and familiarity. If he had really been trying to excite my interest, he could not have succeeded more effectually. I felt towards him much as a man feels in a labyrinth, when every fresh failure in gaining the centre, only produces fresh obstinacy in renewing the effort to arrive at it.

From Margaret I gained no sympathy for my newly-aroused curiosity. She appeared, much to my surprise, to care little about Mr. Mannion; and always changed the conversation, if it related to him, whenever it depended upon her to continue the topic or not.

Mrs. Sherwin's conduct was far from resembling her daughter's, when I spoke to her on the same subject. She always listened intently to what I said; but her answers were invariably brief, confused, and sometimes absolutely incomprehensible. It was only after great difficulty that I induced her to confess her dislike of Mr. Mannion. Whence it proceeded she could never tell. Did she suspect anything? In answering this question, she always stammered, trembled, and looked away from me. "How could she suspect anything? If she did suspect, it would be very wrong without good reason: but she ought not to suspect, and did not, of course."

I never obtained any replies from her more intelligible than these. Attributing their confusion to the nervous agitation which more or less affected her when she spoke on any subject, I soon ceased making any efforts to induce her to explain herself; and determined to search for the clue to Mr. Mannion's character, without seeking assistance from any one.

Accident at length gave me an opportunity of knowing something of his habits and opinions; and so far, therefore, of knowing something about the man himself.

One night, I met him in the hall at North Villa, about to leave the house at the same time that I was, after a business-consultation in private with Mr. Sherwin. We went out together. The sky was unusually black; the night atmosphere unusually oppressive and still. The roll of distant thunder sounded faint and dreary all about us. The sheet lightning, flashing quick and low in the horizon, made the dark firmament look like a thick veil, rising and falling incessantly, over a heaven of dazzling light behind it. Such few foot-passengers as passed us, passed running —for heavy, warning drops were falling already from the sky. We quickened our pace; but before we had walked more than two hundred yards, the rain came down, furious and drenching; and the thunder began to peal fearfully, right over our heads.

"My house is close by," said my companion, just as quietly and deliberately as usual—" pray step in, Sir, until the storm is over."

I followed him down a bye street; he opened a door with his own key; and the next instant I was sheltered under Mr. Mannion's roof.

He led me at once into a room on the ground floor

The fire was blazing in the grate; an arm-chair, with a reading easel attached, was placed by it; the lamp was ready lit; the tea-things were placed on the table; the dark, thick curtains were drawn close over the window; and, as if to complete the picture of comfort before me, a large black cat lay on the rug, basking luxuriously in the heat of the fire. While Mr. Mannion went out to give some directions, as he said, to his servant, I had an opportunity of examining the apartment more in detail. To study the appearance of a man's dwelling-room, is very often nearly equivalent to studying his own character.

The personal contrast between Mr. Sherwin and his clerk was remarkable enough, but the contrast between the dimensions and furnishing of the rooms they lived in, was to the full as extraordinary. The apartment I now surveyed was less than half the size of the sitting-room at North Villa. The paper on the walls was of a dark red; the curtains were of the same colour; the carpet was brown, and if it bore any pattern, that pattern was too quiet and unpretending to be visible by candlelight. One wall was entirely occupied by rows of dark mahogany shelves, completely filled with books, most of them cheap editions of the classical works of ancient and modern literature. The opposite wall was thickly hung with engravings in maple-wood frames from the works of modern painters, English and French. All the minor articles of furniture were of the plainest and neatest order —even the white china tea-pot and tea-cup on the table, had neither pattern nor colouring of any kind. What a contrast was this room to the drawing-room at North Villa!

On his return, Mr. Mannion found me looking at his tea-equipage. "I am afraid, Sir, I must confess myself an epicure and a prodigal in two things," he said; "an epicure in tea, and a prodigal (at least for a person in my situation) in books. However, I receive a liberal salary, and can satisfy my tastes, such as they are, and save money too. What can I offer you, Sir?"

Seeing the preparations on the table, I asked for tea. While he was speaking to me, there was one peculiarity about him that I observed. Almost all men, when they stand on their own hearths, in their own homes, instinctively alter more or less from their out-of-door manner: the stiffest people expand, the coldest thaw a little, by their own firesides. It was not so with Mr. Mannion. He was exactly the same man at his own house that he was at Mr. Sherwin's.

There was no need for him to have told me that he was an epicure in tea; the manner in which he made it would have betrayed that to anybody. He put in nearly treble the quantity which would generally be considered sufficient for two persons; and almost immediately after he had filled the tea-pot with boiling water, began to pour from it into the cups—thus preserving all the aroma and delicacy of flavour in the herb, without the alloy of any of the coarser part of its strength. When we had finished our first cups, there was no pouring of dregs into a basin, or of fresh water on the leaves. A middle-aged female servant, neat and quiet, came up and took away the tray, bringing it to us again with the tea-pot and tea-cups clean and empty, to receive a fresh infusion from fresh leaves. These were trifles to notice; but I thought of other tradesmen's clerks who were drinking their gin-and-water jovially, at home or at a tavern, and found Mr. Mannion a more exasperating mystery to me than ever.

The conversation between us turned at first on trivial subjects, and was but ill sustained on my part—there were peculiarities in my present position which made me thoughtful. Once, our talk ceased altogether; and, just at that moment, the storm began to rise to its height. Hail mingled with the rain, and rattled heavily against the window. The thunder, bursting louder and louder with each successive peal, seemed to shake the house to its foundations. As I listened to the fearful crashing and roaring that seemed to fill the whole measureless void of upper air, and then looked round on the calm, dead-calm face of the man beside me—without one human emotion of any kind even faintly pictured on it—I felt strange, unutterable sensations creeping over me; our silence grew oppressive and sinister; I began to wish, I hardly knew why, for some third person in the room—for somebody else to look at and to speak to.

He was the first to resume the conversation. I should have imagined it impossible for any man, in the midst of such thunder as now raged above our heads, to think or talk of anything but the storm. And yet, when he spoke, it was merely on a subject connected with his introduction to me at North Villa. His attention seemed as far from being attracted or impressed by the mighty elemental tumult without, as if the tranquillity of the night were uninvaded by the slightest murmur of sound.

"May I inquire, Sir," he began, "whether I am right in apprehending that my conduct towards you, since we first met at Mr. Sherwin's house, may have appeared strange, and even discourteous, in your eyes?"

"In what respect, Mr. Mannion?" I asked, a little startled by the abruptness of the question.

"I am perfectly sensible, Sir, that you have kindly set me the example, on many occasions, in trying to better our acquaintance. When such advances are made by one in your station to one in mine, they ought to be immediately and gratefully responded to."

Why did he pause? Was he about to tell me he had discovered that my advances sprang from curiosity to know more about him than he was willing to reveal? I waited for him to proceed.

"I have only failed," he continued, "in the courtesy and gratitude you had a right to expect from me, because, knowing how you were situated with Mr. Sherwin's daughter, I thought any intrusion on my part, while you were with the young lady, might not be so acceptable as you, Sir, in your kindness, were willing to lead me to believe."

"Let me assure you," I answered; relieved to find myself unsuspected, and really impressed by his delicacy—"let me assure you that I fully appreciate the consideration you have shown—"

Just as the last words passed my lips, the thunder pealed awfully over the house. I said no more: the sound silenced me.

"As my explanation has satisfied you, Sir," he went on; his clear and deliberate utterance rising discordantly audible above the long, retiring roll of the last burst of thunder—"may I feel justified in speaking on the subject of your present position in my employer's house, with some freedom? I mean, if I may say so without offence, with the freedom of a friend."

I begged he would use all the freedom he wished; feeling really desirous that he should do so, apart from any purpose of leading him to talk unreservedly on the chance of hearing him talk of himself. The profound respect of manner and phrase which he had hitherto testified—observed by a man of his age, to a man of mine—made me feel ill at ease. He was most probably my equal in acquirements: he had the manners and tastes of a gentleman, and might have the birth too, for aught I knew to the contrary. The difference between us was only in our worldly positions. I had not enough of my father's pride of caste to think that this difference alone, made it right that a man whose years nearly doubled mine, whose knowledge perhaps surpassed mine, should speak to me as Mr. Mannion had spoken up to this time.

"I may tell you then," he resumed, "that while I am anxious to commit no untimely intrusion on your hours at North Villa, I am at the same time desirous of being something more than merely inoffensive towards you. I should wish to be positively useful, as far as I can. In my opinion Mr. Sherwin has held you to rather a hard engagement—he is trying your discretion a little too severely I think, at your years and in your situation. Feeling thus, it is my sincere wish to render what connection and influence I have with the family, useful in making the probation you have still to pass through, as easy as possible. I have more means of doing this, Sir, than you might at first imagine."

His offer took me a little by surprise. I felt with a sort of shame, that candour and warmth of feeling were what I had not expected from him. My attention insensibly wandered away from the storm, to attach itself more and more closely to him, as he went on:

"I am perfectly sensible," he resumed, "that such a proposition as I now make to you, proceeding from one little better than a stranger, may cause surprise and even suspicion, at first. I can only explain it, by asking you to remember that I have known the young lady since childhood; and that, having assisted in forming her mind and developing her character, I feel towards her almost as a second father, and am therefore naturally interested in the gentleman who has chosen her for a wife."

Was there a tremor at last in that changeless voice, as he spoke? I thought so; and looked anxiously to catch the answering gleam of expression, which might now, for the first time, be softening his iron features, animating the blank stillness of his countenance. If any such expression had been visible, I was too late to detect it. Just as I looked at him he stooped down to poke the fire. When he turned towards me again, his face was the same impenetrable face, his eye the same hard, steady, inexpressive eye as before.

"Besides," he continued, "a man must have some object in life for his sympathies to be employed on. I have neither wife nor child; and no near relations to think of— I have nothing but my routine of business in the day, and my books here by my lonely fireside, at night. Our life is not much; but it was made for a little more than this. My former pupil at North Villa is my pupil no longer. I can't help feeling that it would be an object in existence for me to occupy myself with her happiness and yours; to have two young people, in the heyday of youth and first love, looking towards me occasionally for the promotion of some of their pleasures—no matter how trifling. All this will seem odd and incomprehensible to *you*. If you were of my age, Sir, and in my position, you would understand it."

Was it possible that he could speak thus, without his voice faltering, or his eye softening in the slightest degree? Yes: I looked at him and listened to him intently; but there was not the faintest change in his face or his tones—there was nothing to show outwardly whether he felt what he said, or whether he did not. His words had painted such a picture of forlornness on my mind, that I had mechanically half raised my hand to take his, while he was addressing me; but the sight of him when he ceased, checked the impulse almost as soon as it was formed. He did not appear to have noticed either my involuntary gesture, or its immediate repression; and went on speaking.

"I have said perhaps more than I ought," he resumed. "If I have not succeeded in making you understand my explanation as I could wish, we will change the subject, and not return to it again, until you have known me for a much longer time."

"On no account change the subject, Mr. Mannion," I said; unwilling to let it be implied that I would not put trust in him. "I am deeply sensible of the kindness of your offer, and the interest you take in Margaret and me. We shall both, I am sure, accept your good offices—"

I stopped. The storm had decreased a little in violence: but my attention was now struck by the wind, which had risen as the thunder and rain had partially lulled. How drearily it was moaning down the street! It seemed, at that moment, to be wailing over *me*; to be wailing over *him*; to be wailing over all mortal things! The strange sensations I then felt, moved me to listen in silence; but I checked them, and spoke again.

"If I have not answered you as I should," I continued, "you must attribute it partly to the storm, which I confess rather discomposes my ideas; and partly to a little surprise—a very foolish surprise, I own — that you should still be able to feel so strong a sympathy with interests which are generally only considered of importance to the young."

"It is only in their sympathies, that men of my years can, and do, live their youth over again," he said. "You may be surprised to hear a tradesman's clerk talk in this manner; but I was not always what I am now. I have gathered knowledge, and suffered in the gathering. I have grown old before my time—my forty years are like the fifty of other men—"

My heart beat quicker—was he, unasked, about to disclose the mystery which evidently hung over his early life? No: he dropped the subject at once, when he continued. I longed to ask him to resume it, but could not. I feared the same repulse which Mr. Sherwin had received: and remained silent.

"What I was," he proceeded, "matters little; the question is what can I do for you? Any aid I can give, may be poor enough; but it may be of some use notwithstanding. For instance, the other day, if I mistake not, you were a little hurt at Mr. Sherwin's taking his daughter to a party to which the family had been invited. This was very natural. You could not be there to watch over her in your real character, without disclosing a secret which must be kept safe; and you could not know what young men she might meet, who would imagine her to be Miss Sherwin still, and would regulate their conduct accordingly. Now, I think I might be of use here. I have some influence— perhaps in strict truth I ought to say great influence—with my employer; and, if you wished it, I would use that influence to back yours, in inducing him to forego, for the future, any intention of taking his daughter into society, except when you desire it. Again: I think I am not wrong in assuming that you infinitely prefer the company of Mrs. Sherwin to that of Mr. Sherwin, during your interviews with the young lady?"

How he had found that out? At any rate, he was right; and I told him so candidly.

"The preference is on many accounts a very natural one," he said; "but if you suffered it to appear to Mr. Sherwin, it might, for obvious reasons, produce a most unfavourable effect. I might interfere in the matter, however, without suspicion; I should have many opportunities of keeping him away from the room, in the evening, which I could use if you wished it. And more than that, if you wanted longer and more frequent communication with North Villa than you now enjoy, I might be able to effect this also. I do not mention what I could do in these, and in other matters, in any disparagement, Sir, of the influence which you have with Mr. Sherwin, in your own right; but because I know that in what concerns your intercourse with his daughter, my employer *has* asked, and *will* ask my advice, from the habit of doing so in other things. I have hitherto declined giving him this advice in your affairs; but I **will** give it, and in your favour and the young lady's, if you **and** she choose."

I thanked him—but not in such warm terms as I should have employed, if I had seen even the faintest smile on his face, or had heard any change in his steady, deliberate tones, as he spoke. While his words attracted, his immovable looks repelled me, in spite of myself.

"I must again beg you"—he proceeded—"to remember what I have already said, in your estimate of the motives of my offer. If I still appear to be interfering officiously in your affairs, you have only to think that I have presumed impertinently on the freedom you have allowed me, and to treat me no longer on the terms of to-night. I shall not complain of your conduct, and shall try hard not to consider you unjust to me, if you do."

Such an appeal as this was not to be resisted : I answered him at once and unreservedly. What right had I to draw bad inferences from a man's face, voice, and manner, merely because they impressed me, as out of the common ? Did I know how much share the influence of natural infirmity, or the outward traces of unknown sorrow and suffering, might nave had in producing the external peculiarities which had struck me ? He would have every right to upbraid me as unjust—and that in the strongest terms—unless I spoke out fairly in reply.

"I am quite incapable, Mr. Mannion," I said, " of viewing your offer with any other than grateful feelings. You will find I shall prove this by employing your good offices for Margaret and myself in perfect faith, and sooner perhaps than you may imagine."

He bowed and said a few cordial words, which I heard but imperfectly—for, as I addressed him, a blast of wind fiercer than usual, rushed down the street, shaking the window shutter violently as it passed, and dying away in a low, melancholy, dirging swell, like a spirit-cry of lamentation and despair.

When he spoke again, after a momentary silence, it was to make some change in the conversation. He talked of Margaret—dwelling in terms of high praise rather on her moral than on her personal qualities. He spoke of Mr. Sherwin, referring to solid and attractive points in his character which I had not detected. What he said of Mrs. Sherwin appeared to be equally dictated by compassion and respect—he even hinted at her coolness towards himself, considerately attributing it to the involuntary caprice of settled nervousness and ill-health. His language, in touching on these subjects, was just as unaffected, just as devoid of any peculiarities, as I had hitherto found it when occupied by other topics.

It was growing late. The thunder still rumbled at long intervals, with a dull, distant sound; and the wind showed no symptoms of subsiding. But the pattering of the rain against the window ceased to be audible. There was little excuse for staying longer; and I wished to find none. I had acquired quite knowledge enough of Mr. Mannion to assure me, that any attempt on my part at extracting from him, in spite of his reserve, the secrets which might be connected with his early life, would prove perfectly fruitless. If I must judge him at all, I must judge him by the experience of the present, and not by the history of the past. I had heard good, and good only, of him from the shrewd master who knew him best, and had tried him longest. He had shown the greatest delicacy towards my feelings, and the strongest desire to do me service—it would be a mean return for those acts of courtesy, to let curiosity tempt me to pry into his private affairs.

I rose to go. He made no effort to detain me; but, after unbarring the shutter and looking out of the window, simply remarked that the rain had almost entirely ceased, and

that my umbrella would be quite sufficient protection against
all that remained. He followed me into the passage to light
me out. As I turned round upon his door-step to thank
him for his hospitality, and to bid him good night, the
thought came across me, that my manner must have appeared cold and repelling to him—especially when he was
offering his services to my acceptance. If I had really
produced this impression, he was my inferior in station,
and it would be cruel to leave it.* I tried to set myself
right at parting.

"Let me assure you again," I said, "that it will not be
my fault if Margaret and I do not thankfully employ your
good offices, as the good offices of a well-wisher and a
friend."

The lightning was still in the sky, though it only appeared at long intervals. Strangely enough, at the moment
when I addressed him, a flash came, and seemed to pass
right over his face. It gave such a hideously livid hue,
such a spectral look of ghastliness and distortion to his
features, that he absolutely seemed to be glaring and grinning on me like a fiend, in the one instant of its duration.
For the moment, it required all my knowledge of the settled
calmness of his countenance, to convince me that my eyes
must have been only dazzled by an optical illusion produced
by the lightning.

When the darkness had come again, I bade him good
night—first mechanically repeating what I had just said,
almost in the same words.

I walked home thoughtful. That night had given me
much matter to think of.

IV.

About the time of my introduction to Mr. Mannion—or, to speak more correctly, both before and after that period —certain peculiarities in Margaret's character and conduct, which came to my knowledge by pure accident, gave me a little uneasiness and even a little displeasure. Neither of these feelings lasted very long, it is true; for the incidents which gave rise to them were of a trifling nature in themselves. While I now write, however, these domestic occurrences are all vividly present to my recollection. I will mention two of them as instances. Subsequent events, yet to be related, will show that they are not out of place at this part of my narrative.

One lovely autumn morning, I called rather before the appointed time at North Villa. As the servant opened the front garden-gate, the idea occurred to me of giving Margaret a surprise, by entering the drawing room unexpectedly, with a nosegay gathered for her from her own flower-bed. Telling the servant not to announce me, I went round to the back garden, by a gate which opened into it at the side of the house. The progress of my flower-gathering led me on to the lawn under one of the drawing-room windows, which was left a little open. The voices of my wife and her mother reached me from the room. It was this part of their conversation which I unintentionally overheard:—

"I tell you, mamma, I must and will have the dress, whether papa chooses or not."

This was spoken loudly and resolutely; in such tones as I had never heard from Margaret before.

"Pray—pray, my dear, don't talk so," answered the weak, faltering voice of Mrs. Sherwin; "you know you have had more than your year's allowance of dresses already."

"I won't be allowanced. *His* sister isn't allowanced: why should I be?"

"My dear love, surely there is some difference—"

"I'm sure there isn't, now I am his wife. I shall ride some day in my carriage, just as his sister does. *He* gives me my way in everything; and so ought you!"

"It isn't *me*, Margaret: if I could do anything, I'm sure I would; but I really couldn't ask your papa for another new dress, after his having given you so many this year, already."

"That's the way it always is with you, mamma—you can't do this, and you can't do that—you are so excessively tiresome! But I will have the dress, I'm determined. He says his sister wears light blue crape of an evening; and I'll have light blue crape, too—see if I don't! I'll get it somehow from the shop, myself. Papa never takes any notice, I'm sure, what I have on; and he needn't find out anything about what's gone out of the shop, until they 'take stock,' or whatever it is he calls it. And then, if he flies into one of his passions—"

"My dear! my dear! you really ought not to talk so of your papa—it is very wrong, Margaret, indeed—what would Mr. Basil say if he heard you?"

I determined to go in at once, and tell Margaret that I had heard her—resolving, at the same time, to exert some firmness, and remonstrate with her, for her own good, on much of what she had said, which had really surprised and displeased me. On my unexpected entrance, Mrs. Sherwin started, and looked more timid than ever. Margaret, however, came forward to meet me with her wonted smile, and held out her hand with her wonted grace. I said nothing until we had got into our accustomed corner, and were talking together in whispers as usual. Then I began my remonstrance—very tenderly, and in the lowest possible tones. She took precisely the right way to stop me in full career, in spite of all my resolution. Her beautiful eyes filled with tears directly—the first I had ever seen in them: caused, too, by what I had said!—and she murmured a few plaintive words about the cruelty of being angry with her for only wanting to please me by being dressed as my sister was, which upset every intention I had formed but the moment before. I involuntarily devoted myself to soothing her for the rest of the morning. Need I say how the matter ended? I never mentioned the subject more; and I made her a present of the new dress.

Some weeks after the little home-breeze which I have just related, had died away into a perfect calm, I was accidentally witness of another domestic dilemma in which Margaret bore a principal share. On this occasion, as I walked up to the house (in the morning again), I found the front door open. A pail was on the steps—the servant had evidently been washing them, had been interrupted in her work, and had forgotten to close the door when she left it. The nature of the interruption I soon discovered as I entered the hall.

"For God's sake, Miss!" cried the housemaid's voice, from the dining-room, "for God's sake, put down the poker! Missus will be here directly; and it's *her* cat!"*

"I'll kill the vile brute! I'll kill the hateful cat! I don't care whose it is!—my poor dear, dear, dear bird!" The voice was Margaret's. At first, its tones were tones of fury; they were afterwards broken by hysterical sobs.

"Poor thing," continued the servant, soothingly, "I'm sorry for it, and for you too, Miss! But, oh! do please to remember it was you left the cage on the table, in the cat's reach—"

"Hold your tongue, you wretch! How dare you hold me?—let me go!"

"Oh, you mustn't—you mustn't indeed! It's missus's

cat, recollect—poor missus's, who's always ill, and hasn't
got nothing else to amuse her."

"I don't care ! The cat has killed my bird, and the cat
shall be killed for doing it !—it shall !—it shall ! !—it shall ! ! !
I'll call in the first boy from the street to catch it,* and hang
it ! Let me go ! I *will* go !"

"I'll let the cat go first, Miss, as sure as my name's
Susan !"

The next instant, the door was suddenly opened, and puss
sprang past me, out of harm's way, closely followed by the
servant, who stared breathless and aghast at seeing me in
the hall. I went into the dining-room immediately.

On the floor lay a bird-cage, with the poor canary dead
inside (it was the same canary that I had seen my wife
playing with, on the evening of the day when I first met
her). The bird's head had been nearly dragged through
the bent wires of the cage, by the murderous claws of the
cat. Near the fire-place, with the poker she had just
dropped on the floor by her side, stood Margaret. Never
had I seen her look so beautiful as she now appeared, in
the fury of passion which possessed her. Her large black
eyes were flashing grandly through her tears—the blood
was glowing crimson in her cheeks—her lips were parted as
she gasped for breath. One of her hands was clenched, and
rested on the mantel-piece ; the other was pressed tight
over her bosom, with the fingers convulsively clasping her
dress. Grieved as I was at the paroxysm of passion into
which she had allowed herself to be betrayed, I could
repress an involuntary feeling of admiration when my eyes
first rested on her. Even anger itself looked lovely in that
lovely face !

She never moved when she saw me. As I approached
her, she dropped down on her knees by the cage, sobbing
with frightful violence, and pouring forth a perfect torrent
of ejaculations of vengeance against the cat. Mrs. Sher-

win came down; and by her total want of tact and presence of mind, made matters worse. In brief, the scene ended by a fit of hysterics.

To speak to Margaret on that day, as I wished to speak to her, was impossible. To approach the subject of the canary's death afterwards, was useless. If I only hinted in the gentlest way, and with the strongest sympathy for the loss of the bird, at the distress and astonishment she had caused me by the extremities to which she had allowed her passion to hurry her, a burst of tears was sure to be her only reply—just the reply, of all others, which was best calculated to silence me. If I had been her husband in fact, as well as in name; if I had been her father, her brother, or her friend, I should have let her first emotions have their way, and then have expostulated with her afterwards. But I was her lover still; and, to my eyes, Margaret's tears made virtues even of Margaret's faults.

Such occurrences as these, happening but at rare intervals, formed the only interruptions to the generally even and happy tenour of our intercourse. Weeks and weeks glided away, and not a hasty or a hard word passed between us. Neither, after one preliminary difference had been adjusted, did any subsequent disagreement take place between Mr. Sherwin and me. This last element in the domestic tranquillity of North Villa was, however, less attributable to his forbearance, or to mine, than to the private interference of Mr. Mannion.

For some days after my interview with the managing clerk, at his own house, I had abstained from calling his offered services into requisition. I was not conscious of any reason for this course of conduct. All that had been said, all that had happened during the night of the storm, had produced a powerful, though vague impression on me. Strange as it may appear, I could not determine whether my brief but extraordinary experience of my new friend had attracted me towards him, or repelled me from him. I felt an unwillingness to lay myself under an obligation to him, which was not the result of pride, or false delicacy, or sullenness, or suspicion—it was an inexplicable unwillingness, that sprang from the fear of encountering some heavy responsibility ; but of what nature I could not imagine. I delayed and held back, by instinct; and, on his side, Mr. Mannion made no further advances. He maintained the same manner, and continued the same habits, during his intercourse with the family at North Villa, which I had observed as characterising him before I took shelter from the storm, in his house. He never referred again to the conversation of that evening, when we now met.

Margaret's behaviour, when I mentioned to her Mr. Mannion's willingness to be useful to us both, rather increased than diminished the vague uncertainties which perplexed me, on the subject of accepting or rejecting his overtures.

I could not induce her to show the smallest interest about him. Neither his house, his personal appearance, his peculiar habits, or his secrecy in relation to his early life—nothing, in short, connected with him—appeared to excite her attention or curiosity in the slightest degree. On the evening of his return from the continent, she had certainly shown some symptoms of interest in his arrival at North Villa, and some appearance of attention to him, when he joined our party. Now, she seemed completely and incomprehensibly changed on this point. Her manner became almost petulant, if I persisted long in making Mr. Mannion a topic of conversation—it was as if she resented his sharing my thoughts with her in the slightest degree. As to the difficult question whether we should engage him in our interests or not, that was a matter which she always seemed to think too trifling to be discussed between us at all.

Ere long, however, circumstances decided me as to the course I should take with Mr. Mannion.

A ball was given by one of Mr. Sherwin's rich commercial friends, to which he announced his intention of taking Margaret. Besides the jealousy which I felt—naturally enough, in my peculiar situation—at the idea of my wife going out as Miss Sherwin, and dancing in the character of a young unmarried lady with any young gentlemen who were introduced to her, I had also the strongest possible desire to keep Margaret out of the society of her own class, until my year's probation was over, and I could hope to instal her permanently in the society of my class. I had privately mentioned to her my ideas on this subject, and found that she fully agreed with them. She was not wanting in ambition to ascend to the highest degree in the social scale; and had already begun to look with indifference on the society which was offered to her by those in her own rank.

To Mr. Sherwin I could confide nothing of this. I could only object, generally, to his taking Margaret out, when neither she nor I desired it. He declared that she liked parties—that all girls did—that she only pretended to dislike them, to please me—and that he had made no engagement to keep her moping at home a whole year on my account. In the case of the particular ball now under discussion, he was determined to have his own way; and he bluntly told me as much.

Irritated by his obstinacy and gross want of consideration for my defenceless position, I forgot all doubts and scruples; and privately applied to Mr. Mannion to exert the influence which he had promised to use, if I wished it, in my behalf.

The result was as immediate as it was conclusive. The very next evening, Mr. Sherwin came to us with a note which he had just written, and informed me that it was an excuse for Margaret's non-appearance at the ball. He never mentioned Mr. Mannion's name, but sulkily and shortly said, that he had reconsidered the matter, and had altered his first decision for reasons of his own.

Having once taken a first step in the new direction, I soon followed it up, without hesitation, by taking many others. Whenever I wished to call oftener than once a-day at North Villa, I had but to tell Mr. Mannion, and the next morning I found the permission immediately accorded to me by the ruling power. The same secret machinery enabled me to regulate Mr. Sherwin's incomings and out-goings, just as I chose, when Margaret and I were together in the evening. I could feel almost certain, now, of never having any one with us, but Mrs. Sherwin, unless I desired it—which, as may be easily imagined, was seldom enough.

My new ally's ready interference for my advantage was exerted quietly, easily, and as a matter of course. I never knew how, or when, he influenced his employer, and Mr. Sherwin on his part, never breathed a word of that influence to me. He accorded any extra privilege I might demand, as if he acted entirely under his own will, little suspecting how well I knew what was the real motive power which directed him.

I was the more easily reconciled to employing the services of Mr. Mannion, by the great delicacy with which he per-formed them. He did not allow me to think—he did not appear to think himself—that he was obliging me in the smallest degree. He affected no sudden intimacy with me; his manners never altered; he still persisted in not joining us in the evening, but at my express invitation; and if I re-ferred in any way to the advantages I derived from his devo-tion to my interests, he always replied in his brief undemon-strative way, that he considered himself the favoured person, in being permitted to make his services of some use to Mar-garet and me.

I had told Mr. Mannion, when I was leaving him on the night of the storm, that I would treat his offers as the offers of a friend; and I had now made good my words, much sooner and much more unreservedly than I had ever intended, when we parted at his own house-door.

V.

The autumn was now over; the winter—a cold, gloomy winter—had fairly come. Five months had nearly elapsed since Clara and my father had departed for the country. What communication did I hold with them, during that interval?

No personal communication with either—written communication only with my sister. Clara's letters to me were frequent. They studiously avoided anything like a reproach for my long absence; and were confined almost exclusively to such details of country life as the writer thought likely to interest me. Their tone was as affectionate—nay, more affectionate, if possible—than usual; but Clara's gaiety and quiet humour, as a correspondent, were gone. My conscience taught me only too easily and too plainly how to account for this change—my conscience told me who had altered the tone of my sister's letters, by altering all the favourite purposes and favourite pleasures of her country life.

I was selfishly enough devoted to my own passions and my own interests, at this period of my life; but I was not so totally dead to every one of the influences which had guided me since childhood, as to lose all thought of Clara and my father, and the ancient house that was associated with my earliest and happiest recollections. Sometimes, even in Margaret's beloved presence, a thought of Clara put away from me all other thoughts. And, sometimes, in the lonely London house, I dreamed—with the strangest sleeping oblivion of my marriage, and of all the new interests which it had crowded into my life—of country rides with my sister, and of quiet conversations in the old gothic library at the Hall. Under such influences as these, I twice resolved to make amends for my long absence, by joining my father and my sister in the country, even though it were only for a few days—and, each time, I failed in my resolution. On the second occasion, I had actually mustered firmness enough to get as far as the railway station; and only at the last moment faltered and hung back. The struggle that it cost me to part for any length of time from Margaret, I had overcome; but the apprehension, as vivid as it was vague, that something—I knew not what—might happen to her in my absence, turned my steps backward at starting. I felt heartily ashamed of my own weakness; but I yielded to it nevertheless.

At last, a letter arrived from Clara, containing a summons to the country, which I could not disobey.

"I have never asked you," she wrote, "to come and see us for my sake; for I would not interfere with any of your interests or any of your plans; but I now ask you to come here for your own sake—just for one week, and no more, unless you like to remain longer. You remember papa telling you, in your room in London, that he believed you kept some secret from him. I am afraid this is preying on his mind: your long absence is making him uneasy about you. He does not say so; but he never sends any message, when I write; and if I speak about you, he always changes the subject directly. Pray come here, and show yourself for a few days—no questions will be asked, you may be sure. It will do so much good; and will prevent—what I hope and pray may never happen—a serious estrangement between papa and you. Recollect, Basil, in a month or six weeks we shall come back to town; and then the opportunity will be gone."

As I read these lines, I determined to start for the country at once, while the effect of them was still fresh on my mind. Margaret, when I took leave of her, only said that she should like to be going with me—"it would be such a sight for her, to see a grand country house like ours!" Mr. Sherwin laughed as coarsely as usual, at the difficulties I made about only leaving his daughter for a week. Mrs. Sherwin very earnestly, and very unaccountably as I then thought, recommended me not to be away any longer than I had proposed. Mr. Mannion privately assured me, that I might depend on him in my absence from North Villa, exactly as I had always depended on him, during my presence there. It was strange that *his* parting words should be the only words which soothed and satisfied me on taking leave of London.

The winter afternoon was growing dim with the evening darkness, as I drove up to the Hall. Snow on the ground, in the country, has always a cheerful look to me. I could have wished to see it on the day of my arrival at home; but there had been a thaw for the last week—mud and water were all about me—a drizzling rain was falling—a raw, damp wind was blowing—a fog was rising, as the evening stole on—and the ancient leafless elms in the park avenue groaned and creaked above my head drearily, as I approached the house.

My father received me with more ceremony than I liked. I had known, from a boy, what it meant when he chose to be only polite to his own son. What construction he had put on my long absence and my persistence in keeping my secret from him, I could not tell; but it was evident that I had lost my usual place in his estimation, and lost it past regaining merely by a week's visit. The estrangement between us, which my sister had feared, had begun already.

I had been chilled by the desolate aspect of nature, as I approached the Hall; my father's reception of me, when I entered the house, increased the comfortless and melancholy impressions produced on my mind; it required all the affectionate warmth of Clara's welcome, all the pleasure of hearing her whisper her thanks, as she kissed me, for my readiness in following her advice, to restore my equanimity. But even then, when the first hurry and excitement of meeting had passed away, in spite of her kind words and looks, there was something in her face which depressed me. She seemed thinner, and her constitutional paleness was more marked than usual. Cares and anxieties had evidently oppressed her—was I the cause of them?

The dinner that evening proceeded very heavily and gloomily. My father only talked on general and common-place topics, as if a mere acquaintance had been present. When my sister left us, he too quitted the room, to see some one who had arrived on business. I had no heart for the company of the wine bottles, so I followed Clara.

At first, we only spoke of her occupations since she had been in the country; I was unwilling, and she forbore, to touch on my long stay in London, or on my father's evident displeasure at my protracted absence. There was a little restraint between us, which neither had the courage to break through. Before long, however, an accident, trifling enough in itself, obliged me to be more candid; and enabled ner to speak unreservedly on the subject nearest to her heart.

I was seated oppposite to Clara, at the fire-place, and was playing with a favourite dog which had followed me into the room. While I was stooping towards the animal, a locket containing some of Margaret's hair, fell out of its place in my waistcoat, and swung towards my sister by the string which attached it round my neck. I instantly hid it again; but not before Clara, with a woman's quickness, had detected the trinket as something new, and drawn the right inference, as to the use to which I devoted it.

An expression of surprise and pleasure passed over her face; she rose, and putting her hands on my shoulders, as if to keep me still in the place I occupied, looked at me intently.

"Basil!" she exclaimed, "if *that* is all the secret you have been keeping from us, how glad I am! When I see a new locket drop out of my brother's waistcoat—" she continued, observing that I was too confused to speak—"and when I find him colouring very deeply, and hiding it again in a great hurry, I should be no true woman if I did not make my own discoveries, and begin to talk about them directly."

I made an effort—a very poor one—to laugh the thing off. Her expression grew serious and thoughtful, while she still fixed her eyes on me. She took my hand gently, and whispered in my ear: "Are you going to be married, Basil? Shall I love my new sister almost as much as I love you?"

At that moment the servant came in with tea. The interruption gave me a minute for consideration. Should I tell her all? Impulse answered, yes—reflection, no. If I disclosed my real situation, I knew that I must introduce Clara to Margaret. This would necessitate taking her privately to Mr. Sherwin's house, and exposing to her the humiliating terms of dependence and prohibition on which I lived with my own wife. A strange medley of feelings, in which pride was uppermost, forbade me to do that. Then again, to involve my sister in my secret, would be to involve her with me in any consequences which might be produced by its disclosure to my father. The mere idea of making her a partaker in responsibilities which I alone ought to bear, was not to be entertained for a moment. As soon as we were left together again, I said to her:

"Will you not think the worse of me, Clara, if I leave you to draw your own conclusions from what you have seen? only asking you to keep strict silence on the subject to every one. I can't speak yet, love, as I wish to speak: you will know why, some day, and say that my reserve was right. In the meantime, can you be satisfied with the assurance, that when the time comes for making my secret known, you shall be the first to know it—the first I put trust in?"

"As you have not starved my curiosity altogether," said Clara, smiling, "but have given it a little hope to feed on for the present, I think, woman though I am, I can promise all you wish. Seriously, Basil," she continued, "that tell-tale locket of yours has so pleasantly brightened some very gloomy thoughts of mine about you, that I can now live happily on expectation, without once mentioning your secret again, till you give me leave to do so."

Here my father entered the room, and we said no more. His manner towards me had not altered since dinner; and it remained the same during the week of my stay at the Hall. One morning, when we were alone, I took courage, and determined to try the dangerous ground a little, with a view towards my guidance for the future; but I had no sooner begun by some reference to my stay in London, and some apology for it, than he stopped me at once.

"I told you," he said, gravely and coldly, "some months ago, that I had too much faith in your honour to intrude on affairs which you choose to keep private. Until you have perfect confidence in me, and can speak with complete candour, I will hear nothing. You have not that confidence now—you speak hesitatingly—your eyes do not meet mine fairly and boldly. I tell you again, I will hear nothing which begins with such common-place excuses as you have just addressed to me. Excuses lead to prevarications, and prevarications to—what I will not insult you by imagining possible in *your* case. You are of age, and must know your own responsibilities and mine. Choose at once, between saying nothing, and saying all."

He waited a moment after he had spoken, and then quitted the room. If he could only have known how I suffered, at that instant, under the base necessities of concealment, I might have confessed everything; and he must have pitied, though he might not have forgiven me.

This was my first and last attempt at venturing towards the revelation of my secret to my father, by hints and half-admissions. As to boldly confessing it, I persuaded myself into a sophistical conviction that such a course could do no good, but might do much harm. When the wedded happiness I had already waited for, and was to wait for still, through so many months, came at last, was it not best to enjoy my married life in convenient secrecy, as long as I could?—best, to abstain from disclosing my secret to my father, until necessity absolutely obliged, or circumstances absolutely invited me to do so? My inclinations conveniently decided the question in the affirmative; and a decision of any kind, right or wrong, was enough to tranquillise me at that time.

So far as my father was concerned, my journey to the country did no good. I might have returned to London the day after my arrival at the Hall, without altering his opinion of me—but I stayed the whole week nevertheless, for Clara's sake.

In spite of the pleasure afforded by my sister's society, my visit was a painful one. The selfish longing to be back with Margaret, which I could not wholly repress; my father's coldness; and the winter gloom and rain which confined us almost incessantly within doors, all tended in their different degrees to prevent my living at ease in the Hall. But, besides these causes of embarrassment, I had the additional mortification of feeling, for the first time, as a stranger in my own home.

Nothing in the house looked to me what it used to look in former years. The rooms, the old servants, the walks and views, the domestic animals, all appeared to have altered, or to have lost something, since I had seen them last. Particular rooms that I had once been fond of occupying, were favourites no longer : particular habits that I had hitherto always practised in the country, I could only succeed in resuming by an effort which vexed and fretted me. It was as if my life had run into a new channel since my last Autumn and winter at the Hall, and now refused to flow back at my bidding into its old course. Home seemed home no longer, except in name.

As soon as the week was over, my father and I parted exactly as we had met. When I took leave of Clara, she refrained from making any allusion to the shortness of my stay ; and merely said that we should soon meet again in London. She evidently saw that my visit had weighed a little on my spirits, and was determined to give to our short farewell as happy and hopeful a character as possible. We now thoroughly understood each other ; and that was some consolation on leaving her.

Immediately on my return to London I repaired to North Villa.

Nothing, I was told, had happened in my absence, but I remarked some change in Margaret. She looked pale and nervous, and was more silent than I had ever known her to be before, when we met. She accounted for this, in answer to my inquiries, by saying that confinement to the house, in consequence of the raw, wintry weather, had a little affected her ; and then changed the subject. In other directions, household aspects had not deviated from their accustomed monotony. As usual, Mrs. Sherwin was at her post in the drawing-room ; and her husband was reading the evening paper, over his renowned old port, in the dining-room. After the first five minutes of my arrival, I adapted myself again to my old way of life at Mr. Sherwin's, as easily as if I had never interrupted it for a single day. Henceforth, wherever my young wife was, there, and there only, would it be home for *me!*

Late in the evening, Mr. Mannion arrived with some business letters for Mr. Sherwin's inspection. I sent for him into the hall to see me, as I was going away. His hand was never a warm one; but as I now took it, on greeting him, it was so deadly cold that it literally chilled mine for the moment. He only congratulated me, in the usual terms, on my safe return; and said that nothing had taken place in my absence—but in his utterance of those few words, I discovered, for the first time, a change in his voice : his tones were lower, and his articulation quicker than usual. This, joined to the extraordinary coldness of his hand, made me inquire whether he was unwell. Yes, he too had been ill while I was away—harassed with hard work, he said. Then apologising for leaving me abruptly, on account of the letters he had brought with him, he returned to Mr. Sherwin, in the dining-room, with a greater appearance of hurry in his manner than I had ever remarked in it on any former occasion.

I had left Margaret and Mr. Mannion both well—I returned, and found them both ill. Surely this was something that had taken place in my absence, though they all said that nothing had happened. But trifling illnesses seemed to be little regarded at North Villa—perhaps, because serious illness was perpetually present there, in the person of Mrs. Sherwin.

VI.

About six weeks after I had left the Hall, my father and Clara returned to London for the season.

It is not my intention to delay over my life either at home

or at North Villa, during the spring and summer. This
would be merely to repeat much of what has been already
related. It is better to proceed at once to the closing period
of my probation; to a period which it taxes my resolution
severely to write of at all. A few weeks more of toil at
my narrative, and the penance of this poor task-work will
be over.

*   *   *   *   *   *

Imagine then, that the final day of my long year of expectation has arrived; and that on the morrow, Margaret,
for whose sake I have sacrificed and suffered so much, is at
last really to be mine.

On the eve of the great change in my life that was now
to take place, the relative positions in which I, and the different persons with whom I was associated, stood towards
each other, may be sketched thus:—

My father's coldness of manner had not altered since his
return to London. On my side, I carefully abstained from
uttering a word before him, which bore the smallest reference to my real situation. Although when we met, we outwardly preserved the usual relations of parent and child,
the estrangement between us had now become complete.

Clara did not fail to perceive this, and grieved over it in
secret. Other and happier feelings, however, became
awakened within her, when I privately hinted that the time
for disclosing my secret to my sister was not far off. She
grew almost as much agitated as I was, though by very different expectations—she could think of nothing else but
the explanation and the surprise in store for her. Sometimes, I almost feared to keep her any longer in suspense;
and half regretted having said anything on the subject of
the new and absorbing interest of my life, before the period
when I could easily have said all.

Mr. Sherwin and I had not latterly met on the most cordial terms. He was dissatisfied with me for not having boldly approached the subject of my marriage in my father's presence; and considered my reasons for still keeping it secret, as dictated by morbid apprehension, and as showing a total want of proper firmness. On the other hand, he was obliged to set against this omission on my part, the readiness I had shown in meeting his wishes on all remaining points. My life was insured in Margaret's favour;* and I had arranged to be called to the bar immediately, so as to qualify myself in good time for every possible place within place-hunting range. My assiduity in making these preparations for securing Margaret's prospects and mine against any evil chances that might happen, failed in producing the favourable effect on Mr. Sherwin, which they must assuredly have produced on a less selfish man. But they obliged him, at least, to stop short at occasional grumblings about my reserve with my father, and to maintain towards me a sort of sulky politeness, which was, after all, less offensive than the usual infliction of his cordiality, with its unfailing accompaniment of dull stories and duller jokes.

During the spring and summer, Mrs. Sherwin appeared to grow feebler and feebler, from continued ill-health. Occasionally, her words and actions—especially in her intercourse with me—suggested fears that her mind was beginning to give way, as well as her body. For instance, on one occasion, when Margaret had left the room for a minute or two, she suddenly hurried up to me, whispering with eager looks and anxious tones:—"Watch over your wife— mind you watch over her, and keep all bad people from her! *I've* tried to do it—mind *you* do it, too!" I asked immediately for an explanation of this extraordinary injunction; but she only answered by muttering something about a mother's anxieties, and then returned hastily to her place. It was impossible to induce her to be more explicit, try how I might.

Margaret once or twice occasioned me much perplexity
and distress, by certain inconsistencies and variations in her
manner, which began to appear shortly after my return to
North Villa from the country. At one time, she would
become, on a sudden, strangely sullen and silent—at another, irritable and capricious. Then, again, she would
abruptly change to the most affectionate warmth of speech
and demeanour, anxiously anticipating every wish I could
form, eagerly showing her gratitude for the slightest attentions I paid her. These unaccountable alterations of manner vexed and irritated me indescribably. I loved Margaret
too well to be able to look philosophically on the imperfec-
tions of her character; I knew of no cause given by me for
the frequent changes in her conduct, and, if they only proceeded from coquetry, then coquetry, as I once told her,
was the last female accomplishment that could charm me
in any woman whom I really loved. However, these causes of
annoyance and regret—her caprices, and my remonstrances
—all passed happily away, as the term of my engagement
with Mr. Sherwin approached its end. Margaret's better
and lovelier manner returned. Occasionally, she might
betray some symptoms of confusion, some evidences of unusual thoughtfulness—but I remembered how near was the
day of the emancipation of our love, and looked on her embarrassment as a fresh charm, a new ornament to the beauty
of my maiden wife.

Mr. Mannion continued—as far as attention to my interests went—to be the same ready and reliable friend as
ever; but he was, in some other respects, an altered man.
The illness of which he had complained months back, when I
returned to London, seemed to have increased. His face
was still the same impenetrable face which had so powerfully
impressed me when I first saw him, but his manner, hitherto
so quiet and self-possessed, had now grown abrupt and
variable. Sometimes, when he joined us in the drawing-

room at North Villa, he would suddenly stop before we had exchanged more than three or four words, murmur something, in a voice unlike his usual voice, about an attack of spasm and giddiness, and leave the room. These fits of illness had something in their nature of the same secrecy which distinguished everything else connected with him: they produced no external signs of distortion, no unusual paleness in his face—you could not guess what pain he was suffering, or where he was suffering it. Latterly, I abstained from ever asking him to join us; for the effect on Margaret of his sudden attacks of illness was, naturally, such as to discompose her seriously for the remainder of the evening. Whenever I saw him accidentally, at later periods of the year, the influence of the genial summer season appeared to produce no alteration for the better in him. I remarked that his cold hand, which had chilled me when I took it on the raw winter night of my return from the country, was as cold as ever, on the warm summer days which preceded the close of my engagement at North Villa.

Such was the posture of affairs at home, and at Mr. Sherwin's, when I went to see Margaret for the last time in my old character, on the last night which yet remained to separate us from each other.

I had been all day preparing for our reception, on the morrow, in a cottage which I had taken for a month, in a retired part of the country, at some distance from London. One month's unalloyed happiness with Margaret, away from the world and all worldly considerations, was the Eden upon earth towards which my dearest hope and anticipations had pointed for a whole year past—and now, now at last, those aspirations were to be realized! All my arrangements at the cottage were completed in time to allow me to return home, just before our usual late dinner hour. During the meal, I provided for my month's absence from

London, by informing my father that I proposed visiting
one of my country friends. He heard me as coldly and indifferently as usual; and, as I anticipated, did not even
ask to what friend's house I was going. After dinner, I
privately informed Clara that on the morrow, before starting, I would, in accordance with my promise, make her the
depositary of my long-treasured secret—which, as yet,
was not to be divulged to any one besides. This done, I
hurried away, between nine and ten o'clock, for a last half-
hour's visit to North Villa; hardly able to realise my own
situation, or to comprehend the fulness and exaltation of
my own joy.

A disappointment was in store for me. Margaret was
not in the house; she had gone out to an evening party,
given by a maiden aunt of hers, who was known to be very
rich, and was, accordingly, a person to be courted and humoured by the family.

I was angry as well as disappointed at what had taken
place. To send Margaret out, on this evening of all others,
showed a want of consideration towards both of us, which
revolted me. Mr. and Mrs. Sherwin were in the room
when I entered; and to *him* I spoke my opinion on the
subject, in no very conciliatory terms. He was suffering
from a bad attack of headache, and a worse attack of ill-
temper, and answered as irritably as he dared.

"My good Sir!" he said, in sharp, querulous tones, "do,
for once, allow me to know what's best. You'll have it all
your way to-morrow—just let me have *mine*, for the last
time, to-night. I'm sure you've been humoured often enough
about keeping Margaret away from parties—and we should
have humoured you this time, too; but a second letter came
from the old lady, saying she should be affronted if Margaret
wasn't one of her guests. I couldn't go and talk her over,
because of this infernal headache of mine—Hang it! it's
your interest that Margaret should keep in with her aunt;

she'll have all the old girl's money, if she only plays her cards decently well. That's why I sent her to the party— her going will be worth some thousands to both of you one of these days. She'll be back by half-past twelve, or before. Mannion was asked; and though he's all out of sorts, he's gone to take care of her, and bring her back. I'll warrant she comes home in good time, when *he's* with her. So you see there's nothing to make a fuss about, after all."

It was certainly a relief to hear that Mr. Mannion was taking care of Margaret. He was, in my opinion, much fitter for such a trust than her own father. Of all the good services he had done for me, I thought this the best—but it would have been even better still, if he had prevented Margaret from going to the party.

" I must say again," resumed Mr. Sherwin, still more irritably, finding I did not at once answer him, " there's nothing that any reasonable being need make a fuss about. I've been doing everything for Margaret's interests and yours—and she'll be back by twelve—and Mr. Mannion takes care of her—and I don't know what you would have —and it's devilish hard, so ill as I am too, to cut up rough with me like this—devilish hard!"

" I am sorry for your illness, Mr. Sherwin; and I don't doubt your good intentions, or the advantage of Mr. Mannion's protection for Margaret; but I feel disappointed, nevertheless, that she should have gone out to-night."

" I said she oughtn't to go at all, whatever her aunt wrote—*I* said that."

This bold speech actually proceeded from Mrs. Sherwin! I had never before heard her utter an opinion in her husband's presence—such an outburst from *her*, was perfectly inexplicable. She pronounced the words with desperate rapidity, and unwonted power of tone, fixing her eyes all the while on me with a very strange expression.

"Damn it, Mrs. S. !" roared her husband in a fury, "will you hold your tongue? What the devil do you mean by giving *your* opinion, when nobody wants it? Upon my soul I begin to think you're getting a little cracked. You've been meddling and bothering lately, so that I don't know what the deuce has come to you! I'll tell you what it is, Mr. Basil," he continued, turning snappishly round upon me, "you had better stop that fidgetty temper of yours, by going to the party yourself. The old lady told me she wanted gentlemen ; and would be glad to see any friends of mine I liked to send her. You have only to mention my name : Mannion will do the civil in the way of introduction. There! there's an envelope with the address to it—they won't know who you are, or what you are, at Margaret's aunt's—you've got your black dress things on, all right and ready—for Heaven's sake, go to the party yourself, and then I hope you'll be satisfied !"

Here he stopped ; and vented the rest of his ill-humour by ringing the bell violently for " his arrow-root," and abusing the servant when she brought it.

I hesitated about accepting his proposal. While I was in doubt, Mrs. Sherwin took the opportunity, when her husband's eye was off her, of nodding her head at me significantly. She evidently wished me to join Margaret at the party—but why? What did her behaviour mean?

It was useless to inquire. Long bodily suffering and weakness had but too palpably produced a corresponding feebleness in her intellect. What should I do? I was resolved to see Margaret that night ; but to wait for her between two and three hours, in company with her father and mother at North Villa, was an infliction not to be endured. I determined to go to the party. No one there would know anything about me. They would be all people who lived in a different world from mine ; and whose manners and habits I might find some amusement in studying. At any rate, I should spend an hour or two with Margaret, and could make it my own charge to see her safely home. Without further hesitation, therefore I took up the envelope with the address on it, and bade Mr. and Mrs. Sherwin good night.

It struck ten as I left North Villa. The moonlight which was just beginning to shine brilliantly on my arrival there, now appeared but at rare intervals; for the clouds were spreading thicker and thicker over the whole surface of the sky, as the night advanced.

VII.

The address to which I was now proceeding, led me some distance away from Mr. Sherwin's place of abode, in the direction of the populous neighbourhood which lies on the western side of the Edgeware Road. The house of Margaret's aunt was plainly enough indicated to me, as soon as I entered the street where it stood, by the glare of light from the windows, the sound of dance music, and the nondescript group of cabmen and linkmen, with their little train of idlers in attendance, assembled outside the door. It was evidently a very large party. I hesitated about going in.

My sensations were not those which fit a man for exchanging conventional civilities with perfect strangers; I felt that I showed outwardly the fever of joy and expectation within me. Could I preserve my assumed character of a mere friend of the family, in Margaret's presence?— and on this night too, of all others? It was far more probable that my behaviour, if I went to the party, would betray everything to everybody assembled. I determined to walk about in the neighbourhood of the house, until twelve o'clock; and then to go into the hall, and send up my **card** to Mr. Mannion, with a message on it, intimating that I was waiting below to accompany him to North Villa with Margaret.

I crossed the street, and looked up again at the house from the pavement opposite. Then lingered a little, listening to the music as it reached me through the windows, and imagining to myself Margaret's occupation at that moment. After this, I turned away; and set forth eastward on my walk, careless in which direction I traced my steps.

I felt little impatience, and no sense of fatigue; for in less than two hours more I knew that I should see my wife again. Until then, the present had no existence for me— I lived in the past and future. I wandered indifferently along lonely bye-streets, and crowded thoroughfares. Of all the sights which attend a night-walk in a great city, not one attracted my notice. Uninformed and unobservant, neither saddened nor startled, I passed through the glittering highways of London.* All sounds were silent to me save the love-music of my own thoughts; all sights had vanished before the bright form that moved through my bridal dream. Where was my world, at that moment? Narrowed to the cottage in the country which was to receive us on the morrow. Where were the beings in the world? All merged in one— Margaret.

Sometimes, my thoughts glided back, dreamily and voluptuously, to the day when I first met her. Sometimes, I recalled the summer evenings when we sat and read together out of the same book; and, once more, it was as if I breathed with the breath, and hoped with the hopes, and longed with the old longings of those days. But oftenest it was with the morrow that my mind was occupied. The first dream of all young men—the dream of living rapturously with the woman they love, in a secret retirement kept sacred from friends and from strangers alike, was now my dream; to be realised in a few hours, to be realised with my waking on the morning which was already at hand!

For the last quarter of an hour of my walk, I must have been unconsciously retracing my steps towards the house of Margaret's aunt. I came in sight of it again, just as the sound of the neighbouring church clocks, striking eleven, roused me from my abstraction. More cabs were in the street; more people were gathered about the door, by this time. Was all this bustle, the bustle of arrival or of departure? Was the party about to break up, at an hour when parties usually begin? I determined to go nearer to the house, and ascertain whether the music had ceased, or not.

I had approached close enough to hear the notes of the harp and pianoforte still sounding as gaily as ever, when the house-door was suddenly flung open for the departure of a lady and gentleman. The light from the hall-lamps fell full on their faces; and showed me Margaret and Mr. Mannion.

Going home already! An hour and a half before it was time to return! Why?

There could be but one reason. Margaret was thinking of me, and of what I should feel if I called at North Villa, and had to wait for her till past midnight. I ran forward to speak to them, as they descended the steps; but exactly at the same moment, my voice was overpowered, and my further progress barred, by a scuffle on the pavement among the people who stood between us. One man said that his pocket had been picked; others roared to him that they had caught the thief. There was a fight—the police came up— I was surrounded on all sides by a shouting, struggling mob that seemed to have gathered in an instant.

Before I could force myself out of the crowd, and escape into the road, Margaret and Mr. Mannion had hurried into a cab. I just saw the vehicle driving off rapidly, as I got free. An empty cab was standing near me—I jumped into it directly—and told the man to overtake them.   After having waited my time so patiently, to let a mere accident stop me from going home with them, as I had resolved, was not to be thought of for a moment. I was hot and angry, after my contest with the crowd ; and could have flogged on the miserable cab-horse with my own hand, rather than have failed in my purpose.

We were just getting closer behind them : I had just put my head out of the window to call to them, and to bid the man who was driving me, call, too—when their cab abruptly turned down a bye-street, in a direction exactly opposite to the direction which led to North Villa.

What did this mean ?   Why were they not going straight home ?

The cabman asked me whether he should not hail them before they got farther away from us ; frankly confessing, as he put the question, that his horse was nothing like equal to the pace of the horse ahead.   Mechanically, without assignable purpose or motive, I declined his offer, and told him simply to follow at any distance he could.   While the words passed my lips, a strange sensation stole over me : I seemed to be speaking as the mere mouthpiece of some other voice. From feeling hot, and moving about restlessly the moment before, I felt unaccountably cold, and sat still now.   What caused this ?

My cab stopped.   I looked out, and saw that the horse had fallen.   "We've lots of time, Sir," said the driver, as he coolly stepped off the box, "they are just pulling up further down the road."   I gave him some money, and got out immediately—determined to overtake them on foot.

It was a very lonely place—a colony of half-finished streets, and half-inhabited houses, which had grown up in the neighbourhood of a great railway station. I heard the fierce scream of the whistle, and the heaving, heavy throb of the engine starting on its journey, as I advanced along the gloomy Square in which I now found myself. The cab I had been following stood at a turning which led into a long street, occupied towards the farther end, by shops closed for the night, and at the end nearest me, apparently by private houses only. Margaret and Mr. Mannion hastily left the cab, and without looking either to the right or the left, hurried down the street. They stopped at the ninth house. I followed just in time to hear the door closed on them, and to count the number of doors intervening between that door and the Square.

The awful thrill of a suspicion which I hardly knew yet for what it really was, began to creep over me—to creep like a dead-cold touch crawling through and through me to the heart. I looked up at the house. It was an hotel—a neglected, deserted, dreary-looking building.* Still acting mechanically; still with no definite impulse that I could recognise, even if I felt it, except the instinctive resolution to follow them into the house, as I had already followed them through the street—I walked up to the door, and rang the bell.

It was answered by a waiter—a mere lad. As the light in the passage fell on my face, he paused in the act of addressing me, and drew back a few steps. Without stopping for any explanations, I closed the door behind me, and said to him at once:

"A lady and gentleman came into this hotel a little while ago."

"What may your business be?"—He hesitated, and added in an altered tone, "I mean, what may you want with them, Sir?"

"I want you to take me where I can hear their voices, and I want nothing more. Here's a sovereign for you, if you do what I ask."

His eyes fastened covetously on the gold, as I held it before them. He retired a few steps on tiptoe, and listened at the end of the passage. I heard nothing but the thick, rapid beating of my own heart. He came back, muttering to himself: "Master's safe at supper down stairs —I'll risk it! You'll promise to go away directly," he added, whispering to me, "and not disturb the house? We are quiet people here, and can't have anything like a disturbance. Just say at once, will you promise to step soft, and not speak a word?"

"I promise."

"This way then, Sir—and mind you don't forget to step soft."

A strange coldness and stillness, an icy insensibility, a dream-sensation of being impelled by some hidden, irresistible agency, possessed me, as I followed him upstairs. He showed me softly into an empty room; pointed to one of the walls, whispering, "It's only boards papered over—" and then waited, keeping his eyes anxiously and steadily fixed upon all my movements.

I listened; and through the thin partition, I heard voices —*her* voice, and *his* voice. *I heard and I knew*—knew my degradation in all its infamy, knew my wrongs in all their nameless horror. He was exulting in the patience and secrecy which had brought success to the foul plot, foully hidden for months on months; foully hidden until the very day before I was to have claimed as my wife, a wretch as guilty as himself!

I could neither move nor breathe. The blood surged and heaved upward to my brain; my heart strained and writhed in anguish; the life within me raged and tore to get free. Whole years of the direst mental and bodily agony were concentrated in that one moment of helpless, motionless torment. I never lost the consciousness of suffering. I heard the waiter say, under his breath, "My God! he's dying." I felt him loosen my cravat—I knew that he dashed cold water over me; dragged me out of the room;

and, opening a window on the landing, held me firmly where the night-air blew upon my face. I knew all this; and knew when the paroxysm passed, and nothing remained of it, but a shivering helplessness in every limb.

Erelong, the power of thinking began to return to me by degrees.

Misery, and shame, and horror, and a vain yearning to hide myself from all human eyes, and weep out my life in secret, overcame me. Then, these subsided; and ONE THOUGHT slowly arose in their stead—arose, and cast down before it every obstacle of conscience, every principle of education, every care for the future, every remembrance of the past, every weakening influence of present misery, every repressing tie of family and home, every anxiety for good fame in this life, and every idea of the next that was to come. Before the fell poison of that Thought, all other thoughts—good or evil—died. As it spoke secretly within me, I felt my bodily strength coming back; a quick vigour leapt hotly through my frame. I turned, and looked round towards the room we had just left—my mind was looking at the room beyond it, the room *they* were in.

The waiter was still standing by my side, watching me intently. He suddenly started back; and, with pale face and staring eyes, pointed down the stairs.

"You go," he whispered, "go directly! You're well now—I'm afraid to have you here any longer. I saw your look, your horrid look at that room! You've heard what you wanted for your money—go at once; or, if I lose my place for it, I'll call out Murder, and raise the house. And mind this: as true as God's in heaven, I'll warn them both before they go outside our door!"

Hearing, but not heeding him, I left the house. No voice that ever spoke, could have called me back from the course on which I was now bound. The waiter watched me vigilantly from the door, as I went out. Seeing this, I made a circuit, before I returned to the spot where, as I had suspected, the cab they had ridden in was still waiting for them.

The driver was asleep inside. I awoke him; told him I had been sent to say that he was not wanted again that night: and secured his ready departure, by at once paying him on his own terms. He drove off; and the first obstacle on the fatal path which I had resolved to tread unopposed, was now removed.

As the cab disappeared from my sight, I looked up at the sky. It was growing very dark. The ragged black clouds, fantastically parted from each other in island shapes over the whole surface of the heavens, were fast drawing together into one huge, formless, lowering mass, and had already hidden the moon for good. I went back to the street, and stationed myself in the pitch darkness of a passage which led down a mews, situated exactly opposite to the hotel.

In the silence and obscurity, in the sudden pause of action while I now waited and watched, my Thought rose to my lips, and my speech mechanically formed it into words. I whispered softly to myself: *I will kill him when he comes out.* My mind never swerved for an instant from this thought—never swerved towards myself; never swerved towards *her.* Grief was numbed at my heart; and the consciousness of my own misery was numbed with grief. Death chills all before it—and Death and my Thought were one.

Once, while I stood on the watch, a sharp agony of suspense tried me fiercely.

Just as I had calculated that the time was come which would force them to depart, in order to return to North Villa by the appointed hour, I heard the slow, heavy, regular tramp of a footstep advancing along the street. It was the policeman of the district going his round. As he approached the entrance to the mews he paused, yawned, stretched his arms, and began to whistle a tune. If Mannion should come out while he was there! My blood seemed to stagnate on its course, while I thought that this might well happen. Suddenly, the man ceased whistling, looked steadily up and down the street, and tried the door of a house near him—advanced a few steps—then paused again, and tried another door—then muttered to himself, in drowsy tones—"I've seen all safe here already: it's the other street I forgot just now." He turned, and retraced his way. I fixed my aching eyes vigilantly on the hotel, while I heard the sound of his footsteps grow fainter and fainter in the distance. It ceased altogether; and still there was no change—still the man whose life I was waiting for, never appeared.

Ten minutes after this, so far as I can guess, the door opened ; and I heard Mannion's voice, and the voice of the lad who had let me in. "Look about you before you go out," said the waiter, speaking in the passage; "the street's not safe for you." Disbelieving, or affecting to disbelieve, what he heard, Mannion interrupted the waiter angrily ; and endeavoured to reassure his companion in guilt, by asserting that the warning was nothing but an attempt to extort money by way of reward. The man retorted sulkily, that he cared nothing for the gentleman's money, or the gentleman either. Immediately afterwards an inner door in the house banged violently ; and I knew that Mannion had been left to his fate.

There was a momentary silence ; and then I heard him tell his accomplice that he would go alone to look for the cab, and that she had better close the door and wait quietly in the passage till he came back. This was done. He walked out into the street. It was after twelve o'clock. No sound of a strange footfall was audible—no soul was at hand to witness, and prevent. the coming struggle. His life was mine. His death followed him as fast as my feet followed, while I was now walking on his track.

He looked up and down, from the entrance to the street, for the cab. Then, seeing that it was gone, he hastily turned back. At that instant I met him face to face. Before a word could be spoken, even before a look could be exchanged, my hands were on his throat.

He was a taller and heavier man than I was; and struggled with me, knowing that he was struggling for his life. He never shook my grasp on him for a moment; but he dragged me out into the road—dragged me away eight or ten yards from the street. The heavy gasps of approaching suffocation beat thick on my forehead from his open mouth : he swerved to and fro furiously, from side to side; and struck at me, swinging his clenched fists high above his head. I stood firm, and held him away at arm's length. As I dug my feet into the ground to steady myself, I heard the crunching of stones—the road had been newly mended with granite. Instantly, a savage purpose goaded into fury the deadly resolution by which I was possessed. I shifted my hold to the back of his neck, and the collar of his coat, and hurled him, with the whole impetus of the raging strength that was let loose in me, face downwards, on to the stones.

In the mad triumph of that moment, I had already stooped towards him, as he lay insensible beneath me, to lift him again, and beat out of him, on the granite, not life only, but the semblance of humanity as well; when, in the blank stillness that followed the struggle, I heard the door of the hotel in the street open once more. I left him directly, and ran back from the square—I knew not with what motive, or what idea—to the spot.

On the steps of the house, on the threshold of that accursed place, stood the woman whom God's minister had given to me in the sight of God, as my wife.

One long pang of shame and despair shot through my heart as I looked at her, and tortured out of its trance the spirit within me. Thousands on thousands of thoughts seemed to be whirling in the wildest confusion through and through my brain—thoughts, whose track was a track of fire—thoughts that struck me with a hellish torment of dumbness, at the very time when I would have purchased with my life the power of a moment's speech. Voiceless and tearless, I went up to her, and took her by the arm, and drew her away from the house. There was some vague purpose in me, as I did this, of never quitting my hold of her, never letting her stir from me by so much as an inch, until I had spoken certain words to her. What words they were, and when I should utter them, I could not tell.

The cry for mercy was on her lips, but the instant our eyes met, it died away in long, low, hysterical moanings. Her cheeks were ghastly, her features were rigid, her eyes glared like an idiot's; guilt and terror had made her hideous to look upon already.

I drew her onward a few paces towards the Square. Then I stopped, remembering the body that lay face downwards on the road. The savage strength of a few moments before, had left me from the time when I first saw her. I now reeled where I stood, from sheer physical weakness. The sound of her pantings and shudderings, of her abject inarticulate murmurings for mercy, struck me with a supernatural terror. My fingers trembled round her arm, the perspiration dripped down my face, like rain; I caught at the railings by my side, to keep myself from falling. As I did so, she snatched her arm from my grasp, as easily as if I had been a child; and, with a cry for help, fled towards the further end of the street.

Still, the strange instinct of never losing hold of her, influenced me. I followed, staggering like a drunken man. In a moment, she was out of my reach; in another, out of my sight. I went on, nevertheless; on, and on, and on, I knew not whither. I lost all ideas of time and distance. Sometimes I went round and round the same streets, over and over again. Sometimes I hurried in one direction, straight forward. Wherever I went, it seemed to me that she was still just before; that *her* track and *my* track were one; that I had just lost my hold of her, and that she was just starting on her flight.

I remember passing two men in this way, in some great thoroughfare. They both stopped, turned, and walked a few steps after me. One laughed at me, as a drunkard. The other, in serious tones, told him to be silent; for I was not drunk, but mad—he had seen my face as I passed under a gas-lamp, and he knew that I was mad.

" MAD !"—that word, as I heard it, rang after me like a voice of judgment. " MAD !"—a fear had come over me, which, in all its frightful complication, was expressed by that one word—a fear which, to the man who suffers it, is worse even than the fear of death; which no human language ever has conveyed, or ever will convey, in all its horrible reality, to others. I had pressed onward, hitherto, because I saw a vision that led me after it—a beckoning shadow, ahead, darker even than the night darkness. I still pressed on, now; but only because I was afraid to stop.

I know not how far I had gone, when my strength utterly failed me, and I sank down helpless, in a lonely place where the houses were few and scattered, and trees and fields were dimly discernible in the obscurity beyond. I hid my face in my hands, and tried to assure myself that I was still in possession of my senses. I strove hard to separate my thoughts; to distinguish between my recollections; to extricate from the confusion within me any one idea, no matter what—and I could not do it. In that awful struggle for the mastery over my own mind, all that had passed, all the horror of that horrible night, became as nothing to me. I raised myself, and looked up again, and tried to steady my reason by the simplest means—even by endeavouring to count all the houses within sight. The darkness bewildered me. Darkness?—*Was* it dark? or was day breaking yonder, far away in the murky eastern sky? Did I know what I saw? Did I see the same thing for a few moments together? What was this under me? Grass? yes! cold, soft, dewy grass. I bent down my forehead upon it, and tried, for the last time, to steady my faculties by praying; tried if I could utter the prayer which I had known and repeated every day from childhood—the Lord's Prayer. The Divine Words came not at my call—no! not one of them, from the beginning to the end! I started up on my knees. A blaze of lurid sunshine flashed before my eyes; a hell-blaze of brightness, with fiends by millions, raining down out of it on my head; then a rayless darkness—the darkness of the blind—then God's mercy at last—the mercy of utter oblivion.

*   *   *   *   *

When I recovered my consciousness, I was lying on the couch in my own study. My father was supporting me on the pillow; the doctor had his fingers on my pulse; and a policeman was telling them where he had found me, and how he had brought me home.

PART III.

I.

WHEN the blind are operated on for the restoration of sight, the same succouring hand which has opened to them the visible world, immediately shuts out the bright prospect again, for a time. A bandage is passed over the eyes, lest in the first tenderness of the recovered sense, it should be fatally affected by the sudden transition from darkness to light. But between the awful blank of total privation of vision, and the temporary blank of vision merely veiled, there lies the widest difference. In the moment of their restoration, the blind have had one glimpse of light, flashing on them in an overpowering gleam of brightness, which the thickest, closest veiling cannot extinguish. The new darkness is not like the void darkness of old; it is filled with changing visions of brilliant colours and ever-varying forms, rising, falling, whirling hither and thither with every second. Even when the handkerchief is passed over them, the once sightless eyes, though bandaged fast, are yet not blinded as they were before.

It was so with my mental vision. After the utter oblivion and darkness of a deep swoon, consciousness flashed like light on my mind, when I found myself in my father's presence, and in my own home. But, almost at the very moment when I first awakened to the bewildering influence of that sight, a new darkness fell upon my faculties—a darkness, this time, which was not utter oblivion; a peopled darkness, like that which the bandage casts over the opened eyes of the blind.

I had sensations, I had thoughts, I had visions, now—but they all acted in the frightful self-concentration of delirium. The lapse of time, the march of events, the alternation of day and night, the persons who moved about me, the words they spoke, the offices of kindness they did for me—all these were annihilated from the period when I closed my eyes again, after having opened them for an instant on my father, in my own study.

My first sensation (how soon it came after I had been brought home, I know not) was of a terrible heat; a steady, blazing heat, which seemed to have shrivelled and burnt up the whole of the little world around me, and to have left me alone to suffer, but never to consume in it. After this, came a quick, restless, unintermittent toiling of obscure thought, ever in the same darkened sphere, ever on the same impenetrable subject, ever failing to reach some distant and visionary result. It was as if something were imprisoned in my mind, and moving always to and fro in it—moving, but never getting free.

Soon, these thoughts began to take a form that I could recognise.

In the clinging heat and fierce seething fever, to which neither waking nor sleeping brought a breath of freshness or a dream of change, I began to act my part over again, in the events that had passed, but in a strangely altered character. Now, instead of placing implicit trust in others, as I had done; instead of failing to discover a significance and a warning in each circumstance as it arose, I was suspicious from the first—suspicious of Margaret, of her father, of her mother, of Mannion, of the very servants in the house. In the hideous phantasmagoria of my own calamity on which I now looked, my position was reversed. Every event of the

doomed year of my probation was revived. But the doom
itself, the night-scene of horror through which I had passed,
had utterly vanished from my memory. This lost recollection, it was the one unending toil of my wandering mind to
recover, and I never got it back. None who have not suffered as I suffered then, can imagine with what a burning
rage of determination I followed past events in my delirium,
one by one, for days and nights together,—followed, to get
to the end which I knew was beyond, but which I never
could see, not even by glimpses, for a moment at a time.

However my visions might alter in their course of succes-
sion, they always began with the night when Mannion returned from the continent to North Villa. I stood again
in the drawing-room; I saw him enter; I marked the slight
confusion of Margaret; and instantly doubted her. I
noticed his unwillingness to meet her eye or mine; I looked
on the sinister stillness of his face; and suspected him.
From that moment, love vanished, and hatred came in its
place. I began to watch; to garner up slight circumstances
which confirmed my suspicions; to wait craftily for the
day when I should discover, judge, and punish them both—
the day of disclosure and retribution that never came.

Sometimes, I was again with Mannion, in his house, on
the night of the storm. I detected in every word he spoke
an artful lure to trap me into trusting him as my second
father, more than as my friend. I heard in the tempest-
sounds which mysteriously interrupted, or mingled with, my
answers, voices supernaturally warning me of my enemy,
each time that I spoke to him. I saw once more the hideous smile of triumph on his face, as I took leave of him on
the doorstep : and saw it, this time, not as an illusion produced by a flash of lightning, but as a frightful reality
which the lightning disclosed.

Sometimes, I was again in the garden at North Villa
accidentally overhearing the conversation between Margaret

and her mother—overhearing what deceit she was willing
to commit, for the sake of getting a new dress—then going
into the room, and seeing her assume her usual manner on
meeting me, as if no such words as I had listened to but
the moment before, had ever proceeded from her lips. Or,
I saw her on that other morning, when, to revenge the
death of her bird, she would have killed with her own hand
the one pet companion that her sick mother possessed.
Now, no generous, trusting love blinded me to the real
meaning of such events as these. Now, instead of regarding them as little weaknesses of beauty, and little errors of
youth, I saw them as timely warnings, which bade me remember when the day of my vengeance came, that in the
contriving of the iniquity on which they were both bent,
the woman had been as vile as the man.

Sometimes, I was once more on my way to North Villa,
after my week's absence at our country house. I saw again
the change in Margaret since I had left her—the paleness,
the restlessness, the appearance of agitation. I took the
hand of Mannion, and started as I felt its deadly coldness,
and remarked the strange alteration in his manner. When
they accounted for these changes by telling me that both
had been ill, in different ways, since my departure, I detected
the miserable lie at once; I knew that an evil advantage
had been taken of my absence; that the plot against me
was fast advancing towards consummation: and that, at the
sight of their victim, even the two wretches who were com-
passing my dishonour could not repress all outward mani-
festation of their guilt.

Sometimes, the figure of Mrs. Sherwin appeared to me,
wan and weary, and mournful with a ghostly mournfulness.
Again I watched her, and listened to her; but now with
eager curiosity, with breathless attention. Once more, I saw
her shudder when Mannion's cold eyes turned on her face—
I marked the anxious, imploring look that she cast on Mar

garet and on me—I heard her confused, unwilling answer,
when I inquired the cause of her dislike of the man in
whom her husband placed the most implicit trust—I
listened to her abrupt, inexplicable injunction to "watch
continually over my wife, and keep bad people from her."
All these different circumstances occurred again as vividly
as in the reality; but I did not now account for them, as I
had once accounted for them, by convincing myself that
Mrs. Sherwin's mind was wandering, and that her bodily
sufferings had affected her intellect. I saw immediately,
that she suspected Mannion, and dared not openly confess
her suspicions; I saw, that in the stillness, and abandonment, and self-concentration of her neglected life, she had
been watching more vigilantly than others had watched;
I detected in every one of her despised gestures, and looks,
and halting words, the same concealed warning ever lying
beneath the surface; I knew they had not succeeded in
deceiving *her;* I was determined they should not succeed
in deceiving *me.*

It was oftenest at this point, that my restless memory
recoiled before the impenetrable darkness which forbade it
to see further—to see on to the last evening, to the fatal
night. It was oftenest at this point, that I toiled and struggled back, over and over again, to seek once more the lost
events of the End, through the events of the Beginning.
How often my wandering thoughts thus incessantly and
desperately traced and retraced their way over their own
fever track, I cannot tell : but there came a time when they
suddenly ceased to torment me; when the heavy burden
that was on my mind fell off; when a sudden strength and
fury possessed me, and I plunged down through a vast
darkness into a world whose daylight was all radiant flame.
Giant phantoms mustered by millions, flashing white as
lightning in the ruddy air. They rushed on me with hurri-
cane speed; their wings fanned me with fiery breezes; and

the echo of their thunder-music was like the groaning and rending of an earthquake, as they tore me away with them on their whirlwind course.

Away! to a City of Palaces, to measureless halls, and arches, and domes, soaring one above another, till their flashing ruby summits are lost in the burning void, high overhead. On! through and through these mountain-piles, into countless, limitless corridors, reared on pillars lurid and rosy as molten lava. Far down the corridors rise visions of flying phantoms, ever at the same distance before us—their raving voices clanging like the hammers of a thousand forges. Still on and on; faster and faster, for days, years, centuries together, till there comes, stealing slowly forward to meet us, a shadow—a vast, stealthy, gliding shadow—the first darkness that has ever been shed over that world of blazing light! It comes nearer—nearer and nearer softly, till it touches the front ranks of our phantom troop. Then in an instant, our rushing progress is checked: the thunder-music of our wild march stops; the raving voices of the spectres ahead, cease; a horror of blank stillness is all about us— and as the shadow creeps onward and onward, until we are enveloped in it from front to rear, we shiver with icy cold under the fiery air and amid the lurid lava pillars which hem us in on either side.

A silence, like no silence ever known on earth; a darkening of the shadow, blacker than the blackest night in the thickest wood—a pause—then, a sound as of the heavy air being cleft asunder; and then, an apparition of two figures coming on out of the shadow—two monsters stretching forth their gnarled yellow talons to grasp at us; leaving on their track a green decay, oozing and shining with a sickly light. Beyond and around me, as I stood in the midst of them, the phantom troop dropped into formless masses, while the monsters advanced. They came close to me; and I alone, of all the myriads around, changed not at their approach. Each laid a talon on my shoulder—each raised a veil which was one hideous net-work of twining worms. I saw through the ghastly corruption of their faces the look that told me who they were—the monstrous iniquities incarnate in monstrous forms ; the fiend-souls made visible in fiend-shapes—Margaret and Mannion !

A moment more ! and I was alone with those two. Not a wreck of the phantom-multitude remained ; the towering city, the gleaming corridors, the fire-bright radiance had vanished. We stood on a wilderness—a still, black lake of dead waters was before us ; a white, faint, misty light shone on us. Outspread over the noisome ground lay the ruins of a house, rooted up and overthrown to its foundations. The demon figures, still watching on either side of me, drew me slowly forward to the fallen stones, and pointed to two dead bodies lying among them.

My father !—my sister !—both cold and still, and whiter than the white light that showed them to me. The demons at my side stretched out their crooked talons, and forbade me to kneel before my father, or to kiss Clara's wan face, before I went to torment. They struck me motionless where I stood*—and unveiled their hideous faces once more, jeering at me in triumph. Anon, the lake of black waters heaved up and overflowed, and noiselessly sucked us away into its central depths—depths that were endless ; depths of rayless darkness, in which we slowly eddied round and round, deeper and deeper down at every turn. I felt the bodies of my father and my sister touching me in cold contact : I stretched out my arms to clasp them and sink with them ; and the demon pair glided between us, and separated me from them. This vain striving to join myself to my dead kindred when we touched each other in the slow, endless whirlpool, ever continued and was ever frustrated in the same way. Still we sank apart, down the black gulphs of the lake ; still there was no light, no sound, no change, no pause of repose—and this was eternity : the eternity of Hell !

*　　　*　　　*　　　*　　　*

Such was one dream-vision out of many that I saw. It must have been at this time that men were set to watch me day and night (as I afterwards heard), in order that I might be held down in my bed, when a paroxysm of convulsive strength made me dangerous to myself and to all about me. The period too when the doctors announced that the fever had seized on my brain, and was getting the better of their skill, must have been *this* period.

But though they gave up my life as lost, I was not to die. There came a time, at last, when the gnawing fever lost its hold; and I awoke faintly one morning to a new exist-ence—to a life frail and helpless as the life of a new-born babe.

I was too weak to move, to speak, to open my eyes, to exert in the smallest degree any one faculty, bodily or men-tal, that I possessed. The first sense of which I regained the use, was the sense of hearing; and the first sound that I recognised, was of a light footstep which mysteri-ously approached, paused, and then retired again gently outside my door. The hearing of this sound was my first pleasure, the waiting for its repetition my first source of happy expectation, since I had been ill. Once more the footsteps approached—paused a moment—then seemed to retire as before—then returned slowly. A sigh, very faint and trembling ; a whisper of which I could not yet distin-guish the import, caught my ear—and after that, there was silence. Still I waited (oh, how happily and calmly !) to hear the whisper soon repeated, and to hear it better when it next came. Ere long, for the third time, the footsteps advanced, and the whispering accents sounded again. I could now hear that they pronounced my name—once, twice, three times—very softly and imploringly, as if to beg the answer which I was still too weak to give. But I knew the voice: I knew it was Clara's. Long after it had ceased, the whisper lingered gently on my ear, like a lullaby that alternately soothed me to slumber, and welcomed me to wakefulness. It seemed to be thrilling through my frame with a tender, reviving influence—the same influence which the sunshine had, weeks afterwards, when I enjoyed it for the first time out of doors.

The next sound that came to me was audible in my room; audible sometimes, close at my pillow. It was the simplest sound imaginable—nothing but the soft rustling of a woman's dress. And yet, I heard in it innumerable harmonies, sweet changes, and pauses minute beyond all definition. I could only open my eyes for a minute at a time, and even then, could not fix them steadily on anything; but I knew that the rustling dress was Clara's; and fresh sensations seemed to throng upon me, as I listened to the sound which told me that she was in the room. I felt the soft summer air on my face; I enjoyed the sweet scent of flowers, wafted on that air; and once, when my door was left open for a moment, the twittering of birds in the aviary down stairs, rang with exquisite clearness and sweetness on my ear. It was thus that my faculties strengthened, hour by hour, always in the same gradual way, from the time when I first heard the footstep and the whisper outside my chamber-door.

One evening I awoke from a cool, dreamless sleep; and, seeing Clara sitting by my bedside, faintly uttered her name, and moved my wasted hand to take hers. As I saw the calm, familiar face bending over me; the anxious eyes looking tenderly and lovingly into mine—as the last melancholy glory of sunset hovered on my bed, and the air, sinking already into its twilight repose, came softly and more softly into the room—as my sister took me in her arms, and raising me on my weary pillow, bade me for *her* sake lie hushed and patient a little longer—tne memory of the ruin and the shame that had overwhelmed me; the memory of my love that had become an infamy; and of my brief year's hope miserably fulfilled by a life of despair, swelled darkly over my heart. The red, retiring rays of sunset just lingered at that moment on my face. Clara knelt down by my pillow, and held up her handkerchief to shade my eyes—" God has given you back to us, Basil," she whispered, "to make us happier than ever." As she spoke, the springs of the grief so long pent up within me were loosened; hot tears dropped heavily and quickly from my eyes; and I wept for the first time since the night of horror which had stretched me where I now lay—wept in my sister's arms, at that quiet evening hour, for the lost honour, the lost hope, the lost happiness that had gone from me for ever in my youth!

II.

Darkly and wearily the days of my recovery went on. After that first outburst of sorrow on the evening when I recognised my sister, and murmured her name as she sat by my side, there sank over all my faculties a dull, heavy trance of mental pain.

I dare not describe what remembrances of the guilty woman who had deceived and ruined me, now gnawed unceasingly and poisonously at my heart. My bodily strength feebly revived; but my mental energies never showed a sign of recovering with them. My father's considerate forbearance, Clara's sorrowful reserve in touching on the subject of my long illness, or of the wild words which had escaped me in my delirium, mutely and gently warned me that the time was come when I owed the tardy atonement of confession to the family that I had disgraced; and still, I had no courage to speak, no resolution to endure. The

great misery of the past, shut out from me the present and
the future alike—every active power of my mind seemed to
be destroyed hopelessly and for ever.

There were moments—most often at the early morning
hours, while the heaviness of the night's sleep still hung
over me in my wakefulness—when I could hardly realise
the calamity which had overwhelmed me; when it seemed
that I must have dreamt, during the night, of scenes of
crime and woe and heavy trial which had never actually
taken place.* What was the secret of the terrible influence
which—let her even be the vilest of the vile—Mannion
must have possessed over Margaret Sherwin, to induce her
to sacrifice me to him? Even the crime itself was not more
hideous and more incredible than the mystery in which its
evil motives, and the manner of its evil ripening, were still
impenetrably veiled.

Mannion! It was a strange result of the mental malady
under which I suffered, that, though the thought of Mannion was now inextricably connected with every thought of
Margaret, I never once asked myself, or had an idea of asking myself, for days together, after my convalescence, what
had been the issue of our struggle, for *him*. In the despair of
first awakening to a perfect sense of the calamity which had
been hurled on me from the hand of my wife—in the misery
of first clearly connecting together, after the wanderings of
delirium, the Margaret to whom with my hand I had given
all my heart, with the Margaret who had trampled on the
gift and ruined the giver—all minor thoughts and minor
feelings, all motives of revengeful curiosity or of personal
apprehension were suppressed. And yet, the time was soon
to arrive when that lost thought of inquiry into Mannion's
fate, was to become the one master-thought that possessed
me—the thought that gave back its vigilance to my intellect,
and its manhood to my heart.

One evening I was sitting alone in my room. My father

had taken Clara out for a little air and exercise, and the servant had gone away at my own desire. It was in this quiet and solitude, when the darkness was fast approaching, when the view from my window was at its loneliest, when my mind was growing listless and confused as the weary day wore out—it was exactly at this time that the thought suddenly and mysteriously flashed across me: Had Mannion been taken up from the stones on which I had hurled him, a living man or a dead?

I instinctively started to my feet with something of the vigour of my former health; repeating the question to myself, and feeling, as I unconsciously murmured aloud the few words which expressed it, that my life had purposes and duties, trials and achievements, which were yet to be fulfilled. How could I instantly solve the momentous doubt which had now, for the first time, crossed my mind?

One moment I paused in eager consideration—the next, I descended to the library. A daily newspaper was kept there, filed for reference. I might possibly decide the fatal question in a few moments by consulting it. In my burning anxiety and impatience I could hardly handle the leaves or see the letters, as I tried to turn back to the right date— the day (oh anguish of remembrance!) on which I was to have claimed Margaret Sherwin as my wife!

At last, I found the number I desired; but the closely-printed columns swam before me as I looked at them. A glass of water stood on a table near me—I dipped my handkerchief in it, and cooled my throbbing eyes. The destiny of my future life might be decided by the discovery I was now about to make!

I locked the door to guard against all intrusion, and then returned to my task—returned to my momentous search— slowly tracing my way through the paper, paragraph by paragraph, column by column.

On the last page, and close to the end, I read these lines :

"MYSTERIOUS OCCURRENCE.

"About one o'clock this morning, a gentleman was discovered lying on his face in the middle of the road, in
Westwood Square, by the policeman on duty. The unfortunate man was to all appearance dead. He had fallen on
a part of the road which had been recently macadamised*;
and his face, we are informed, is frightfully mutilated by
contact with the granite. The policeman conveyed him to
the neighbouring hospital,* where it was discovered that he
was still alive, and the promptest attentions were immediately paid him. We understand that the surgeon in attendance considers it absolutely impossible that he could have
been injured as he was, except by having been violently
thrown down on his face, either by a vehicle driven at a
furious rate, or by a savage attack from some person or persons unknown. In the latter case, robbery could not have
been the motive ; for the unfortunate man's watch, purse,
and ring were all found about him. No cards of address
or letters of any kind were discovered in his pockets, and
his linen and handkerchief were only marked with the letter
M. He was dressed in evening costume—entirely in black.
After what has been already said about the injuries to his
face, any recognisable personal description of him is, for the
present, unfortunately out of the question. We wait with
much anxiety to gain some further insight into this mysterious affair, when the sufferer is restored to consciousness.
The last particulars which our reporter was able to collect
at the hospital were, that the surgeon expected to save his
patient's life, and the sight of one of his eyes. The sight
of the other is understood to be entirely destroyed."

With sensations of horror which I could not then, and
cannot now analyse, I turned to the next day's paper ; but

found in it no further reference to the object of my search. In the number for the day after, however, the subject was resumed in these words:

"The mystery of the accident in Westwood Square thickens. The sufferer is restored to consciousness; he is perfectly competent to hear and understand what is said to him, and is able to articulate, but not very plainly, and only for a moment or so, at a time. The authorities at the hospital anticipated, as we did, that, on the patient's regaining his senses, some information of the manner in which the terrible accident from which he is suffering was caused, would be obtained from him. But, to the astonishment of every one, he positively refuses to answer any questions as to the circumstances under which his frightful injuries were inflicted. With the same unaccountable secrecy, he declines to tell his name, his place of abode, or the names of any friends to whom notice of his situation might be communicated. It is quite in vain to press him for any reason for this extraordinary course of conduct—he appears to be a man of very unusual firmness of character; and his refusal to explain himself in any way, is evidently no mere caprice of the moment. All this leads to the conjecture that the injuries he has sustained were inflicted on him from some motive of private vengeance; and that certain persons are concerned in this disgraceful affair, whom he is unwilling to expose to public odium, for some secret reason which it is impossible to guess at. We understand that he bears the severe pain consequent upon his situation, in such a manner as to astonish every person about him—no agony draws from him a word or a sigh. He displayed no emotion even when the surgeons informed him that the sight of one of his eyes was hopelessly destroyed; and merely asked to be supplied with writing materials as soon as he could see to use them, when he was told that the sight of the other would be saved.

He further added, we are informed, that he was in a position to reward the hospital authorities for any trouble he gave, by making a present to the funds of the charity, as soon as he should be discharged as cured. His coolness in the midst of sufferings which would deprive most other men of all power of thinking or speaking, is as remarkable as his unflinching secrecy—a secrecy which, for the present at least, we cannot hope to penetrate."

I closed the newspaper. Even then, a vague forewarning of what Mannion's inexplicable reserve boded towards me, crossed my mind. There was yet more difficulty, danger, and horror to be faced, than I had hitherto confronted. The slough of degradation and misery into which I had fallen, had its worst perils yet in store for me.

As I became impressed by this conviction, the enervating remembrance of the wickedness to which I had been sacrificed, grew weaker in its influence over me; the bitter tears that I had shed in secret for so many days past, dried sternly at their sources; and I felt the power to endure and to resist coming back to me with my sense of the coming strife. On leaving the library, I ascended again to my own room. In a basket, on my table, lay several unopened letters, which had arrived for me during my illness. There were two which I at once suspected, in hastily turning over the collection, might be all-important in enlightening me on the vile subject of Mannion's female accomplice. The addresses of both these letters were in Mr. Sherwin's handwriting. The first that I opened was dated nearly a month back, and ran thus:

"North Villa, Hollyoake Square.

"DEAR SIR,

"With agonised feelings which no one but a parent, and I will add, an affectionate parent, can possibly form an idea of, I address you on the subject of the act of atrocity com-

mitted by that perjured villain, Mannion. You will find
that I and my innocent daughter have been, like you, vic-
tims of the most devilish deceit that ever was practised on
respectable and unsuspecting people.

"Let me ask you, Sir, to imagine the state of my feelings on the night of that most unfortunate party, when I
saw my beloved Margaret, instead of coming home quietly
as usual, rush into the room in a state bordering on distrac-
tion, with a tale the most horrible that ever was addressed
to a father's ears. The double-faced villain (I really can't
mention his name again) had, I blush to acknowledge, attempted to take advantage of her innocence and confidence
—of all our innocences and confidences, I may say*—but my
dear Margaret showed a virtuous courage beyond her years,
the natural result of the pious principles and the moral
bringing up which I have given her from her cradle. Need
I say what was the upshot? Virtue triumphed, as virtue
always does, and the villain left her to herself. It was when
she was approaching the door-step to fly to the bosom of
her home that, I am given to understand, you, by a most
remarkable accident, met her. As a man of the world,
you will easily conceive what must have been the feelings
of a young female, under such peculiar and shocking circumstances. Besides this, your manner, as I am informed,
was so terrrifying and extraordinary, and my poor Margaret
felt so strongly that deceitful appearances might be against
her, that she lost all heart, and fled at once, as I said before,
to the bosom of her home.

"She is still in a very nervous and unhappy state; she
fears that you may be too ready to believe appearances;
but I know better. Her explanation will be enough for
you, as it was for me. We may have our little differences
on minor topics, but we have both the same manly confidence, I am sure—you in your wife, and me in my daughter.

"I called at your worthy father's mansion, to have a fuller

explanation with you than I can give here, the morning after this to-all-parties-most-distressing occurrence happened: and was then informed of your serious illness, for which pray accept my best condolences. The next thing I thought of doing was to write to your respected father, requesting a private interview. But on maturer consideration, I thought it perhaps slightly injudicious to take such a step, while you, as the principal party concerned, were ill in bed, and not able to come forward and back me. I was anxious, you will observe, to act for your interests, as well as the interests of my darling girl—of course, knowing at the same time that I had the marriage certificate in my possession, if needed as a proof, and supposing I was driven to extremities and obliged to take my own course in the matter. But, as I said before, I have a fatherly and friendly confidence in your feeling as convinced of the spotless innocence of my child as I do. So will write no more on this head.

" Having determined, as best under all circumstances, to wait till your illness was over, I have kept my dear Margaret in strict retirement at home (which, as she is your wife, you will acknowledge I had no obligation to do), until you were well enough to come forward and do her justice before her family and yours. I have not omitted to make almost daily inquiries after you, up to the time of penning these lines, and shall continue so to do until your convalescence, which I sincerely hope may be speedily at hand. I am unfortunately obliged to ask that our first interview, when you are able to see me and my daughter, may not take place at North Villa, but at some other place, any you like to fix on. The fact is, my wife, whose wretched health has been a trouble and annoyance to us for years past, has now, I grieve to say, under pressure of this sad misfortune, quite lost her reason. I am sorry to say that she would be capable of interrupting us here, in a most undesirable manner

to all parties, and therefore request that our first happy
meeting may not take place at my house.

"Trusting that this letter will quite remove all unpleasant feelings from your mind, and that I shall hear from you
soon, on your much-to-be-desired recovery,

"I remain, dear Sir,

"Your faithful, obedient servant,

"STEPHEN SHERWIN.

"P.S.—I have not been able to find out where that scoundrel, Mannion, has betaken himself to; but if you should
know, or suspect, I wish to tell you, as a proof that my in-
dignation at his villany is as great as yours, that I am ready
and anxious to pursue him with the utmost rigour of the
law, if law can only reach him—paying out of my own
pocket all expenses of punishing him and breaking him for
the rest of his life, if I go through every court in the
country to do it!—S. S."

Hurriedly as I read over this wretched and revolting
letter, I detected immediately how the new plot had been
framed to keep me still deceived; to heap wrong after wrong
on me with the same impunity. She was not aware that
I had followed her into the house, and had heard all from
her voice and Mannion's—she believed that I was still ignorant of everything, until we met at the door-step; and in
this conviction she had forged the miserable lie which her
father's hand had written down. Did he really believe it,
or was he writing as her accomplice? It was not worth
while to inquire: the worst and darkest discovery which it
concerned me to make, had already proclaimed itself—she
was a liar and a hypocrite to the very last!

And it was this woman's lightest glance which had once
been to me as the star that my life looked to!—it was for
this woman that I had practised a deceit on my family

which it now revolted me to think of; had braved whatever my father's anger might inflict; had risked cheerfully the loss of all that birth and fortune could bestow! Why had I ever risen from my weary bed of sickness?—it would have been better, far better, that I had died!

But, while life remained, life had its trials and its toils, from which it was useless to shrink. There was still another letter to be opened: there was yet more wickedness which I must know how to confront.

The second of Mr. Sherwin's letters was much shorter than the first, and had apparently been written not more than a day or two back. His tone was changed; he truckled to me no longer—he began to threaten. I was reminded that the servant's report pronounced me to have been convalescent for several days past: and was asked why, under these circumstances, I had never even written. I was warned that my silence had been construed greatly to my disadvantage; and that if it continued longer, the writer would assert his daughter's cause loudly and publicly, not to my father only, but to all the world. The letter ended by according to me three days more of grace, before the fullest disclosure would be made.

For a moment, my indignation got the better of me. I rose, to go that instant to North Villa and unmask the wretches who still thought to make their market of me as easily as ever. But the mere momentary delay caused by opening the door of my room, restored me to myself. I felt that my first duty, my paramount obligation, was to confess all to my father immediately; to know and accept my future position in my own home, before I went out from it to denounce others. I returned to the table, and gathered up the letters scattered on it. My heart beat fast, my head felt confused; but I was resolute in my determination to tell my father, at all hazards, the tale of degradation which I have told in these pages.

I waited in the stillness and loneliness, until it grew nearly dark. The servant brought in candles. Why could I not ask him whether my father and Clara had come home yet? Was I faltering in my resolution already?

Shortly after this, I heard a step on the stairs and a knock at my door.—My father? No! Clara. I tried to speak to her unconcernedly, when she came in.

"Why, you have been walking till it is quite dark, Clara!"

"We have only been in the garden of the Square—neither papa nor I noticed how late it was. We were talking on a subject of the deepest interest to us both."

She paused a moment, and looked down; then hurriedly came nearer to me, and drew a chair to my side. There was a strange expression of sadness and anxiety in her face, as she continued:

"Can't you imagine what the subject was? It was you, Basil. Papa is coming here directly, to speak to you."

She stopped once more. Her cheeks reddened a little, and she mechanically busied herself in arranging some books that lay on the table. Suddenly, she abandoned this employment; the colour left her face; it was quite pale when she addressed me again, speaking in very altered tones; so altered, that I hardly recognised them as hers.

"You know, Basil, that for a long time past, you have kept some secret from us; and you promised that I should know it first; but I—I have changed my mind; I have no wish to know it, dear: I would rather we never said anything about it." (She coloured, and hesitated a little again, then proceeded quickly and earnestly:) "But I hope you will tell it all to papa: he is coming here to ask you—oh, Basil! be candid with him, and tell him everything; let us all be to one another what we were before this time last year! You have nothing to fear, if you only speak openly; for I have begged him to be gentle and forgiving with you, and

you know he refuses me nothing. I only came here to prepare you; to beg you to be candid and patient. Hush!
there is a step on the stairs. Speak out, Basil, for *my* sake
—pray, pray, speak out, and then leave the rest to me."

She hurriedly left the room. The next minute, my
father entered it.

Perhaps my guilty conscience deceived me, but I thought
he looked at me more sadly and severely than I had ever
seen him look before. His voice, too, was troubled when
he spoke. This was a change, which meant much in *him*.

"I have come to speak to you," he said, "on a subject
about which I had much rather you had spoken to me
first."

"I think, Sir, I know to what subject you refer. I—"

"I must beg you will listen to me as patiently as you
can," he rejoined; "I have not much to say."

He paused, and sighed heavily. I thought he looked at
me more kindly. My heart grew very sad; and I yearned
to throw my arms round his neck, to give freedom to the
repressed tears which half choked me, to weep out on his
bosom my confession that I was no more worthy to be
called his son. Oh, that I had obeyed the impulse which
moved me to do this!

"Basil," pursued my father, gravely and sadly; "I hope
and believe that I have little to reproach myself with in my
conduct towards you. I think I am justified in saying, that
very few fathers would have acted towards a son as I have
acted for the last year or more. I may often have grieved
over the secresy which has estranged you from us; I may
even have shown you by my manner that I resented it;
but I have never used my authority to force you into the
explanation of your conduct, which you have been so uni-
formly unwilling to volunteer. I rested on that implicit
faith in the honour and integrity of my son, which I will
not yet believe to have been ill-placed, but which, I fear,

has led me to neglect too long the duty of inquiry which I owed to your own well-being, and to my position towards you. I am now here to atone for this omission; circumstances have left me no choice. It deeply concerns my interest as a father, and my honour as the head of our family, to know what heavy misfortune it was (I can imagine it to be nothing else) that stretched my son senseless in the open street, and afflicted him afterwards with an illness which threatened his reason and his life. You are now sufficiently recovered to reveal this; and I only use my legitimate authority over my own children, when I tell you that I must now know all. If you persist in remaining silent, the relations between us must henceforth change for life."

"I am ready to make my confession, Sir. I only ask you to believe beforehand, that if I have sinned grievously against you, I have been already heavily punished for the sin. I am afraid it is impossible that your worst forebodings can have prepared you——"

"The words you spoke in your delirium—words which I heard, but will not judge you by—justified the worst forebodings."

"My illness has spared me the hardest part of a hard trial, Sir, if it has prepared you for what I have to confess; if you suspect——"

"I do not *suspect*—I feel but too *sure*, that you, my second son, from whom I had expected far better things, have imitated in secret—I am afraid, outstripped—the worst vices of your elder brother."

"My brother!—my brother's faults mine! Ralph!"

"Yes, Ralph. It is my last hope that you will now imitate Ralph's candour. Take example from that best part of him, as you have already taken example from the worst."

My heart grew faint and cold as he spoke. Ralph's example! Ralph's vices!—vices of the reckless hour, or the idle day!—vices whose stain, in the world's eye, was not a stain for life!—convenient, reclaimable vices, that men were mercifully unwilling to associate with grinning infamy and irreparable disgrace! How far—how fearfully far, my father was from the remotest suspicion of what had really happened! I tried to answer his last words, but the apprehension of the life-long humiliation and grief which my confession might inflict on him—absolutely incapable, as he appeared to be, of foreboding even the least degrading part of it—kept me speechless. When he resumed, after a momentary silence, his tones were stern, his looks searching —pitilessly searching, and bent full upon my face.

"A person has been calling, named Sherwin," he said, "and inquiring about you every day. What intimate connection between you authorises this perfect stranger to *me* to come to the house as frequently as he does, and to make his inquiries with a familiarity of tone and manner which has struck every one of the servants who have, on different occasions, opened the door to him? Who is this Mr. Sherwin?"

"It is not with him, Sir, that I can well begin. I must go back——"

"You must go back farther, I am afraid, than you will be able to return. You must go back to the time when you had nothing to conceal from me, and when you could speak to me with the frankness and directness of a gentleman."

"Pray be patient with me, Sir; give me a few minutes to collect myself. I have much need for a little self-possession before I tell you all."

"All? your tones mean more than your words—*they* are candid, at least! Have I feared the worst, and yet not feared as I ought? Basil!—do you hear me, Basil? You are trembling very strangely; you are growing pale!"

"I shall be better directly, Sir. I am afraid I am not quite so strong yet as I thought myself. Father! I am heart-broken and spirit-broken: be patient and kind to me, or I cannot speak to you."

I thought I saw his eyes moisten. He shaded them a moment with his hand, and sighed again—the same long, trembling sigh that I had heard before. I tried to rise from my chair, and throw myself on my knees at his feet. He mistook the action, and caught me by the arm, believing that I was fainting.

"No more to-night, Basil," he said, hurriedly, but very gently; "no more on this subject till to-morrow."

"I can speak now, Sir; it is better to speak at once."

"No: you are too much agitated; you are weaker than I thought. To-morrow, in the morning, when you are stronger after a night's rest. No! I will hear nothing more. Go to bed now; I will tell your sister not to disturb you to-night. To-morrow, you shall speak to me; and speak in your own way, without interruption. Good-night, Basil, good-night."

Without waiting to shake hands with me, he hastened to the door, as if anxious to hide from my observation the grief and apprehension which had evidently overcome him. But, just at the moment when he was leaving the room, he hesitated, turned round, looked sorrowfully at me for an instant, and then, retracing his steps, gave me his hand, pressed mine for a moment in silence, and left me.

After the morrow was over, would he ever give me that hand again?

III.

The morning which was to decide all between my father and me, the morning on whose event hung the future of my home life, was the brightest and loveliest that my eyes ever looked on. A cloudless sky, a soft air, sunshine so joyous and dazzling that the commonest objects looked beautiful in its light, seemed to be mocking at me for my heavy heart, as I stood at my window, and thought of the hard duty to be fulfilled, on the harder judgment that might be pronounced, before the dawning of another day.

During the night, I had arranged no plan on which to conduct the terrible disclosure which I was now bound to make—the greatness of the emergency deprived me of all power of preparing myself for it. I thought on my father's character, on the inbred principles of honour which ruled him with the stern influence of a fanaticism: I thought on his pride of caste, so unobtrusive, so rarely hinted at in words, and yet so firmly rooted in his nature, so intricately entwined with every one of his emotions, his aspirations, his simplest feelings and ideas: I thought on his almost feminine delicacy in shrinking from the barest mention of impurities which other men could carelessly discuss, or could laugh over as good material for an after-dinner jest. I thought over all this, and when I remembered that it was to such a man that I must confess the infamous marriage which I had contracted in secret, all hope from his fatherly affection deserted me; all idea of appealing to his chivalrous generosity became a delusion in which it was madness to put a moment's trust.

The faculties of observation are generally sharpened, in proportion as the faculties of reflection are dulled, under the influence of an absorbing suspense. While I now waited alone in my room, the most ordinary sounds and events in the house, which I never remembered noticing before, absolutely enthralled me. It seemed as if the noise of a footstep, the echo of a voice, the shutting or opening of doors down stairs, must, on this momentous day, presage some mysterious calamity, some strange discovery, some secret project formed against me, I knew not how, or by whom. Two or three times I found myself listening intently on the staircase, with what object I could hardly tell. It was always, however, on those occasions, that a dread, significant quiet appeared to have fallen suddenly on the house. Clara never came to me, no message arrived from my father; the door-bell seemed strangely silent, the servants strangely neglectful of their duties above stairs. I caught myself returning to my own room softly, as if I expected that some hidden catastrophe might break forth, if the sound of my footsteps were heard.

Would my father seek me again in my own room, or would he send for me down stairs? It was not long before the doubt was decided. One of the servants knocked at my door—the servant whose special duty it had been to wait on me in my illness. I longed to take the man's hand, and implore his sympathy and encouragement while he addressed me.

"My master, Sir, desires me to say that, if you feel well enough, he wishes to see you in his own room."

I rose, and immediately followed the servant. On our way, we passed the door of Clara's private sitting-room—it opened, and my sister came out and laid her hand on my arm. She smiled as I looked at her; but the tears stood thick in her eyes, and her face was deadly pale.

"Think of what I said last night, Basil," she whispered, "and, if hard words are spoken to you, think of *me*. All that our mother would have done for you, if she had been still among us, *I* will do. Remember that, and keep heart and hope to the very last."

She hastily returned to her room, and I went on down stairs. In the hall, the servant was waiting for me, with a letter in his hand.

"This was left for you, Sir, a little while ago. The messenger who brought it said he was not to wait for an answer."

It was no time for reading letters—the interview with my father was too close at hand. I hastily put the letter into my pocket, barely noticing, as I did so, that the handwriting on the address was very irregular, and quite unknown to me.

I went at once into my father's room.

He was sitting at his table, cutting the leaves of some new books that lay on it. Pointing to a chair placed opposite to him, he briefly inquired after my health; and then added, in a lower tone—

"Take any time you like, Basil, to compose and collect yourself. This morning my time is yours."

He turned a little away from me, and went on cutting the leaves of the books placed before him. Still utterly incapable of preparing myself in any way for the disclosure expected from me; without thought or hope, or feeling of any kind, except a vague sense of thankfulness for the reprieve granted me before I was called on to speak—I mechanically looked round and round the room, as if I expected to see the sentence to be pronounced against me, already written on the walls, or grimly foreshadowed in the faces of the old family portraits which hung above the fireplace.

What man has ever felt that all his thinking powers were absorbed, even by the most poignant mental misery that could occupy them? In moments of imminent danger, the mind can still travel of its own accord over the past, in spite of the present—in moments of bitter affliction, it can still recur to every-day trifles, in spite of ourselves. While I now sat silent in my father's room, long-forgotten associations of childhood connected with different parts of it, began to rise on my memory in the strangest and most startling independence of any influence or control, which my present agitation and suspense might be supposed to exercise over them. The remembrances that should have been the last to be awakened at this time of heavy trial, were the very remembrances which now moved within me.

With burdened heart and aching eyes I looked over the

walls around me. There, in that corner, was the red cloth door which led to the library. As children, how often Ralph and I had peeped curiously through that very door, to see what my father was about in his study, to wonder why he had so many letters to write, and so many books to read. How frightened we both were, when he discovered us one day, and reproved us severely! How happy the moment afterwards, when we had begged him to pardon us, and were sent back to the library again with a great picture-book to look at, as a token that we were both forgiven! Then, again, there was the high, old-fashioned, mahogany press before the window, with the same large illustrated folio about Jewish antiquities lying on it, which, years and years ago, Clara and I were sometimes allowed to look at, as a special treat, on Sunday afternoons; and which we always examined and re-examined with never-ending delight —standing together on two chairs to reach up to the thick, yellow-looking leaves, and turn them over with our own hands. And there, in the recess between two book-cases, still stood the ancient desk-table, with its rows of little inlaid drawers; and on the bracket above it the old French clock, which had once belonged to my mother, and which always chimed the hours so sweetly and merrily. It was at that table that Ralph and I always bade my father farewell, when we were going back to school after the holidays, and were receiving our allowance of pocket-money, given to us out of one of the tiny inlaid drawers, just before we started. Near that spot, too, Clara—then a little rosy child —used to wait gravely and anxiously, with her doll in her arms, to say good-bye for the last time, and to bid us come back soon, and then never go away again. I turned, and looked abruptly towards the window; for such memories as the room suggested were more than I could bear.

Outside, in the dreary strip of garden, the few stunted, dusky trees were now rustling as pleasantly in the air, as if the breeze that stirred them came serenely over an open meadow, or swept freshly under their branches from the rippling surface of a brook. Distant, but yet well within hearing, the mighty murmur from a large thoroughfare—the great mid-day voice of London—swelled grandly and joyously on the ear. While, nearer still, in a street that ran past the side of the house, the notes of an organ rang out shrill and fast; the instrument was playing its liveliest waltz tune—a tune which I had danced to in the ball-room over and over again. What mocking memories within, what mocking sounds without, to herald and accompany such a confession as I had now to make!

Minute after minute glided on, inexorably fast; and yet I never broke silence. My eyes turned anxiously and slowly on my father.

He was still looking away from me, still cutting the leaves of the books before him. Even in that trifling action, the strong emotions which he was trying to conceal, were plainly and terribly betrayed. His hand, usually so steady and careful, trembled perceptibly; and the paper-knife tore through the leaves faster and faster—cutting them awry, rending them one from another, so as to spoil the appearance of every page. I believe he *felt* that I was looking at him; for he suddenly discontinued his employment, turned round towards me, and spoke—

"I have resolved to give you your own time," he said, "and from that resolve I have no wish to depart—I only ask you to remember that every minute of delay adds to the suffering and suspense which I am enduring on your account." He opened the books before him again, adding in lower and colder tones, as he did so—"In *your* place, Ralph would have spoken before this."

Ralph, and Ralph's example quoted to me again!—I could remain silent no longer.

"My brother's faults towards you, and towards his family,

are not such faults as mine, Sir," I began. "I have *not* imitated his vices; I have acted as he would *not* have acted. And yet, the result of my error will appear far more humiliating, and even disgraceful, in your eyes, than the results of any errors of Ralph's."

As I pronounced the word "disgraceful," he suddenly looked me full in the face. His eyes lightened up sternly, and the warning red spot rose on his pale cheeks.

"What do you mean by 'disgraceful?'" he asked abruptly; "what do you mean by associating such a word as *disgrace* with your conduct—with the conduct of a son of mine?"

"I must reply to your question indirectly, Sir," I continued. "You asked me last night who the Mr. Sherwin was who has called here so often—"

"And this morning I ask it again. I have other questions to put to you, besides—you called constantly on a woman's name in your delirium. But I will repeat last night's question first—who is Mr. Sherwin?"

"He lives—"

"I don't ask where he lives. Who is he? What is he?"

"Mr. Sherwin is a linendraper—"

"You owe him money?—you have borrowed money of him? Why did you not tell me this before? You have degraded my house by letting a man call at the door—I know it!—in the character of a dun. He has inquired about you as his 'friend,'—the servants told me of it. This money-lending tradesman, your '*friend!*' If I had heard that the poorest labourer on my land called you 'friend,' I should have held you honoured by the attachment and gratitude of an honest man. When I hear that name given to you by a tradesman and money-lender, I hold you contaminated by connection with a cheat. You were right, Sir!—this *is* disgrace; how much do you owe? Where are your dishonoured acceptances? Where have you used *my*

name and ` *my* credit ?   Tell me at once—I insist on
it !" `

He spoke rapidly and contemptuously, and rising from his
chair as he ended, walked impatiently up and down the
room.

"I owe no money to Mr. Sherwin, Sir—no money to any
one."

He stopped suddenly :

"No money to any one ?" he repeated very slowly, and
in very altered tones. "You spoke of disgrace just now.
There is a worse disgrace then that you have hidden from
me, than debts dishonourably contracted ?"

At this moment, a step passed across the hall. He instantly turned round, and locked the door on that side of
the room—then continued :

"Speak ! and speak honestly if you can. How have you
been deceiving me ? A woman's name escaped you constantly, when your delirium was at its worst. You used
some very strange expressions about her, which it was impossible altogether to comprehend ; but you said enough to
show that her character was one of the most abandoned ;
that her licentiousness—it is too revolting to speak of *her*—
I return to *you*. I insist on knowing how far your vices
have compromised you with that vicious woman."

"She has wronged me—cruelly, horribly, wronged me—"

I could say no more. My head drooped on my breast ;
my shame overpowered me.

"Who is she ?   You called her Margaret, in your illness
—who is she ?"

"She is Mr. Sherwin's daughter—" The words that I
would fain have spoken next, seemed to suffocate me. I
was silent again.

I heard him mutter to himself :

"*That* man's daughter !—a worse bait than the bait of
money !"

He bent forward, and looked at me searchingly. A frightful paleness flew over his face in an instant.

"Basil!" he cried, "in God's name, answer me at once! What is Mr. Sherwin's daughter to *you?*"

"She is my wife!"

I heard no answer—not a word, not even a sigh. My eyes were blinded with tears, my face was bent down; I saw nothing at first. When I raised my head, and dashed away the blinding tears, and looked up, the blood chilled at my heart.

My father was leaning against one of the book-cases, with his hands clasped over his breast. His head was drawn back; his white lips moved, but no sound came from them. Over his upturned face there had passed a ghastly change, as indescribable in its awfulness as the change of death.

I ran horror-stricken to his side, and attempted to take his hand. He started instantly into an erect position, and thrust me from him furiously, without uttering a word. At that fearful moment, in that fearful silence, the sounds out of doors penetrated with harrowing distinctness and merriment into the room. The pleasant rustling of the trees mingled musically with the softened, monotonous rolling of carriages in the distant street, while the organ-tune, now changed to the lively measure of a song, rang out clear and cheerful above both, and poured into the room as lightly and happily as the very sunshine itself.

For a few minutes we stood apart, and neither of us moved or spoke. I saw him take out his handkerchief, and pass it over his face, breathing heavily and thickly, and leaning against the book-case once more. When he withdrew the handkerchief and looked at me again, I knew that the sharp pang of agony had passed away, that the last hard struggle between his parental affection and his family pride was over, and that the great gulph which was hence-

forth to separate father and son, had now opened between
us for ever.

He pointed peremptorily to me to go back to my former
place, but did not return to his own chair. As I obeyed, I
saw him unlock the door of the book-case against which he
had been leaning, and place his hand on one of the books
inside. Without withdrawing it from its place, without
turning or looking towards me, he asked if I had anything
more to say to him.

The chilling calmness of his tones, the question itself, and
the time at which he put it, the unnatural repression of a
single word of rebuke, of passion, or of sorrow, after such
a confession as I had just made, struck me speechless. He
turned a little away from the book-case—still keeping his
hand on the book inside—and repeated the question. His
eyes, when they met mine, had a pining, weary look, as if
they had been long condemned to rest on woful and revolting objects; his expression had lost its natural refine-
ment, its gentleness of repose, and had assumed a hard,
lowering calmness, under which his whole countenance appeared to have shrunk and changed—years of old age
seemed to have fallen on it, since I had spoken the last fatal
words !

" Have you anything more to say to me ?"

On the repetition of that terrible question, I sank down
in the chair at my side, and hid my face in my hands. Unconscious how I spoke, or why I spoke; with no hope in
myself, or in him; with no motive but to invite and bear
the whole penalty of my disgrace, I now disclosed the miserable story of my marriage, and of all that followed it. I
remember nothing of the words I used·—nothing of what I
urged in my own defence. The sense of bewilderment and
oppression grew heavier and heavier on my brain; I spoke
more and more rapidly, confusedly, unconsciously, until I
was again silenced and recalled to myself by the sound of

my father's voice. I believe I had arrived at the last, worst part of my confession, when he interrupted me

"Spare me any more details," he said, bitterly, "you have humiliated me sufficiently—you have spoken enough."

He removed the book on which his hand had hitherto rested from the case behind him, and advanced with it to the table—paused for a moment, pale and silent—then slowly opened it at the first page, and resumed his chair.

I recognised the book instantly. It was a biographical history of his family, from the time of his earliest ancestors down to the date of the births of his own children. The thick quarto pages were beautifully illuminated in the manner of the ancient manuscripts; and the narrative, in written characters, had been produced under his own inspection. This book had cost him years of research and perseverance. The births and deaths, the marriages and possessions, the battle achievements and private feuds of the old Norman barons from whom he traced his descent, were all enrolled in regular order on every leaf—headed, sometimes merely by representations of the Knight's favourite weapon; sometimes by copies of the Baron's effigy on his tombstone in a foreign land. As the history advanced to later dates, beautiful miniature portraits were inlaid at the top of each leaf; and the illuminations were so managed as to symbolize the remarkable merits or the peculiar tastes of the subject of each biography. Thus, the page devoted to my mother was surrounded by her favourite violets, clustering thickest round the last melancholy lines of writing which told the story of her death.

Slowly and in silence, my father turned over the leaves of the book which, next to the Bible, I believe he most reverenced in the world, until he came to the last-written page but one—the page which I knew, from its position, to be occupied by my name. At the top, a miniature portrait of me, when a child, was let into the leaf. Under it, was the record of my birth and names, of the School and College at which I had been taught, and of the profession that I had adopted. Below, a large blank space was left for the entry of future particulars. On this page my father now looked, still not uttering a word, still with the same ghastly calmness on his face. The organ-notes sounded no more; but the trees rustled as pleasantly, and the roar of the distant carriages swelled as joyously as ever on the ear. Some children had come out to play in the garden of a neighbouring house. As their voices reached us, so fresh, and clear, and happy—but another modulation of the thanksgiving song to God which the trees were singing in the summer air—I saw my father, while he still looked on the page before him, clasp his trembling hands over my portrait so as to hide it from sight.

Then he spoke; but without looking up, and more as if he were speaking to himself than to me. His voice, at other times clear and gentle in its tones, was now so hard and harsh in its forced calmness and deliberation of utterance, that it sounded like a stranger's.

"I came here, this morning," he began, "prepared to hear of faults and misfortunes which should pain me to the heart; which I might never, perhaps, be able to forget, however willing and even predetermined to forgive. But I did *not* come prepared to hear, that unutterable disgrace had been cast on me and mine, by my own child. I have no words of rebuke or of condemnation for this: the reproach and the punishment have fallen already where the guilt was —and not there only. My son's infamy defiles his brother's birthright, and puts his father to shame. Even his sister's name—"

He stopped, shuddering. When he proceeded, his voice faltered, and his head drooped low.

"I say it again:—you are below all reproach and all condemnation; but I have a duty to perform towards my two children who are absent, and I have a last word to say to *you* when that duty is done. On this page—" (as he pointed to the family history, his tones strengthened again)—" on this page there is a blank space left, after the last entry, for writing the future events of your life. Here, then, if I still acknowledge you to be my son; if I think your presence and the presence of my daughter possible in the same house, must be written such a record of dishonour and degradation as has never yet defiled a single page of this book—here, the foul stain of your marriage, and its consequences, must be admitted to spread over all that is pure before it, and to taint to the last whatever comes after. This shall not be. I have no faith or hope in you more. I know you now, only as an enemy to me and to my house— it is mockery and hypocrisy to call you son; it is an insult to Clara, and even to Ralph, to think of you as my child. In this record your place is destroyed—and destroyed for ever. Would to God I could tear the past from my memory, as I tear the leaf from this book!"

As he spoke, the hour struck; and the old French clock rang out gaily the same little silvery chime which my mother had so often taken me into her room to listen to, in the bygone time. The shrill, lively peal mingled awfully with the sharp, tearing sound, as my father rent out from the book before him the whole of the leaf which contained my name; tore it into fragments, and cast them on the floor.

He rose abruptly, after he had closed the book again. His cheeks flushed once more ; and when he next spoke, his voice grew louder and louder with every word he uttered. It seemed as if he still distrusted his resolution to abandon me; and sought, in his anger, the strength of purpose which, in his calmer mood, he might even yet have been unable to command.

"Now, Sir," he said, "we treat together as strangers.

You are Mr. Sherwin's son—not mine. You are the husband of his daughter—not a relation of my family. Rise,
as I do: we sit together no longer in the same room.
Write!" (he pushed pen, ink, and paper before me,) "write
your terms there—I shall find means to keep you to a written engagement—the terms of your absence, for life, from
this country; and of hers: the terms of your silence, and
of the silence of your accomplices; of all of them. Write
what you please; I am ready to pay dearly for your absence,
your secrecy, and your abandonment of the name you have
degraded. My God! that I should live to bargain for hushing up the dishonour of my family, and to bargain for it
with *you*."

I had listened to him hitherto without pleading a word in
my own behalf; but his last speech roused me. Some of
his pride stirred in my heart against the bitterness of his
contempt. I raised my head, and met his eye steadily for
the first time—then, thrust the writing materials away from
me, and left my place at the table.

"Stop!" he cried. "Do you pretend that you have not
understood me?"

"It is *because* I have understood you, Sir, that I go. I
have deserved your anger, and have submitted without a
murmur to all that it could inflict. If you see in my conduct towards you no mitigation of my offence; if you cannot view the shame and wrong inflicted on me, with such
grief as may have some pity mixed with it—I have, I
think, the right to ask that your contempt may be silent,
and your last words to me, not words of insult."

"Insult! After what has happened, is it for *you* to utter
that word in the tone in which you have just spoken it? I
tell you again, I insist on your written engagement as I
would insist on the engagement of a stranger—I will have
it, before you leave this room!"

"All, and more than all, which that degrading engagement

could imply, I will do. But I have not fallen so low yet as to be bribed to perform a duty. You may be able to forget that you are my father; I can never forget that I am your son."

"The remembrance will avail you nothing as long as I live. I tell you again, I insist on your written engagement, though it were only to show that I have ceased to believe in your word. Write at once—do you hear me?—Write!"

I neither moved nor answered. His face changed again, and grew livid; his fingers trembled convulsively, and crumpled the sheet of paper, as he tried to take it up from the table on which it lay.

"You refuse?" he said quickly.

"I have already told you, Sir—"

"Go!" he interrupted, pointing passionately to the door, "go out from this house, never to return to it again—go, not as a stranger to me, but as an enemy! I have no faith in a single promise you have made: there is no baseness which I do not believe you will yet be guilty of. But I tell you, and the wretches with whom you are leagued, to take warning: I have wealth, power, and position; and there is no use to which I will not put them against the man or woman who threatens the fair fame of this family. Leave me, remembering that—and leave me for ever!"

Just as he uttered the last word, just as my hand was on the lock of the door, a faint sound—something between breathing and speaking—was audible in the direction of the library. He started, and looked round. Impelled, I know not how, I paused on the point of going out. My eyes followed his, and fixed on the cloth door which led into the library.

It opened a little—then shut again—then opened wide. Slowly and noiselessly, Clara came into the room.

The silence and suddenness of her entrance at such a mo-

ment; the look of terror which changed to unnatural
vacancy the wonted softness and gentleness of her eyes, her
pale face, her white dress, and slow, noiseless step, made her
first appearance in the room seem almost supernatural; it
was as if an apparition had been walking towards us, and
not Clara herself! As she approached my father, he pronounced her name in astonishment; but his voice sank to a
whisper, while he spoke it. For an instant, she paused,
hesitating—I saw her tremble as her eyes met his—then, as
they turned towards me, the brave girl came on; and,
taking my hand, stood and faced my father, standing by my
side.

"Clara!" he exclaimed again, still in the same whispering
tones.

I felt her cold hand close fast on mine; the grasp of the
chill, frail fingers was almost painful to me. Her lips moved,
but her quick, hysterical breathing made the few words she
uttered inarticulate.

"Clara!" repeated my father, for the third time, his voice
rising, but sinking again immediately—when he spoke his
next words, "Clara," he resumed, sadly and gently, "let
go his hand; this is not a time for your presence, I beg you
to leave us. You must not take his hand! He has ceased
to be my son, or your brother. Clara, do you not hear
me?"

"Yes, Sir, I hear you," she answered. "God grant that
my mother in heaven may not hear you too!"

He was approaching while she replied; but at her last
words, he stopped instantly, and turned his face away from
us. Who shall say what remembrances of other days shook
him to the heart?

"You have spoken, Clara, as you should not have spoken,"
he went on, without looking up. "Your mother—" his
voice faltered and failed him. "Can you still hold his hand
after what I have said? I tell you again, he is unworthy to

be in your presence; my house is his home no longer—must I *command* you to leave him?"

The deeply planted instinct of gentleness and obedience prevailed; she dropped my hand, but did not move away from me, even yet.

"Now leave us, Clara," he said. "You were wrong, my love, to be in that room, and wrong to come in here. I will speak to you up-stairs—you must remain here no longer."

She clasped her trembling fingers together, and sighed heavily.

"I cannot go, Sir," she said quickly and breathlessly.

"Must I tell you for the first time in your life, that you are acting disobediently?" he asked.

"I cannot go," she repeated in the same manner, "till you have said you will let him atone for his offence, and will forgive him."

"For *his* offence there is neither atonement nor forgiveness. Clara! are you so changed, that you can disobey me to my face?"

He walked away from us as he said this.

"Oh, no! no!" She ran towards him; but stopped half-way, and looked back at me affrightedly, as I stood near the door. "Basil," she cried, "you have not done what you promised me; you have not been patient. Oh, Sir, if I have ever deserved kindness from you, be kind to him for *my* sake! Basil! speak, Basil! Ask his pardon on your knees. Father, I promised him he should be forgiven, if I asked you. Not a word; not a word from either? Basil! you are not going yet—not going at all! Remember, Sir, how good and kind he has always been to *me*. My poor mother, (I *must* speak of her), my poor mother's favourite son—you have told me so yourself! and he has always been my favourite brother; I think because my mother loved him so! His first fault, too! his first grief! And will you tell him for this, that our home is *his* home no longer? Punish *me*,

Sir! I have done wrong like him; when I heard your voices so loud, I listened in the library. He's going! No, no, no! not yet!"

She ran to the door as I opened it, and pushed it to again. Overwhelmed by the violence of her agitation, my father had sunk into a chair while she was speaking.

"Come back—come back with me to his knees!" she whispered, fixing her wild, tearless eyes on mine, flinging her arms round my neck, and trying to lead me with her from the door. "Come back, or you will drive me mad!" she repeated loudly, drawing me away towards my father.

He rose instantly from his chair.

"Clara," he said, "I command you, leave him!" He advanced a few steps towards me. "Go!" he cried; "if you are human in your villany, you will release me from this!"

I whispered in her ear, "I will write, love—I will write," and disengaged her arms from my neck—they were hanging round it weakly, already! As I passed the door, I turned back, and looked again into the room for the last time.

Clara was in my father's arms, her head lay on his shoulder, her face was as still in its heavenly calmness as if the world and the world's looks knew it no more, and the only light that fell on it now, was light from the angel's eyes. She had fainted.

He was standing with one arm round her, his disengaged hand was searching impatiently over the wall behind him for the bell, and his eyes were fixed in anguish and in love unutterable on the peaceful face, hushed in its sad repose so close beneath his own. For one moment, I saw him thus, ere I closed the door—the next, I had left the house.

I never entered it again—I have never seen my father since.

IV.

We are seldom able to discover under any ordinary conditions of self-knowledge, how intimately that spiritual part of us, which is undying, can attach to itself and its operations the poorest objects of that external world around us, which is perishable. In the ravelled skein, the slightest threads are the hardest to follow. In analysing the associations and sympathies which regulate the play of our passions, the simplest and homeliest are the last that we detect. It is only when the shock comes, and the mind recoils before it—when joy is changed into sorrow, or sorrow into joy—that we really discern what trifles in the outer world our noblest mental pleasures, or our severest mental pains, have made part of themselves; atoms which the whirlpool has drawn into its vortex, as greedily and as surely as the largest mass.

It was reserved for me to know this, when—after a moment's pause before the door of my father's house, more homeless, then, than the poorest wretch who passed me on the pavement, and had wife or kindred to shelter him in a garret that night—my steps turned, as of old, in the direction of North Villa.

Again I passed over the scene of my daily pilgrimage, always to the same shrine, for a whole year; and now, for the first time, I knew that there was hardly a spot along the entire way, which my heart had not unconsciously made beautiful and beloved to me by some association with Margaret Sherwin. Here was the friendly, familiar shop-window, filled with the glittering trinkets which had so often lured me in to buy presents for her, on my way to the house. There was the noisy street corner, void of all adornment in itself, but once bright to me with the fairy-land architecture of a dream, because I knew that at that place

I had passed over half the distance which separated my
home from hers. Further on, the Park trees came in sight
—trees that no autumn decay or winter nakedness could
make dreary, in the bygone time; for she and I had walked
under them together. And further yet, was the turning
which led from the long, suburban road into Hollyoake
Square—the lonely, dust-whitened place, around which my
past happiness and my wasted hopes had flung their golden
illusions, like jewels hung round the coarse wooden image
of a Roman saint. Dishonoured and ruined, it was among
such associations as these—too homely to have been recognised by me in former times—that I journeyed along the
well-remembered way to North Villa.

I went on without hesitating, without even a thought of
turning back. I had said that the honour of my family
should not suffer by the calamity which had fallen on me;
and, while life remained, I was determined that nothing
should prevent me from holding to my word. It was from
this resolution that I drew the faith in myself, the confidence
in my endurance, the sustaining calmness under my father's
sentence of exclusion, which nerved me to go on. I must
inevitably see Mr. Sherwin (perhaps even suffer the humiliation of seeing *her!*)—must inevitably speak such words,
disclose such truths, as should show him that deceit was
henceforth useless. I must do this : and more, I must be
prepared to guard the family to which—though banished
from it—I still belonged, from every conspiracy against
them that detected crime or shameless cupidity could form,
whether in the desire of revenge, or in the hope of gain.
A hard, almost an impossible task—but, nevertheless, a task
that must be done!

I kept the thought of this necessity before my mind unceasingly; not only as a duty, but as a refuge from another
thought, to which I dared not for a moment turn. The
still, pale face which I had seen lying hushed on my father's

breast—CLARA!—That way, lay the grief that weakens, the yearning and the terror that are near despair; that way was not for *me*.

The servant was at the garden-gate of North Villa—the same servant whom I had seen and questioned in the first days of my fatal delusion. She was receiving a letter from a man, very poorly dressed, who walked away the moment I approached. Her confusion and surprise were so great as she let me in, that she could hardly look at, or speak to me. It was only when I was ascending the door-steps that she said—

"Miss Margaret"—(she still gave her that name!)— "Miss Margaret is upstairs, Sir. I suppose you would like—"

"I have no wish to see her: I want to speak to Mr. Sherwin."

Looking more bewildered, and even frightened, than before, the girl hurriedly opened one of the doors in the passage. I saw, as I entered, that she had shown me, in her confusion, into the wrong room. Mr. Sherwin, who was in the apartment, hastily drew a screen across the lower end of it, apparently to hide something from me; which, however, I had not seen as I came in.

He advanced, holding out his hand; but his restless eyes wandered unsteadily, looking away from me towards the screen.

"So you have come at last, have you? Just let's step into the drawing-room: the fact is—I thought I wrote to you about it—?"

He stopped suddenly, and his outstretched arm fell to his side. I had not said a word. Something in my look and manner must have told him already on what errand I had come.

"Why don't you speak?" he said, after a moment's pause. "What are you looking at me like that for? Stop!

Let's say our say in the other room." He walked past me towards the door, and half opened it.

Why was he so anxious to get me away? Who, or what, was he hiding behind the screen? The servant had said his daughter was upstairs; remembering this, and suspecting every action or word that came from him, I determined to remain in the room, and discover his secret. It was evidently connected with me.

"Now then," he continued, opening the door a little wider, "it's only across the hall, you know; and I always receive visitors in the best room."

"I have been admitted here," I replied, "and have neither time nor inclination to follow you from room to room, just as you like. What I have to say is not much; and, unless you give me fit reasons to the contrary, I shall say it here."

"You will, will you? Let me tell you that's damned like what we plain mercantile men call downright incivility. I say it again—incivility; and rudeness too, if you like it better." He saw I was determined, and closed the door as he spoke, his face twitching and working violently, and his quick, evil eyes turned again in the direction of the screen.

"Well," he continued, with a sulky defiance of manner and look, "do as you like; stop here—you'll wish you hadn't before long, I'll be bound! You don't seem to hurry yourself much about speaking, so *I* shall sit down. *You* can do as you please. Now then! just let's cut it short—do you come here in a friendly way, to ask me to send for *my* girl downstairs, and to show yourself the gentleman, or do you not?"

"You have written me two letters, Mr. Sherwin—"

"Yes: and took devilish good care you should get them— I left them myself."

"In writing those letters, you were either grossly deceived; and, in that case, are only to be pitied, or—"

"Pitied! what the devil do you mean by that? Nobody wants your pity here."

"Or you have been trying to deceive me; and in that case, I have to tell you that deceit is henceforth useless. I know all—more than you suspect: more, I believe, than you would wish me to have known."

"Oh, that's your tack, is it? By God, I expected as much the moment you came in! What! you don't believe *my* girl—don't you? You're going to fight shy, and behave like a scamp—are you? Damn your infernal coolness and your aristocratic airs and graces! You shall see I'll be even with you—you shall. Ha! ha! look here!—here's the marriage certificate safe in my pocket. You won't do the honourable by my poor child—won't you? Come out! Come away! You'd better—I'm off to your father to blow the whole business; I am, as sure as my name's Sherwin!"

He struck his fist on the table, and started up, livid with passion. The screen trembled a little, and a slight rustling noise was audible behind it, just as he advanced towards me. He stopped instantly, with an oath, and looked back.

"I warn you to remain here," I said. "This morning, my father has heard all from my lips. He has renounced me as his son, and I have left his house for ever."

He turned round quickly, staring at me with a face of mingled fury and dismay.

"Then you come to me a beggar!" he burst out; "a beggar who has taken me in about his fine family, and his fine prospects; a beggar who can't support my child—Yes! I say it again, a beggar who looks me in the face, and talks as you do. I don't care a damn about you or your father! I know my rights; I'm an Englishman, thank God! I know my rights, and *my* Margaret's rights; and I'll have them in spite of you both. Yes! you may stare as angry as you like; staring aon't hurt. I'm an honest man, and *my* girl's an honest girl!"

I was looking at him, at that moment, with the contempt that I really felt; his rage produced no other sensation in me. All higher and quicker emotions seemed to have been dried at their sources by the events of the morning.

"I say *my* girl's an honest girl," he repeated, sitting down again; "and I dare you, or anybody—I don't care who—to prove the contrary. You told me you knew all, just now. What *all?* Come! we'll have this out before we do anything else. She says she's innocent, and I say she's innocent: and if I could find out that damnation scoundrel Mannion, and get him here, I'd make him say it too. Now, after all that, what have you got against her?—against your lawful wife; and I'll make you own her as such, and keep her as such, I can promise you!"

"I am not here to ask questions, or to answer them," I replied—"my errand in this house is simply to tell you, that the miserable falsehoods contained in your letter, will avail you as little as the foul insolence of language by which you are now endeavouring to support them. I told you before, and I now tell you again, I know all. I had been inside that house, before I saw your daughter at the door; and had heard, from *her* voice and *his* voice, what such shame and misery as you cannot comprehend forbid me to repeat. To your past duplicity, and to your present violence, I have but one answer to give:—I will never see your daughter again."

"But you *shall* see her again—yes! and keep her too! Do you think I can't see through you and your precious story? Your father's cut you off with a shilling; and now you want to curry favour with him again by trumping up a case against *my* girl, and trying to get her off your hands that way. But it won't do! You've married her, my fine gentleman, and you shall stick to her! Do you think I wouldn't sooner believe her, than believe you? Do you think I'll stand this? Here she is up-stairs, half heart-broken, on my hands; here's my wife"—(his voice sank suddenly as he said this)—" with her mind in such a state that I'm kept away from business, day after day, to look after her; here's all this crying and misery and mad goings-on in my house, because you choose to behave like a scamp—and do you think I'll put up with it quietly? I'll make you do your duty to *my* girl, if she goes to the parish to appeal against you! *Your* story indeed! Who'll believe that a young female, like Margaret, could have taken to a fellow like Mannion? and kept it all a secret from you? Who believes that, I should like to know?"

" *I believe it!* "

The third voice which pronounced those words was Mrs. Sherwin's.

But was the figure that now came out from behind the screen, the same frail, shrinking figure which had so often moved my pity in the past time? the same wan figure of sickness and sorrow, ever watching in the background of the fatal love-scenes at North Villa; ever looking like the same spectre-shadow, when the evenings darkened in as I sat by Margaret's side?

Had the grave given up its dead? I stood awe-struck, neither speaking nor moving while she walked towards me. She was clothed in the white garments of the sick-room— they looked on *her* like the raiment of the tomb. Her figure, which I only remembered as drooping with premature infirmity, was now straightened convulsively to its proper height; her arms hung close at her side, like the arms of a corpse; the natural paleness of her face had turned to an earthy hue; its natural expression, so meek, so patient, so melancholy in uncomplaining sadness, was gone; and, in its stead, was left a pining stillness that never changed; a weary repose of lifeless waking—the awful seal

of Death stamped ghastly on the living face; the awful look
of Death staring out from the chill, shining eyes.

Her husband kept his place, and spoke to her as she
stopped opposite to me. His tones were altered, but his
manner showed as little feeling as ever.

"There now!" he began, "you said you were sure he'd
come here, and that you'd never take to your bed, as the
Doctor wanted you, till you'd seen him and spoken to him.
Well, he *has* come; there he is. He came in while you
were asleep, I rather think; and I let him stop, so that if
you woke up and wanted to see him, you might. You can't
say—nobody can say—I haven't given in to your whims and
fancies after that. There! you've had your way, and you've
said you believe him; and now, if I ring for the nurse,
you'll go up-stairs at last, and make no more worry about it
—Eh?"

She moved her head slowly, and looked at him. As those
dying eyes met his, as that face on which the light of life
was darkening fast, turned on him, even *his* gross nature
felt the shock. I saw him shrink—his sallow cheeks whit-
ened, he moved his chair away, and said no more.

She looked back to me again, and spoke. Her voice was
still the same soft, low voice as ever. It was fearful to hear
how little it had altered, and then to look on the changed
face.

"I am dying," she said to me. "Many nights have
passed since that night when Margaret came home by herself, and I felt something moving down into my heart, when
I looked at her, which I knew was death—many nights,
since I have been used to say my prayers, and think I had
said them for the last time, before I dared shut my eyes in
the darkness and the quiet. I have lived on till to-day,
very weary of my life ever since that night when Margaret
came in; and yet, I could not die, because I had an atonement to make to *you,* and you never came to hear it and

forgive me. I was not fit for God to take me till you came—I know that, know it to be truth from a dream."

She paused, still looking at me, but with the same deathly blank of expression. The eye had ceased to speak already ; nothing but the voice was left.

"My husband has asked, who will believe you?" she went on; her weak tones gathering strength with every fresh word she uttered. "I have answered that *I* will; for you have spoken the truth. Now, when the light of this world is fading from my eyes ; here, in this earthly home of much sorrow and suffering, which I must soon quit—in the presence of my husband—under the same roof with my sinful child—I bear you witness that you have spoken the truth. I, her mother, say it of her : Margaret Sherwin is guilty ; she is no more worthy to be called your wife."

She pronounced the last words slowly, distinctly, solemnly. Till that fearful denunciation was spoken, her husband had been looking sullenly and suspiciously towards us, as we stood together ; but while she uttered it, his eyes fell, and he turned away his head in silence.

He never looked up, never moved, or interrupted her, as she continued, still addressing me ; but now speaking very slowly and painfully, pausing longer and longer between every sentence.

"From this room I go to my death-bed. The last words I speak in this world shall be to my husband, and shall change his heart towards you. I have been weak of purpose," (as she said this, a strange sweetness and mournfulness began to steal over her tones,) "miserably, guiltily weak, all my life. Much sorrow and pain and heavy disappointment, when I was young, did some great harm to me which I have never recovered since. I have lived always in fear of others, and doubt of myself; and this has made me guilty of a great sin towards *you*. Forgive me before I die! I suspected the guilt that was preparing—I foreooded the shame that was to come—they hid it from others' eyes; but, from the first, they could not hide it from mine —and yet I never warned you as I ought! *That man* had the power of Satan over me! I always shuddered before him, as I used to shudder at the darkness when I was a little child! My life has been all fear—fear of *him;* fear of my husband, and even of my daughter; fear, worse still, of my own thoughts, and of what I had discovered that should be told to *you.* When I tried to speak, you were too generous to understand me—I was afraid to think my suspicions were right, long after they should have been suspicions no longer. It was misery!—oh, what misery from then till now!'

Her voice died away for a moment, in faint, breathless murmurings. She struggled to recover it, and repeated in a whisper:

"Forgive me before I die! I have made a terrible atonement; I have borne witness against the innocence of my own child. My own child! I dare not bid God bless her, if they bring her to my bedside!—forgive me!—forgive me before I die!"

She took my hand, and pressed it to her cold lips. The tears gushed into my eyes, as I tried to speak to her.

"No tears for *me!*" she murmured gently. "Basil!— let me call you as your mother would call you if she was alive—Basil! pray that I may be forgiven in the dreadful Eternity to which I go, as *you* have forgiven me! And, for *her?*—oh! who will pray for *her* when I am gone?"

Those words were the last I heard her pronounce. Exhausted beyond the power of speaking more, though it were only in a whisper, she tried to take my hand again, and express by a gesture the irrevocable farewell. But her strength failed her even for this—failed her with awful suddennesss. Her hand moved halfway towards mine; then stopped and trembled for a moment in the air; then fell to her side, with the fingers distorted and clenched together. She reeled where she stood, and sank helplessly as I stretched out my arms to support her.

Her husband rose fretfully from his chair, and took her from me. When his eyes met mine, the look of sullen self-restraint in his countenance was crossed, in an instant, by an expression of triumphant malignity. He whispered to me: "If you don't change your tone by to-morrow!"—paused—and then, without finishing the sentence, moved away abruptly, and supported his wife to the door.

Just when her face was turned towards where I stood, as he took her out, I thought I saw the cold, vacant eyes soften as they rested on me, and change again tenderly to the old look of patience and sadness which I remembered so well. Was my imagination misleading me? or had the light of that meek spirit shone out on earth, for the last time at parting, in token of farewell to mine? She was gone to *me*, gone for ever—before I could look nearer, and know.

* * * * *

I was told, afterwards, how she died.

For the rest of that day, and throughout the night, she lay speechless, but still alive. The next morning, the faint pulse still fluttered. As the day wore on, the doctors applied fresh stimulants, and watched her in astonishment; for they had predicted her death as impending every moment, at least twelve hours before. When they spoke of this to her husband, his behaviour was noticed as very altered and unaccountable by every one. He sulkily refused to believe that her life was in danger; he roughly accused anybody who spoke of her death, as wanting to fix on him the imputation of having ill-used her, and so being the cause of her illness; and more than this, he angrily vindicated himself to every one about her—even to the servants—by quoting the indulgence he had shown to her fancy for seeing me when I called, and his patience while she was (as he termed it) wandering in her mind in trying to talk to me. The doctors, suspecting how his uneasy conscience was accusing him, forbore in disgust all expostulation. Except when he was in his daughter's room, he was shunned by everybody in the house.

Just before noon, on the second day, Mrs. Sherwin rallied a little under the stimulants administered to her, and asked to see her husband alone. Both her words and manner gave the lie to his assertion that her faculties were impaired—it was observed by all her attendants, that whenever she had strength to speak, her speech never wandered in the slightest degree. Her husband quitted her room more fretfully uneasy, more sullenly suspicious of the words and looks of those about him than ever—went instantly to seek his daughter—and sent her in alone to her mother's bedside. In a few minutes, she hurriedly came out again, pale, and violently agitated; and was heard to say, that she had been spoken to so unnaturally, and so shockingly, that she could not, and would not, enter that room again until her mother was better. Better! the father and daughter were both agreed in that; both agreed that she was not dying, but only out of her mind.

During the afternoon, the doctors ordered that Mrs. Sherwin should not be allowed to see her husband or her child again, without their permission. There was little need of taking such a precaution to preserve the tranquillity of her last moments. As the day began to decline, she sank again into insensibility : her life was just not death, and that was all. She lingered on in this quiet way, with her eyes peacefully closed, and her breathing so gentle as to be quite inaudible, until late in the evening. Just as it grew quite dark, and the candle was lit in the sick room, the servant who was helping to watch by her, drew aside the curtain to look at her mistress; and saw that, though her eyes were still closed, she was smiling. The girl turned round, **and** beckoned to the nurse to come to the bedside. When **they** lifted the curtains again to look at her, she was dead.

*　　*　　*　　*　　*　　*

Let me return to the day of my last visit to North Villa. More remains to be recorded, before my narrative can advance to the morrow.

After the door had closed, and I knew that I had looked my last on Mrs. Sherwin in this world, I remained a few minutes alone in the room, until I had steadied my mind sufficiently to go out again into the streets. As I walked down the garden-path to the gate, the servant whom I had seen on my entrance, ran after me, and eagerly entreated that I would wait one moment and speak to her.

When I stopped and looked at the girl, she burst into tears. " I'm afraid I've been doing wrong, Sir," she sobbed out, " and at this dreadful time too, when my poor mistress is dying ! If you please, Sir, I *must* tell you about it !"

I gave her a little time to compose herself; and then asked what she had to say.

" I think you must have seen a man leaving a letter with me, Sir," she continued, " just when you came up to the door, a little while ago ?"

" Yes : I saw him."

" It was for Miss Margaret, Sir, that letter ; and I was to keep it secret ; and—and—it isn't the first I've taken in for her. It's weeks and weeks ago, Sir, that the same man came with a letter, and gave me money to let nobody see it but Miss Margaret—and that time, Sir, he waited ; and she sent me with an answer to give him, in the same secret way. And now, here's this second letter ; I don't know who it comes from—but I haven't taken it to her yet ; I waited to show it to you, Sir, as you came out, because—"

" Why, Susan ?—tell me candidly why ?"

" I hope you won't take it amiss, Sir, if I say that having

lived in the family so long as I have, I can't help knowing a little about what you and Miss Margaret used to be to each other, and that something's happened wrong between you lately; and so, Sir, it seems to be very bad and dishonest in me (after first helping you to come together, as I did), to be giving her strange letters, unknown to you. They may be bad letters. I'm sure I wouldn't wish to say anything disrespectful, or that didn't become my place; but—"

"Go on, Susan—speak as freely and as truly to me as ever."

"Well, Sir, Miss Margaret's been very much altered, ever since that night when she came home alone, and frightened us so. She shuts herself up in her room, and won't speak to anybody except my master; she doesn't seem to care about anything that happens; and sometimes she looks so at me, when I'm waiting on her, that I'm almost afraid to be in the same room with her. I've never heard her mention your name once, Sir; and I'm fearful there's something on her mind that there oughtn't to be. He's a very shabby man that leaves the letters—would you please to look at this, and say whether you think it's right in me to take it up-stairs."

She held out a letter. I hesitated before I looked at it.

"Oh, Sir! please, please do take it!" said the girl earnestly. "I did wrong, I'm afraid, in giving her the first; but I can't do wrong again, when my poor mistress is dying in the house. I can't keep secrets, Sir, that may be bad secrets, at such a dreadful time as this; I couldn't have laid down in my bed to-night, when there's likely to be death in the house, if I hadn't confessed what I've done; and my poor mistress has always been so kind and good to us servants—better than ever we deserved."

Weeping bitterly as she said this, the kind-hearted girl held out the letter to me once more. This time I took it from her, and looked at the address.

Though I did not know the handwriting, still there was something in those unsteady characters which seemed familiar to me. Was it possible that I had ever seen them before? I tried to consider; but my memory was confused, my mind wearied out, after all that had happened since the morning. The effort was fruitless: I gave back the letter.

"I know as little about it, Susan, as you do."

"But ought I to take it up-stairs, Sir? only tell me that!"

"It is not for *me* to say. All interest or share on my part, Susan, in what she—in what your young mistress receives, is at an end."

"I'm very sorry to hear you say that, Sir; very, very sorry. But what would you advise me to do?"

"Let me look at the letter once more."

On a second view, the handwriting produced the same effect on me as before, ending too with just the same result I returned the letter again.

"I respect your scruples, Susan, but I am not the person to remove or to justify them. Why should you not apply in this difficulty to your master?"

"I dare not, Sir; I dare not for my life. He's been worse than ever, lately; if I said as much to him as I've said to you, I believe he'd kill me!" She hesitated, then continued more composedly; "Well, at any rate I've told *you*, Sir, and that's made my mind easier; and—and I'll give her the letter this once, and then take in no more—if they come, unless I hear a proper account of them."

She curtseyed; and, bidding me farewell very sadly and anxiously, returned to the house with the letter in her hand. If I had guessed at that moment who it was written by! If I could only have suspected what were its contents!

I left Hollyoake Square in a direction which led to some fields a little distance on. It was very strange; but that unknown handwriting still occupied my thoughts: that

wretched trifle absolutely took possession of my mind, at
such a time as this; in such a position as mine was now.

I stopped wearily in the fields at a lonely spot, away from
the footpath. My eyes ached at the sunlight, and I shaded
them with my hand. Exactly at the same instant, the lost
recollection flashed back on me so vividly that I started
almost in terror. The handwriting shown me by the servant at North Villa, was the same as the handwriting on
that unopened and forgotten letter in my pocket, which I
had received from the servant at home—received in the
morning, as I crossed the hall to enter my father's room.

I took out the letter, opened it with trembling fingers,
and looked through the cramped, closely-written pages for
the signature.

It was "ROBERT MANNION."

V.

Mannion! I had never suspected that the note shown
to me at North Villa might have come from him. And yet,
the secrecy with which it had been delivered; the person
to whom it was addressed; the mystery connected with it
even in the servant's eyes, all pointed to the discovery which
I had so incomprehensibly failed to make. I had suffered a
letter, which might contain written proof of her guilt, to be
taken, from under my own eyes, to Margaret Sherwin!
How had my perceptions become thus strangely blinded? The
confusion of my memory, the listless incapacity of all my faculties, answered the question but too readily, of themselves.

"Robert Mannion!" I could not take my eyes from that
name: I still held before me the crowded, closely-written
lines of his writing, and delayed to read them. Something
of the horror which the presence of the man himself would
have inspired in me, was produced by the mere sight of his
letter, and that letter addressed to *me*. The vengeance

which my own hands had wreaked on him, he was, of all men, the surest to repay. Perhaps, in these lines, the dark future through which his way and mine might lie, would be already shadowed forth. Margaret too! Could he write so much, and not write of *her?* not disclose the mystery in which the motives of *her* crime were still hidden? I turned back again to the first page, and resolved to read the letter.

It began abruptly, in the following terms:—

"St. Helen's Hospital.

"You may look at the signature when you receive this, and may be tempted to tear up my letter, and throw it from you unread. I warn you to read what I have written, and to estimate, if you can, its importance to yourself. Destroy these pages afterwards if you like—they will have served their purpose.

"Do you know where I am, and what J suffer? I am one of the patients of this hospital, hideously mutilated for life by your hand. If I could have known certainly the day of my dismissal, I should have waited to tell you with my own lips what I now write—but I am ignorant of this. At the very point of recovery I have suffered a relapse.

"You will silence any uneasy upbraidings of conscience, should you feel them, by saying that I have deserved death at your hands. I will tell you, in answer, what you deserve and shall receive at mine.

"But I will first assume that it was knowledge of your wife's guilt which prompted your attack on me. I am well aware that she has declared herself innocent, and that her father supports her declaration. By the time you receive this letter (my injuries oblige me to allow myself a whole fortnight to write it in), I shall have taken measures which render further concealment unnecessary. Therefore, if my confession avail you aught, you have it here :—She is guilty: *willingly* guilty, remember, whatever she may say to the contrary. You may believe this, and believe all I write hereafter. Deception between us two is at an end.

"I have told you Margaret Sherwin is guilty. Why was she guilty? What was the secret of my influence over her?

"To make you comprehend what I have now to communicate, it is necessary for me to speak of myself, and of my early life. To-morrow, I will undertake this disclosure—to-day, I can neither hold the pen, nor see the paper any longer. If you could look at my face, where I am now laid, you would know why!"

"When we met for the first time at North Villa, I had not been five minutes in your presence before I detected your curiosity to know something about me, and perceived that you doubted, from the first, whether I was born and bred for such a situation as I held under Mr. Sherwin. Failing—as I knew you would fail—to gain any information about me from my employer or his family, you tried, at various times, to draw me into familiarity, to get me to talk unreservedly to you; and only gave up the attempt to penetrate my secret, whatever it might be, when we parted after our interview at my house on the night of the storm. On that night, I determined to baulk your curiosity, and yet to gain your confidence; and I succeeded. You little thought, when you bade me farewell at my own door, that you had given your hand and your friendship to a man, who—long before you met with Margaret Sherwin—had inherited the right to be the enemy of your father, and of every descendant of your father's house.

"Does this declaration surprise you? Read on, and you will understand it.

"I am the son of a gentleman. My father's means were miserably limited, and his family was not an old family, like yours. Nevertheless, he was a gentleman in anybody's sense of the word; he knew it, and that knowledge was his ruin. He was a weak, kind, careless man; a worshipper of conventionalities; and a great respecter of the wide gaps which lay between social stations in his time. Thus, he determined to live like a gentleman, by following a gentleman's pursuit—a profession, as distinguished from a trade. Failing in this, he failed to follow out his principle, and starve like a gentleman. He died the death of a felon; leaving me no inheritance but the name of a felon's son.

"While still a young man, he contrived to be introduced to a gentleman of great family, great position, and great wealth. He interested, or fancied he interested, this gentleman; and always looked on him as the patron who was to make his fortune, by getting him the first government sinecure (they were plenty enough in those days!) which might fall vacant. In firm and foolish expectation of this, he lived far beyond his little professional income—lived among rich people without the courage to make use of them as a poor man. It was the old story: debts and liabilities of all kinds pressed heavy on him—creditors refused to wait— exposure and utter ruin threatened him—and the prospect of the sinecure was still as far off as ever.

"Nevertheless he believed in the advent of this office; and all the more resolutely now, because he looked to it as his salvation. He was quite confident of the interest of his patron, and of its speedy exertion in his behalf. Perhaps, that gentleman had overrated his own political influence; perhaps, my father had been too sanguine, and had misinterpreted polite general promises into special engagements. However it was, the bailiffs came into his house one morning, while help from a government situation, or any situation, was as unattainable as ever—came to take him to prison: to seize everything, in execution, even to the very bed on which my mother (then seriously ill) was lying.

The whole fabric of false prosperity which he had been
building up to make the world respect him, was menaced
with instant and shameful overthrow. He had not the courage to let it go; so he took refuge from misfortune in a
crime.

  "He forged a bond, to prop up his credit for a little time
longer. The name he made use of was the name of his
patron. In doing this, he believed—as all men who commit crime believe—that he had the best possible chance of
escaping consequences. In the first place, he might get
the long-expected situation in time to repay the amount of
the bond before detection. In the second place, he had almost the certainty of a legacy from a rich relative, old and
in ill-health, whose death might be fairly expected from
day to day. If both these prospects failed (and they *did*
fail), there was still a third chance—the chance that his
rich patron would rather pay the money than appear against
him. In those days they hung for forgery.* My father believed it to be impossible that a man at whose table he had
sat, whose relatives and friends he had amused and instructed by his talents, would be the man to give evidence
which should condemn him to be hanged on the public
scaffold.

  "He was wrong. The wealthy patron held strict principles of honour which made no allowance for temptations
and weaknesses; and was moreover influenced by high-flown
notions of his responsibilities as a legislator (he was a member of Parliament) to the laws of his country. He appeared
accordingly, and gave evidence against the prisoner; who
was found guilty, and left for execution.

  "Then, when it was too late, this man of pitiless honour
thought himself at last justified in leaning to the side of
mercy, and employed his utmost interest, in every direction,
to obtain a mitigation of the sentence to transportation for
life. The application failed; even a reprieve of a few days

was denied. At the appointed time, my father died on the scaffold by the hangman's hand.

'Have you suspected, while reading this part of my letter, who the high-born gentleman was whose evidence hung him? If you have not, I will tell you. That gentleman was *your father*. You will now wonder no longer how I could have inherited the right to be his enemy, and the enemy of all who are of his blood.

"The shock of her husband's horrible death deprived my mother of reason. She lived a few months after his execution; but never recovered her faculties. I was their only child; and was left penniless to begin life as the son of a father who had been hanged, and of a mother who had died in a public mad-house.

"More of myself to-morrow—my letter will be a long one: I must pause often over it, as I pause to-day."

———

"Well: I started in life with the hangman's mark on me—with the parent's shame for the son's reputation. Wherever I went, whatever friends I kept, whatever acquaintances I made—people knew how my father had died: and showed that they knew it. Not so much by shunning or staring at me (vile as human nature is, there were not many who did that), as by insulting me with over-acted sympathy, and elaborate anxiety to sham entire ignorance of my father's fate. The gallows-brand was on my forehead; but they were too benevolently blind to see it. The gallows-infamy was my inheritance; but they were too resolutely generous to discover it! This was hard to bear. However, I was strong-hearted even then, when my sensations were quick, and my sympathies young: so I bore it.

"My only weakness was my father's weakness—the notion that I was born to a station ready made for me, and

that the great use of my life was to live up to it. My
station! I battled for that with the world for years and
years, before I discovered that the highest of all stations is
the station a man makes for himself: and the lowest, the
station that is made for him by others.

"At starting in life, your father wrote to make me offers
of assistance—assistance, after he had ruined me! Assistance to the child, from hands which had tied the rope
round the parent's neck! I sent him back his letter. He
knew that I was his enemy, his son's enemy, and his son's
son's enemy, as long as I lived. I never heard from him
again.

"Trusting boldly to myself to carve out my own way,
and to live down my undeserved ignominy; resolving in the
pride of my integrity to combat openly and fairly with misfortune, I shrank, at first, from disowning my parentage
and abandoning my father's name. Standing on my own
character, confiding in my intellect and my perseverance,
I tried pursuit after pursuit, and was beaten afresh at every
new effort. Whichever way I turned, the gallows still
rose as the same immovable obstacle between me and fortune, between me and station, between me and my fellow-
men. I was morbidly sensitive on this point. The slightest
references to my father's fate, however remote or accidental,
curdled my blood. I saw open insult, or humiliating compassion, or forced forbearance, in the look and manner of
every man about me. So I broke off with old friends, and
tried new; and, in seeking fresh pursuits, sought fresh connections, where my father's infamy might be unknown.
Wherever I went, the old stain always broke out afresh,
just at the moment when I had deceived myself into the
belief that it was utterly effaced. I had a warm heart
then—it was some time before it turned to stone, and felt
nothing. Those were the days when failure and humiliation
could still draw tears from me: that epoch in my life

is marked in my memory as the epoch when I could weep.

"At last, I gave way before difficulty, and conceded the first step to the calamity which had stood front to front with me so long. I left the neighbourhood where I was known, and assumed the name of a schoolfellow who had died. For some time this succeeded; but the curse of my father's death followed me, though I saw it not. After various employments—still, mind, the employments of a gentleman!—had first supported, then failed me, I became an usher at a school. It was there that my false name was detected, and my identity discovered again—I never knew through whom. The exposure was effected by some enemy, anonymously. For several days, I thought everybody in the school treated me in an altered way. The cause came out, first in whispers, then in reckless jests, while I was taking care of the boys in the playground. In the fury of the moment I struck one of the most insolent, and the eldest of them, and hurt him rather seriously. The parents heard of it, and threatened me with prosecution; the whole neighbourhood was aroused. I had to leave my situation secretly, by night, or the mob would have pelted the felon's son out of the parish.

"I went back to London, bearing another assumed name; and tried, as a last resource to save me from starvation, the resource of writing. I served my apprenticeship to literature as a hack-author of the lowest degree. Knowing I had talents which might be turned to account, I tried to vindicate them by writing an original work. But my expérience of the world had made me unfit to dress my thoughts in popular costume: I could only tell bitter truths bitterly; I exposed licenced hypocrisies too openly; I saw the vicious side of many respectabilities, and said I saw it—in short, I called things by their right names; and no publisher would treat with me. So I stuck to my low task-work;

my penny-a lining in third-class newspapers; my translating from Frenchmen and Germans, and plagiarising from dead authors, to supply the raw material for bookmongering by more accomplished bookmongers than I. In this life, there was one advantage which compensated for much misery and meanness, and bitter, biting disappointment: I could keep my identity securely concealed. Character was of no consequence to me; nobody cared to know who I was, or to inquire what I had been—the gallows-mark was smoothed out at last!

"While I was living thus on the offal of literature, I met with a woman of good birth, and fair fortune, whose sympathies or whose curiosity I happened to interest. She and her father and mother received me favourably, as a gentleman who had known better days, and an author whom the public had undeservedly neglected. How I managed to gain their confidence and esteem, without alluding to my parentage, it is not worth while to stop to describe. That I did so you will easily imagine, when I tell you that the woman to whom I refer, consented, with her father's full approval, to become my wife.

"The very day of the marriage was fixed. I believed I had successfully parried all perilous inquiries—but I was wrong. A relation of the family, whom I had never seen, came to town a short time before the wedding. We disliked each other on our first introduction. He was a clever, resolute man of the world, and privately inquired about me to much better purpose in a few days, than his family had done in several months. Accident favoured him strangely, everything was discovered—literally everything—and I was contemptuously dismissed the house. Could a lady of respectability marry a man (no matter how worthy in *her* eyes) whose father had been hanged, whose mother had died in a madhouse, who had lived under assumed names, who had been driven from an excellent country neighbourhood, for cruelty to a harmless school-boy? Impossible!

"With this event, my long strife and struggle with the world ended.

"My eyes opened to a new view of life, and the purpose of life. My first aspirations to live up to my birth-right position, in spite of adversity and dishonour, to make my name sweet enough in men's nostrils, to cleanse away the infamy on my father's, were now no more. The ambition which—whether I was a hack-author, a travelling portrait-painter, or an usher at a school—had once whispered to me: low down as you are in dark, miry ways, you are on the path which leads upward to high places in the sun-shine afar-off; you are not working to scrape together wealth for another man; you are independent, self-reliant, labouring in your own cause—the daring ambition which had once counselled thus, sank dead within me at last. The strong, stern spirit was beaten by spirits stronger and sterner yet—Infamy and Want.

"I wrote to a man of character and wealth; one of my friends of early days, who had ceased to hold communication with me, like other friends, but, unlike them, had given me up in genuine sorrow: I wrote, and asked him to meet me privately by night. I was too ragged to go to his house, too sensitive still (even if I had gone and had been ad-mitted) to risk encountering people there, who either knew my father, or knew how he had died. I wished to speak to my former friend, unseen, and made the appointment ac-cordingly. He kept it.

"When we met, I said to him:—I have a last favour to ask of you. When we parted years ago, I had high hopes and brave resolutions—both are worn out. I then believed that I could not only rise superior to my misfortune, but could make that very misfortune the motive of my rise. You told me I was too quick of temper, too morbidly sensitive about the slightest reference to my father's death, too fierce and changeable under undeserved trial and disappointment. This might have been true then; but I am altered now: pride and ambition have been persecuted and starved out of me. An obscure, monotonous life, in which thought and spirit may be laid asleep, never to wake again, is the only life I care for. Help me to lead it. I ask you, first, as a beggar, to give me from your superfluity, apparel decent enough to bear the daylight. I ask you next, to help me to some occupation which will just give me my bread, my shelter, and my hour or two of solitude in the evening. You have plenty of influence to do this, and you know I am honest. You cannot choose me too humble and obscure an employment; let me descend low enough to be lost to sight beneath the world I have lived in; let me go among people who want to know that I work honestly for them, and want to know nothing more. Get me a mean hiding-place to conceal myself and my history in for ever, and then neither attempt to see me nor communicate with me again. If former friends chance to ask after me, tell them I am dead, or gone into another country. The wisest life is the life the animals lead: I want, like them, to serve my master for food, shelter, and liberty to lie asleep now and then in the sunshine, without being driven away as a pest or a trespasser. Do you believe in this resolution?—it is my last.

"He *did* believe in it; and he granted what I asked. Through his interference and recommendation, I entered the service of Mr. Sherwin.—

"I must stop here for to-day. To-morrow I shall come to disclosures of vital interest to you. Have you been surprised that I, your enemy by every cause of enmity that one man can have against another, should write to you so fully about the secrets of my early life? I have done so, because I wish the strife between us to be an open strife on *my* side; because I desire that you should know thoroughly what you have to expect from my character, after such a life as I have led. There was purpose in my deceit, when I deceived you—there is purpose in my frankness, when I now tell you all."

"I began in Mr. Sherwin's employment, as the lowest clerk in his office. Both the master and the men looked a little suspiciously on me, at first. My account of myself was always the same—simple and credible; I had entered the counting-house with the best possible recommendation, and I acted up to it. These circumstances in my favour, joined to a manner that never varied, and to a steadiness at my work that never relaxed, soon produced their effect— all curiosity about me gradually died away: I was left to pursue my avocations in peace. The friend who had got me my situation, preserved my secret as I had desired him; of all the people whom I had formerly known, pitiless enemies and lukewarm adherents, not one ever suspected that my hiding-place was the back office of a linen-draper's shop. For the first time in my life, I felt that the secret of my father's misfortune was mine, and mine only; that my security from exposure was at length complete.

"Before long, I rose to the chief place in the counting-house. It was no very difficult matter for me to discover, that my new master's character had other elements besides that of the highest respectability. In plain terms, I found him to be a pretty equal compound by nature, of the fool, the tyrant, and the coward. There was only one direction in which what grovelling sympathies he had, could be touched to some purpose. Save him waste, or get him profit; and he was really grateful. I succeeded in working both these marvels. His managing man cheated him; I found it out; refused to be bribed to collusion; and exposed the fraud to Mr. Sherwin. This got me his **con-fidence**, and the place of chief clerk. In that position, I discovered a means, which had never occurred to my employer, of greatly enlarging his business and its profits, with the least possible risk. He tried my plan, and it succeeded. This gained me his warmest admiration, an increase of salary, and a firm footing in his family circle. My projects were more than fulfilled: I had money enough, and leisure enough; and spent my obscure existence exactly as I had proposed.

"But my life was still not destined to be altogether devoid of an animating purpose. When I first knew Margaret Sherwin, she was just changing from childhood to girlhood. I marked the promise of future beauty in her face and figure; and secretly formed the resolution which you afterwards came forward to thwart, but which I have executed, and will execute, in spite of you.

"The thoughts out of which that resolution sprang, counselled me more calmly than you can suppose. I said within myself: 'The best years of my life have been irrevocably wasted; misery and humiliation and disaster have followed my steps from my youth; of all the pleasant draughts which other men drink to sweeten existence, not one has passed my lips. I will know happiness before I die; and this girl shall confer it. She shall grow up to maturity for *me*: I will imperceptibly gain such a hold on her affections, while they are yet young and impressible, that, when the time comes, and I speak the word— though my years more than double hers, though I am dependent on her father for the bread I eat, though parents' voice and lover's voice unite to call her back—she shall still come to my side, and of her own free will put her hand in mine, and follow me wherever I go; my wife, my mistress, my servant, which I choose.

"This was my project. To execute it, time and **oppor-**

tunity were mine ; and I steadily and warily made use of them, hour by hour, day by day, year by year. From first to last, the girl's father never suspected me. Besides the security which he felt in my age, he had judged me by his own small commercial standard, and had found me a model of integrity. A man who had saved him from being cheated, who had so enlarged and consolidated his business as to place him among the top dignitaries of the trade ; who was the first to come to the desk in the morning, and the last to remain there in the evening ; who had not only never demanded, but had absolutely refused to take, a single holiday—such a man as this was, morally and intellectually, a man in ten thousand ; a man to be admired and trusted in every relation of life !

"His confidence in me knew no bounds. He was uneasy if I was not by to advise him in the simplest matters. My ears were the first to which he confided his insane ambition on the subject of his daughter—his anxiety to see her marry above her station—his stupid resolution to give her the false, flippant, fashionable education which she subsequently received. I thwarted his plans in nothing, openly—counteracted them in everything, secretly. The more I strengthened my sources of influence over Margaret, the more pleased he was. He was delighted to hear her constantly referring to me about her home-lessons ; to see her coming to me, evening after evening, to learn new occupations and amusements. He suspected I had been a gentleman ; he had been told I spoke pure English ; he felt sure I had received a first-rate education—I was nearly as good for Margaret as good society itself ! When she grew older, and went to the fashionable school, as her father had declared she should, my offer to keep up her lessons in the holidays, and to examine what progress she had made, when she came home regularly every fortnight for the Sunday, was accepted with greedy readiness, and acknowledged with servile gratitude.

At this time, Mr. Sherwin's own estimate of me, among his friends, was, that he had got me for half nothing, and that I was worth more to him than a thousand a-year.

"But there was one member of the family who suspected my intentions from the first. Mrs. Sherwin—the weak, timid, sickly woman, whose opinion nobody regarded, whose character nobody understood—Mrs. Sherwin, of all those who dwelt in the house, or came to the house, was the only one whose looks, words, and manner kept me constantly on my guard. The very first time we saw each other, that woman doubted *me*, as I doubted *her;* and for ever afterwards, when we met, she was on the watch. This mutual distrust, this antagonism of our two natures, never openly proclaimed itself, and never wore away. My chance of security lay, not so much in my own caution, and my perfect command of look and action under all emergencies, as in the self-distrust and timidity of her nature; in the helpless inferiority of position to which her husband's want of affection, and her daughter's want of respect, condemned her in her own house; and in the influence of repulsion— at times, even of absolute terror—which my presence had the power of communicating to her. Suspecting what I am assured she suspected—incapable as she was of rendering her suspicions certainties—knowing beforehand, as she must have known, that no words she could speak would gain the smallest respect or credit from her husband or her child— that woman's life, while I was at North Villa, must have been a life of the direst mental suffering to which any human being was ever condemned.

"As time passed, and Margaret grew older, her beauty both of face and form approached nearer to perfection than I had foreseen, closely as I watched her. But neither her mind nor her disposition kept pace with her beauty.* I studied her closely, with the same patient, penetrating observation, which my experience of the world has made it a

habit with me to direct on every one with whom I am brought in contact—I studied her, I say, intently ; and found her worthy of nothing, not even of the slave-destiny which I had in store for her.

"She had neither heart nor mind, in the higher sense of those words. She had simply instincts—most of the bad instincts of an animal; none of the good. The great motive power which really directed her, was Deceit. I never met with any human being so inherently disingenuous, so naturally incapable of candour even in the most trifling affairs of life, as she was. The best training could never have wholly overcome this vice in her : the education she actually got — an education under false pretences—encouraged it. Everybody has read, some people have known, of young girls who have committed the most extraordinary impostures, or sustained the most infamous false accusations ; their chief motive being often the sheer enjoyment of practising deceit. Of such characters was the character of Margaret Sherwin.

"She had strong passions, but not their frequent accompaniment—strong will, and strong intellect. She had some obstinacy, but no firmness. Appeal in the right way to her vanity, and you could make her do the thing she had declared she would not do, the minute after she had made the declaration. As for her mind, it was of the lowest school-girl average. She had a certain knack at learning this thing, and remembering that ; but she understood nothing fairly, felt nothing deeply. If I had not had my own motive in teaching her, I should have shut the books again, the first time she and I opened them together, and have given her up as a fool.

"All, however, that I discovered of bad in her character, never made me pause in the prosecution of my design ; I had carried it too far for that, before I thoroughly knew her. Besides, what mattered her duplicity to *me ?*—I could see through it. Her strong passions?—I could control them. Her obstinacy?—I could break it. Her poverty of intellect?—I cared nothing about her intellect. What I wanted was youth and beauty; she was young and beautiful, and I was sure of her.

"Yes; sure. Her showy person, showy accomplishments, and showy manners dazzled all eyes but mine—of all the people about her, I alone found out what she really was; and in that lay the main secret of my influence over her. I dreaded no rivalry. Her father, prompted by his ambitious hopes, kept most young men of her class away from the house; the few who did come were not dangerous; *they* were as incapable of inspiring, as *she* was of feeling, real love. Her mother still watched me, and still discovered nothing; still suspected me behind my back, and still trembled before my face. Months passed on monotonously, year succeeded to year; and I bided my time as patiently, and kept my secret as cautiously as at the first. No change occurred, nothing happened to weaken or alter my influence at North Villa, until the day arrived when Margaret left school and came home for good.

"Exactly at the period to which I have referred, certain business transactions of great importance required the presence of Mr. Sherwin, or of some confidential person to represent him, at Lyons. Secretly distrusting his own capabilities, he proposed to me to go; saying that it would be a pleasant trip for me, and a good introduction to his wealthy manufacturing correspondents. After some consideration, I accepted his offer.

"I had never hinted a word of my intentions towards her to Margaret; but she understood them well enough—I was certain of that, from many indications which no man could mistake. For reasons which will presently appear, I resolved not to explain myself until my return from Lyons. My private object in going there, was to make interest secretly with Mr. Sherwin's correspondents for a situation in their house. I knew that when I made my proposals to Margaret, I must be prepared to act on them on the instant; I knew that her father's fury when he discovered that I had been helping to educate his daughter only for myself, would lead him to any extremities; I knew that we must fly to some foreign country; and, lastly, I knew the importance of securing a provision for our maintenance, when we got there. I had saved money, it is true—nearly two-thirds of my salary, every year—but had not saved enough for two. Accordingly, I left England to push my own interests, as well as my employer's; left it, confident that my short absence would not weaken the result of years of steady influence over Margaret. The sequel showed that, cautious and calculating as I was, I had nevertheless overlooked the chances against me, which my own experience of her vanity and duplicity ought to have enabled me thoroughly to foresee.

"Well: I had been some time at Lyons; had managed my employer's business (from first to last, I was faithful, as I had engaged to be, to his commercial interests); and had arranged my own affairs securely and privately. Already, I was looking forward, with sensations of happiness which were new to me, to my return and to the achievement of the one success, the solitary triumph of my long life of humiliation and disaster, when a letter arrived from Mr. Sherwin. It contained the news of your private marriage, and of the extraordinary conditions that had been attached to it with your consent.

"Other people were in the room with me when I read that letter; but my manner betrayed nothing to them. My hand never trembled when I folded the sheet of paper again; I was not a minute late in attending a business

engagement which I had accepted; the slightest duties of
other kinds which I had to do, I rigidly fulfilled.   Never
did I more thoroughly and fairly earn the evening's leisure
by the morning's work, than I earned it that day.

"Leaving the town at the close of afternoon, I walked on
till I came to a solitary place on the bank of the great river
which runs near Lyons.   There I opened the letter for the
second time, and read it through again slowly, with no
necessity now for self-control, because no human being was
near to look at me.   There I read your name, constantly
repeated in every line of writing; and knew that the man
who, in my absence, had stepped between me and my prize
—the man who, in his insolence of youth, and birth, and
fortune, had snatched from me the one long-delayed reward
for twenty years of misery, just as my hands were stretched
forth to grasp it, was the son of that honourable and high-
born gentleman who had given my father to the gallows,
and had made me the outcast of my social privileges for life.

"The sun was setting when I looked up from the letter;
flashes of rose-light leapt on the leaping river; the birds
were winging nestward to the distant trees, and the ghostly
stillness of night was sailing solemnly over earth and sky, as
the first thought of the vengeance I would have on father
and son began to burn fiercely at my heart, to move like a
new life within me, to whisper to my spirit—Wait: be patient; they are both in your power; you can now foul the
father's name as the father fouled yours—you can yet
thwart the son, as the son has thwarted *you*.

"In the few minutes that passed, while I lingered in that
lonely place after reading the letter, I imagined the whole
scheme which it afterwards took a year to execute.   I laid
the whole plan against you and your father, the first half of
which, through the accident that led you to your discovery,
has alone been carried out.   I believed then, as I believe
now, that I stood towards you both in the place of an in-

jured man, whose right it was, in self-defence and self-assertion, to injure you. Judged by your ideas, this may read wickedly; but to me, after having lived and suffered as I have, the modern common-places current in the world are so many brazen images which society impudently worships—like the Jews of old*—in the face of living Truth.

"Let us get back to England.

"That evening, when we met for the first time, did you observe that Margaret was unusually agitated before I came in? I detected some change, the moment I saw her. Did you notice that I avoided speaking to her, or looking at her? it was because I was afraid to do so. I saw that, with my return, my old influence over her was coming back: and I still believe that, hypocritical and heartless though she was, and blinded though you were by your passion for her, she would unconsciously have betrayed everything to you on that evening, if I had not acted as I did. Her mother, too! how her mother watched me from the moment when I came in!

"Afterwards, while you were trying hard to open, undetected, the sealed history of my early life, I was warily discovering from Margaret all that I desired to know. I say 'warily,' but the word poorly expresses my consummate caution and patience, at that time. I never put myself in her power, never risked offending, or frightening, or revolting her; never lost an opportunity of bringing her back to her old habits of familiarity; and, more than all, never gave her mother a single opportunity of detecting me. This was the sum of what I gathered up, bit by bit, from secret and scattered investigations, persevered in through many weeks.

"Her vanity had been hurt, her expectations disappointed, at my having left her for Lyons, with no other parting words than such as I might have spoken to any other woman whom I looked on merely as a friend. That she felt any genuine love for me I never have believed, and never shall: but I had that practical ability, that firmness of will, that obvious personal ascendancy over most of those with whom I came in contact, which extorts the respect and admiration of women of all characters, and even of women of no character at all. As far as her senses, her instincts, and her pride could take her, I had won her over to me; but no farther—because no farther could she go. I mention pride among her motives, advisedly. She was proud of being the object of such attentions as I had now paid to her for years, because she fancied that, through those attentions, I, who, more or less, ruled everyone else in her sphere, had yielded to her the power of ruling *me*. The manner of my departure from England showed her too plainly that she had miscalculated her influence, and that the power, in her case, as in the case of others, was all on my side. Hence the wound to her vanity, to which I have alluded.

"It was while this wound was still fresh that you met her, and appealed to her self-esteem in a new direction. You must have seen clearly enough, that such proposals as yours far exceeded the most ambitious expectations formed by her father. No man's alliance could have lifted her much higher out of her own class: she knew this, and from that knowledge married you—married you for your station, for your name, for your great friends and connections, for your father's money, and carriages, and fine houses; for everything, in short, but yourself.

"Still, in spite of the temptations of youth, wealth, and birth which your proposals held out to her, she accepted them at first (I made her confess it herself) with a secret terror and misgiving, produced by the remembrance of me. These sensations, however, she soon quelled, or fancied she quelled; and these, it was now my last, best chance to revive. I had a whole year for the work before me; and I felt certain of success.

"On your side, you had immense advantages. You had social superiority; you had her father's full approbation; and you were married to her. If she had loved you for yourself, loved you for anything besides her own sensual interests, her vulgar ambition, her reckless vanity, every effort I could have made against you would have been defeated from the first. But, setting this out of the question, in spite of the utter heartlessness of her attachment to you, if you had not consented to that condition of waiting a year for her after marriage; or, consenting to it, if you had broken it long before the year was out—knowing, as you should have known, that in most women's eyes a man is not dishonoured by breaking his promise, so long as he breaks it for a woman's sake—if, I say, you had taken either of these courses, I should still have been powerless against you. But you remained faithful to your promise, faithful to the condition, faithful to the ill-directed modesty of your love; and that very fidelity put you in my power. A pure-minded girl would have loved you a thousand times better for acting as you did—but Margaret Sherwin was not a pure-minded girl, not a maidenly girl: I have looked into her thoughts, and I know it.*

"Such were your chances against me; and such was the manner in which you misused them. On *my* side, I had indefatigable patience; personal advantages equal, with the exception of birth and age, to yours: long-established influence; freedom to be familiar; and more than all, that stealthy, unflagging strength of purpose which only springs from the desire of revenge. I first thoroughly tested your character, and discovered on what points it was necessary for me to be on my guard against you, when you took shelter under my roof from the storm. If your father had been with you on that night, there were moments, while the tempest was wrought to its full fury, when, if my voice could have called the thunder down on the house to crush it and every one in it to atoms, I would have spoken the word, and ended the strife for all of us.   The wind, the hail, and the lightning maddened my thoughts of your father and you — I was nearly letting you see it, when that flash came between us as we parted at my door.

"How I gained your confidence, you know ; and you know also, how I contrived to make you use me, afterwards, as the secret friend who procured you privileges with Margaret which her father would not grant at your own request. This, at the outset, secured me from suspicion on your part; and I had only to leave it to your infatuation to do the rest. With you my course was easy—with her it was beset by difficulties; but I overcame them. Your fatal consent to wait through a year of probation, furnished me with weapons against you, which I employed to the most unscrupulous purpose. I can picture to myself what would be your in-dignation and your horror, if I fully described the use which I made of the position in which your compliance with her father's conditions placed you towards Margaret. I spare you this avowal—it would be useless now. Con-sider me what you please; denounce my conduct in any terms you like : my justification will always be the same. I was the injured man, you were the aggressor; I was right-ing myself by getting back a possession of which you had robbed me, and any means were sanctified by such an end as that.

"But my success, so far, was of little avail, in itself, against the all-powerful counter-attraction which you pos-sessed. Contemptible, or not, you still had this superiority over me—you could make a fine lady of her. From that fact sprang the ambition which all my influence, dating as it did from her childhood, could not destroy. There, was fastened the main-spring which regulated her selfish devotion to you, and which it was next to impossible to snap asunder. I never made the attempt.

"The scheme which I proposed to her, when she was fully prepared to hear it, and to conceal that she had heard it, left her free to enjoy all the social advantages which your alliance could bestow—free to ride in her carriage, and go into her father's shop (that was one of her ambitions!) as a new customer added to his aristocratic connection—free even to become one of your family, unsuspected, in case your rash marriage was forgiven. Your credulity rendered the execution of this scheme easy. In what manner it was to be carried out, and what object I proposed to myself in framing it, I abstain from avowing; for the simple reason that the discovery at which you arrived by following us on the night of the party, made my plan abortive, and has obliged me since to renounce it. I need only say, in this place, that it threatened your father as well as you, and that Margaret recoiled from it at first—not from any horror of the proposal, but through fear of discovery. Gradually, I overcame her apprehensions: very gradually, for I was not thoroughly secure of her devotion to my purpose, until your year of probation was nearly out.

"Through all that year, daily visitor as you were at North Villa, you never suspected either of us! And yet, had you been one whit less infatuated, how many warnings you might have discovered, which, in spite of her duplicity and my caution, would then have shown themselves plainly enough to put you on your guard! Those abrupt changes in her manner, those alternate fits of peevish silence and capricious gaiety, which sometimes displayed themselves even in your presence, had every one of them their meaning—though you could not discern it. Sometimes, they meant fear of discovery, sometimes fear of me: now, they might be traced back to hidden contempt; now, to passions swelling under fancied outrage; now, to secret remem-

brance of disclosures I had just made, or eager anticipation
of disclosures I had yet to reveal. There were times at
which every step of the way along which I was advancing
was marked, faintly yet significantly, in her manner and her
speech, could you only have interpreted them aright. My
first renewal of my old influence over her, my first words
that degraded you in her eyes, my first successful pleading
of my own cause against yours, my first appeal to those
passions in her which I knew how to move, my first proposal to her of the whole scheme which I had matured in
solitude, in the foreign country, by the banks of the great
river—all these separate and gradual advances on my part
towards the end which I was vowed to achieve, were outwardly shadowed forth in her, consummate as were her
capacities for deceit, and consummately as she learnt to use
them against you.

"Do you remember noticing, on your return from the
country, how ill Margaret looked, and how ill I looked?
We had some interviews during your absence, at which I
spoke such words to her as would have left their mark on
the face of a Jezebel, or a Messalina. Have you forgotten
how often, during the latter days of your year of expectation, I abruptly left the room after you had called me in
to bear you company in your evening readings? My pre-
text was sudden illness; and illness it was, but not of the
body. As the time approached, I felt less and less secure
of my own caution and patience. With you, indeed, I
might still have considered myself safe: it was the presence
of Mrs. Sherwin that drove me from the room. Under
that woman's fatal eye I shrank, when the last days drew
near—I, who had defied her detection, and stood firmly on
my guard against her sleepless, silent, deadly vigilance, for
months and months—gave way as the end approached! I
knew that she had once or twice spoken strangely to you,
and I dreaded lest her wandering, incoherent words might

yet take in time a recognisable direction, a palpable shape. They did not; the instinct of terror bound her tongue to the last. Perhaps, even if she had spoken plainly, you would not have believed her; you would have been still true to yourself and to your confidence in Margaret. Enemy as I am to you, enemy as I will be to the day of your death, I will do you justice for the past:—Your love for that girl was a love which even the purest and best of women could never have thoroughly deserved.

———

" My letter is nearly done: my retrospect is finished. I have brought it down to the date of events, about which you know as much as I do. Accident conducted you to a discovery which, otherwise, you might not have made, perhaps for months, perhaps not at all, until I had led you to it of my own accord. I say accident, positively; knowing that from first to last I trusted no third person. What you know, you knew by accident alone.

" But for that chance discovery, you would have seen me bring her back to North Villa at the appointed time, in my care, just as she went out. I had no dread of her meeting you.* But enough of her! I shall dispose of her future, as I had resolved to dispose of it years ago; careless how she may be affected when she first sees the hideous alteration which your attack has wrought in me. Enough, I say, of the Sherwins—father, mother, and daughter—your destiny lies not with *them*, but with *me*.

" Do you still exult* in having deformed me in every feature, in having given me a face to revolt every human being who looks at me? Do you triumph in the remembrance of this atrocity, as you triumphed in the acting of it—believing that you had destroyed my future with Margaret, in destroying my very identity as a man? I tell you, that with the hour when I leave this hospital your day of

triumph will be over, and your day of expiation will begin
—never to end till the death of one of us. You shall live
—refined educated gentleman as you are—to wish, like a
ruffian, that you had killed me; and your father shall live
to wish it too.

"Am I trying to awe you with the fierce words of a
boaster and a bully? Test me, by looking back a little,
and discovering what I have abstained from for the sake of
my purpose, since I have been here. A word or two from
my lips, in answer to the questions with which I have been
baited, day after day, by those about me, would have called
you before a magistrate to answer for an assault—a shocking and a savage assault, even in this country, where hand
to hand brutality is a marketable commodity between the
Prisoner and the Law. Your father's name might have
been publicly coupled with your dishonour, if I had but
spoken; and I was silent. I kept the secret—kept it,
because to avenge myself on you by a paltry scandal, which
you and your family (opposing to it wealth, position, previous character, and general sympathy) would live down in
a few days, was not *my* revenge : because to be righted
before magistrates and judges by a beggarman's exhibition
of physical injury, and a coward's confession of physical
defeat, was not *my* way of righting myself. I have a life-
long retaliation in view, which laws and lawgivers are powerless either to aid or to oppose—the retaliation which set a
mark upon Cain (as I will set a mark on you); and then
made his life his punishment (as I will make your life
yours).

"How? Remember what my career has been; and
know that I will make your career like it. As my father's
death by the hangman affected *my* existence, so the events
of that night when you followed me shall affect *yours*.
Your father shall see you living the life to which his evidence
against *my* father condemned *me*—shall see the foul stain

of your disaster clinging to you wherever you go. The infamy with which I am determined to pursue you, shall be your own infamy that you cannot get quit of—for you shall never get quit of me, never get quit of the wife who has dishonoured you. You may leave your home, and leave England; you may make new friends, and seek new employments; years and years may pass away—and still, you shall not escape us: still, you shall never know when we are near, or when we are distant; when we are ready to appear before you, or when we are sure to keep out of your sight. My deformed face and her fatal beauty shall hunt you through the world. The terrible secret of your dishonour, and of the atrocity by which you avenged it, shall ooze out through strange channels, in vague shapes, by tortuous intangible processes; ever changing in the manner of its exposure, never remediable by your own resistance, and always directed to the same end—your isolation as a marked man, in every fresh sphere, among every new community to which you retreat.

"Do you call this a very madness of malignity and revenge? It is the only occupation in life for which your mutilation of me has left me fit; and I accept it, as work worthy of my deformity. In the prospect of watching how you bear this hunting through life, that never quite hunts you down; how long you resist the poison-influence, as slow as it is sure, of a crafty tongue that cannot be silenced, of a denouncing presence that cannot be fled, of a damning secret torn from you and exposed afresh each time you have hidden it—there is the promise of a nameless delight which it sometimes fevers, sometimes chills my blood to think of. Lying in this place at night, in those hours of darkness and stillness when the surrounding atmosphere of human misery presses heavy on me in my heavy sleep, prophecies of dread things to come between us, trouble my spirit in dreams. At those times, I know, and shudder in knowing, that there is something besides the motive of retaliation, something less earthly and apparent than that, which urges me horribly and supernaturally to link myself to you for life; which makes me feel as the bearer of a curse that shall follow you; as the instrument of a fatality pronounced against you long ere we met—a fatality beginning before our fathers were parted by the hangman; perpetuating itself in you and me; ending who shall say how, or when?

"Beware of comforting yourself with a false security, by despising my words, as the wild words of a madman, dreaming of the perpetration of impossible crimes. Throughout this letter I have warned you of what you may expect; because I will not assail you at disadvantage, as you assailed me; because it is my pleasure to ruin you, openly resisting me at every step. I have given you fair play, as the huntsmen give fair play at starting to the animal they are about to run down. Be warned against seeking a false hope in the belief that my faculties are shaken, and that my resolves are visionary—false, because such a hope is only despair in disguise.

"I have done. The time is not far distant when my words will become deeds. They cure fast in a public hospital*; we shall meet soon!

                                        "ROBERT MANNION."

"We shall meet soon!"

How? Where? I looked back at the last page of writing. But my attention wandered strangely; I confused one paragraph with another; the longer I read, the less I was able to grasp the meaning, not of sentences merely, but even of the simplest words.

From the first lines to the last, the letter had produced no distinct impressions on my mind. So utterly was I worn out by the previous events of the day, that even those earlier portions of Mannion's confession, which revealed the connection between my father and his, and the terrible manner of their separation, hardly roused me to more than a momentary astonishment. I just called to remembrance that I had never heard the subject mentioned at home, except once or twice in vague hints dropped mysteriously by an old servant, and little regarded by me at the time, as referring to matters which had happened before I was born. I just reflected thus briefly and languidly on the narrative at the commencement of the letter; and then mechanically read on. Except the passages which contained the exposure of Margaret's real character, and those which described the origin and progress of Mannion's infamous plot, nothing in the letter impressed me, as I was afterwards destined to be impressed by it, on a second reading. The lethargy. of all feeling into which I had now sunk, seemed a very lethargy of death.

I tried to clear and concentrate my faculties by thinking of other subjects; but without success. All that I had heard and seen since the morning, now recurred to me more and more vaguely and confusedly. I could form no plan either for the present or the future. I knew as little how to meet Mr. Sherwin's last threat of forcing me to acknowledge his guilty daughter, as how to defend myself against the life-long hostility with which I was menaced by Mannion. A feeling of awe and apprehension, which I could trace to no distinct cause, stole irresistibly and mysteriously over me. A horror of the searching brightness of daylight, a suspicion of the loneliness of the place to which I had retreated, a yearning to be among my fellow-creatures again, to live where there was life—the busy life of London —overcame me. I turned hastily, and walked back from the suburbs to the city.

It was growing towards evening as I gained one of the great thoroughfares. Seeing some of the inhabitants of the houses, as I walked along, sitting at their open windows to enjoy the evening air, the thought came to me for the first time that day:—where shall I lay my head tonight? Home I had none. Friends who would have gladly received me were not wanting; but to go to them would oblige me to explain myself, to disclose something of the secret of my calamity; and this I was determined to keep concealed, as I had told my father I would keep it. My last-left consolation was my knowledge of still preserving that resolution, of still honourably holding by it at all hazards, cost what it might.

So I thought no more of succour or sympathy from any one of my friends. As a stranger I had been driven from my home, and as a stranger I was resigned to live, until I had learnt how to conquer my misfortune by my own vigour and endurance. Firm in this determination, though firm in nothing else, I now looked around me for the first shelter I could purchase from strangers—the humbler the better.

I happened to be in the poorest part, and on the poorest side of the great street along which I was walking—among the inferior shops, and the houses of few stories. A room to let was not hard to find here. I took the first I saw; escaped questions about names and references by paying my week's rent in advance; and then found myself left in possession of the one little room which I must be resigned to look on for the future—perhaps for a long future!—as my home.

Home! A dear and a mournful remembrance was revived in the reflections suggested by that simple word. Through the darkness that thickened over my mind, there now passed one faint ray of light which gave promise of the morning—the light of the calm face that I had last looked on when it was resting on my father's breast.

Clara! My parting words to her, when I had unclasped

from my neck those kind arms which would fain have held me to home for ever, had expressed a promise that was yet unfulfilled. I trembled as I now thought on my sister's situation. Not knowing whither I had turned my steps on leaving home; uncertain to what extremities my despair might hurry me; absolutely ignorant even whether she might ever see me again—it was terrible to reflect on the suspense under which she might be suffering, at this very moment, on my account. My promise to write to her, was of all promises the most vitally important, and the first that should be fulfilled.

My letter was very short. I communicated to her the address of the house in which I was living (well knowing that nothing but positive information on this point would effectually relieve her anxiety)—I asked her to write in reply, and let me hear some news of her, the best that she could give—and I entreated her to believe implicitly in my patience and courage under every disaster; and to feel assured that, whatever happened, I should never lose the hope of soon meeting her again. Of the perils that beset me, of the wrong and injury I might yet be condemned to endure, I said nothing. Those were truths which I was determined to conceal from her, to the last. She had suffered for me more than I dared think of, already!

I sent my letter by hand, so as to ensure its immediate delivery. In writing those few simple lines, I had no suspicion of the important results which they were destined to produce. In thinking of to-morrow, and of all the events which to-morrow might bring with it, I little thought whose voice would be the first to greet me the next day, whose hand would be held out to me as the helping hand of a friend.

VI.

It was still early in the morning, when a loud knock sounded at the house-door, and I heard the landlady calling to the servant: "A gentleman to see the gentleman who came in last night." The moment the words reached me, my thoughts recurred to the letter of yesterday—Had Mannion found me out in my retreat? As the suspicion crossed my mind, the door opened, and the visitor entered.

I looked at him in speechless astonishment. It was my elder brother! It was Ralph himself who now walked into the room!

"Well, Basil! how are you?" he said, with his old off-hand manner and hearty voice.

"Ralph! You in England!—you here!"

"I came back from Italy last night. Basil, how awfully you're changed! I hardly know you again."

His manner altered as he spoke the last words. The look of sorrow and alarm which he fixed on me, went to my heart. I thought of holiday-time, when we were boys; of Ralph's boisterous ways with me; of his good-humoured school-frolics, at my expense; of the strong bond of union between us, so strangely compounded of my weakness and his strength; of my passive and of his active nature; I saw how little *he* had changed since that time, and knew, as I never knew before, how miserably *I* was altered. All the shame and grief of my banishment from home came back on me, at sight of his friendly, familiar face. I strug- gled hard to keep my self-possession, and tried to bid him welcome cheerfully; but the effort was too much for me. I turned away my head, as I took his hand; for the old school-boy feeling of not letting Ralph see that I was in tears, influenced me still.

"Basil! Basil! what are you about? This won't do. Look up, and listen to me. I have promised Clara to pull you through this wretched mess; and I'll do it. Get a chair, and give me a light. I'm going to sit on your bed, smoke a cigar, and have a long talk with you."

While he was lighting his cigar, I looked more closely at him than before. Though he was the same as ever in manner; though his expression still preserved its reckless levity of former days, I now detected that he had changed a little in some other respects. His features had become coarser—dissipation had begun to mark them. His spare, active, muscular figure had filled out; he was dressed rather carelessly; and of all his trinkets and chains of early times, not one appeared about him now. Ralph looked prematurely middle-aged, since I had seen him last.

"Well," he began, "first of all, about my coming back. The fact is, the morganatic Mrs. Ralph—" (he referred to his last mistress) "wanted to see England, and I was tired of being abroad. So I brought her back with me; and we're going to live quietly, somewhere in the Brompton neighbourhood.* That woman has been my salvation—you must come and see her. She has broke me of gaming altogether; I was going to the devil as fast as I could, when she stopped me—but you know all about it, of course. Well: we got to London yesterday afternoon; and in the evening I left her at the hotel, and went to report myself at home. There, the first thing I heard, was that you had cut me out of my old original distinction of being the family scamp. Don't look distressed, Basil; I'm not laughing at you; I've come to do something better than that. Never mind my talk: nothing in the world ever was serious to *me*, and nothing ever will be."

He stopped to knock the ash off his cigar, and settle himself more comfortably on my bed; then proceeded.

"It has been my ill-luck to see my father pretty seriously offended on more than one occasion; but I never
saw him so very quiet and so very dangerous as last night
when he was telling me about you. I remember well enough
how he spoke and looked, when he caught me putting away
my trout-flies in the pages of that family history of his;
but it was nothing to see him or hear him then, to what it
is now. I can tell you this, Basil—if I believed in what the
poetical people call a broken heart (which I don't), I should
be almost afraid that *he* was broken-hearted. I saw it was
no use to say a word for you just yet, so I sat quiet and
listened to him till I got my dismissal for the evening. My
next proceeding was to go up-stairs, and see Clara. Up-
stairs, I give you my word of honour, it was worse still.
Clara was walking about the room with your letter in her
hand—just reach me the matches : my cigar's out. Some
men can talk and smoke in equal proportions—I never
could.

"You know as well as I do," he continued when he had
relit his cigar, "that Clara is not usually demonstrative. I
always thought her rather a cold temperament—but the
moment I put my head in at the door, I found I'd been just
as great a fool on that point as on most others. Basil, the
scream Clara gave when she first saw me, and the look in
her eyes when she talked about you, positively frightened me.
I can't describe anything; and I hate descriptions by other men
(most likely on that very account): so I won't describe what
she said and did. I'll only tell you that it ended in my promising to come here the first thing this morning ; promising
to get you out of the scrape ; promising, in short, everything
she asked me. So here I am, ready for your business before my own. The fair partner of my existence* is at the
hotel, half-frantic because I won't go lodging-hunting with
her ; but Clara is paramount, Clara is the first thought.
Somebody must be a good boy at home ; and now you have

resigned, I'm going to try and succeed you, by way of a change!"

"Ralph! Ralph! can you mention Clara's name, and that woman's name, in the same breath? Did you leave Clara quieter and better! For God's sake be serious about that, though serious about nothing else!"

"Gently, Basil! *Doucement mon ami!* I *did* leave her quieter: my promise made her look almost like herself again. As for what you say about mentioning Clara and Mrs. Ralph in the same breath, I've been talking and smoking till I have no second breaths left to devote to second-rate virtue. There is an unanswerable reason for you, if you want one! And now let us get to the business that brings me here. I don't want to worry you by raking up this miserable mess again, from beginning to end, in your presence; but I must make sure at the same time that I have got hold of the right story, or I can't be of any use to you. My father was a little obscure on certain points. He talked enough, and more than enough, about consequences to the family, about his own affliction, about his giving you up for ever; and, in short, about everything but the case itself, as it really stands against us. Now that is just what I ought to be put up to, and *must* be put up to. Let me tell you in three words what I was told last night."

"Go on, Ralph: speak as you please."

"Very good. First of all, I understand that you took a fancy to some shopkeeper's daughter—so far, mind, I don't blame you: I've spent time very pleasantly among the ladies of the counter myself. But in the second place, I'm told that you actually married the girl! I don't wish to be hard upon you, my good fellow, but there was an unparalleled insanity about that act, worthier of a patient in Bedlam than of my brother. I am not quite sure whether I understand exactly what virtuous behaviour is; but if *that* was virtuous behaviour — there! there! don't look shocked. Let's have done with the marriage, and get on. Well, you made the girl your wife; and then innocently consented to a very queer condition of waiting a year for her (virtuous behaviour again, I suppose!) At the end of that time— don't turn away your head, Basil! I *may* be a scamp; but I am not blackguard enough to make a joke—either in your presence, or out of it—of this part of the story. I will pass it over altogether, if you like; and only ask you a question or two. You see, my father either could not or would not speak plainly of the worst part· of the business; and you know him well enough to know why. But some- body must be a little explicit, or I can do nothing. About that man? You found the scoundrel out? Did you get within arm's length of him?"

I told my brother of the struggle with Mannion in the Square.

He heard me almost with his former schoolboy delight, when I had succeeded, to his satisfaction, in a feat of strength or activity. He jumped off the bed, and seized both my hands in his strong grasp; his face radiant, his eyes spark- ling. "Shake hands, Basil! Shake hands, as we haven't shaken hands yet: this makes amends for everything! One word more, though, about that fellow; where is he now?"

"In the hospital."

Ralph laughed heartily, and jumped back on the bed. I remembered Mannion's letter, and shuddered as I thought of it.

"The next question is about the girl," said my brother. "What has become of her? Where was she all the time of your illness?"

"At her father's house; she is there still."

"Ah, yes! I see; the old story; innocent, of course. And her father backs her, doesn't he? To be sure, that's the old story too. I have got at our difficulty now; we are threatened with an exposure, if you don't acknowledge her. Wait a minute! Have you any evidence against her, besides your own?"

"I have a letter, a long letter from her accomplice, containing a confession of his guilt and hers."

"She is sure to call that confession a conspiracy. It's of no use to us, unless we dared to go to law—and we daren't. We must hush the thing up at any price; or it will be the death of my father. This is a case for money, just as I thought it would be. Mr. and Miss Shopkeeper have got a large assortment of silence to sell; and we must buy it of them, over the domestic counter, at so much a yard. Have you been there yet, Basil, to ask the price and strike the bargain?"

"I was at the house, yesterday."

"The deuce you were! And who did you see?—The father? Did you bring him to terms? did you do business with Mr. Shopkeeper?"

"His manner was brutal: his language, the language of a bully—?"

"So much the better. Those men are easiest dealt with: if he will only fly into a passion with *me*, I engage for success beforehand. But the end—how did it end?"

"As it began:—in threats on his part, in endurance on mine."

"Ah! we'll see how he likes *my* endurance next: he'll find it rather a different sort of endurance from yours. By the-bye, Basil, what money had you to offer him?"

"I made no offer to him then. Circumstances happened which rendered me incapable of thinking of it. I intended to go there again, to-day; and if money would bribe him to silence, and save my family from sharing the dishonour which has fallen on *me*, to abandon to him the only money I have of my own—the little income left me by our mother."

"Do you mean to say that your only resource is in that wretched trifle, and that you ever really intend to let it go, and start in the world without a rap? Do you mean to say that my father gave you up without making the smallest provision for you, in such a mess as your's? Hang it! do him justice. He has been hard enough on you, I know; but he can't have coolly turned you over to ruin in that way."

"He offered me money, at parting; but with such words of contempt and insult that I would have died rather than take it. I told him that, unaided by his purse, I would preserve him, and preserve his family from the infamous consequences of my calamity—though I sacrificed my own happiness and my own honour for ever in doing it. And I go to-day to make that sacrifice. The loss of the little I have to depend on, is the least part of it. He may not see his injustice in doubting me, till too late; but he *shall* see it."

"I beg your pardon, Basil; but this is almost as great an insanity, as the insanity of your marriage. I honour the independence of your principle, my dear fellow; but, while I am to the fore, I'll take good care that you don't ruin yourself gratuitously, for the sake of any principles whatever! Just listen to me, now. In the first place, remember that what my father said to you, he said in a moment of violent exasperation. You had been trampling the pride of his life in the mud: no man likes that—my father least of any. And, as for the offer of your poor little morsel of an income to stop these people's greedy mouths, it isn't a quarter enough for them. They know our family is a wealthy family; and they will make their demand accordingly. Any other sacrifice, even to taking the girl back (though you never could bring yourself to do that!), would be of no earthly use. Nothing but money will do; money cunningly doled out, under the strongest possible stipulations.

Now, I'm just the man to do that, and I have got the money—or, rather, my father has, which comes to the same thing. Write me the fellow's name and address; there's no time to be lost—I'm off to see him at once!"

"I can't allow you, Ralph, to ask my father for what I would not ask him myself—"

"Give me the name and address, or you will sour my excellent temper for the rest of my life. Your obstinacy won't do with *me*, Basil—it didn't at school, and it won't now. I shall ask my father for money for myself, and use as much of it as I think proper for your interests. He'll give me anything I want, now I have turned good boy. I don't owe fifty pounds, since my last debts were paid off—thanks to Mrs. Ralph, who is the most managing woman in the world. By-the-bye, when you see her, don't seem surprised at her being older than I am. Oh! this is the address, is it? Hollyoake Square? Where the devil's that! Never mind, I'll take a cab, and shift the responsibility of finding the place on the driver. Keep up your spirits, and wait here till I come back. You shall have such news of Mr. Shopkeeper and his daughter as you little expect! *Au revoir*, my dear fellow—*au revoir*."

He left the room as rapidly as he had entered it. The minute afterwards, I remembered that I ought to have warned him of the fatal illness of Mrs. Sherwin. She might be dying—dead for aught I knew—when he reached the house. I ran to the window, to call him back: it was too late. Ralph was gone.

Even if he were admitted at North Villa, would he succeed? I was little capable of estimating the chances. The unexpectedness of his visit; the strange mixture of sympathy and levity in his manner, of worldly wisdom and boyish folly in his conversation, appeared to be still confusing me in his absence, just as they had confused me in his presence. My thoughts imperceptibly wandered away from

Ralph, and the mission he had undertaken on my behalf, to a subject which seemed destined, for the future, to steal on my attention, irresistibly and darkly, in all my lonely hours. Already, the fatality denounced against me in Mannion's letter had begun to act: already, that terrible confession of past misery and crime, that monstrous declaration of enmity which was to last with the lasting of life, began to exercise its numbing influence on my faculties, to cast its blighting shadow over my heart.

I opened the letter again, and re-read the threats against me at its conclusion. One by one, the questions now arose in my mind: how can I resist, or how escape the vengeance of this evil spirit? how shun the dread deformity of that face, which is to appear before me in secret? how silence that fiend's tongue, or make harmless the poison which it will pour drop by drop into my life? When should I first look for that avenging presence?—now, or not till months hence? Where should I first see it? in the house?—or in the street? At what time would it steal to my side? by night—or by day? Should I show the letter to Ralph?——it would be useless. What would avail any advice or assistance which his reckless courage could give, against an enemy who combined the ferocious vigilance of a savage with the far-sighted iniquity of a civilised man?

As this last thought crossed my mind, I hastily closed the letter; determining (alas! how vainly!) never to open it again. Almost at the same instant, I heard another knock at the house-door. Could Ralph have returned already? impossible! Besides, the knock was very different from his —it was only just loud enough to be audible where I now sat.

Mannion? But would he come thus? openly, fairly, in the broad daylight, through the populous street?

A light, quick step ascended the stairs—my heart bounded; I started to my feet. It was the same step which I used to listen for, and love to hear, in my illness. I ran to the door, and opened it. My instinct had not deceived me! it was my sister!

"Basil!" she exclaimed, before I could speak—"has Ralph been here?"

"Yes, love—yes."

"Where has he gone? what has he done for you? He promised me—"

"And he has kept his promise nobly, Clara: he is away helping me now."

"Thank God! thank God!"

She sank breathless into a chair, as she spoke. Oh, the pang of looking at her at that moment, and seeing how she was changed!—seeing the dimness and weariness of the gentle eyes; the fear and the sorrow that had already over-shadowed the bright young face!

"I shall be better directly," she said, guessing from my expression what I then felt—"but, seeing you in this strange place, after what happened yesterday; and having come here so secretly, in terror of my father finding it out—I can't help feeling your altered position and mine a little painfully at first. But we won't complain, as long as I can get here sometimes to see you: we will only think of the future now. What a mercy, what a happiness it is that Ralph has come back! We have always done him injustice; he is far kinder and far better than we ever thought him. But, Basil, how worn and ill you are looking! Have you not told Ralph everything? Are you in any danger?"

"None, Clara—none, indeed!"

"Don't grieve too deeply about yesterday! Try and forget that horrible parting, and all that brought it about. He has not spoken of it since, except to tell me that I must never know more of your fault and your misfortune, than the little—the very little—I know already. And I have resolved not to think about it, as well as not to ask about it, for the future. I have a hope already, Basil—very, very far off fulfilment—but still a hope. Can you not think what it is?"

"Your hope is far off fulfilment, indeed, Clara, if it is hope from my father!"

"Hush! don't say so; I know better. Something occurred, even so soon as last night—a very trifling event—but enough to show that he thinks of you, already, in grief far more than in anger."

"I wish I could believe it, love; but my remembrance of yesterday—"

"Don't trust that remembrance; don't recall it! I will tell you what occurred. Some time after you had gone, and after I had recovered myself a little in my own room, I went downstairs again to see my father; for I was too terrified and too miserable at what had happened, to be alone. He was not in his room when I got there. As I looked round me for a moment, I saw the pieces of your page in the book about our family, scattered on the floor; and the miniature likeness of you, when you were a child, was lying among the other fragments. It had been torn out of its setting in the paper, but not injured. I picked it up, Basil, and put it on the table, at the place where he always sits; and laid my own little locket, with your hair in it, by the side, so that he might know that the miniature had not been accidentally taken up and put there by the servant. Then, I gathered together the pieces of the page and took them away with me, thinking it better that he should not see them again. Just as I had got through the door that leads into the library, and was about to close it, I heard the other door, by which you enter the study from the hall, opening; and he came in, and went directly to the table. His back was towards me, so I could look at him unperceived. He observed the miniature directly, and stood quite still with it in his hand; then sighed—sighed so bitterly!—and then took the portrait of our dear mother from one of the drawers of the table, opened the case in which it is kept, and put your miniature inside, very gently and tenderly. I could not trust myself to see any more, so I went up to my room again : and shortly afterwards he came in with my locket, and gave it me back, only saying—' You left this on my table, Clara.' But if you had seen his face then, you would have hoped all things from him in the time to come, as I hope now."

" And as I *will* hope, Clara, though it be from no stronger motive than gratitude to you."

"Before I left home," she proceeded, after a moment's silence, " I thought of your loneliness in this strange place —knowing that I could seldom come to see you, and then only by stealth ; by committing a fault which, if my father found it out—but we won't speak of that ! I thought of your lonely hours here ; and I have brought with me an old, forgotten companion of yours, to bear you company, and to keep you from thinking too constantly on what you have suffered. Look, Basil ! won't you welcome this old friend again ?"

She gave me a small roll of manuscript, with an effort to resume her kind smile of former days, even while the tears stood thick in her eyes. I untied the leaves, glanced at the handwriting, and saw before me, once more, the first few chapters of my unfinished romance ! Again I looked on the patiently-laboured pages, familiar relics of that earliest and best ambition which I had abandoned for love ; too faithful records of the tranquil, ennobling pleasures which I had lost for ever ! Oh, for one Thought-Flower now, from the dream-garden of the happy Past !

" I took more care of those leaves of writing, after you had thrown them aside, than of anything else I had," said Clara. " I always thought the time would come, when you would return again to the occupation which it was once

your greatest pleasure to pursue, and my greatest pleasure
to watch. And surely that time has arrived. I am certain,
Basil, your book will help you to wait patiently for happier
times, as nothing else can. This place must seem very
strange and lonely; but the sight of those pages, and the
sight of me sometimes (when I can come), may make it
look almost like home to you! The room is not—not
very—"

She stopped suddenly. I saw her lip tremble, and her
eyes grow dim again, as she looked round her. When I
tried to speak all the gratitude I felt, she turned away
quickly, and began to busy herself in re-arranging the
wretched furniture; in setting in order the glaring ornaments on the chimney-piece; in hiding the holes in the
ragged window-curtains; in changing, as far as she could,
all the tawdry discomfort of my one miserable little room.
She was still absorbed in this occupation, when the church-
clocks of the neighbourhood struck the hour—the hour that
warned her to stay no longer.

"I must go," she said; "it is later than I thought.
Don't be afraid about my getting home: old Martha came
here with me, and is waiting downstairs to go back (you
know we can trust her). Write to me as often as you can;
I shall hear about you every day, from Ralph; but I should
like a letter sometimes, as well. Be as hopeful and as patient yourself, dear, under misfortune, as you wish *me* to be;
and I shall despair of nothing. Don't tell Ralph I have
been here—he might be angry. I will come again, the first
opportunity. Good-bye, Basil! Let us try and part happily, in the hope of better days. Good-bye, dear—good-
bye, only for the present!"

Her self-possession nearly failed her, as she kissed me,
and then turned to the door. She just signed to me not to
follow her down-stairs, and, without looking round again,
hurried from the room.

It was well for the preservation of our secret, that she had so resolutely refrained from delaying her departure. She had been gone but for a few minutes—the lovely and consoling influence of her presence was still fresh in my heart—I was still looking sadly over the once precious pages of manuscript which she had restored to me—when Ralph returned from North Villa. I heard him leaping, rather than running, up the ricketty wooden stairs. He burst into my room more impetuously than ever.

"All right!" he said, jumping back to his former place on the bed. "We can buy Mr. Shopkeeper for anything we like—for nothing at all, if we choose to be stingy. His inno-cent daughter has made the best of all confessions, just at the right time. Basil, my boy, she has left her father's house!"

"What do you mean?"

"She has eloped to the hospital!"

"Mannion!"

"Yes, Mannion: I have got his letter to her. She is criminated by it, even past her father's contradiction—and he doesn't stick at a trifle! But I'll begin at the beginning, and tell you everything. Hang it, Basil, you look as if I'd brought you bad news instead of good!"

"Never mind how I look, Ralph—pray go on!"

"Well: the first thing I heard, on getting to the house, was that Sherwin's wife was dying. The servant took in my name: but I thought of course I shouldn't be admitted. No such thing! I was let in at once, and the first words this fellow, Sherwin, said to me, were, that his wife was only ill, that the servants were exaggerating, and that he was quite ready to hear what Mr. Basil's 'highly-respected' brother (fancy calling *me* 'highly-respected!') had to say to him. The fool, however, as you see, was cunning enough to try civility to begin with. A more ill-looking human mongrel I never set eyes on! I took the measure of my man directly, and in two minutes told him exactly what I came for, without softening a single word."

"And how did he answer you?"

"As I anticipated, by beginning to bluster immediately. I took him down, just as he swore his second oath. 'Sir,' I said very politely, 'if you mean to make a cursing and a swearing conference of this, I think it only fair to inform you before-hand that you are likely to get the worst of it. When the whole collection of British oaths is exhausted, I can swear fluently in five foreign languages: I have always made it a principle to pay back abuse at compound interest, and I don't exaggerate in saying, that I am quite capable of swearing you out of your senses, if you persist in setting me the example. And now, if you like to go on, pray do —I'm ready to hear you.' While I was speaking, he stared at me in a state of helpless astonishment; when I had done, he began to bluster again—but it was a pompous, dignified, parliamentary sort of bluster, now, ending in his pulling your unlucky marriage-certificate out of his pocket, asserting for the fiftieth time, that the girl was innocent, and declaring that he'd make you acknowledge her, if he went before a magistrate to do it. That's what he said when *you* saw him, I suppose?"

"Yes: almost word for word."

"I had my answer ready for him, before he could put the certificate back in his pocket. 'Now, Mr. Sherwin,' I said, 'have the goodness to listen to me. My father has certain family prejudices and nervous delicacies, which I do not inherit from him, and which I mean to take good care to prevent you from working on. At the same time, I beg you to understand that I have come here without his knowledge. I am not my father's ambassador, but my brother's —who is unfit to deal with you, himself, because he is not half hard-hearted, or half worldly enough. As my brother's envoy, therefore, and out of consideration for my father's peculiar feelings, I now offer you, from my own resources, a certain annual sum of money, far more than sufficient for all your daughter's expenses—a sum payable quarterly, on condition that neither you nor she shall molest us; that you shall never make use of our name anywhere; and that the fact of my brother's marriage (hitherto preserved a secret) shall for the future be consigned to oblivion. *We* keep our opinion of your daughter's guilt—*you* keep your opinion of her innocence. *We* have silence to buy, and *you* have silence to sell, once a quarter; and if either of us break our conditions, we both have our remedy—*your's* the easy remedy, *our's* the difficult. This arrangement—a very unfair and dangerous for us; a very advantageous and safe one for you—I understand that you finally refuse?' 'Sir,' says he, solemnly, 'I should be unworthy the name of a father—' 'Thank you'—I remarked, feeling that he was falling back on paternal sentiment—'thank you; I quite understand. We will get on, if you please, to the reverse side of the question.'"

"The reverse side! What reverse side, Ralph? What could you possibly say more?"

"You shall hear. 'Being, on your part, thoroughly determined,' I said, 'to permit no compromise, and to make my brother (his family of course included) acknowledge a woman, of whose guilt they entertain not the slightest doubt, you think you can gain your object by threatening an exposure. Don't threaten any more! Make your exposure! Go to the magistrate at once, if you like! Gibbet our names in the newspaper report, as a family connected by marriage with Mr. Sherwin the linendraper's daughter, whom they believe to have disgraced herself as a woman and a wife for ever. Do your very worst; make public every shameful particular that you can—what advantage will you get by it? Revenge, I grant you. But will revenge put a halfpenny into your pocket? Will revenge

pay a farthing towards your daughter's keep? Will revenge make us receive her? Not a bit of it! We shall be
driven into a corner; we shall have no exposure to dread
after you have exposed us; we shall have no remedy left,
but a desperate remedy, and we'll go to law—boldly, openly
go to law, and get a divorce. We have written evidence, which
you know nothing about, and can call testimony which you
cannot gag. I am no lawyer, but I'll bet you five hundred
to one (quite in a friendly way, my dear Sir!) that we get
our case. What follows? We send you back your daughter,
without a shred of character left to cover her; and we comfortably wash our hands of *you* altogether."

"Ralph! Ralph! how could you——"

"Stop! hear the end of it. Of course I knew that we
couldn't carry out this divorce-threat, without its being the
death of my father; but I thought a little quiet bullying on
my part might do Mr. Shopkeeper Sherwin some good.
And I was right. You never saw a man sit sorer on the
sharp edges of a dilemma than he did. I stuck to my point in
spite of everything; silence and money, or exposure and
divorce—just which he pleased. 'I deny every one of your
infamous imputations,' said he. 'That's not the question,'
said I. 'I'll go to your father,' said he. 'You won't be
let in,' said I. 'I'll write to him,' said he. 'He won't
receive your letter,' said I. There we came to a pull-up.
He began to stammer, and *I* refreshed myself with a pinch
of snuff. Finding it wouldn't do, he threw off the Roman
at last, and resumed the Tradesman. 'Even supposing I
consented to this abominable compromise, what is to become of my daughter?' he asked. 'Just what becomes of
other people who have comfortable annuities to live on,'
I answered. 'Affection for my deeply-wronged child half
inclines me to consult her wishes, before we settle anything
—I'll go up-stairs,' said he. 'And I'll wait for you down
here,' said I.

" Did he object to that ?"

" Not he.   He went up-stairs, and in a few minutes ran down again, with an open letter in his hand, looking as if the devil was after him before his time.   At the last three or four stairs, he tripped, caught at the bannisters, dropped the letter over them in doing so, tumbled into the passage in such a fury and fright that he looked like a madman, tore his hat off a peg, and rushed out.   I just heard him say his daughter should come back,* if he put a straight waistcoat* on her, as he passed the door.   Between his tumble, his passion, and his hurry, he never thought of coming back for the letter he had dropped over the bannisters.   I picked it up before I went away, suspecting it might be good evidence on our side; and I was right.   Read it yourself, Basil; you have every moral and legal claim on the precious document—and here it is."

I took the letter, and read (in Mannion's handwriting) these words, dated from the hospital :—

" I have received your last note, and cannot wonder that you are getting impatient under restraint.   But, remember, that if you had not acted as I warned you beforehand to act in case of accidents—if you had not protested innocence to your father, and preserved total silence towards your mother; if you had not kept in close retirement, behaving like a domestic martyr, and avoiding, in your character of a victim, all voluntary mention of your husband's name—your position might have been a very awkward one.   Not being able to help you, the only thing I could do was to teach you how to help yourself.   I gave you the lesson, and you have been wise enough to profit by it.

" The time has now come for a change in my plans.   I have suffered a relapse; and the date of my discharge from this place is still uncertain.   I doubt the security, both on your account, and on mine, of still leaving you at your

father's house, to await my cure. Come to me here, therefore, to-morrow, at any hour when you can get away unperceived. You will be let in as a visitor, and shown to my
bedside, if you ask for Mr. Turner—the name I have given
to the hospital authorities. Through the help of a friend
outside these walls, I have arranged for a lodging in which
you can live undiscovered, until I am discharged and can
join you. You can come here twice a week, if you like,
and you had better do so, to accustom yourself to the sight
of my injuries. I told you in my first letter how and where
they had been inflicted—when you see them with your own
eyes, you will be best prepared to hear what my future
purposes are, and how you can aid them. R. M."

This was evidently the letter about which I had been
consulted by the servant at North Villa; the date corresponded with the date of Mannion's letter to me. I noticed
that the envelope was missing, and asked Ralph whether he
had got it.

"No," he replied; "Sherwin dropped the letter just in
the state in which I have given it to you. I suspect the
girl took away the envelope with her, thinking that the
letter which she left behind her was inside. But the loss
of the envelope doesn't matter. Look there: the fellow
has written her name at the bottom of the leaf, as coolly as
if it was an ordinary correspondence. She is identified with
the letter, and that's all we want in our future dealings
with her father."

"But, Ralph, do you think——"

"Do I think her father will get her back? If he's in
time to catch her at the hospital, he assuredly will. If not,
we shall have some little trouble on our side, I suspect. This
seems to me to be how the matter stands now, Basil:—After
that letter, and her running away, Sherwin will have nothing
for it but to hold his tongue about her innocence; we may

consider *him* as settled and done with. As for the other rascal, Mannion, he certainly writes as if he meant to do something dangerous. If he really does attempt to annoy us, we will mark him again (I'll do it next time, by way of a little change!) ; *he* has no marriage certificate to shake over our heads, at 'any rate. What's the matter now?—you're looking pale again."

I *felt* that my colour was changing, while he spoke. There was something ominous in the contrast which, at that moment, I could not fail to draw between Mannion's enmity, as Ralph ignorantly estimated it, and as I really knew it. Already the first step towards the conspiracy with which I was threatened, had been taken by the departure of Sherwin's daughter from her father's house. Should I, at this earliest warning of coming events, show my brother the letter I had received from Mannion? No! such defence against the dangers threatened in it as Ralph would be sure to counsel, and to put in practice, might only include *him* in the life-long persecution which menaced *me*. When he repeated his remark about my sudden paleness, I merely accounted for it by some common-place excuse, and begged him to proceed.

"I suppose, Basil," he said, "the truth is, that you can't help being a little shocked—though you could expect nothing better from the girl—at her boldly following this fellow Mannion, even to the hospital" (Ralph was right ; in spite of myself, this feeling was one among the many which now influenced me.) "Setting that aside, however, we are quite ready, I take it, to let her stick to her choice, and live just as she pleases, so long as she doesn't live under our name. There is the great fear and great difficulty now! If Sherwin can't find her, *we* must; otherwise, we can never feel certain that she is not incurring all sorts of debts as your wife. If her father gets her back, I shall be able to bring her to terms at North Villa; if not, I must get speech of her, wherever she happens to be hidden. She's the only thorn in our side now, and we must pull her out with gold pincers immediately. Don't you see that, Basil?"

"I see it, Ralph!"

"Very well. Either to-night or to-morrow morning, I'll communicate with Sherwin, and find out whether he has laid hands on her. If he hasn't, we must go to the hospital, and see what we can discover for ourselves. Don't look miserable and downhearted, Basil, I'll go with you: you needn't see her again, or the man either; but you must come with me, for I may be obliged to make use of you. And now, I'm off for to-day, in good earnest. I must get back to Mrs. Ralph (unfortunately she happens to be one of the most sensitive women in the world), or she will be sending to advertise me in the newspapers. We shall pull through this, my dear fellow—you will see we shall! By the bye, you don't know of a nice little detached house in the Brompton neighbourhood, do you? Most of my old theatrical friends live about there—a detached house, mind! The fact is, I have taken to the violin lately (I wonder what I shall take to next?); Mrs. Ralph accompanies me on the pianoforte; and we might be an execrable nuisance to very near neighbours—that's all! You don't know of a house? Never mind; I can go to an agent, or something of that sort. Clara shall know to-night that we are moving prosperously, if I can only give the worthiest creature in the world the slip: she's a little obstinate, but, I assure you, a really superior woman. Only think of my dropping down to playing the fiddle, and paying rent and taxes in a suburban villa! How are the fast men fallen! Good bye, Basil, good bye!"

VII.

The next morning, Ralph never appeared—the day passed on, and I heard nothing—at last, when it was evening, a letter came from him.

The letter informed me that my brother had written to Mr. Sherwin, simply asking whether he had recovered his daughter. The answer to this question did not arrive till late in the day; and was in the negative—Mr. Sherwin had not found his daughter. She had left the hospital before he got there; and no one could tell him whither she had gone. His language and manner, as he himself admitted, had been so violent that he was not allowed to enter the ward where Mannion lay. When he returned home, he found his wife at the point of death; and on the same evening she expired. Ralph described his letter, as the letter of a man half out of his senses. He only mentioned his daughter, to declare, in terms almost of fury, that he would accuse her before his wife's surviving relatives, of having been the cause of her mother's death; and called down the most terrible denunciations on his own head, if he ever spoke to his child again, though he should see her starving before him in the streets. In a postscript, Ralph informed me that he would call the next morning, and concert measures for tracking Sherwin's daughter to her present retreat.

Every sentence in this letter bore warning of the crisis which was now close at hand; yet I had as little of the desire as of the power to prepare for it. A superstitious conviction that my actions were governed by a fatality which no human foresight could alter or avoid, began to strengthen within me. From this time forth, I awaited events with the uninquiring patience, the helpless resignation of despair.

My brother came, punctual to his appointment. When he proposed that I should at once accompany him to the hospital, I never hesitated at doing as he desired. We reached our destination; and Ralph approached the gates to make his first enquiries.

He was still speaking to the porter, when a gentleman advanced towards them, on his way out of the hospital. I saw him recognise my brother, and heard Ralph exclaim:

"Bernard! Jack Bernard! Have *you* come to England, of all the men in the world!"

"Why not?" was the answer. "I got every surgical testimonial the *Hôtel Dieu* could give me,* six months ago; and couldn't afford to stay in Paris only for my pleasure. Do you remember calling me a 'mute, inglorious Liston,*' long ago, when we last met? Well, I have come to England to soar out of my obscurity and blaze into a shining light of the profession. Plenty of practice at the hospital, here—very little anywhere else, I am sorry to say."

"You don't mean that you belong to *this* hospital?"

"My dear fellow, I am regularly on the staff; I'm here every day of my life."

"You're the very man to enlighten us. Here, Basil, cross over, and let me introduce you to an old Paris friend of mine. Mr. Bernard—my brother. You've often heard me talk, Basil, of a younger son of old Sir William Bernard's, who preferred a cure of bodies to a cure of souls; and actually insisted on working in a hospital when he might have idled in a family living. This is the man—the best of doctors and good fellows."

"Are you bringing your brother to the hospital to follow my mad example?" asked Mr. Bernard, as he shook hands with me.

"Not exactly, Jack! But we really have an object in coming here. Can you give us ten minutes' talk, somewhere in private? We want to know about one of your patients."

He led us into an empty room, on the ground-floor of the building. "Leave the matter in my hands," whispered Ralph to me, as we sat down. "I'll find out everything."

"Now, Bernard," he said, "you have a man here, who calls himself Mr. Turner?"

"Are *you* a friend of that mysterious patient? Wonderful! The students call him 'The Great Mystery of London;' and I begin to think the students are right. Do you want to see him? When he has not got his green shade on, he's rather a startling sight, I can tell you, for unprofessional eyes."

"No, no—at least, not at present; my brother here, not at all. The fact is, certain circumstances have happened which oblige us to look after this man; and which I am sure you won't inquire into, when I tell you that it is our interest to keep them secret."

"Certainly not!"

"Then, without any more words about it, our object here, to-day, is to find out everything we can about Mr. Turner, and the people who have been to see him. Did a woman come, the day before yesterday?"

"Yes; and behaved rather oddly, I believe. I was not here when she came, but was told she asked for Turner, in a very agitated manner. She was directed to the Victoria Ward, where he is; and when she got there, looked excessively flurried and excited—seeing the Ward quite full, and, perhaps, not being used to hospitals. However it was, though the nurse pointed out the right bed to her, she ran in a mighty hurry to the wrong one."

"I understand," said Ralph; "just as some women run into the wrong omnibus, when the right one is straight before them."

"Exactly. Well, she only discovered her mistake (the room being rather dark), after she had stooped down close over the stranger, who was lying with his head away from her. By that time, the nurse was at her side, and led her to the right bed. There, I'm told, another scene happened. At sight of the patient's face, which is very frightfully dis-

figured, she was on the point (as the nurse thought) of
going into a fit; but Turner stopped her in an instant. He
just laid his hand on her arm, and whispered something to
her; and, though she turned as pale as ashes, she was quiet
directly. The next thing they say he did, was to give her
a slip of paper, coolly directing her to go to the address
written on it, and to come back to the hospital again, as
soon as she could show a little more resolution. She went
away at once—nobody knows where."

" Has nobody asked where?"

" Yes; a fellow who said he was her father, and who behaved like a madman. He came here about an hour after
she had left, and wouldn't believe that we knew nothing
about her (how the deuce *should* we know anything!) He
threatened Turner (whom, by the bye, he called Manning,
or some such name) in such an outrageous manner, that we
were obliged to refuse him admission. Turner himself will
give no information on the subject; but I suspect that his
injuries are the result of a quarrel with the father about the
daughter—a pretty savage quarrel, I must say, looking to
the consequences—I beg your pardon, but your brother
seems ill! I'm afraid," (turning to me), " you find the room
rather close?"

" No, indeed; not at all. I have just recovered from a
serious illness—but pray go on."

" I have very little more to say. The father went away
in a fury, just as he came; the daughter has not yet made
her appearance a second time. But, after what was reported
to me of the first interview, I daresay she *will* come. She
must, if she wants to see Turner; he won't be out, I suspect, for another fortnight. He has been making himself
worse by perpetually writing letters; we were rather afraid
of erysipelas,* but he'll get over that danger, I think."

" About the woman," said Ralph; " it is of the greatest
importance that we should know where she is now living.

Is there any possibility (we will pay well for it) of getting some sharp fellow to follow her home from this place, the next time she comes here?"

Mr. Bernard hesitated a moment, and considered.

"I think I can manage it for you with the porter, after you are gone," he said, "provided you leave me free to give any remuneration I may think necessary."

"Anything in the world, my dear fellow. Have you got pen and ink? I'll write down my brother's address; you can communicate results to him, as soon as they occur."

While Mr. Bernard went to the opposite end of the room, in search of writing materials, Ralph whispered to me—

"If he wrote to *my* address, Mrs. Ralph might see the letter. She is the most amiable of her sex; but if written information of a woman's residence, directed to me, fell into her hands—you understand, Basil! Besides, it will be easy to let me know, the moment you hear from Jack. Look up, young one! It's all right—we are sailing with wind and tide."

Here Mr. Bernard brought us pen and ink. While Ralph was writing my address, his friend said to me:

"I hope you will not suspect me of wishing to intrude on your secrets, if (assuming your interest in Turner to be the reverse of a friendly interest) I warn you to look sharply after him when he leaves the hospital. Either there has been madness in his family, or his brain has suffered from his external injuries. Legally, he may be quite fit to be at large; for he will be able to maintain the appearance of perfect self-possession in all the ordinary affairs of life. But, morally, I am convinced that he is a dangerous mono-maniac; his mania being connected with some fixed idea which evidently never leaves him day or night. I would lay a heavy wager that he dies in a prison or a madhouse."

"And I'll lay another wager, if he's mad enough to annoy

us, that we are the people to shut him up," said Ralph.
" There is the address. And now, we needn't waste your
time any longer. I have taken a little place at Brompton,
Jack,—you and Basil must come and dine with me, as soon
as the carpets are down."

We left the room. As we crossed the hall, a gentleman
came forward, and spoke to Mr. Bernard.

" That man's fever in the Victoria Ward has declared itself at last," he said. " This morning the new symptoms
have appeared."

" And what do they indicate ?"

" Typhus of the most malignant character—not a doubt
of it. Come up, and look at him."

I saw Mr. Bernard start, and glance quickly at my brother. Ralph fixed his eyes searchingly on his friend's face ;
exclaimed : " Victoria Ward ! why you mentioned that— ;"
and then stopped, with a very strange and sudden alteration in his expression. The next moment he drew Mr.
Bernard aside, saying : " I want to ask you whether the
bed in Victoria Ward, occupied by this man whose fever
has turned to typhus, is the same bed, or near the bed
which—" The rest of the sentence was lost to me as they
walked away.

After talking together in whispers for a few moments,
they rejoined me. Mr. Bernard was explaining the different
theories of infection* to Ralph.

" *My* notion," he said, " is, that infection is taken through
the lungs ; one breath inhaled from the infected atmosphere
hanging immediately around the diseased person, and generally extending about a foot from him, being enough to communicate his malady to the breather—provided there exists,
at the time, in the individual exposed to catch the malady,
a constitutional predisposition to infection. This predisposition we know to be greatly increased by mental agitation,
or bodily weakness ; but, in the case we have been talking

of," (he looked at me,) " the chances of infection or non-infection may be equally balanced. At any rate, I can predict nothing about them at this stage of the discovery."

" You will write the moment you hear anything?" said Ralph, shaking hands with him.

" The very moment. I have your brother's address safe in my pocket."

We separated. Ralph was unusually silent and serious on our way back. He took leave of me at the door of my lodging, very abruptly; without referring again to our visit to the hospital.

A week passed away, and I heard nothing from Mr. Bernard. During this interval, I saw little of my brother; he was occupied in moving into his new house. Towards the latter part of the week, he came to inform me that he was about to leave London for a few days. My father had asked him to go to the family house, in the country, on business connected with the local management of the estates. Ralph still retained all his old dislike of the steward's accounts and the lawyer's consultations; but he felt bound, out of gratitude for my father's special kindness to him since his return to England, to put a constraint on his own inclinations, and go to the country as he was desired. He did not expect to be absent more than two or three days; but earnestly charged me to write to him, if I had any news from the hospital while he was away.

During the week, Clara came twice to see me—escaping from home by stealth, as before. On each occasion, she showed the same affectionate anxiety to set me an example of cheerfulness, and to sustain me in hope. I saw, with a sorrow and apprehension which I could not altogether conceal from her, that the weary look in her face had never changed, never diminished since I had first observed it. Ralph had, from motives of delicacy, avoided increasing the hidden anxieties which were but too evidently preying upon

her health, by keeping her in perfect ignorance of our visit
to the hospital, and, indeed, of the particulars of all our
proceedings since his return. I took care to preserve the
same secrecy, during her short interviews with me. She
bade me farewell after her third visit, with a sadness which
she vainly endeavoured to hide. I little thought, then, that
the tones of her sweet, clear voice had fallen on my ear for
the last time, before I wandered to the far West of England
where I now write.

At the end of the week—it was on a Saturday, I remember—I left my lodgings early in the morning, to go into the
country; with no intention of returning before evening. I
had felt a sense of oppression, on rising, which was almost
unendurable. The perspiration stood thick on my forehead,
though the day was not unusually hot; the air of London
grew harder and harder to breathe, with every minute; my
heart felt tightened to bursting; my temples throbbed with
fever-fury; my very life seemed to depend on escaping
into pure air, into some place where there was shade from
trees, and water that ran cool and refreshing to look on.
So I set forth, careless in what direction I went; and remained in the country all day. Evening was changing into
night as I got back to London.

I inquired of the servant at my lodging, when she let me
in, whether any letter had arrived for me. She answered,
that one had come just after I had gone out in the morning,
and that it was lying on my table. My first glance at it,
showed me Mr. Bernard's name written in the corner of
the envelope. I eagerly opened the letter, and read these
words:

"Private.   "Friday.

    "MY DEAR SIR,

    "On the enclosed slip of paper you will find the address
of the young woman, of whom your brother spoke to me

when we met at the hospital. I regret to say, that the circumstances under which I have obtained information of her residence, are of the most melancholy nature.

"The plan which I arranged for discovering her abode, in accordance with your brother's suggestion, proved useless. The young woman never came to the hospital a second time. Her address was given to me this morning, by Turner himself, who begged that I would visit her professionally, as he had no confidence in the medical man who was then in attendance on her. Many circumstances combined to make my compliance with his request anything but easy or desirable; but knowing that you—or your brother I ought, perhaps, rather to say—were interested in the young woman, I determined to take the very earliest opportunity of seeing her, and consulting with her medical attendant. I could not get to her till late in the afternoon. When I arrived, I found her suffering from one of the worst attacks of Typhus* I ever remember to have seen; and I think it my duty to state candidly, that I believe her life to be in imminent danger. At the same time, it is right to inform you that the gentleman in attendance on her does not share my opinion : he still thinks there is a good chance of saving her.

"There can be no doubt whatever, that she was infected with Typhus at the hospital. You may remember my telling you, how her agitation appeared to have deprived her of self-possession, when she entered the ward; and how she ran to the wrong bed, before the nurse could stop her. The man whom she thus mistook for Turner, was suffering from fever which had not then specifically declared itself; but which did so declare itself, as a Typhus fever, on the morning when you and your brother came to the hospital. This man's disorder must have been infectious when the young woman stooped down close over him, under the impression that he was the person she had come to see. Although she

started back at once, on discovering her mistake, she had
breathed the infection into her system—her mental agitation
at the time, accompanied (as I have since understood) by
some physical weakness, rendering her specially liable to the
danger to which she had accidentally exposed herself.

" Since the first symptoms of her disease appeared, on
Saturday last, I cannot find that any error has been committed in the medical treatment, as reported to me. I remained some time by her bedside to-day, observing her.
The delirium which is, more or less, an invariable result of
Typhus, is particularly marked in her case, and manifests
itself both by speech and gesture. It has been found impossible to quiet her, by any means hitherto tried. While
I was watching by her, she never ceased calling on your
name, and entreating to see you. I am informed by her
medical attendant, that her wanderings have almost invariably taken this direction for the last four-and-twenty
hours. Occasionally she mixes other names with yours, and
mentions them in terms of abhorrence; but her persistency in
calling for your presence, is so remarkable that I am
tempted, merely from what I have heard myself, to suggest
that you really should go to her, on the bare chance that
you might exercise some tranquillising influence. At the
same time, if you fear infection, or for any private reasons
(into which I have neither the right nor the wish to inquire)
feel unwilling to take the course I have pointed out, do not
by any means consider it your duty to accede to my proposal. I can conscientiously assure you that duty is not
involved in it.

" I have, however, another suggestion to make, which is
of a positive nature, and which I am sure will meet with
your approval. It is, that her parents, or some of her
other relations, if her parents are not alive, should be informed of her situation. Possibly, you may know something of her connections, and can therefore do this good

office. She is dying in a strange place, among people who avoid her as they would avoid a pestilence. Even though it be only to bury her, some relation ought to be immediately summoned to her bed-side.

"I shall visit her twice to-morrow, in the morning and at night. If you are not willing to risk seeing her (and I repeat that it is in no sense imperative that you should combat such unwillingness), perhaps you will communicate with me at my private address.

"I remain, dear Sir,
"Faithfully yours,
"JOHN BERNARD.

"P.S.—I open my letter again, to inform you that Turner, acting against all advice, has left the hospital to-day. He attempted to go on Tuesday last, when, I believe, he first received information of the young woman's serious illness, but was seized with a violent attack of giddiness, on attempting to walk, and fell down just outside the door of the ward. On this second occasion, however, he has succeeded in getting away without any accident—as far, at least, as the persons employed about the hospital can tell."

When the letter fell from my trembling hand, when I first asked of my own heart the fearful question :—"Have I, to whom the mere thought of ever seeing this woman again, has been as a pollution to shrink from, the strength to stand by her death-bed, the courage to see her die ?"— then, and not till then, did I really know how suffering had fortified, while it had humbled me; how affliction has the power to purify, as well as to pain.

All bitter memory of the ill that she had done me, of the misery I had suffered at her hands, lost its hold on my mind. Once more, her mother's last words of earthly lament—" Oh, who will pray for her when I am gone ?"

seemed to be murmuring in my ear—murmuring in harmony with the divine words in which the Voice from the
Mount of Olives taught forgiveness of injuries to all mankind.

She was dying: dying among strangers in the pining
madness of fever—and the one being of all who knew her,
whose presence at her bedside might yet bring calmness to
her last moments, and give her quietly and tenderly to death,
was the man whom she had pitilessly deceived and dishonoured, whose youth she had ruined, whose hopes she
had wrecked for ever. Strangely had destiny brought us
together—terribly had it separated us—awfully would it
now unite us again, at the end!

What were my wrongs, heavy as they had been; what
my sufferings, poignant as they still were, that they should
stand between this dying woman, and the last hope of
awakening her to the consciousness that she was going
before the throne of God? The sole resource for her
which human skill and human pity could now suggest, em-
braced the sole chance that she might still be recovered for
repentance, before she was resigned to death. How did I
know, but that in those ceaseless cries which had uttered
my name, there spoke the last earthly anguish of the tortured spirit, calling upon me for one drop of water to cool
its burning guilt—one drop from the waters of Peace?

I took up Mr. Bernard's letter from the floor on which it
had fallen, and re-directed it to my brother; simply writing
on a blank place in the inside, "I have gone to soothe her
last moments." Before I departed, I wrote to her father,
and summoned him to her bedside. The guilt of his absence
—if his heartless and hardened nature did not change towards her—would now rest with him, and not with me. I
forbore from thinking how he would answer my letter; for
I remembered his written words to my brother, declaring
that he would accuse his daughter of having caused her

mother's death ; and I suspected him even then, of wishing
to shift the shame of his conduct towards his unhappy wife
from himself to his child.

After writing this second letter, I set forth instantly for
the house to which Mr. Bernard had directed me. No thought
of myself; no thought, even, of the peril suggested by the
ominous disclosure about Mannion, in the postscript to the
surgeon's letter, ever crossed my mind. In the great stillness, in the heavenly serenity that had come to my spirit,
the wasting fire of every sensation which was only of this
world, seemed quenched for ever.

It was eleven o'clock when I arrived at the house. A
slatternly, sulky woman opened the door to me. "Oh! I
suppose you're another doctor," she muttered, staring at me
with scowling eyes. "I wish you were the undertaker, to
get her out of my house before we all catch our deaths of
her! There! there's the other doctor coming down stairs;
he'll show you the room—I won't go near it."

As I took the candle from her hand, I saw that Mr. Bernard was approaching me from the stairs.

"You can do no good, I am afraid," he said, "but I am
glad you have come."

"There is no hope, then ?"

"In my opinion, none. Turner came here this morning,
whether she recognised him, or not, in her delirium, I cannot say; but she grew so much worse in his presence, that
I insisted on his not seeing her again, except under medical
permission. Just now, there is no one in the room—are you
willing to go up stairs at once?"

"Does she still speak of me in her wanderings ?"

"Yes, as incessantly as ever."

"Then I am ready to go to her bedside."

"Pray believe that I feel deeply what a sacrifice you are
making. Since I wrote to you, much that she has said in
her delirium has told me"—(he hesitated)—"has told me

more, I am afraid, than you would wish me to have known, as a comparative stranger to you. I will only say, that secrets unconsciously disclosed on the death-bed are secrets sacred to me, as they are to all who pursue my calling; and that what I have unavoidably heard above stairs, is doubly-sacred in my estimation, as affecting a near and dear relative of one of my oldest friends." He paused, and took my hand very kindly; then added: "I am sure you will think yourself rewarded for any trial to your feelings to-night, if you can only remember in years to come, that your presence quieted her in her last moments!"

I felt his sympathy and delicacy too ˙strongly to thank him in words; I could only *look* my gratitude as he asked me to follow him up stairs.

We entered the room softly. Once more, and for the last time in this world, I stood in the presence of Margaret Sherwin.

Not even to see her, as I had last seen her, was such a sight of misery as to behold her now, forsaken on her death-bed, to look at her, as she lay with her head turned from me, fretfully covering and uncovering her face with the loose tresses of her long black hair, and muttering my name incessantly in her fever-dream: "Basil! Basil! Basil! I'll never leave off calling for him, till he comes. Basil! Basil! Where is he? Oh, where, where, where!"

"He is here," said the doctor, taking the candle from my hand, and holding it, so that the light fell full on my face. "Look at her and speak to her as usual, when she turns round," he whispered to me.

Still she never moved; still those hoarse, fierce, quick tones —that voice, once the music that my heart beat to; now the discord that it writhed under—muttered faster and faster: "Basil! Basil! Bring him here! bring me Basil!"

"He *is* here," repeated Mr. Bernard loudly. "Look! look up at him!"

She turned in an instant, and tore the hair back from her face. For a moment, I forced myself to look at her; for a moment, I confronted the smouldering fever in her cheeks; the glare of the bloodshot eyes; the distortion of the parched lips; the hideous clutching of the outstretched fingers at the empty air—but the agony of that sight was more than I could endure: I turned away my head, and hid my face in horror.

"Compose yourself," whispered the doctor. "Now she is quiet, speak to her; speak to her before she begins again; call her by her name."

Her name! Could my lips utter it at such a moment as this?

"Quick! quick!" cried Mr. Bernard. "Try her while you have the chance."

I struggled against the memories of the past, and spoke to her—God knows as gently, if not as happily, as in the bygone time!

"Margaret," I said, "Margaret, you asked for me, and I have come."

She tossed her arms above her head with a shrill scream, frightfully prolonged till it ended in low moanings and murmurings; then turned her face from us again, and pulled her hair over it once more.

"I am afraid she is too far gone," said the doctor; "but make another trial."

"Margaret," I said again, "have you forgotten me? Margaret!"

She looked at me once more. This time, her dry, dull eyes seemed to soften, and her fingers twined themselves less passionately in her hair. She began to laugh—a low, vacant, terrible laugh.

"Yes, yes," she said, "I know he's come at last; I can make him do anything. Get me my bonnet and shawl; any shawl will do, but a mourning shawl is best, because we are going to the funeral of our wedding. Come, Basil!

let's go back to the church, and get unmarried again; that's what I wanted you for. We don't care about each other; Robert Mannion wants me more than you do—*he's* not ashamed of me because my father's a tradesman; *he* won't make believe that he's in love with me, and then marry me to spite the pride of his family. Come! I'll tell the clergyman to read the service backwards; that makes a marriage no marriage at all, everybody knows."

As the last wild words escaped her, some one below stairs called to Mr. Bernard. He went out for a minute, then returned again, telling me that he was summoned to a case of sudden illness which he must attend without a moment's delay.

"The medical man whom I found here when I first came," he said, "was sent for this evening into the country, to be consulted about an operation, I believe. But if anything happens, I shall be at your service. There is the address of the house to which I am now going" (he wrote it down on a card); "you can send, if you want me. I will get back, however, as soon as possible, and see her again; she seems to be a little quieter already, and may become quieter still, if you stay longer. The night-nurse is below—I will send her up as I go downstairs. Keep the room well ventilated, the windows open as they are now. Don't breathe too close to her, and you need fear no infection. Look! her eyes are still fixed on you. This is the first time I have seen her look in the same direction for two minutes together; one would think she really recognised you. Wait till I come back, if you possibly can—I won't be a moment longer than I can help."

He hastily left the room. I turned to the bed, and saw that she was still looking at me. She had never ceased murmuring to herself while Mr. Bernard was speaking; and she did not stop when the nurse came in.

The first sight of this woman, on her entrance, sickened

and shocked me. All that was naturally repulsive in her, was made doubly revolting by the characteristics of the habitual drunkard, lowering and glaring at me in her purple, bloated face. To see her heavy hands shaking at the pillow, as they tried mechanically to arrange it; to see her stand, alternately leering and scowling by the bedside, an incarnate blasphemy in the sacred chamber of death, was to behold the most horrible of all mockeries, the most impious of all profanations. No loneliness in the presence of mortal agony could try me to the quick, as the sight of that foul old age of degradation and debauchery, defiling the sick room, now tried me. I determined to wait alone by the bedside till Mr. Bernard returned.

With some difficulty, I made the wretched drunkard understand that she might go downstairs again; and that I would call her if she was wanted. At last, she comprehended my meaning, and slowly quitted the room. The door closed on her; and I was left alone to watch the last moments of the woman who had ruined me!

As I sat down near the open window, the sounds outside in the street told of the waning of the night. There was an echo of many footsteps, a hoarse murmur of conflicting voices, now near, now afar off. The public houses were dispersing their drunken crowds—the crowds of a Saturday night: it was twelve o'clock.

Through those street-sounds of fierce ribaldry and ghastly mirth, the voice of the dying woman penetrated, speaking more slowly, more distinctly, more terribly than it had spoken yet.

"I see him," she said, staring vacantly at me, and moving her hands slowly to and fro in the air. "I see him! But he's a long way off; he can't hear our secrets, and he does not suspect you as mother does. Don't tell me that about him any more; my flesh creeps at it! What are you looking at me in that way for? You make me feel on fire.

You know I like you, because I *must* like you; because I can't help it.* It's no use saying hush: I tell you he can't hear us, and can't see us. He can see nothing; you make a fool of him, and I make a fool of him. But mind! I *will* ride in my own carriage: you must keep things secret enough to let me do that. I say I *will* ride in my carriage: and I'll go where father walks to business: I don't care if I splash him with *my* carriage wheels! I'll be even with him for some of the passions he's been in with me. You see how I'll go into our shop and order dresses! (be quiet! I say he can't hear us). I'll have velvet where his sister has silk, and silk where she has muslin: I'm a finer girl than she is, and I'll be better dressed. Tell *him* anything, indeed! What have I ever let out? It's not so easy always to make believe I'm in love with him, after what you have told me. Suppose he found us out?—Rash? I'm no more rash than you are! Why didn't you come back from France in time, and stop it all? Why did you let me marry him? A nice wife I've been to him, and a nice husband he has been to me—a husband who waits a year! Ha! ha! he calls himself a man, doesn't he? A husband who waits a year!"

I approached nearer to the bedside, and spoke to her again, in the hope to win her tenderly towards dreaming of better things. I know not whether she heard me, but her wild thoughts changed—changed darkly to later events.

"Beds! beds!" she cried, " beds everywhere, with dying men on them! And one bed the most terrible of all—look at it! The deformed face, with the white of the pillow all round it! *His* face? *his* face, that hadn't a fault in it? Never! It's the face of a devil; the finger-nails of the devil are on it! Take me away! drag me out! I can't move for that face: it's always before me: it's walling me up among the beds: it's burning me all over. Water! water drown me in the sea; drown me deep, away from the burning face!"

"Hush, Margaret! hush! drink this, and you will be cool again." I gave her some lemonade, which stood by the bedside.

"Yes, yes; hush, as you say. Where's Robert? Robert Mannion? Not here! then I've got a secret for you. When you go home to-night, Basil, and say your prayers, pray for a storm of thunder and lightning; and pray that I may be struck dead in it, and Robert too. It's a fortnight to my aunt's party; and in a fortnight you'll wish us both dead, so you had better pray for what I tell you in time. We shall make handsome corpses. Put roses into my coffin—scarlet roses, if you can find any, because that stands for Scarlet Woman—in the Bible, you know. Scarlet? What do I care! It's the boldest colour in the world. Robert will tell you, and all your family, how many women are as scarlet as I am—virtue wears it at home, in secret; and vice wears it abroad, in public: that's the only difference, he says. Scarlet roses! scarlet roses! throw them into the coffin by hundreds; smother me up in them; bury me down deep; in the dark, quiet street—where there's a broad door-step in front of a house, and a white, wild face, something like Basil's, that's always staring on the door-step awfully. Oh, why did I meet him! why did I marry him! oh, why! why!"

She uttered the last words in slow, measured cadence— the horrible mockery of a chaunt which she used to play to us at North Villa, on Sunday evenings. Then her voice sank again; her articulation thickened, and grew indistinct. It was like the change from darkness to daylight, in the sight of sleepless eyes, to hear her only murmuring now, after hearing her last terrible words.

The weary night-time passed on. Longer and longer grew the intervals of silence between the scattered noises from the streets; less and less frequent were the sounds of distant carriage-wheels, and the echoing rapid footsteps of late pleasure-seekers hurrying home. At last, the heavy tramp of the policeman going his rounds, alone disturbed the silence of the early morning hours. Still, the voice from the bed muttered incessantly; but now, in drowsy, languid tones: still, Mr. Bernard did not return: still, the father of the dying girl never came, never obeyed the letter which summoned him for the last time to her side.

(There was yet one more among the absent—one from whose approach the death-bed must be kept sacred; one, whose evil presence was to be dreaded as a pestilence and a scourge. Mannion!—where was Mannion?)

I sat by the window, resigned to wait in loneliness till the end came, watching mechanically the vacant eyes that ever watched *me*—when, suddenly, the face of Margaret seemed to fade out of my sight. I started and looked round. The candle, which I had placed at the opposite end of the room, had burnt down without my noticing it, and was now expiring in the socket. I ran to light the fresh candle which lay on the table by its side, but was too late. The wick flickered its last; the room was left in darkness.

While I felt among the different objects under my hands for a box of matches: Margaret's voice strengthened again.

"Innocent! innocent!" I heard her cry mournfully through the darkness. "I'll swear I'm innocent, and father is sure to swear it too. Innocent Margaret! Oh, me! what innocence!"

She repeated these words over and over again, till the hearing them seemed to bewilder all my senses. I hardly knew what I touched. Suddenly, my searching hands stopped of themselves, I could not tell why. Was there some change in the room? Was there more air in it, as if a door had been opened? Was there something moving over the floor? Had Margaret left her bed?—No! the mournful voice was speaking unintermittingly, and speaking from the same distance.

I moved to search for the matches on a chest of drawers, which stood near the window. Though the morning was at its darkest, and the house stood midway between two gas-lamps, there was a glimmering of light in this place. I looked back into the room from the window, and thought I saw something shadowy moving near the bed. "Take him away!" I heard Margaret scream in her wildest tones. "His hands are on me: he's feeling my face, to feel if I'm dead!"

I ran to her, stiking against some piece of furniture in the darkness. Something passed swiftly between me and the bed, as I got near it. I thought I heard a door close. Then there was silence for a moment; and then, as I stretched out my hands, my right hand encountered the little table placed by Margaret's side, and the next moment I felt the match-box that had been left on it.

As I struck a light, her voice repeated close at my ear:

"His hands are on me: he's feeling my face to feel if I'm dead!"

The match flared up. As I carried it to the candle, I looked round, and noticed for the first time that there was a second door, at the further corner of the room, which lighted some inner apartment through glass panes at the top. When I tried this door, it was locked on the inside, and the room beyond was dark.

Dark and silent. But was no one there, hidden in that darkness and silence? Was there any doubt now, that stealthy feet had approached Margaret, that stealthy hands had touched her, while the room was in obscurity?— Doubt? There was none on that point, none on any other. Suspicion shaped itself into conviction in an instant, and identified the stranger who had passed in the darkness between me and the bedside, with the man whose presence I had dreaded, as the presence of an evil spirit in the chamber of death.

He was waiting secretly in the house—waiting for her last moments; listening for her last words; watching his opportunity, perhaps, to enter the room again, and openly profane it by his presence! I placed myself by the door, resolved, if he approached, to thrust him back, at any hazard, from the bedside. How long I remained absorbed in watching before the darkness of the inner room, I know not—but some time must have elapsed before the silence around me forced itself suddenly on my attention. I turned towards Margaret; and, in an instant, all previous thoughts were suspended in my mind, by the sight that now met my eyes.

She had altered completely. Her hands, so restless hitherto, lay quite still over the coverlid; her lips never moved; the whole expression of her face had changed—the fever-traces remained on every feature, and yet the fever-look was gone. Her eyes were almost closed; her quick breathing had grown calm and slow. I touched her pulse; it was beating with a wayward, fluttering gentleness. What did this striking alteration indicate? Recovery? Was it possible? As the idea crossed my mind, every one of my faculties became absorbed in the sole occupation of watching her face; I could not have stirred an instant from the bed, for worlds.

The earliest dawn of day was glimmering faintly at the window, before another change appeared—before she drew a long, sighing breath, and slowly opened her eyes on mine. Their first look was very strange and startling to behold; for it was the look that was natural to her; the calm look of consciousness, restored to what it had always been in the past time. It lasted only for a moment. She recognised me; and, instantly, an expression of anguish and shame flew over the first terror and surprise of her face. She struggled vainly to lift her hands—so busy all through the night; so idle now! A faint moan of supplication breathed from her lips; and she slowly turned her head on the pillow, so as to hide her face from my sight.

"Oh, my God! my God!" she murmured, in low, wailing tones, "I've broken his heart, and he still comes here to be kind to me! This is worse than death! I'm too bad to be forgiven—leave me! leave me!—oh, Basil, leave me to die!"

I spoke to her; but desisted almost immediately—desisted even from uttering her name. At the mere sound of my voice, her suffering rose to agony; the wild despair of the soul wrestling awfully with the writhing weakness of the body, uttered itself in words and cries horrible, beyond all imagination, to hear. I sank down on my knees by the bedside; the strength which had sustained me for hours, gave way in an instant, and I burst into a passion of tears, as my spirit poured from my lips in supplication for hers —tears that did not humiliate me; for I knew, while I shed them, that I had forgiven her!

The dawn brightened. Gradually, as the fair light of the new day flowed in lovely upon her bed; as the fresh morning breeze lifted tenderly and playfully the scattered locks of her hair that lay over the pillow—so, the calmness began to come back to her voice and the stillness of repose to her limbs. But she never turned her face to me again; never, when the wild words of her despair grew fewer and fainter; never, when the last faint supplication to me, to leave her to die forsaken as she deserved, ended mournfully in a long, moaning gasp for breath. I waited after this— waited a long time—then spoke to her softly—then waited once more; hearing her still breathe, but slowly and more slowly with every minute—then spoke to her for the second time, louder than before. She never answered, and never moved. Was she sleeping? I could not tell. Some influence seemed to hold me back from going to the other side of the bed, to look at her face, as it lay away from me, almost hidden in the pillow.

The light strengthened faster, and grew mellow with the clear beauty of the morning sunshine. I heard the sound of rapid footsteps advancing along the street; they stopped under the window: and a voice which I recognized, called me by my name. I looked out: Mr. Bernard had returned at last.

"I could not get back sooner," he said; "the case was desperate, and I was afraid to leave it. You will find a key on the chimney-piece—throw it out to me, and I can let myself in; I told them not to bolt the door before I went out."

I obeyed his directions. When he entered the room, I thought Margaret moved a little, and signed to him with my hand to make no noise. He looked towards the bed without any appearance of surprise, and asked me in a whisper when the change had come over her, and how. I told him very briefly, and inquired whether he had known of such changes in other cases, like hers.

"Many," he answered, "many changes just as extraordinary, which have raised hopes that I never knew realised. Expect the worst from the change you have witnessed; it is a fatal sign."

Still, in spite of what he said, it seemed as if he feared to wake her, for he spoke in his lowest tones, and walked very softly when he went close to the bedside.

He stopped suddenly, just as he was about to feel her pulse, and looked in the direction of the glass door—listened attentively—and said, as if to himself—"I thought I heard some one moving in that room, but I suppose I am mistaken; nobody can be up in the house yet." With those words he looked down at Margaret, and gently parted back her hair from her forehead.

"Don't disturb her," I whispered, "she is asleep; surely she is asleep!"

He paused before he answered me, and placed his hand on her heart. Then softly drew up the bed-linen, till it hid her face.

"Yes, she *is* asleep," he said gravely; "asleep, never to wake again. She is dead."

I turned aside my head in silence, for my thoughts, at that moment, were not the thoughts which can be spoken by man to man.

"This has been a sad scene for any one at your age," he resumed kindly, as he left the bedside, "but you have borne it well. I am glad to see that you can behave so calmly under so hard a trial."

Calmly?

Yes! at that moment it was fit that I should be calm; for I could remember that I had forgiven her.

VIII.

On the fourth day from the morning when she had died, I stood alone in the churchyard by the grave of Margaret Sherwin.

It had been left for me to watch her dying moments; it was left for me to bestow on her remains the last human charity which the living can extend to the dead. If I could have looked into the future on our fatal marriage-day, and could have known that the only home of my giving which she would ever inhabit, would be the home of the grave!—

Her father had written me a letter, which I destroyed at the time; and which, if I had it now, I should forbear from copying into these pages. Let it be enough for me to relate here, that he never forgave the action by which she thwarted him in his mercenary designs upon me and upon my family; that he diverted from himself the suspicion and

disgust of his wife's surviving relatives (whose hostility he
had some pecuniary reasons to fear), by accusing his
daughter, as he had declared he would accuse her, of having
been the real cause of her mother's death; and that he
took care to give the appearance of sincerity to the indignation which he professed to feel against her, by refusing to
follow her remains to the place of burial.

Ralph had returned to London, as soon as he received the
letter from Mr. Bernard which I had forwarded to him.
He offered me his assistance in performing the last duties
left to my care, with an affectionate earnestness that I had
never seen him display towards me before. But Mr. Bernard had generously undertaken to relieve me of every
responsibility which could be assumed by others; and on
this occasion, therefore, I had no need to put my brother's
ready kindness in helping me to the test.

I stood alone by the grave. Mr. Bernard had taken leave
of me; the workers and the idlers in the churchyard had
alike departed. There was no reason why I should not
follow them; and yet I remained, with my eyes fixed upon
the freshly-turned earth at my feet, thinking of the dead.

Some time had passed thus, when the sound of approaching footsteps attracted my attention. I looked up, and
saw a man, clothed in a long cloak drawn loosely around
his neck, and wearing a shade over his eyes, which hid the
whole upper part of his face, advancing slowly towards me,
walking with the help of a stick. He came on straight to
the grave, and stopped at the foot of it—stopped opposite
me, as I stood at the head.

"Do you know me again?" he said. "Do you know me
for Robert Mannion?" As he pronounced his name, he
raised the shade and looked at me.

The first sight of that appalling face, with its ghastly dis-
colouration of sickness, its hideous deformity of feature, its
fierce and changeless malignity of expression glaring full on

me in the piercing noonday sunshine—glaring with the
same unearthly look of fury and triumph which I had seen
flashing through the flashing lightning, when I parted from
him on the night of the storm—struck me speechless where
I stood, and has never left me since. I must not, I dare
not, describe that frightful sight; though it now rises before my imagination, vivid in its horror as on the first day
when I saw it—though it moves hither and thither before
me fearfully, while I write; though it lowers at my window,
a noisome shadow on the radiant prospect of earth, and sea,
and sky, whenever I look up from the page I am now writing towards the beauties of my cottage view.

"Do you know me for Robert Mannion?" he repeated.
"Do you know the work of your own hands, now you see
it? Or, am I changed to you past recognition, as *your*
father might have found *my* father changed, if he had seen
him on the morning of his execution, standing under the
gallows, with the cap over his face?"

Still I could neither speak nor move. I could only look
away from him in horror, and fix my eyes on the ground.

He lowered the shade to its former position on his face,
then spoke again.

"Under this earth that we stand on," he said, setting his
foot on the grave; "down here, where you are now looking,
lies buried with the buried dead, the last influence which
might one day have gained you respite and mercy at my
hands. Did you think of the one, last chance that you
were losing, when you came to see her die? I watched
you, and I watched *her*. I heard as much as you heard; I
saw as much as you saw; I know when she died, and how,
as you know it; I shared her last moments with you, to the
very end. It was my fancy not to give her up, as your sole
possession, even on her death-bed: it is my fancy, now, not
to let you stand alone—as if her corpse was your property
—over her grave!"

While he uttered the last words, I felt my self-possession returning. I could not force myself to speak, as I would fain have spoken—I could only move away, to leave him.

"Stop," he said, "what I have still to say concerns you. I have to tell you, face to face, standing with you here, over her dead body, that what I wrote from the hospital, is what I will do; that I will make your whole life to come, one long expiation of this deformity;" (he pointed to his face), "and of that death" (he set his foot once more on the grave). "Go where you will, this face of mine shall never be turned away from you; this tongue, which you can never silence but by a crime, shall awaken against you the sleeping superstitions and cruelties of all mankind. The noisome secret of that night when you followed us, shall reek up like a pestilence in the nostrils of your fellow-beings, be they whom they may. You may shield yourself behind your family and your friends—I will strike at you through the dearest and the bravest of them! Now you have heard me, go! The next time we meet, you shall acknowledge with your own lips that I can act as I speak. Live the free life which Margaret Sherwin has restored to you by her death—you will know it soon for the life of Cain!"

He turned from the grave, and left me by the way that he had come; but the hideous image of him, and the remembrance of the words he had spoken, never left me. Never for a moment, while I lingered alone in the churchyard; never, when I quitted it, and walked through the crowded streets. The horror of the fiend-face was still before my eyes, the poison of the fiend-words was still in my ears, when I returned to my lodging, and found Ralph waiting to see me as soon as I entered my room.

"At last you have come back!" he said; "I was determined to stop till you did, if I stayed all day. Is anything the matter? Have you got into some worse difficulty than ever?"

"No, Ralph—no. What have you to tell me?"

"Something that will rather surprise you, Basil: I have to tell you to leave London at once! Leave it for your own interests and for everybody else's. My father has found out that Clara has been to see you."

"Good heavens! how?"

"He won't tell me. But he has found it out. You know how you stand in his opinion—I leave you to imagine what he thinks of Clara's conduct in coming here."

"No! no! tell me yourself, Ralph—tell me how she bears his displeasure!"

"As badly as possible. After having forbidden her ever to enter this house again, he now only shows how he is offended, by his silence; and it is exactly that, of course, which distresses her. Between her notions of implicit obedience to *him*, and her opposite notions, just as strong, of her sisterly duties to *you*, she is made miserable from morning to night. What she will end in, if things go on like this, I am really afraid to think; and I'm not easily frightened, as you know. Now, Basil, listen to me: it is *your* business to stop this, and *my* business to tell you how."

"I will do anything you wish—anything for Clara's sake!"

"Then leave London; and so cut short the struggle between her duty and her inclination. If you don't, my father is quite capable of taking her at once into the country, though I know he has important business to keep him in London. Write a letter to her, saying that you have gone away for your health, for change of scene and peace of mind—gone away, in short, to come back better some day. Don't say where you're going, and don't tell me, for she is sure to ask, and sure to get it out of me if I know. Then she might be writing to you, and that might be found out, too. She can't distress herself about your absence, if you account for it properly, as she distresses herself now—that is one consideration. And you will serve your own interests, as well as Clara's, by going away—that is another."

"Never mind *my* interests. Clara! I can only think of Clara!"

"But you *have* interests, and you must think of them. I told my father of the death of that unhappy woman, and of your noble behaviour when she was dying. Don't interrupt me, Basil—it *was* noble; I couldn't have done what you did, I can tell you! I saw he was more struck by it than he was willing to confess. An impression has been made on him by the turn circumstances have taken. Only leave that impression to strengthen, and you're safe. But if you destroy it by staying here, after what has happened, and keeping Clara in this new dilemma—my dear fellow, you destroy your best chance! There is a sort of defiance of him in stopping; there is a downright concession to him in going away."

"I *will* go, Ralph; you have more than convinced me that I ought! I will go to-morrow, though where—"

"You have the rest of the day to think where. *I* should go abroad and amuse myself; but your ideas of amusement are, most likely, not mine. At any rate, wherever you go, I can always supply you with money, when you want it; you can write to me, after you have been away some little time, and I can write back, as soon as I have good news to tell you. Only stick to your present determination, Basil, and, I'll answer for it, you will be back in your own study at home, before you are many months older!"

"I will put it out of my power to fail in my resolution, by writing to Clara at once, and giving you the letter to place in her hands to-morrow evening, when I shall have left London some hours."

"That's right, Basil! that's acting and speaking like a man!"

I wrote immediately, accounting for my sudden absence as Ralph had advised me—wrote, with a heavy heart, all that I thought would be most reassuring and cheering to Clara; and then, without allowing myself time to hesitate or to think, gave the letter to my brother.

"She shall have it to-morrow night," he said, "and my father shall know why you have left town, at the same time. Depend on me in this, as in everything else. And now, Basil, I must say good bye—unless you're in the humour for coming to look at my new house this evening. Ah! I see that won't suit you just now, so, good bye, old fellow! Write when you are in any necessity—get back your spirits and your health—and never doubt that the step you are now taking will be the best for Clara, and the best for yourself!"

He hurried out of the room, evidently feeling more at saying farewell than he was willing to let me discover. I was left alone for the rest of the day, to think whither I should turn my steps on the morrow.

I knew that it would be best that I should leave England; but there seemed to have grown within me, suddenly, a yearning towards my own country that I had never felt before—a home-sickness for the land in which my sister lived. Not once did my thoughts wander away to foreign places, while I now tried to consider calmly in what direction I should depart when I left London.

While I was still in doubt, my earliest impressions of childhood came back to my memory; and influenced by them, I thought of Cornwall. My nurse had been a Cornish woman; my first fancies and first feelings of curiosity had been excited by her Cornish stories, by the descriptions of the scenery, the customs, and the people of her native land, with which she was ever ready to amuse me. As I grew older, it had always been one of my favourite projects to go to Cornwall, to explore the wild western land, on foot, from hill to hill throughout. And now, when no motive of

pleasure could influence my choice—now, when I was going
forth homeless and alone, in uncertainty, in grief, in peril—
the old fancy of long-past days still kept its influence, and
pointed out my new path to me among the rocky boundaries
of the Cornish shore.

My last night in London was a night made terrible by
Mannion's fearful image in all my dreams—made mournful,
in my waking moments, by thoughts of the morrow which
was to separate me from Clara. But I never faltered in
my resolution to leave London for her sake. When the
morning came, I collected my few necessaries, added to them
one or two books, and was ready to depart.

My way through the streets took me near my father's
house. As I passed by the well-remembered neighbourhood, my self-control so far deserted me, that I stopped and
turned aside into the Square, in the hope of seeing Clara
once more before I went away. Cautiously and doubtfully,
as if I was a trespasser even on the public pavement, I
looked up at the house which was no more my home—at
the windows, side by side, of my sister's sitting-room and
bed-room. She was neither standing near them, nor passing
accidentally from one room to another at that moment. Still
I could not persuade myself to go on. I thought of many
and many an act of kindness that she had done for me,
which I seemed never to have appreciated until now—I
thought of what she had suffered, and might yet suffer, for
my sake—and the longing to see her once more, though only
for an instant, still kept me lingering near the house and
looking up vainly at the lonely windows.

It was a bright, cool, autumnal morning; perhaps she
might have gone out into the garden of the square : it used
often to be her habit, when I was at home, to go there and
read at this hour. I walked round, outside the railings,
searching for her between gaps in the foliage ; and had
nearly made the circuit of the garden thus, before the figure

of a lady sitting alone under one of the trees, attracted my attention. I stopped—looked intently towards her—and saw that it was Clara.

Her face was almost entirely turned from me; but I knew her by her dress, by her figure—even by her position, simple as it was. She was sitting with her hands on a closed book which rested on her knee. A little spaniel that I had given her lay asleep at her feet: she seemed to be looking down at the animal, as far as I could tell by the position of her head. When I moved aside, to try if I could see her face, the trees hid her from sight. I was obliged to be satisfied with the little I could discern of her, through the one gap in the foliage which gave me a clear view of the place where she was sitting. To speak to her, to risk the misery to both of us of saying farewell, was more than I dared trust myself to do. I could only stand silent, and look at her—it might be for the last time!—until the tears gathered in my eyes, so that I could see nothing more. I resisted the temptation to dash them away. While they still hid her from me—while I could not see her again, if I would—I turned from the garden view, and left the Square.

Amid all the thoughts which thronged on me, as I walked farther and farther away from the neighbourhood of what was once my home; amid all the remembrances of past events—from the first day when I met Margaret Sherwin to the day when I stood by her grave—which were recalled by the mere act of leaving London, there now arose in my mind, for the first time, a doubt, which from that day to this has never left it; a doubt whether Mannion might not be tracking me in secret along every step of my way.

I stopped instinctively, and looked behind me. Many figures were moving in the distance; but the figure that I had seen in the churchyard was nowhere visible among them. A little further on, I looked back again, and still with the same result. After this, I let a longer interval elapse before I stopped; and then, for the third time, I turned round, and scanned the busy street-scene behind me, with eager, suspicious eyes. Some little distance back, on the opposite side of the way, I caught sight of a man who was standing still (as I was standing), amid the moving throng. His height was like Mannion's height; and he wore a cloak like the cloak I had seen on Mannion, when he approached me at Margaret's grave. More than this I could not detect, without crossing over. The passing vehicles and foot-passengers constantly intercepted my view, from the position in which I stood.

Was this figure, thus visible only by intervals, the figure of Mannion? and was he really tracking my steps? As the suspicion strengthened in my mind that it was so, the remembrance of his threat in the churchyard: "You may shield yourself behind your family and your friends: I will strike at you through the dearest and the bravest of them—" suddenly recurred to me; and brought with it a thought which urged me instantly to proceed on my way. I never looked behind me again, as I now walked on; for I said within myself:—"If he is following me, I must not, and will not avoid him: it will be the best result of my departure, that I shall draw after me that destroying presence; and thus at least remove it far and safely away from my family and my home!"

So, I neither turned aside from the straight direction, nor hurried my steps, nor looked back any more. At the time I had resolved on, I left London for Cornwall, without making any attempt to conceal my departure. And though I knew that he must surely be following me, still I never saw him again: never discovered how close or how far off he was on my track.

————

Two months have passed since that period; and I know no more about him *now* than I knew *then*.

JOURNAL.

October 19th.—My retrospect is finished. I have traced the history of my errors and misfortunes, of the wrong I have done and the punishment I have suffered for it, from the past to the present time.

The pages of my manuscript (many more than I thought to write at first) lie piled together on the table before me. I dare not look them over: I dare not read the lines which my own hand has traced. There may be much in my manner of writing that wants alteration; but I have no heart to return to my task, and revise and reconsider as I might if I were intent on producing a book which was to be published during my lifetime. Others will be found, when I am no more, to carve, and smooth, and polish to the popular taste of the day this rugged material of Truth which I shall leave behind me.

But now, while I collect these leaves, and seal them up, never to be opened again by my hands, can I feel that I have related all which it is necessary to tell? No! While Mannion lives—while I am ignorant of the changes that may yet be wrought in the home from which I am exiled—there remains for me a future which must be recorded, as the necessary sequel to the narrative of the past. What may yet happen worthy of record, I know not: what sufferings I may yet undergo, which may unfit me for continuing the labour now terminated for a time, I cannot foresee. I have not hope enough in the future, or in

myself, to believe that I shall have the time or the energy
to write hereafter, as I have written already, from recollection. It is best, then, that I should note down events
daily as they occur; and so ensure, as far as may be, a
continuation of my narrative, fragment by fragment, to the
very last.

But, first, as a fit beginning to the Journal I now propose to keep, let me briefly reveal something, in this place,
of the life that I am leading in my retirement on the
Cornish coast.

The fishing hamlet in which I have written the preceding
pages, is on the southern shore of Cornwall, not more than
a few miles distant from the Land's End. The cottage I
inhabit is built of rough granite, rudely thatched, and has
but two rooms. I possess no furniture but my bed, my
table, and my chair; and some half-dozen fishermen and
their families are my only neighbours. But I feel neither
the want of luxuries, nor the want of society: all that
I wished for in coming here, I have—the completest
seclusion.

My arrival produced, at first, both astonishment and
suspicion.* The fishermen of Cornwall still preserve almost
all the superstitions, even to the grossest, which were held
dear by their humble ancestors, centuries back. My simple neighbours could not understand why I had no business
to occupy me; could not reconcile my worn, melancholy
face with my youthful years. Such loneliness as mine
looked unnatural—especially to the women. They questioned me curiously; and the very simplicity of my answer,
that I had only come to Cornwall to live in quiet, and
regain my health, perplexed them afresh. They waited,
day after day, when I was first installed in the cottage, to
see letters sent to me—and no letters arrived: to see my
friends join me—and no friends came. This deepened the
mystery to their eyes. They began to recall to memory

old Cornish legends of solitary, secret people who had lived, years and years ago, in certain parts of the county —coming, none knew whence; existing, none knew by what means; dying and disappearing, none knew when. They felt half inclined to identify me with these mysterious visitors—to consider me as some being, a stranger to the whole human family, who had come to waste away under a curse, and die ominously and secretly among them. Even the person to whom I first paid money for my necessaries, questioned, for a moment, the lawfulness and safety of receiving it!

But these doubts gradually died away; this superstitious curiosity insensibly wore off, among my poor neighbours. They became used to my solitary, thoughtful, and (to them) inexplicable mode of existence. One or two little services of kindness which I rendered, soon after my arrival, to their children, worked wonders in my favour; and I am pitied now, rather than distrusted. When the results of the fishing are abundant, a little present has been often made to me, out of the nets. Some weeks ago, after I had gone out in the morning, I found on my return, two or three gulls' eggs placed in a basket before my door. They had been left there by the children, as ornaments for my cottage window—the only ornaments they had to give; the only ornaments they had ever heard of.

I can now go out unnoticed, directing my steps up the ravine in which our hamlet is situated, towards the old grey stone church which stands solitary on the hill-top, surrounded by the lonesome moor. If any children happen to be playing among the scattered tombs, they do not start and run away, when they see me sitting on the coffin stone at the entrance of the churchyard, or wandering round the sturdy granite tower, reared by hands which have mouldered into dust centuries ago. My approach has ceased to be of evil omen for my little neighbours. They just look up at me, for a moment, with bright smiles, and then go on with their game.

From the churchyard, I look down the ravine, on fine days, towards the sea. Mighty piles of granite soar above the fishermen's cottages on each side; the little strip of white beach which the cliffs shut in, glows pure in the sunlight; the inland stream that trickles down the bed of the rocks, sparkles, at places, like a rivulet of silver-fire; the round white clouds, with their violet shadows and bright wavy edges, roll on majestically above me; the cries of the sea-birds, the endless, dirging murmur of the surf, and the far music of the wind among the ocean caverns, fall, now together, now separately on my ear. Nature's voice and Nature's beauty—God's soothing and purifying angels of the soul—speak to me most tenderly and most happily, at such times as these.

It is when the rain falls, and wind and sea arise together —when, sheltered among the caverns in the side of the precipice, I look out upon the dreary waves and the leaping spray—that I feel the unknown dangers which hang over my head in all the horror of their uncertainty. Then, the threats of my deadly enemy strengthen their hold fearfully on all my senses. I see the dim and ghastly personification of a fatality that is lying in wait for me, in the strange shapes of the mist which shrouds the sky, and moves, and whirls, and brightens, and darkens in a weird glory of its own over the heaving waters. Then, the crash of the breakers on the reef howls upon me with a sound of judgment; and the voice of the wind, growling and battling behind me in the hollows of the cave, is, ever and ever, the same thunder-voice of doom and warning in my ear.

Does this foreboding that Mannion's eye is always on me, that his footsteps are always secretly following mine, proceed only from the weakness of my worn-out energies? Could others in my situation restrain themselves from fearing, as I do, that he is still incessantly watching me in secret? It is possible. It may be, that his terrible connection with all my sufferings of the past, makes me attach credit too easily to the destroying power which he arrogates to himself in the future. Or it may be, that all resolution to resist him is paralysed in me, not so much by my fear of his appearance, as by my uncertainty of the time when it will take place—not so much by his menaces themselves, as by the delay in their execution. Still, though I can estimate fairly the value of these considerations, they exercise over me no lasting influence of tranquillity. I remember what this man *has* done; and in spite of all reasoning, I believe in what he has told me he will yet do. Madman though he may be, I have no hope of defence or escape from him in any direction, look where I will.

But for the occupation which the foregoing narrative has given to my mind; but for the relief which my heart can derive from its thoughts of Clara, I must have sunk under the torment of suspense and suspicion in which my life is now passed. My sister! Even in this self-imposed absence from her, I have still found a means of connecting myself remotely with something that she loves. I have taken, as the assumed name under which I live, and shall continue to live until my father has given me back his confidence and his affection, the name of a little estate that once belonged to my mother, and that now belongs to her daughter. Even the most wretched have their caprice, their last favourite fancy. I possess no memorial of Clara, not even a letter. The name that I have taken from the place which she was always fondest and proudest of, is, to me, what a lock of hair, a ring, any little loveable keepsake, is to others happier than I am.

I have wandered away from the simple details of my life in this place. Shall I now return to them? Not to-day; my head burns, my hand is weary. If the morrow should

bring with it no event to write of, on the morrow I can
resume the subject from which I now break off.

October 20*th.*—After laying aside my pen, I went out
yesterday for the purpose of renewing that former friendly
intercourse with my poor neighbours, which has been interrupted for the last three weeks by unintermitting labour at
the latter portions of my narrative.

In the course of my walk among the cottages and up to
the old church on the moor, I saw fewer of the people of
the district than usual. The behaviour of those whom I
did chance to meet, seemed unaccountably altered; perhaps
it was mere fancy, but I thought they avoided me. One
woman abruptly shut her cottage door as I approached. A
fisherman, when I wished him good day, hardly answered;
and walked on without stopping to gossip with me as usual.
Some children, too, whom I overtook on the road to the
church, ran away from me, making gestures to each other
which I could not understand. Is the first superstitious
distrust of me returning after I thought it had been entirely overcome? Or are my neighbours only showing their
resentment at my involuntary neglect of them for the last
three weeks? I must try to find out to-morrow.

21*st.*—I have discovered all! The truth, which I was
strangely slow to suspect yesterday, has forced itself on me
to-day.

I went out this morning, as I had purposed, to discover
whether my neighbours had really changed towards me, or
not, since the interval of my three weeks' seclusion. At
the cottage-door nearest to mine, two young children were
playing, whom I knew I had succeeded in attaching to me
soon after my arrival. I walked up to speak to them; but,
as I approached, their mother came out, and snatched them
from me with a look of anger and alarm. Before I could
question her, she had taken them inside the cottage, and had
closed the door.

Almost at the same moment, as if by a preconcerted signal, three or four other women came out from their abodes at a little distance, warned me in loud, angry voices not to come near them, or their children; and disappeared, shutting their doors. Still not suspecting the truth, I turned back, and walked towards the beach. The lad whom I employ to serve me with provisions, was lounging there against the side of an old boat. At seeing me, he started up, and walked away a few steps—then stopped, and called out—

"I'm not to bring you anything more; father says he won't sell to you again, whatever you pay him."

I asked the boy why his father had said that; but he ran back towards the village without answering me.

"You had best leave us," muttered a voice behind me. "If you don't go of your own accord, our people will starve you out of the place."

The man who said these words, had been one of the first to set the example of friendliness towards me, after my arrival; and to him I now turned for the explanation which no one else would give me.

"You know what we mean, and why we want you to go, well enough," was his reply.

I assured him that I did not; and begged him so earnestly to enlighten me, that he stopped as he was walking away.

"I'll tell you about it," he said; "but not now; I don't want to be seen with you." (As he spoke he looked back at the women, who were appearing once more in front of their cottages.) "Go home again, and shut yourself up; I'll come at dusk."

And he came as he had promised. But when I asked him to enter my cottage, he declined, and said he would talk to me outside, at my window. This disinclination to be under my roof, reminded me that my supplies of food had, for the last week, been left on the window-ledge, instead of being brought into my room as usual. I had been too constantly occupied to pay much attention to the circumstance at the time; but I thought it very strange now.

"Do you mean to tell me you don't suspect why we want to get you out of our place here?" said the man, looking in distrustfully at me through the window.

I repeated that I could not imagine why they had all changed towards me, or what wrong they thought I had done them.

"Then I'll soon let you know it," he continued. "We want you gone from here, because—"

"Because," interrupted another voice behind him, which I recognised as his wife's, "because you're bringing a blight on us, and our houses—because *we want our children's faces left as God made them*—"

"Because," interposed a second woman, who had joined her, "you're bringing devil's vengeances among Christian people! Come back, John! he's not safe for a true man to speak to."

They dragged the fisherman away with them before he could say another word. I had heard enough. The fatal truth burst at once on my mind. Mannion *had* followed me to Cornwall; his threats were executed to the very letter!

(10 *o'clock.*)—I have lit my candle for the last time in this cottage, to add a few lines to my journal. The hamlet is quiet; I hear no footstep outside—and yet, can I be certain that Mannion is not lurking near my door at this moment?

I must go when the morning comes; I must leave this quiet retreat, in which I have lived so calmly until now. There is no hope that I can reinstate myself in the opinions of my poor neighbours. He has arrayed against me the pitiless hostility of their superstition. He has found out the dormant cruelties, even in the hearts of these simple people; and has awakened them against me, as he said he would. The evil work must have been begun within the last three weeks, while I was much within doors, and there was little chance of meeting me in my usual walks. How that work was accomplished it is useless to inquire; my only object now, must be to prepare myself at once for departure.

(11 *o'clock.*)—While I was putting up my few books, a minute ago, a little embroidered marker fell out of one of them, which I had not observed in the pages before; and which I recognised as having been worked for me by Clara. I have a memorial of my sister in my possession, after all! Trifling as it is, I shall preserve it about me, as a messenger of consolation in the time of adversity and peril.

(1 *o'clock.*)—The wind sweeps down on us, from off the moorland, in fiercer and fiercer gusts; the waves dash heavily against our rock promontory; the rain drifts wildly past my windows; and the densest darkness overspreads the whole sky. The storm which has been threatening for some days, is gathering fast.

(*Village of Treen,** *October* 22*nd.*)—The events of this one day have changed the whole future of my life. I must force myself to write of them at once. Something warns me that if I delay, though only till to-morrow, I shall be incapable of relating them at all.

It was still early in the morning—I think about seven o'clock—when I closed my cottage door behind me, never to open it again. I met only one or two of my neighbours as I left the hamlet. They drew aside to let me advance, without saying a word. With a heavy heart, grieved more than I could have imagined possible at departing as an enemy from among the people with whom I had lived as a friend, I passed slowly by the last cottages, and ascended the cliff path which led to the moor.

The storm had raged at its fiercest some hours back. Soon after daylight the wind sank; but the majesty of the mighty sea had lost none of its terror and grandeur as yet. The huge Atlantic waves still hurled themselves, foaming and furious, against the massive granite of the Cornish cliffs. Overhead, the sky was hidden in a thick white mist, now hanging, still and dripping, down to the ground; now rolling in shapes like vast smoke-wreaths before the light wind which still blew at intervals. At a distance of more than a few yards, the largest objects were totally invisible. I had nothing to guide me, as I advanced, but the ceaseless roaring of the sea on my right hand.

It was my purpose to get to Penzance by night. Beyond that, I had no project, no thought of what refuge I should seek next. Any hope I might have formerly felt of escaping from Mannion, had now deserted me for ever. I could not discover by any outward indications, that he was still fol-lowing my footsteps. The mist obscured all objects behind me from view; the ceaseless crashing of the shore-waves overwhelmed all landward sounds, but I never doubted for a moment that he was watching me, as I proceeded along my onward way.

I walked slowly, keeping from the edge of the precipices only by keeping the sound of the sea always at the same distance from my ear; knowing that I was advancing in the proper direction, though very circuitously, as long as I heard the waves on my right hand. To have ventured on the shorter way, by the moor and the cross-roads beyond it, would have been only to have lost myself past all chance of extrication, in the mist.

In this tedious manner I had gone on for some time, before it struck me that the noise of the sea was altering completely to my sense of hearing. It seemed to be sounding very strangely on each side of me—both on my right hand and on my left. I stopped and strained my eyes to look through the mist, but it was useless. Crags only a few yards off, seemed like shadows in the thick white vapour. Again, I went on a little; and, ere long, I heard rolling towards me, as it were, under my own feet, and under the roaring of the sea, a howling, hollow, intermittent sound, like thunder at a distance. I stopped again, and rested against a rock. After some time, the mist began to part to seaward, but remained still as thick as ever on each side of me. I went on towards the lighter sky in front—the thunder-sound booming louder and louder, in the very heart, as it seemed, of the great cliff.

The mist brightened yet a little more, and showed me a landmark to ships, standing on the highest point of the surrounding rocks. I climbed to it, recognised the glaring red and white pattern in which it was painted, and knew that I had wandered, in the mist, away from the regular line of coast, out on one of the great granite promontories which project into the sea, as natural breakwaters, on the southern shore of Cornwall.

I had twice penetrated as far as this place, at the earlier period of my sojourn in the fishing-hamlet, and while I now listened to the thunder-sound, I knew from what cause it proceeded.

Beyond the spot where I stood, the rocks descended suddenly, and almost perpendicularly, to the range below them. In one of the highest parts of the wall-side of granite thus formed, there opened a black, yawning hole* that slanted nearly straight downwards, like a tunnel, to unknown and unfathomable depths below, into which the waves found entrance through some subterranean channel. Even at calm times the sea was never silent in this frightful abyss, but on stormy days its fury was terrific. The wild waves boiled and thundered in their imprisonment, till they seemed to convulse the solid cliff about them, like an earthquake. But, high as they leapt up in the rocky walls of the chasm, they never leapt into sight from above. Nothing but clouds of spray indicated to the eye, what must be the horrible tumult of the raging waters below.

With my recognition of the place to which I had now wandered, came remembrance of the dangers I had left behind me on the rock-track that led from the mainland to the promontory—dangers of narrow ledges and treacherous precipices, which I had passed safely, while unconscious of them in the mist, but which I shrank from tempting again, now that I recollected them, until the sky had cleared, and I could see my way well before me. The atmosphere was still brightening slowly over the tossing, distant waves : I determined to wait until it had lost all its obscurity, before I ventured to retrace my steps.

I moved down towards the lower range of rocks, to seek a less exposed position than that which I now occupied. As I neared the chasm, the terrific howling of the waves inside it was violent enough to drown, not only the crashing sound of the surf on the outward crags of the promontory, but even the shrill cries of the hundreds on hundreds of sea-birds that whirled around me, except when their flight was immediately over my head. At each side of the abyss, the rocks, though very precipitous, afforded firm hold for hand and foot. As I descended them, the morbid longing to look on danger, which has led many a man to the very brink of a precipice, even while he dreaded it, led me to advance as near as I durst to the side of the great hole, and to gaze down into it. I could see but little of its black, shining, interior walls, or of the fragments of rock which here and there jutted out from them, crowned with patches of long, lank, sea-weed waving slowly to and fro in empty space—I could see but little of these things, for the spray from the bellowing water in the invisible depths below, steamed up almost incessantly, like smoke, and shot, hissing in clouds out of the mouth of the chasm, on to a huge flat rock, covered with sea-weed, that lay beneath and in front of it. The very sight of this smooth, slippery plane of granite, shelving steeply downward, right into the gaping depths of the hole, made my head swim; the thundering of the water bewildered and deafened me—I moved away while I had the power: away, some thirty or forty yards in a lateral direction, towards the edges of the promontory which looked down on the sea. Here, the rocks rose again in wild shapes, forming natural caverns and penthouses. Towards one of these I now advanced, to shelter myself till the sky had cleared.

I had just entered the place, close to the edge of the cliff, when a hand was laid suddenly and firmly on my arm; and, through the crashing of the waves below, the thundering of the water in the abyss behind, and the shrieking of the sea-birds overhead, I heard these words, spoken close to my ear :—

"Take care of your life. It is not your's to throw away —it is *mine !*"*

I turned, and saw Mannion standing by me. No shade concealed the hideous distortion of his face. His eye was on me, as he pointed significantly down to the surf foaming two hundred feet beneath us.

"Suicide!" he said slowly—"I suspected it, and, this time, I followed close : followed, to fight with death, which should have you."

As I moved back from the edge of the precipice, and shook him from me, I marked the vacancy that glared even through the glaring triumph of his eye, and remembered how I had been warned against him at the hospital.

The mist was thickening again, but thickening now in clouds that parted and changed minute by minute, under the influence of the light behind them. I had noticed these sudden transitions before, and knew them to be the signs which preceded the speedy clearing of the atmosphere.

When I looked up at the sky, Mannion stepped back a few paces, and pointed in the direction of the fishing-hamlet from which I had departed.

"Even in that remote place," he said, "and among those ignorant people, my deformed face has borne witness against you, and Margaret's death has been avenged, as I said it should. You have been expelled as a pest and a curse, by a community of poor fishermen; you have begun to live your life of excommunication, as I lived mine. Superstition!—barbarous, monstrous superstition, which I found ready made to my use, is the scourge with which I have driven you from that hiding-place. Look at me now! I have got back my strength; I am no longer the sick refuse of the hospital. Where you go, I have the limbs and the endurance to go too! I tell you again, we are linked together for life; I cannot leave you if I would. The horrible joy of hunting you through the world, leaps in my blood like fire! Look! look out on those tossing waves. There is no rest for *them;* there shall be no rest for *you!*"

The sight of him, standing close by me in that wild solitude; the hoarse sound of his voice, as he raised it almost to raving in his exultation over my helplessness; the incessant crashing of the sea on the outer rocks; the roaring of the tortured waters imprisoned in the depths of the abyss behind us; the obscurity of the mist, and the strange, wild shapes it began to take, as it now rolled almost over our heads—all that I saw, all that I heard, seemed suddenly to madden me, as Mannion uttered his last words. My brain felt turned to fire; my heart to ice. A horrible temptation to rid myself for ever of the wretch before me, by hurling him over the precipice at my feet, seized on me. I felt my hands stretching themselves out towards him without my willing it—if I had waited another instant, I should have dashed him or myself to destruction. But I turned back in time ; and, reckless of all danger, fled from the sight of him, over the rugged and perilous surface of the cliff.

The shock of a fall among the rocks, before I had advanced more than a few yards, partly restored my self-possession. Still, I dared not look back to see if Mannion was following me, so long as the precipice behind him was within view.

I began to climb to the higher range of rocks almost at the same spot by which I had descended from them—judging by the close thunder of the water in the chasm. Half-way up, I stopped at a broad resting-place ; and found that I must proceed a little, either to the right or to the left, in a horizontal direction, before I could easily get higher. At that moment, the mist was slowly brightening again. I looked first to the left, to see where I could get good foot-hold—then to the right, towards the outer sides of the riven rocks close at hand.

At the same instant, I caught sight dimly of the figure of Mannion, moving shadow-like below and beyond me, skirting the farther edge of the slippery plane of granite that shelved into the gaping mouth of the hole. The brightening atmosphere showed him that he had risked himself, in the mist, too near to a dangerous place. He stopped—looked up and saw me watching him—raised his hand—and shook it threateningly in the air. The ill-calculated violence of his action, in making that menacing gesture, destroyed his equilibrium—he staggered—tried to recover himself—swayed half round where he stood—then fell heavily backward, right on to the steep shelving rock.

The wet sea-weed slipped through his fingers, as they madly clutched at it. He struggled frantically to throw himself towards the side of the declivity ; slipping further and further down it at every effort. Close to the mouth of the abyss, he sprang up as if he had been shot. A tremendous jet of spray hissed out upon him at the same moment. I heard a scream so shrill, so horribly unlike any

human cry, that it seemed to silence the very thundering
of the water. The spray fell. For one instant, I saw two
livid and bloody hands tossed up against the black walls of
the hole, as he dropped into it. Then, the waves roared
again fiercely in their hidden depths; the spray flew out
once more; and when it cleared off, nothing was to be seen
at the yawning mouth of the chasm—nothing moved over
the shelving granite, but some torn particles of sea-weed
sliding slowly downwards in the running ooze.

The shock of that sight must have paralysed within me
the power of remembering what followed it; for I can recall nothing, after looking on the emptiness of the rock
below, except that I crouched on the ledge under
my feet, to save myself from falling off it—that there
was an interval of oblivion — and that I seemed to
awaken again, as it were, to the thundering of the water
in the abyss. When I rose and looked around me, the
seaward sky was lovely in its clearness; the foam of the
leaping waves flashed gloriously in the sunlight: and all
that remained of the mist was one great cloud of purple
shadow, hanging afar off over the whole inland view.

I traced my way back along the promotory feebly and
slowly. My weakness was so great, that I trembled in every
limb. A strange uncertainty about directing myself in
the simplest actions, overcame my mind. Sometimes, I
stopped short, hesitating in spite of myself at the slightest
obstacles in my path. Sometimes, I grew confused without any cause, about the direction in which I was proceeding, and fancied I was going back to the fishing village.
The sight that I had witnessed, seemed to be affecting me
physically, far more than mentally. As I dragged myself
on my weary way along the coast, there was always the
same painful vacancy in my thoughts: there seemed to be
no power in them, yet, of realising Mannion's appalling death.

By the time I arrived at this village, my strength was so
utterly exhausted, that the people at the inn were obliged

to help me upstairs. Even now, after some hours' rest, the mere exertion of dipping my pen in the ink begins to be a labour and a pain to me. There is a strange fluttering at my heart; my recollections are growing confused again—I can write no more.

23rd.—The frightful scene that I witnessed yesterday still holds the same disastrous influence over me. I have vainly endeavoured to think, not of Mannion's death, but of the free prospect which that death has opened to my view. Waking or sleeping, it is as if some fatality kept all my faculties imprisoned within the black walls of the chasm. I saw the livid, bleeding hands flying past them again, in my dreams, last night. And now, while the morning is clear and the breeze is fresh, no repose, no change comes to my thoughts. The bright beauty of unclouded daylight seems to have lost the happy influence over me which it used for-merly to possess.

25th.—All yesterday I had not energy enough even to add a line to this journal. The strength to control myself seems to have gone from me. The slightest accidental noise in the house, throws me into a fit of trembling which I can-not subdue. Surely, if ever the death of one human being brought release and salvation to another, the death of Man-nion has brought them to me; and yet, the effect left on my mind by the horror of having seen it, is still not les-sened—not even by the knowledge of all that I have gained by being freed from the deadliest and most determined enemy that man ever had.

26th.—Visions—half waking, half dreaming—all through the night. Visions of my last lonely evening in the fish-ing-hamlet—of Mannion again—the livid hands whirling to and fro over my head in the darkness—then, glimpses of home; of Clara reading to me in my study—then, a change to the room where Margaret died—the sight of her again, with her long black hair streaming over her face—then, ob-livion for a little while—then, Mannion once more; walk-

ing backwards and forwards by my bedside—his death,
seeming like a dream; his watching me through the night
like a reality to which I had just awakened—Clara walking
opposite to him on the other side—Ralph between them,
pointing at me.

27*th*.—I am afraid my mind is seriously affected; it must
have been fatally weakened before I passed through the
terrible scenes among the rocks of the promontory. My
nerves must have suffered far more than I suspected at
the time, under the constant suspense in which I have been
living since I left London, and under the incessant strain
and agitation of writing the narrative of all that has happened to me. Shall I send a letter to Ralph? No—not yet.
It might look like impatience, like not being able to bear
my necessary absence as calmly and resolutely as I ought.

28*th*.—A wakeful night—tormented by morbid apprehensions that the reports about me in the fishing-village may
spread to this place; that inquiries may be made after
Mannion; and that I may be suspected of having caused his
death.

29*th*.—The people at the inn have sent to get me medical
advice. The doctor came to-day. He was kindness itself;
but I fell into a fit of trembling, the moment he entered the
room—grew confused in attempting to tell him what was
the matter with me—and, at last, could not articulate a
single word distinctly. He looked very grave as he examined me and questioned the landlady. I thought I
heard him say something about sending for my friends, but
could not be certain.

31*st*.—Weaker and weaker. I tried in despair, to-day,
to write to Ralph; but knew not how to word the letter.
The simplest forms of expression confused themselves inextricably in my mind. I was obliged to give it up. It is
a surprise to me to find that I can still add with my pencil
to the entries in this Journal! When I am no longer able
to continue, in some sort, the employment to which I have

been used for so many weeks past, what will become of me? Shall I have lost the only safeguard that keeps me in my senses?

*   *   *   *   *

Worse! worse! I have forgotten what day of the month it is; and cannot remember it for a moment together, when they tell me—cannot even recollect how long I have been confined to my bed. I feel as if my heart was wasting away. Oh! if I could only see Clara again.

*   *   *   *   *

The doctor and a strange man have been looking among my papers.

My God! am I dying? dying at the very time when there is a chance of happiness for my future life?

*   *   *   *   *

Clara!—far from her—nothing but the little book-marker she worked for me—leave it round my neck when I—

I can't move, or breathe, or think—if I could only be taken back—if my father could see me as I am now! Night again—the dreams that *will* come—always of home; sometimes, the untried home in heaven, as well as the familiar home on earth—

*   *   *   *   *

Clara! I shall die out of my senses, unless Clara—break the news gently—it may kill her—

Her face so bright and calm! her watchful, weeping eyes always looking at me, with a light in them that shines steady through the quivering tears. While the light lasts, I shall live; when it begins to die out—*

NOTE BY THE EDITOR

* There are some lines of writing beyond this point; but they are illegible.

LETTERS IN CONCLUSION.

LETTER I.

FROM WILLIAM PENHALE, MINER, AT BARTALLOCK, IN CORN-
WALL, TO HIS WIFE IN LONDON.

MY DEAR MARY,

I received your letter yesterday, and was more glad than
I can say, at hearing that our darling girl Susan has got
such a good place in London, and likes her new mistress so
well.   My kind respects to your sister and her husband, and
say I don't grumble about the money that's been spent in
sending you with Susan to take care of her.   She was too
young, poor child, to be trusted to make the journey alone;
and, as I was obliged to stop at home and work to keep the
other children, and pay back what we borrowed for the trip,
of course you were the proper person, after me, to go with
Susan—whose welfare is a more precious possession to us
than any money, I am sure.   Besides, when I married you,
and took you away to Cornwall, I always promised you a
trip to London to see your friends again; and now that
promise is performed.   So, once again, don't fret about the
money that's been spent : I shall soon pay it back.

I've got some very strange news for you, Mary. You know
how bad work was getting at the mine, before you went
away—so bad, that I thought to myself after you had gone
" Hadn't I better try what I can do in the fishing at Treen ?"

And I went there; and, thank God, have got on well by it. I can turn my hand to most things; and the fishing has been very good this year. So I have stuck to my work. And now I come to my news.

The landlady at the inn here, is, as you know, a sort of relation of mine. Well, the third afternoon after you had gone, I was stopping to say a word to her at her own door, on my way to the beach, when we saw a young gentleman, quite a stranger, coming up to us. He looked very pale and wild-like, I thought, when he asked for a bed; and then got faint all of a sudden—so faint and ill, that I was obliged to lend a hand in getting him upstairs. The next morning I heard he was worse: and it was just the same story the morning after. He quite frightened the landlady, he was so restless, and talked to himself in such a strange way; specially at night. He wouldn't say what was the matter with him, or who he was: we could only find out that he had been stopping among the fishing people further west: and that they had not behaved very well to him at last—more shame for them! I'm sure they could take no hurt from the poor young fellow, let him be whom he may. Well, the end of it was that I went and fetched the doctor for him myself, and when we got into his room, we found him all pale and trembling, and looking at us, poor soul, as if he thought we meant to murder him. The doctor gave his complaint some hard names which I don't know how to write down; but it seems there's more the matter with his mind than his body, and that he must have had some great fright which has shaken his nerves all to pieces. The only way to do him good, as the doctor said, was to have him carefully nursed by his relations, and kept quiet among people he knew; strange faces about him being likely to make him worse. The doctor asked where his friends lived; but he wouldn't say, and, lately, he's got so much worse that he can't speak clearly to us at all.

Yesterday evening, he gave us all a fright. The doctor hearing me below, asking after him, said I was to come up stairs and help to move him to have his bed made. As soon as I raised him up (though I'm sure I touched him as gently as I could), he fainted dead away. While he was being brought to, a little piece of something that looked like card-board, prettily embroidered with beads and silk, came away from a string that held it round his neck, and dropped off the bedside. I picked it up; for I remembered the time, Mary, when you and I were courting, and how precious the least thing was to me that belonged to you. So I took care of it for him, thinking it might be a keepsake from his sweetheart. And sure enough, when he came to, he put up his thin white hands to his neck, and looked so thankful at me when I tied the little thing again to the string! Just as I had done that the doctor beckons me to the other end of the room.

"This won't do," says he to me in a whisper. "If he goes on like this, he'll lose his reason, if not his life. I must search his papers, to find out what friends he has; and you must be my witness."

So the doctor opens his little bag, and takes out a square sealed packet first; then two or three letters tied together; the poor soul looking all the while as if he longed to prevent us from touching them. Well, the doctor said there was no occasion to open the packet, for the direction was the same on all the letters, and the name corresponded with his initials marked on his linen.

"I'm next to certain this is where he lives, or did live; so this is where I'll write," says the doctor.

"Shall my wife take the letter, Sir?" says I. "She's in London with our girl, Susan; and, if his friends should be gone away from where you are writing to, she may be able to trace them."

"Quite right, Penhale!" says he; "we'll do that. Write to your wife, and put my letter inside yours."

I did as he told me, at once; and his letter is inside this, with the direction of the house and the street.

Now, Mary, dear, go at once, and see what you can find out. The direction on the doctor's letter may be his home; and if it isn't, there may be people there who can tell you where it is. So go at once, and let us know directly what luck you have had, for there is no time to be lost; and if you saw the young gentleman, you would pity him as much as we do.

This has got to be such a long letter, that I have no room left to write any more. God bless you, Mary, and God bless my darling Susan! Give her a kiss for father's sake, and believe me,

Your loving husband,

WILLIAM PENHALE.

LETTER II.

FROM MARY PENHALE TO HER HUSBAND.

DEAREST WILLIAM,

Susan sends a hundred kisses, and best loves to you and her brothers and sisters. She's getting on nicely; and her mistress is as kind and fond of her as can be. Best respects, too, from my sister Martha, and her husband. And now I've done giving you all my messages, I'll tell you some good news for the poor young gentleman who is so bad at Treen.

As soon as I had seen Susan, and read your letter to her, I went to the place where the doctor's letter directed me. Such a grand house, William! I was really afraid to knock at the door. So I plucked up courage, and gave a pull at the bell; and a very fat, big man, with his head all plastered over with powder, opened the door, almost before I had done ringing. "If you please, Sir," says I, showing

him the name on the doctor's letter, " do any friends of this
gentleman live here?" " To be sure they do," says he;
" his father and sister live here : but what do you want to
know for?" " I want them to read this letter," says I.
" It's to tell them that the young gentleman is very bad in
health down in our country." " You can't see my master,"
says he, " for he's confined to his bed by illness : and Miss
Clara is very poorly too—you had better leave the letter
with me." Just as he said this, an elderly lady crossed the
hall (I found out she was the housekeeper, afterwards), and
asked what I wanted. When I told her, she looked quite
startled. " Step this way, ma'am," says she; " you will do
Miss Clara more good than all the doctors put together.
But you must break the news to her carefully, before she
sees the letter. Please to make it out better news than it
is, for the young lady is in very delicate health." We went
upstairs—such stair-carpets! I was almost frightened to
step on them, after walking through the dirty streets. The
housekeeper opened a door, and said a few words inside,
which I could not hear, and then let me in where the young
lady was.

Oh, William! she had the sweetest, kindest face I ever
saw in my life. But it was so pale, and there was such a
sad look in her eyes when she asked me to sit down, that it
went to my heart, when I thought of the news I had to tell
her. I couldn't speak just at first ; and I suppose she
thought I was in some trouble—for she begged me not to
tell her what I wanted, till I was better. She said it with
such a voice and such a look, that, like a great fool, I burst
out crying, instead of answering as I ought. But it did me
good, though, and made me able to tell her about her brother (breaking it as gently as I could) before I gave her the
doctor's letter. She never opened it ; but stood up before
me as if she was turned to stone—not able to cry, or speak,
or move. It frightened me so, to see her in such a dreadful

state, that I forgot all about the grand house, and the difference there was between us; and took her in my arms,
making her sit down on the sofa by me—just as I should
do, if I was consoling our own Susan under some great
trouble. Well! I soon made her look more like herself,
comforting her in every way I could think of: and she laid
her poor head on my shoulder, and I took and kissed her,
(not remembering a bit about its being a born lady and a
stranger that I was kissing); and the tears came at last,
and did her good. As soon as she could speak, she thanked
God her brother was found, and had fallen into kind hands.
She hadn't courage to read the doctor's letter herself, and
asked me to do it. Though he gave a very bad account of
the young gentleman, he said that care and nursing, and
getting him away from a strange place to his own home and
among his friends, might do wonders for him yet. When I
came to this part of the letter, she started up, and asked
me to give it to her. Then she inquired when I was going
back to Cornwall; and I said, "as soon as possible," (for
indeed, it's time I was home, William). "Wait; pray wait
till I have shown this letter to my father!" says she. And
she ran out of the room with it in her hand.

After some time, she came back with her face all of a
flush, like; looking quite different to what she did before,
and saying that I had done more to make the family happy
by coming with that letter, than she could ever thank me
for as she ought. A gentleman followed her in, who was
her eldest brother (she said); the pleasantest, liveliest gentleman I ever saw. He shook hands as if he had known me
all his life; and told me I was the first person he had ever
met with who had done good in a family by bringing them
bad news. Then he asked me whether I was ready to go to
Cornwall the next morning with him, and the young lady,
and a friend of his who was a doctor. I had thought already of getting the parting over with poor Susan, that very

day : so I said, "Yes."   After that, they wouldn't let me go
away till I had had something to eat and drink ; and the
dear, kind young lady asked me all about Susan, and where
she was living, and about you and the children, just as if
she had known us like neighbours.   Poor thing ! she was so
flurried, and so anxious for the next morning, that it was all
the gentleman could do to keep her quiet, and prevent her
falling into a sort of laughing and crying fit, which it seems
she had been liable to lately.   At last they let me go away ;
and I went and stayed with Susan as long as I could before
I bid her good-bye.   She bore the parting bravely—poor,
dear child !   God in heaven bless her ; and I'm sure he will ;
for a better daughter no mother ever had.

My dear husband, I am afraid this letter is very badly
written ; but the tears are in my eyes, thinking of Susan ;
and I feel so wearied and flurried after what has happened.
We are to go off very early to-morrow morning in a carriage,
which is to be put on the railway.   Only think of my riding
home in a fine carriage, with gentlefolks !—how surprised
Willie, and Nancy, and the other children will be !   I shall
get to Treen almost as soon as my letter ; but I thought I
would write, so that you might have the good news, the first
moment it could get to you, to tell the poor young gentleman.   I'm sure it must make him better, only to hear that
his brother and sister are coming to fetch him home.

I can't write any more, dear William, I'm so very tired ;
except that I long to see you and the little ones again ; and
that I am,

Your loving and dutiful wife,

MARY PENHALE.

LETTER III.

TO MR. JOHN BERNARD, FROM THE WRITER OF THE FORE-
GOING AUTOBIOGRAPHY.

[This letter is nearly nine years later in date than the letters which
precede it.]

Lanreath Cottage, Breconshire.

My dear Friend,

I find, by your last letter, that you doubt whether I still
remember the circumstances under which I made a certain
promise to you, more than eight years ago. You are mistaken: not one of those circumstances has escaped my
memory. To satisfy you of this, I will now recapitulate
them. You will own, I think, that I have forgotten nothing.

After my removal from Cornwall (shall I ever forget the
first sight of Clara and Ralph at my bedside!), when the
nervous malady from which I suffered so long, had yielded
to the affectionate devotion of my family—aided by the
untiring exercise of your skill—one of my first anxieties
was to show that I could gratefully appreciate your exer-
tions for my good, by reposing the same confidence in you,
which I should place in my nearest and dearest relatives.
From the time when we first met at the hospital, your services were devoted to me, through much misery of mind and
body, with the delicacy and the self-denial of a true friend.
I felt that it was only your due that you should know by
what trials I had been reduced to the situation in which
you found me, when you accompanied my brother and sister
to Cornwall—I felt this; and placed in your hands, for
your own private perusal, the narrative which I had written
of my error and of its terrible consequences. To tell you
all that had happened to me, with my own lips, was more

than I could do then—and even after this lapse of years, would be more than I could do now.

After you had read the narrative, you urged me, on returning it into my possession, to permit its publication during my lifetime. I granted the justness of the reasons which led you to counsel me thus;* but I told you, at the same time, that an obstacle, which I was bound to respect, would prevent me from following your advice. While my father lived, I could not suffer a manuscript in which he was represented (no matter under what excess of provocation) as separating himself in the bitterest hostility from his own son, to be made public property. I could not suffer events of which we never afterwards spoke ourselves, to be given to others in the form of a printed narrative which might perhaps fall under his own eye. You acknowledged, I remember, the justice of these considerations; and promised, in case I died before him, to keep back my manuscript from publication as long as my father lived. In binding yourself to that engagement, however, you stipulated, and I agreed, that I should reconsider your arguments in case I outlived him. This was my promise, and these were the circumstances under which it was made. You will allow, I think, that my memory is more accurate than you had imagined it to be.

And now, you write to remind me of *my* part of our agreement—forbearing, with your accustomed delicacy, to introduce the subject, until more than six months have elapsed since my father's death. You have done well. I have had time to feel all the consolation afforded to me by the remembrance that, for years past, my life was of some use in sweetening my father's; that his death has occurred in the ordinary course of Nature; and that I never, to my own knowledge, gave him any cause to repent the full and loving reconciliation which took place between us, as soon as we could speak together freely after my return to home.

Still I am not answering your question:—Am I now willing to permit the publication of my narrative, provided all names and places mentioned in it remained concealed, and I am known to no one but yourself, Ralph, and Clara, as the writer of my own story? I reply that I *am* willing. In a few days, you will receive the manuscript by a safe hand. Neither my brother nor my sister object to its being made public on the terms I have mentioned; and I feel no hesitation in accepting the permission thus accorded to me. I have not glossed over the flightiness of Ralph's character; but the brotherly kindness and manly generosity which lie beneath it, are as apparent, I hope, in my narrative as they are in fact. And Clara, dear Clara!—all that I have said of her is only to be regretted as unworthy of the noblest subject that my pen, or any other pen, can have to write on !

One difficulty, however, still remains :— How are the pages which I am about to send you to be concluded? In the novel-reading sense of the word, my story has no real conclusion. The repose that comes to all of [us after trouble—to *me*, a repose in life : to others, how often a repose only in the grave !—is the end which must close this autobiography : an end, calm, natural, and uneventful; yet not, perhaps, devoid of all lesson and value. Is it fit that I should set myself, for the sake of effect, to *make* a conclusion, and terminate by fiction what has begun, and thus far, has proceeded in truth ? In the interests of Art, as well as in the interests of Reality, surely not !

Whatever remains to be related after the last entry in my journal, will be found expressed in the simplest, and therefore, the best form, by the letters from William and Mary Penhale, which I send you with this. When I revisited Cornwall, to see the good miner and his wife, I found, in the course of the inquiries which I made as to the past, that they still preserved the letters they had written about me, while I lay ill at Treen. I asked permission to take copies of these two documents, as containing materials, which I could but ill supply from my own resources, for filling up a gap in my story. They at once consented; telling me that they had always kept each other's letters after marriage, as carefully as they kept them before, in token that their first affection remained to the last unchanged. At the same time they entreated me, with the most earnest simplicity, to polish their own homely expressions; and turn them, as they phrased it, into proper reading. You may easily imagine that I knew better than to do this; and you will, I am sure, agree with me that both the letters I send should be printed as literally as they were copied by my hand.

Having now provided for the continuation of my story to the period of my return home, I have a word or two to say on the subject of preparing the autobiography for press. Failing in the resolution, even now, to look over my manuscript again, I leave the corrections it requires to others— but on one condition. Let none of the passages in which I have related events, or described characters, be either softened or suppressed. I am well aware of the tendency, in some readers, to denounce truth itself as improbable, unless their own personal experience has borne witness to it; and it is on this very account that I am firm in my determination to allow of no cringing beforehand to anticipated incredulities. What I have written is Truth; and it shall go into the world as Truth should—entirely uncompromised. Let my style be corrected as completely as you will; but leave characters and events which are taken from realities, real as they are.

In regard to the surviving persons with whom this narrative associates me, I have little to say which it can concern the reader to know. The man whom I have presented in the preceding pages under the name of Sherwin is, I believe still alive, and still residing in France—whither he retreated soon after the date of the last events mentioned in my autobiography. A new system had been [introduced into his business by his assistant, which, when left to his own unaided resources, he failed to carry out. His affairs became involved; a commercial crisis occurred, which he was wholly unable to meet; and he was made a bankrupt, having first dishonestly secured to himself a subsistence for life, out of the wreck of his property. I accidentally heard of him, a few years since, as maintaining among the English residents of the town he then inhabited, the character of a man who had undeservedly suffered from severe family misfortunes, and who bore his afflictions with the most exemplary piety and resignation.

To those once connected with him, who are now no more, I need not and cannot refer again. That part of the dreary Past with which they are associated, is the part which I still shrink in terror from thinking on. There are two names which my lips have not uttered for years; which, in this life, I shall never pronounce again. The night of Death is over them: a night to look away from for evermore.

To look away from—but, towards what object? The Future? That way, I see but dimly even yet. It is on the Present that my thoughts are fixed, in the contentment which desires no change.

For the last five months I have lived here with Clara— here, on the little estate which was once her mother's, which is now hers. Long before my father's death we often talked, in the great country house, of future days which we might pass together, as we pass them now, in this place. Though we may often leave it for a time, we shall always look back to Lanreath Cottage as to our home. The years of retirement which I spent at the Hall, after my recovery, have not awakened in me a single longing to return to the

busy world. Ralph—now the head of our family; now
aroused by his new duties to a sense of his new position—
Ralph, already emancipated from many of the habits which
once enthralled and degraded him, has written, bidding me
employ to the utmost the resources which his position ena-
bles him to offer me, if I decide on entering into public
life. But I have no such purpose; I am still resolved to
live on in obscurity, in retirement, in peace. I have suffered
too much; I have been wounded too sadly, to range myself
with the heroes of Ambition, and fight my way upward from
the ranks. The glory and the glitter which I once longed
to look on as my own, would dazzle and destroy me, now.
Such shocks as I have endured, leave that behind them
which changes the character and the purpose of a life. The
mountain-path of Action is no longer a path for *me;* my
future hope pauses with my present happiness in the shadowed valley of Repose.

Not a repose which owns no duty, and is good for no
use; not a repose which Thought cannot ennoble, and Affection cannot sanctify. To serve the cause of the poor and
the ignorant, in the little sphere which now surrounds me;
to smooth the way for pleasure and plenty, where pain and
want have made it rugged too long; to live more and more
worthy, with every day, of the sisterly love which, never
tiring, never changing, watches over me in this last retreat,
this dearest home—these are the purposes, the only purposes left, which I may still cherish. Let me but live to
fulfil them, and life will have given to me all that I can
ask!

I may now close my letter. I have communicated to you
all the materials I can supply for the conclusion of my autobiography, and have furnished you with the only directions
I wish to give in reference to its publication. Present it to
the reader in any form, and at any time, that you think fit.
On its reception by the public I have no wish to speculate.

It is enough for me to know that, with all its faults, it has been written in sincerity and in truth. I shall not feel false shame at its failure, or false pride at its success.

If there be any further information which you think it necessary to possess, and which I have forgotten to communicate, write to me on the subject—or, far better, come here yourself, and ask of me with your own lips all that you desire to know. Come, and judge of the life I am now leading, by seeing it as it really is. Though it be only for a few days, pause long enough in your career of activity and usefulness, of fame and honour, to find leisure time for a visit to the cottage where we live. This is as much Clara's invitation as mine. She will never forget (even if I could!) all that I have owed to your friendship—will never weary (even if I should tire!) of showing you that we are capable of deserving it. Come, then, and see *her* as well as *me*—see her, once more, my sister of old times! I remember what you said of Clara, when we last met, and last talked of her; and I believe you will be almost as happy to see her again in her old character as I am.

Till then, farewell! Do not judge hastily of my motives for persisting in the life of retirement which I have led for so many years past. Do not think that calamity has chilled my heart, or enervated my mind. Past suffering may have changed, but it has not deteriorated me. It has fortified my spirit with an abiding strength; it has told me plainly, much that was but dimly revealed to me before; it has shown me uses to which I may put my existence, that have their sanction from other voices than the voices of fame; it has taught me to feel that bravest ambition which is vigorous enough to overleap the little life here! Is there no aspiration in the purposes for which I would now live? —Bernard! whatever we can do of good, in this world, with our affections or our faculties, rises to the Eternal World above us, as a song of praise from Humanity to God.

Amid the thousand, thousand tones ever joining to swell the music of that song, are those which sound loudest and grandest *here*, the tones which travel sweetest and purest to the Imperishable Throne; which mingle in the perfectest harmony with the anthem of the angel-choir! Ask your own heart that question—and then say, may not the obscurest life—even a life like mine—be dignified by a lasting aspiration, and dedicated to a noble aim?

I have done. The calm summer evening has stolen on me while I have been writing to you; and Clara's voice—now the happy voice of the happy old times—calls to me from our garden seat to come out and look at the sunset over the distant sea. Once more—farewell!

EXPLANATORY NOTES

xxxv *Letter of Dedication*: in 1862 Collins made extensive cuts in the original Letter: four and a half paragraphs after the first paragraph, two pages after page v, and a paragraph at the end.

Charles James Ward, Esq.: Charles James Ward, an employee of Coutts bank, was a lifelong friend of Collins and named as executor of his will in 1882. His brother, Edward Ward the painter, was an even closer friend. See next note.

I have founded the main event . . . a fact within my own knowledge: in 1848 Collins played an important part in arranging the secret marriage of Henrietta and Edward Ward; the secrecy was due to her parents' opposition to the match—the bride was not yet sixteen years old. Collins gave the bride away. Afterwards she returned to the parental home for three months until an elopement in August which was also masterminded by Collins.

Twelve years after Collins's death, Thomas Seccombe's entry in the *Dictionary of National Biography* claimed that 'intimacies formed as a young man led to [Collins] being harrassed after he became famous, in a manner which proved very prejudicial to his peace of mind'. Is it possible that this refers to a secret marriage? Such a hypothesis would explain why Collins married neither Caroline Graves nor Martha Rudd. Kenneth Robinson, Collins's most level-headed biographer, writes that 'it is probable that Wilkie had recently undergone a violent emotional experience and wrote *Basil* as a form of catharsis' (Wilkie Collins (London, 1951), 64).

xxxviii *Nobody can assert that such scenes are unproductive of useful results*: in the first edition this reads 'Nobody can assert that such scenes are either useless or immoral in their effect on the reader.'

In deriving the lesson: in the first edition this reads 'In deriving the moral lesson'. The outraged response to *Basil* may have induced Collins to minimize his claims as to the moral value of the novel.

xxxix *condemned off-hand . . . an outrage on their sense of propriety*: for examples of contemporary attitudes to *Basil*, see Introduction, pp. xxi–xxii. With these remarks Collins began his lifelong habit of writing prefaces and introductions attacking the prudery of contemporary critics.

1 *it may be put to some warning use*: in 1862 Collins deleted after this, 'There have been men who, on their deathbeds, have left directions that their bodies should be anatomised, as an offering to science. In these pages, written on the death-bed of enjoyment and hope, I give my heart, already anatomised, as an offering to human nature.

'Perhaps, while desiring to write a confession, I desire to write an apology as well.'

3 *The story of my boyhood and youth*: in 1862 Collins deleted before this, three pages on Basil's mother, which include references to 'some great sorrow' in her life.

My life at college has not left me a single pleasant recollection: further derogatory comments on university life in *Hide and Seek* (1854) and *A Rogue's Life* (1856) suggest that the opposition to Collins senior's plan of sending his son 'to the University of Oxford, with a view to my entering the Church' came from Wilkie Collins himself (Wilkie Collins, 'Memorandum Relating to the Life and Writings of Wilkie Collins', in M. D. Parrish, *Wilkie Collins and Charles Reade* (London, 1940), p. 4). Though his apprenticeship to Antrobus the tea merchant was little to his taste, it seems less inappropriate than the Church.

4 *'livings'*: livings were endowed Church offices which could be bestowed by patronage and yielded an income to the holder.

11 *a single-stick player*: a single-stick was a wooden stick used in sporting contests, especially fencing.

12 *Richmond; ascended in balloons at Vauxhall*: Richmond had not at this time been swallowed by the London conurbation, but remained a pretty country town, fashionable for summer parties. Vauxhall Gardens (opened *c.*1660) were public pleasure gardens, popular with Londoners from their formal reopening in 1732 until their closure in 1859. The first balloon ascent at Vauxhall was in Sept. 1835; thereafter they were continuously offered as part of the entertainments.

13 *a catch club . . . a pic-nic club*: a catch-club was a social club originally formed for the purpose of singing part-songs, especially rounds. The Picnic Society was a group of fashion-

able people in London at the beginning of the nineteenth century meeting for social entertainment, private theatricals, and so on, to which each member contributed a share. Ralph's club was more likely to be of this kind rather than one devoted exclusively to *al fresco* outdoor meals.

he liked the idea of living on the continent: in 1862 Collins deleted, after this, 'and he was tired of the tenant's daughter'. This was one of several deletions which minimized Ralph's dissolute behaviour.

14 *cabriolet . . . the opera-dancers*: a cabriolet was a light, two-wheeled, horse-drawn carriage with two seats and a folding hood. Opera-dancers held a place in the Victorian imagination similar to that of chorus girls in this century.

French novels: at the time French novels were considered to be especially salacious.

a Cyprian temple: the cabinet with which Ralph replaces the chest of drawers may have been in the form of a classical temple: a Cyprian temple would be devoted to the orgiastic worship of Aphrodite on Cyprus.

16 *grisettes*: they were French working girls—particularly shop-girls and seamstresses—often regarded as being especially pretty or flirtatious.

24 *Even at my worst moments of despair*: in 1862 Collins deleted, after this, '—even when my trust in God falters—'.

25 *I am engaged in writing a historical romance . . . been abroad*: Wilkie Collins's own first extended work of fiction was also a historical romance set abroad—*Antonina: or, The Fall of Rome* (1850). On the evidence of the greatly scored and rewritten manuscript of *Basil*, Basil's description of the painstaking difficulty with which he wrote his romance (see p. 56) may reflect Collins's own laborious care.

keeping the key of the door when I am not in need of it: in 1862 Collins deleted after this, 'Nay, she must do more than this. Wherever I have marked passages for extract in books of reference, she volunteers to make the extracts, so as to leave me all my time for original composition. I am anxious to spare her this task; but she answers laughingly that she is determined to go down to posterity with me, and be mentioned as the amanuensis of the illustrious author, when his biography is written for future generations.'

26 *bait*: to bait is to feed a horse, especially during a break in a journey.

27 *I had often before ridden in omnibuses . . . observing the passengers*: horse-drawn omnibuses were first introduced from Paris in 1829, travelling along the New Road from Paddington to the City. They rapidly proved a popular and genteel alternative to the private carriage. By the 1850s advertisements for villas in the new suburbs (see note to p. 31 below) stressed their proximity to omnibus routes.

    as various even as the varieties of the human face: in 1862 Collins deleted after this, 'Riding in an omnibus was always, to me, like reading for the first time, an entertaining book.'

28 *the omnibus stopped to give admission to two ladies*: in 1862, before this, Collins made his longest deletion, a ten-page scene featuring a veterinarian. The passage is comic in tone despite its recounting the veterinarian's self-cauterization of mad-dog bites which deformed his face, and his unsuccessful attempts to impose similar remedies on a friend.

29 *before experience has guided us with a single fact in relation to their characters!*: in 1862 Collins deleted, after this, two pages on supernatural attraction. This deletion, and others nearby, diminish the themes of influence and fatality.

31 *a suburb of new houses*: the rise in the population of London from 1.6 million to 2.3 million between 1831 and 1851 was accompanied by a boom in speculative building of both working-class terraces and middle-class villas. North Villa, the Sherwin's 'partly detached' house in Hollyoake Square, is in 'a suburb of new houses', which is 'unfinished like everything else in the neighbourhood'. From it Basil walks to 'Regent's Park, the northern portion of which was close at hand' (32). On this evidence it seems likely that the Sherwins lived in Chalcots, an area stretching from St John's Wood to Haverstock Hill and from Primrose Hill to Belsize Park, which was developed in the 1840s and 1850s. Catching the essence of their attraction to the Sherwin family exactly, the houses have been described as 'nondescript . . . inoffensive . . . built to please respectable but undiscerning clients' (H. C. Prince, in J. T. Coppock and H. C.

Prince, eds., *Great London* [London: Faber & Faber, 1963], p. 174).

48 '*Hope is a lover's staff . . . despairing thoughts*': Shakespeare, *Two Gentlemen of Verona*, III. i. 246–7. It is ironic that Basil innocently quotes from a play which contrasts the idealistic love affairs of the aristocracy with the crude affairs of their servants, and in which Proteus betrays Valentine's trust to gain Silvia for himself.

49 *mighty vitality of the great city . . . interest in the sight*: there was a growing awareness among Victorian authors of the unique nature of contemporary urban life and a sub-genre of literature describing London grew up, typified by such works as Pierce Egan's *Life in London* (1820–1) and G. A. Sala's *Twice Round the Clock* (1858). This passage is reminiscent of Dickens's 'The Streets—Morning' in *Sketches by Boz* (1836).

Collins met Dickens in 1851 when he took the part of his valet in Dickens's amateur production of Bulwer-Lytton's *Not So Bad as We Seem*. During the summer of 1852 when he was writing *Basil*, Collins went on an extensive provincial tour with the play. In September, Collins showed Dickens the manuscript; he not only approved but gave Collins good advice on the financial negotiations with his publisher. In later years the two men were the closest of friends.

59 *no right to expect one*: in 1862 Collins deleted four passages from this page, three concerning Margaret's response to Basil.

61 *Tonbridge toys*: ornaments made of Tonbridge ware. Named after Tunbridge Wells where it was perfected, this is a simple technique of veneering, whereby differently coloured strips of wood are glued together and sliced horizontally.

70 *a very small independence . . . no certain prospects*: before 1862 Collins was more definite about Basil's financial situation. Rather than *a very small independence* he had 'two hundred a-year' and instead of having *no certain prospects*, Basil says, 'I am entirely dependent on my father.'

72 *bran-new*: an uncommon formation of brand-new.

73 *Ewell*: this was an area Collins came to know well during the writing of *Basil*. Collins's brother Charley (then mistakenly considered a leader of the Pre-Raphaelite Brotherhood by contemporary art critics) took lodgings with Millais and

Holman Hunt in a farmhouse near Ewell in the summer of 1851. Collins, perhaps worried about Charley's growing asceticism, visited them frequently that autumn. Millais's portrait of Collins dates from this period.

75 *Poor Mrs. Sherwin!*: Mrs Sherwin is the first of a series of disoriented, mentally unstable women whom Collins described sympathetically in his fiction. She and Sarah Leeson in *The Dead Secret* (1857) are prototypes of the more famous Anne Catherick in *The Woman in White* (1859).

restless timidity: in 1862 Collins deleted 'vigilant' from between *restless* and *timidity*.

79 *in an educational point of view*: before 1862 Mr Sherwin says, after this, 'too young in a medical point of view; too young altogether. I hold strong opinions on this subject, Sir, having one sad example already in my family (in a collateral branch) of the evils, physical and—and in fact of the evils of marrying too early.'

83 *only saw in the strange plan he proposed to me*: before 1862 Basil adds after this, 'a guarantee of the possession of Margaret'.

97 *until the year was over, and she*: in 1862 Collins substituted this for 'The fair flower I had longed for, was now promised me beyond recall: a year's tending and watching over it, a year to study its value and beauty; and then it.'

130 *If I had really produced this impression . . . cruel to leave it*: the awkwardness of this sentence may suggest that a line has been omitted but it is correct to both the first edition and the manuscript.

133 *For God's sake . . . cat!*: before 1862 the housemaid added, 'Oh, Lord, miss! you couldn't go for to do it!—I'm sure you couldn't!' and Margaret answered, 'I will do it. I'll kill that infamous, horrid, brutal cat!'

134 *I'll call in the first boy from the street to catch it*: before 1862 Margaret adds, 'and poison it, and hang it!' Both this and the previous deletion serve to diminish Margaret's passionate cruelty.

149 *My life was insured in Margaret's favour*: in 1862 Collins deleted after this, 'I had made the proper applications, in the proper quarters, for the first good official situation which might fall vacant.'

155 *linkmen*: before the introduction of street lighting, linkmen were
      paid to carry torches for pedestrians in dark streets. Gas
      lighting was first installed, in Pall Mall, in 1807 and was fairly
      common from 1816 onwards.

156 *I passed through the glittering highways of London*: in 1862 Collins
      deleted after this two pages describing Basil's walk 'amid all
      the appealing beauty and all the revolting horror of the hours
      of dark'.

159 *a neglected, deserted, dreary-looking building*: despite Collins's often
      repeated defiance of contemporary Puritanism—and Basil's
      own instructions that 'none of the passages in which I have
      related events, or described characters, be either softened or
      suppressed . . . it shall go into the world as Truth should—
      entirely uncompromised' (p. 340)—there is evidence that
      Collins bowed to his publisher's objections and made the house
      of assignation less recognizable. He wrote to Bentley: 'I sent
      you Volume 1—now at last ready for the press. As I have
      managed the alteration now, I think the difficulty in the last
      chapter is got over altogether. If you look at Folio 104, you will
      see that I have only mentioned the hotel as a deserted, dreary-
      looking building' (quoted in Nuel Pharr Davis, *The Life of
      Wilkie Collins* (Urbana, 1956) p. 125). In the extant manu-
      script it is a house, not a hotel.

160 *foully hidden until the very day*: in 1862 Collins substituted this for
      'foully matured on the very day'.

174 *They struck me motionless where I stood*: in 1862 Collins deleted
      after this, 'they leapt in their pollution upon each fair, pure
      corpse'.

178 *which had never actually taken place*: in 1862 Collins deleted after
      this, 'And was there not, in truth, an incredible maturity of
      corruptness in her iniquity? I had given to this young girl all
      that man could resign; I had accumulated, throughout a whole
      year, proof on proof of the sincerity, the devotion, the
      inexhaustible self-denial of my love—where could reason be
      found for such a foul and horrible return, on her part, to all
      that I had offered, to all that I have conferred, to all that I had
      yet to give? Where could a parallel be discovered for the
      accursed perfection of hypocrisy which had concealed the
      conspiracy from me, for months on months; or, had at most,
      only shown its progress on rare occasions, by such slight, faint

signs as no generous, trusting nature could ever have discerned?' This and the previous two deletions are part of a series
of excisions which serve to lessen the emphasis on Margaret's
moral depravity.

180 *macadamised*: named after John McAdam (1756–1836), maca-
damization is a method of composing a road surface out of
compressed layers of small broken stones often bound together
with tar or asphalt. On p. 164 Basil refers to hearing 'the
crunching of stones—the road had been recently mended with
granite'.

neighbouring hospital: after travelling for some time from 'the
western side of the Edgeware Road' (p. 155) Margaret and
Mannion 'abruptly turned down a bye-street, in a direction
exactly opposite to the direction which led to North Villa'
arriving in 'the neighbourhood of a great railway station' (p.
158). After Basil's attack, Mannion is taken to a 'neighbouring
hospital' ('St. Helen's', p. 225) which takes students (p. 279).
Collins may have had no particular hospital in mind; but if, of
the five railway stations then built, we discard Fenchurch
Street, London Bridge, and Waterloo as too distant, the station
must be either Euston or King's Cross, in which case it seems
likely that the hospital is based on University College Hospital.

183 *I may say*: in 1862 Collins deleted a number of sentences from
Mr Sherwin's denunciation of Mannion and defence of
Margaret, including, after 'I may say', 'lured my unsuspecting
child into some hotel; and there, while she was in his power,
had the impudence to make the most immoral proposals to
her'. Margaret 'denounced the wretch, I am happy to say,
with an indignation which absolutely frightened him' and, says
Mr Sherwin, 'She is still a child in purity and innocence; and
she acted like a child—poor, dear thing!—on this very
lamentable occasion.'

197 *Mr. Sherwin is a linendraper*: before 1862 Basil identified Mr
Sherwin as a linendraper in Oxford Street.

228 *In those days they hung for forgery*: the death penalty for forgery
was not removed until 1835.

238 *neither her mind nor her disposition kept pace with her beauty*: in 1862
Collins deleted after this, 'This did not surprise me: while she
was little better than a child I had doubted her character; and
now I found all my doubts confirmed. Few if any of her faults

escaped me; it was not in my age nor in my purpose to let her personal beauty blind me to her mental defects and moral deformities.'

243 *so many brazen images . . . like the Jews of old*: there are no specific references in the Old Testament to the worship of brazen images; Mannion is making a general reference to the Jews' recurrent lapses into the worship of pagan idols, perhaps most memorably in Exodus 32: 1–35 when in Moses' absence they choose Aaron as their leader and worship a golden bull.

245 *I have looked into her thoughts, and I know it*: in 1862 Collins deleted after this, 'She was fit to be any man's mistress no man's wife.'

248 *As the time approached*: in 1862 Collins deleted after this, 'for the consummation of my success and your defeat'.

249 *I had no dread of her meeting you*: in 1862 Collins deleted after this, 'She had been guilty in thought and in purpose so long, that she was fit to be guilty in act without a chance of betraying herself.'

 Do you still exult: in 1862 Collins deleted, before this, three sentences including, 'I have made good my prior right to Margaret, as I purposed'.

252 *a public hospital*: Victorian hospitals generally were established by charitable donations, accepting patients with letters of reference from subscribers. Most would, however, also accept accident and emergency cases, of whom Mannion would be one.

257 *somewhere in the Brompton neighbourhood*: describing the Brompton of 1851 E. A. Bowring wrote, 'The secluded region of Brompton Park, with its fine old trees, and quaint dwellings . . . formed the favourite abode of leading actors' ('South Kensington', *Nineteenth Century*, 1 (1877), 563–4). Despite the reformatory qualities of his mistress Ralph did not choose to live in the most conventionally respectable part of London.

258 *The fair partner of my existence*: before 1862 Ralph referred to *The fair partner of my existence* and *Mrs. Ralph* just as 'Madame'.

269 *'All right!' he said*: before 1862 Ralph spoke rather more robustly: Collins substituted *"All right!" he said* for ' "Victory! victory!" he cried'; *she has left her father's house!* for 'she's bolted';

and *She has eloped to the hospital!* for 'Bolted, by Jupiter. Gone off to the hospital! gone to see how you have marked that fellow—what's his name?'

273 *say his daughter should come back*: in 1862 Collins substituted this for 'say: "Damn her! she shall come back".'

a straight waistcoat: this is a jacket made of strong material, probably canvas, for restraining violent prisoners or mental patients; the modern term would be strait-jacket.

274 *how you can aid them*: before 1862 Mannion's letter continues, 'You need trouble yourself no longer to act innocence, or to deceive your mock-husband: you will know why when we meet. Your future destiny lies with *me*: a new and adventurous career is before you [etc.]'.

278 *every surgical testimonial the Hôtel Dieu could give me*: one of Europe's great teaching hospitals, the *Hôtel Dieu* is believed to date from between 641 and 691, though the first indisputable record is not until 829. France, and Paris in particular, were regarded by knowledgeable Victorians as at the forefront of medical progress: most developments in medicine between 1800 and 1850 came from France. Lydgate, George Eliot's doctor in *Middlemarch* (1871–2), trained there.

a 'mute inglorious Liston': Thomas Gray, in 'Elegy Written in a Country Churchyard', wonders whether 'Some mute inglorious Milton here may rest'. Robert Liston (1794–1847), surgeon, anatomist, and medical author, was noted in the age immediately prior to the introduction of anaesthetics for his remarkable speed and dexterity as a surgeon.

280 *erysipelas*: this is an acute infectious disease of the skin, often called St Anthony's fire.

281 *monomaniac . . . some fixed idea*: the term monomania—a form of insanity in which the patient is irrational on one subject only— was of fairly recent date in 1852. Collins uses it in 'The Twin Sisters' (1851); and in 'Mad Monkton', written in 1852, he uses the term 'fixed idea'. Collins's interest in mental illness continued throughout his writing life. See note to p. 75 above.

282 *the different theories of infection*: this would be an engrossing topic for a young doctor fresh from the excitement of Parisian medical advances (see note to p. 278 above). 'The confusion surrounding infection and contagion which endured in medical

minds for some three hundred years began to dissipate as the germ theory developed in the last half of the nineteenth century.' R. P. Hudson, *Disease and Its Control* (Westport Connecticut and London: Greenwood Press, 1983).

285 *Typhus*: the subsequent description of Margaret's illness follows quite closely the account Collins gave of his Uncle Frank's death from typhus in *Memoirs of the Life of William Collins, Esq. R.A.* (1848). See i. 32.

293 *degradation and debauchery, defiling the sick room*: nurses enjoyed exceedingly low social status, equivalent perhaps to that of a scullery maid; they were untrained and generally lacked even rudimentary education. The most famous literary example of the type is Dickens's Mrs Sairey Gamp (*Martin Chuzzlewit*, 1843). The nursing reforms begun in the 1840s culminated in Florence Nightingale's work.

294 *because I can't help it*: in 1862 Collins deleted after this, '*You* are a man; a strong, daring, conquering man: he's a——.'

295 *Scarlet Woman—in the Bible*: see Revelation 17: 1–6. The phrase is commonly used to indicate a sexually promiscuous woman.

307 *to go to Cornwall, to explore the wild western land*: during the summer of 1850 Collins took a walking tour through Cornwall with his friend the illustrator Henry Brandling. The general ignorance about Cornwall before the opening of Brunel's great bridge at Saltash is reflected in Collins's title for the book which resulted from the tour: *Rambles Beyond Railways: Notes in Cornwall Taken A-Foot* (1851). He also used Cornish scenery in *The Dead Secret*.

312 *astonishment and suspicion*: in *Rambles* Collins writes that he and Brandling 'were curiously regarded at an awful distance, and respectfully questioned in circumlocutory phrases as to our secret designs in walking through the country'. Wilkie Collins, *Rambles Beyond Railways* (London: Anthony Mott Ltd., 1982, pp. 44–5). All subsequent quotations from *Rambles* are from this edition.

319 *Treen*: Basil's journey from his 'fishing hamlet . . . on the southern shore on Cornwall, not more than a few miles distance from the Land's End' (p. 312) to Treen was one which Collins made in reverse during his walk through Cornwall; in *Rambles* he used the contemporary spelling Trereen. '[I]t

is . . . the walk to the Land's End along the southern coast . . . which displays the grandest combinations of scenery in which this grandest part of Cornwall abounds . . . On approaching the wondrous landscapes between Treen and the Land's End . . . granite and granite alone . . . appears everywhere . . . presenting an appearance of adamantine solidity and strength . . . In these wild districts, the sea rolls and roars in fiercer agitation, and the mists fall thicker, and at the same time fade and change faster, than elsewhere . . . You go on, guided . . . by the *sound* of the sea, when you stray instinctively from the edge of the cliff' (*Rambles*, pp. 99–100.

321 *a black, yawning hole*: the locale of the encounter may have been suggested by a geographic phenomenon near Kynance Cove. Describing 'The Devil's Throat' in *Rambles* Collins writes, 'our rock track is narrow, rugged, and slippery; the sea roars bewilderingly below; and a single false step would not be attended with agreeable consequences. Soon, however, we . . . come to a halt before a wide, tunnelled opening . . a black, gaping hole, into the bottom of which the sea is driven through the aptly-named "Devil's Throat." . . . [T]he rocks thundering with a fearful noise, which rises in hollow echoes through the aptly-named "Devils Throat." . . . [T]he rocks rose wild, jagged, and precipitous, all around it' (*Rambles*, pp. 75–6).

323 *Take care of your life. It is not your's to throw away—it is mine!*: in 1862 Collins substituted this for 'Your life is *mine*. Would you steal it from me by a suicide?'

330 *Bartallock, in Cornwall*: William Penhale has come to Treen because of the difficulty of finding work in a mine which is within walking distance fo Bartallock. While there were hundreds of mines in Cornwall at the time, the similarity in names, proximity to Treen, and Collins's visit to it, suggest he may have had Botallack mine in mind. Chapter IX of *Rambles*, which describes Collins's own descent of Botallack mine, is one of the highlights of the book.

338 *the reasons which led you to counsel me thus*: in 1862 Collins deleted after this, 'I admitted the security which concealment of names, places, and dates gave against the chance that the identity of any one of the actors in my story might be discovered—'.

THE WORLD'S CLASSICS

A Select List

HANS ANDERSEN: Fairy Tales
Translated by L. W. Kingsland
Introduction by Naomi Lewis
Illustrated by Vilhelm Pedersen and Lorenz Frølich

JANE AUSTEN: Emma
Edited by James Kinsley and David Lodge

Mansfield Park
Edited by James Kinsley and John Lucas

J. M. BARRIE: Peter Pan in Kensington Gardens & Peter and Wendy
Edited by Peter Hollindale

WILLIAM BECKFORD: Vathek
Edited by Roger Lonsdale

CHARLOTTE BRONTË: Jane Eyre
Edited by Margaret Smith

THOMAS CARLYLE: The French Revolution
Edited by K. J. Fielding and David Sorensen

LEWIS CARROLL: Alice's Adventures in Wonderland
and Through the Looking Glass
Edited by Roger Lancelyn Green
Illustrated by John Tenniel

MIGUEL DE CERVANTES: Don Quixote
Translated by Charles Jarvis
Edited by E. C. Riley

GEOFFREY CHAUCER: The Canterbury Tales
Translated by David Wright

ANTON CHEKHOV: The Russian Master and Other Stories
Translated by Ronald Hingley

JOSEPH CONRAD: Victory
Edited by John Batchelor
Introduction by Tony Tanner

DANTE ALIGHIERI: The Divine Comedy
Translated by C. H. Sisson
Edited by David Higgins

VIRGIL: The Aeneid
Translated by C. Day Lewis
Edited by Jasper Griffin

HORACE WALPOLE: The Castle of Otranto
Edited by W. S. Lewis

IZAAK WALTON and CHARLES COTTON:
The Compleat Angler
Edited by John Buxton
Introduction by John Buchan

OSCAR WILDE: Complete Shorter Fiction
Edited by Isobel Murray

The Picture of Dorian Gray
Edited by Isobel Murray

VIRGINIA WOOLF: Orlando
Edited by Rachel Bowlby

ÉMILE ZOLA:
The Attack on the Mill and other stories
Translated by Douglas Parmée

A complete list of Oxford Paperbacks, including The World's Classics, OPUS, Past Masters, Oxford Authors, Oxford Shakespeare, and Oxford Paperback Reference, is available in the UK from the Arts and Reference Publicity Department (BH), Oxford University Press, Walton Street, Oxford OX2 6DP.

In the USA, complete lists are available from the Paperbacks Marketing Manager, Oxford University Press, 200 Madison Avenue, New York, NY 10016.

Oxford Paperbacks are available from all good bookshops. In case of difficulty, customers in the UK can order direct from Oxford University Press Bookshop, Freepost, 116 High Street, Oxford, OX1 4BR, enclosing full payment. Please add 10 per cent of published price for postage and packing.